IZETTE

The Last Days of Childhood

Viv Packer

Pen Press Publishers Ltd

© Viv Packer 2006

All rights reserved

No part of this publication may be reproduced,
stored in a retrieval system, or transmitted
in any form or by any means, without
the prior permission in writing of the publisher,
nor be otherwise circulated in any form of binding or cover
other than that in which it is published and without a similar
condition including this condition being imposed on the
subsequent purchaser.

First published in Great Britain by
Pen Press Publishers Ltd
The Old School
39 Chesham Road
Brighton BN2 1NB

ISBN: 1-905621-36-1
ISBN13: 978-1-905621-36-1

Printed and bound in the UK

A catalogue record of this book is available from
the British Library

Cover design by Jacqueline Abromeit

for John

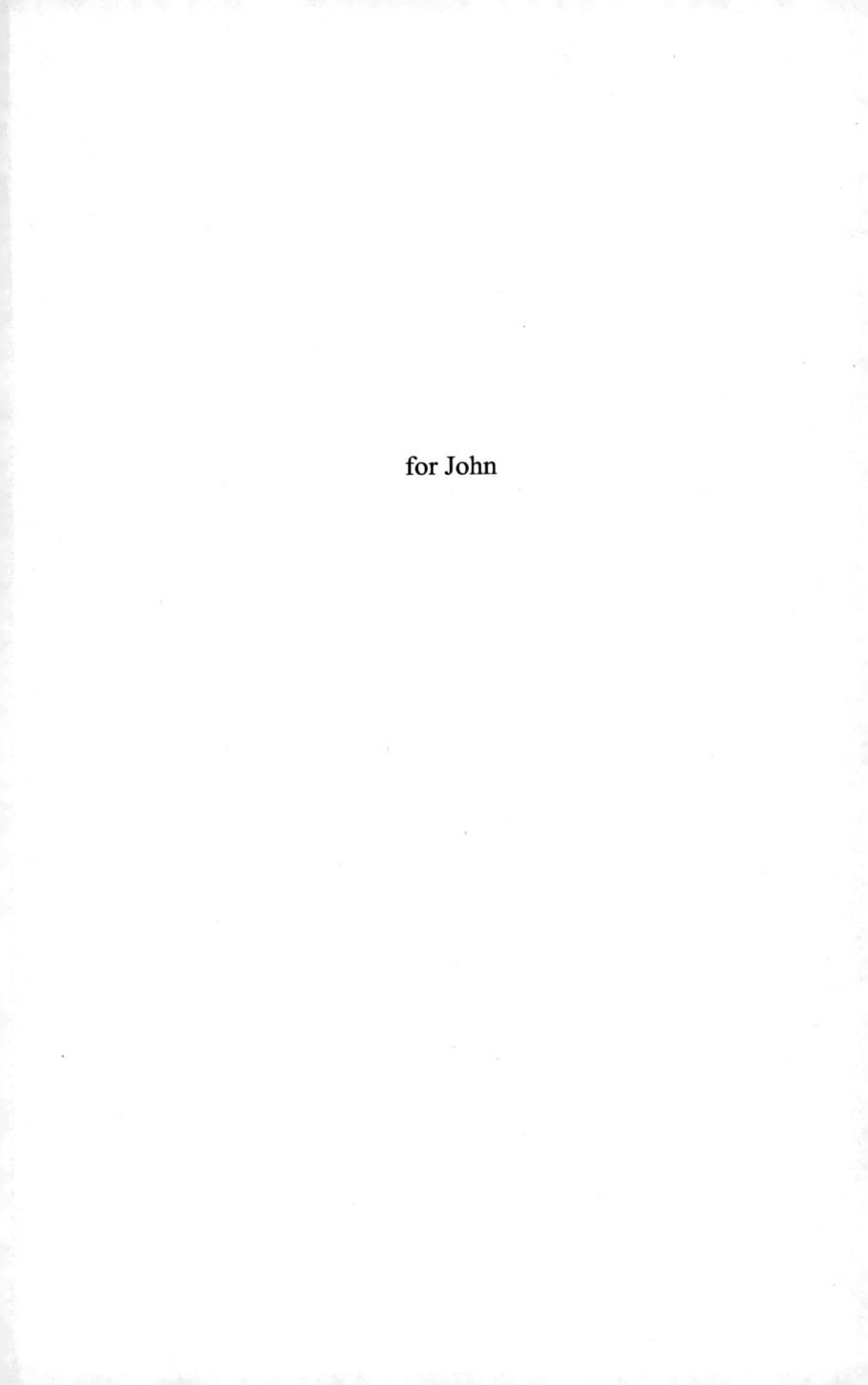

ACKNOWLEDGEMENTS

My thanks go to W M Ginns, Esq M.B.E. of the Channel Islands Occupation Society, for much valuable assistance, to the Société Jersiaise Museum and the Lord Coutanche Library both of which gave generous access to their archives of information on the occupation and to my husband, John, for uncomplainingly searching through wartime records while under the impression that he had come to Jersey for a holiday and, above all, for his unfailing support.

ABOUT THE AUTHOR

Born and raised in Manchester, Viv Packer graduated from the University of Manchester with an honours degree in drama. She then married and relocated to Cheltenham, Gloucestershire, where, after a false start in the Civil Service (having decided she was temperamentally unsuited to government work!) she started showing and breeding St Bernard dogs. She later joined a local conservationist in setting up and running an environmental conservation and study centre for overseas students, a job she enjoyed and stayed with for seventeen years, producing two sons along the way.

Divorced and remarried seven years ago, Viv started writing as a serious hobby around this time. She worked at the University of Gloucestershire for four years until she was able to take advantage of an extraordinarily early retirement scheme, which enabled her to up sticks and move to the Sierra Nevada region of Andalucia in Spain. Viv and John bought an old Moorish house in the Alpujarran village of Yegen, made famous by the British writer Gerald Brenan in his book, *South from Granada*, where they live happily today.

CHAPTER 1

It was very quiet that day, strangely so. Even the seagulls seemed to be huddled in brooding silence, stilled by the air of unease that hung over the island. Izette dug her fingers into the sand, wishing it would all go away, this war business. She wrinkled her nose to dislodge a fly, feeling the tightness of sun-scorched skin across her forehead. The soft skin in the creases of her elbows felt a little sore. Her mum had said to take the cream but she had forgotten it, deliberately. How could you flop down on the sand if you were covered in cream? She lay, limbs spread-eagled, imagining herself a beached starfish, her eyes closed to the sky and sun, letting the droplets of seawater dry to crusty circles of salt on her skin. Later, she would lick them off, the smell of sun-scorched skin filling her nostrils.

Now, late in the afternoon, the sand was comfortably warm against her body, not searingly hot as it had been earlier, burning the soles of her feet as she'd hopped and jumped towards the cool damp margin at the edge of the water. The late afternoon sun hung over the western side of the bay, drawing a converging line of golden ripples towards itself. At the appointed time the sun would plunge into hiding beyond the headland and the little ripples would lose their sparkle and disperse, deceived yet again by the daily ritual.

She opened one eye and screwed her head round to see what Nancy was up to. The beach was nearly deserted now, mothers having taken their little ones home for tea, bath and bed. Nancy was on her hands and knees by an abandoned sandcastle, poking at it with a stick. It was a grandiose structure, or, at least, it had been before Nancy turned her attention to it.

'What are you doing, Nancy?' Izette called, partly stifling a yawn.

'Nothing,' Nancy replied, then stood up, letting fly a rock that shattered one of the corner towers, a great fissure appearing in the fragile, battlemented walls.

Izette closed her eyes again. Her friend Nancy had two elder brothers, Tom and George, whose boys' toys had always been passed down to her . She was as boyish as them, brought up with their games, wearing their cast off clothes, her hair cropped short as a lad's. Since early childhood, Nancy and Izette had scrambled round the island in the boys' wake, beaches, fields and cliffs their playground, free as savages. Now the boys were away, one in the army, one at work but their patterns of play were continued by the two girls. Izette yawned again. It had been one of those perfect beach days, a long day of toasting and idleness, of poking around in rock pools and collecting shells to be carried home proudly and displayed on her dressing table until layers of dust masked their delicate pastel shades and they were scooped into her mother's dustpan and forgotten.

The drone of an aircraft engine slowly became audible. Izette didn't open her eyes. For the past few days, planes had been flying low over the island but nothing had happened.

Photographs of them appeared in the evening paper over which Dad and Mr Birrell next door shook their heads solemnly. Dad had drawn the wing markings for her a couple of days ago but she wasn't sure she could remember which was which. Circles and crosses? Like noughts and crosses? She shuffled her feet deeper into the sand, feeling the cool, dense weight of it press down on her toes.

'Any tomato sandwiches left, Nancy?'

'No. There's just an apple and a squashed bun,' came the reply.

Izette sighed. What she really wanted was an ice cream but the ice cream man had cycled away when the tots were taken home for tea.

For the last few days, when the wind was in the right direction, they'd heard the dull thump of explosions from the French mainland and seen dark clouds of smoke hanging above the horizon. She'd watched the men look with troubled faces across the narrow expanse of sea that separated the island from France. All noise had to stop when the news bulletins came on the wireless and the war news in the Evening Post was discussed interminably. Surrounded by long faces, Izette was reminded of the time when Granny died. Everyone had been solemn then. Dark blinds were screwed to the windows and drawn down during the daytime as a sign of mourning. This time the blinds were there for the blackout and had been drawn down every night for months and months. That was why it was good to be here on the beach, away from all that gloom.

This day of release on the beach with Nancy was an unexpected treat. Mum had been against it. She didn't want to let any of them out of her sight but Dad overruled her. 'Where's the harm, Betty? They've been shut in for days. It'll do them good to get a bit of fresh air. Nothing much seems to be happening at the moment. They can't stay shut in forever. Let them go.' Mum hadn't been pleased but she packed them a picnic. They had put their bathers and towels in the bag and rushed out of the house before she could change her mind. Like young heifers let out to grass after a long winter, they'd run and skipped all the way to town to catch a bus for the coast road.

*

A deafening crash brought Izette abruptly upright, her heart suddenly pounding. The ground shook beneath her. Looking round as she scrambled rapidly to her feet, she saw Nancy kneeling, staring across the bay towards town to where great dark clouds of smoke billowed into the sky. There were aeroplanes over the harbour, flying very low. As they watched, disbelieving, strings of bombs fell from beneath the planes , glinting briefly in the lowering sunlight. There was a short pause then a series of deep explosions boomed around the bay. Both on their feet by now, the girls were running for shelter when they heard the crackle of machine-gun fire.

'Behind there! Quick!' screamed Izette and they flung themselves down behind a low stone breakwater at the top of the beach, crouching down close together. Nancy gripped Izette's arm tightly.

'It's them, Izette! The Germans. They've come.' Her voice was high and shrill.

'Shh. I know. Just keep down!' Izette was bewildered. Dad had said nothing would happen today.

'But what are we going to do?' whispered Nancy.

'I don't know. Can you see anyone about?'

They raised their heads cautiously to look around but the beach was now completely empty. It looked as though the few remaining people had fled, abandoning towels and bags on the sand. Only a small dog remained in the open, yapping excitedly. There was a terrific noise coming from the harbour and smoke drifted in huge dark clouds over Fort Regent and the town. Horrified, the girls saw the planes, three of them, wheel away from the port and turn to fly directly towards them across the bay.

'Get down,' shrieked Izette, pulling her friend down on to the sand.

The planes roared overhead, machine guns blazing a trail of bullets along the coast road. They cowered, hands over ears, faces almost in the sand, waiting for the awful noise to stop. When the roar of the engines faded a little they risked lifting their heads again to see what was happening. The planes were at the western end of the bay now and the girls heard them open fire on St Aubins, saw the flames from the guns clearly in the gathering dusk. Banking sharply to avoid the headland, the planes turned and flew back across the bay towards St Helier. Once more they swooped low over the town, dropping another string of bombs before disappearing over Fort Regent.

Suddenly it was quiet again. The girls waited, listening for the returning roar of the engines. Long minutes passed. Nothing happened. From some distance along the beach a child could be heard crying, a small child's wail, eerie in the shocked silence. Beside her, Nancy let out a sobbing gasp. Izette looked at her anxiously. Nancy's face was white and smudged with sand and she looked as Izette imagined people might look if they'd seen a ghost, sort of quivery. They looked at one another in confusion, not knowing what to do.

'I want to go home,' moaned Nancy.

Izette, only now remembering Mum and Dad, Edmund and Irene back there in St Helier, felt a wave of panic. 'Yes, we've got to get home! Come on.'

'Our clothes....'

'Quick! Let's get them.'

Izette pulled Nancy to her feet and they ran back down the beach. Several other people had emerged from their hiding places and were running as well. The girls hurriedly pulled their clothes over still damp bathing costumes. There being no time to fiddle with the stiff buckles on her new sandals, Izette just grabbed them and ran towards the road in her bare feet, shouting to Nancy to hurry. It was a steep incline up to the road and they were out of breath by the time they reached the roadside and the bus stop.

'What shall we do?' gasped Nancy, 'Shall we wait for the bus?'

Izette was clutching her side, trying to catch her breath. There was no sign of a bus.

'It might not come, not now, with all this.' Izette waved her hand in the direction of the spreading pall of smoke. They looked around but there was no one they could ask. Where had everyone gone?

'We'd better walk then.'

'I suppose so.' Izette wondered if she could manage it. Her legs felt wobbly and weak, as though she'd just jumped down from a horse after riding all day. 'Just a minute, I'll have to put my sandals on.'

She sat on the road and pulled on her T-bar sandals, struggling with the stiffness of the leather. The sand sticking to her feet chafed the soft skin of her toes. Hearing a coughing noise she looked round to see Nancy being sick at the roadside. She got up and stood awkwardly by Nancy's side until she'd finished, then handed her a handkerchief. Nancy looked awful.

'Are you all right, Nance?' she asked anxiously.

Nancy nodded miserably, close to tears.

'Come on, then, we must hurry. Give me the bag.'

Nancy handed it over and Izette set off at a trot, hoping Nancy would be able to keep up. Looking ahead all she could see was a sky full of smoke. The road stretched a long way into the distance. How far was it back to town? One mile? Two? She glanced back at Nancy who was lagging behind but seemed to be managing. Izette calculated it would take them at least three-quarters of an hour to get home if no buses came along. But they couldn't keep up this pace for long. Already she could feel the beginnings of another stitch in her side. A little further on an elderly man came into sight, hurrying in the opposite direction. When he reached them he stopped.

'Are you all right, dears? Where are you going?'

'Yes, thank you.' Izette panted, 'We're going home ...to town.'

He grunted grimly, 'Mm. Well, be very careful. If you hear any of those Hun aircraft again, you get down in the ditch straight away and stay there until they've gone. You hear me?'

The girls nodded, 'Yes, thank you.' Anxious to be away, they didn't give him the opportunity to say any more but set off again at a run.

'I hope everyone is safe,' said Nancy.

'What?' shouted Izette over her shoulder.

Nancy speeded up until she was alongside Izette. 'I said, I hope everyone is safe - at home I mean. What time is it?'

'I don't know. It must be about six o'clock, or perhaps seven.' She'd lost track of time.

'Our dads will be home from work then, but Tom sometimes goes out again down to town after tea.'

Izette didn't need to be told that. Nancy's house was her second home. She knew their habits as well as she knew her own. Tom usually met his friends in town in the evenings.

Not having much money to spend in the bars, they would lean on the railings at the pier head, smoking cigarettes as they talked over the war situation and watched the fishermen working on their boats. The harbour was one of their meeting places. Nancy must be thinking along those lines too.

'Don't worry, Nancy. Tom'll be all right.'

The distant sound of an engine brought the girls to a frightened halt. Turning towards the sound, they were relieved to see the St Helier bus hurtling along the road towards them.

'It's the bus, Izette. Do you think he'll stop? We're not at a bus stop.'

'Of course he will, idiot. This is an emergency.'

Emboldened by their situation, Izette stepped into the middle of the road and stood there determinedly with her hand held up to stop the bus. The bus braked harshly to a halt and the conductor hurried them on.

'Come on, young ladies, on you get, quickly. We'll get you home safely.'

The bus was only half full. The girls walked towards the front seats, falling into them as the driver accelerated away fiercely. A woman with two small children huddled awkwardly on her lap smiled anxiously at them and asked if they were all right. Izette fumbled in the bag for their bus-fares and held the coins ready in her hand. The passengers scanned the sky nervously. Izette and Nancy sat clutching their belongings fearfully, bracing themselves against the lurching of the bus, watching the huge cloud of smoke ahead. An elderly couple sat side by side, holding hands. Izette took Nancy's hand and squeezed it reassuringly. She was the elder by ten months and two weeks, and thus felt a degree of responsibility for her friend. Moreover she would celebrate her 14th birthday in two days time so she thought of herself as almost grown-up really. They were best friends, had been so for as long as they could remember. Their houses and gardens were joined, set high on a hill overlooking the town of St Helier and the two families were closer than most relatives. Izette knew both sets of parents would be terribly worried about them at this very minute but, at this speed, it wouldn't take them long to reach home.

'Phew! I've never travelled this fast on a bus before,' said Izette.

'Me neither. Where's your Edmund? Will he be at home?' asked Nancy.

'Oh, he'll be at home, no fear of that,' replied Izette with a small smile. 'You know Edmund, he never goes anywhere.'

At nine, Izette's brother Edmund was the baby of the family and the only boy. He didn't have the thick, dark hair or olive skin of the rest of the Vaubert family. Izette was five when Edmund was born. When she was allowed her first peep at the new baby in his cot and saw his delicate, pale features and fine golden hair sticking up in a tuft, she was sure Jesus had brought her an elf. As the months and years passed and the tiny, magical baby grew into a toddler, Izette's wonder and excitement faded but she never completely lost her pride in this strange sibling. She found him uncannily beautiful with his slender limbs and wide, pale blue eyes. She was sure Edmund would be safely at home now up in his room, head buried in a book probably.

Dad didn't seem to know what to make of Edmund sometimes. It was Izette who was the tomboy of the family, always happiest when she was outdoors, returning at dusk with grazed knees and elbows, filthy and utterly content. Edmund would join their wild games occasionally but his real passion was for books and he would happily pass the glorious summer days in his bedroom, reading voraciously. Bill found this difficult to understand. Books are all right, he would say to Edmund's mother, but who wants to be stuck inside on a day like this?

*

As the bus came into town the girls could see people hurrying in all directions. The bus was forced to slow down. Cars, lorries and carts had been abandoned anywhere and everywhere. They saw a fire engine trying to thread its way through people and vehicles. Despite the shrill ringing of the bells and the driver shouting and sounding his horn, people continued to run across the road in front of it, blindly intent on reaching their destinations. Eventually the bus came to a standstill.

'I can't get any closer to the Weighbridge,' the driver shouted back to the passengers. 'It's chaos. I'm afraid you'll have to make your own way from here.'

There was a rush to get off the bus, passengers infected by the sense of panic on the streets. Bewildered, the girls followed the others, Izette still clutching the pennies for their fares in her hand. She paused on the pavement but the conductor was nowhere to be seen. Guiltily, she stuffed the pennies back into her bag. Izette and Nancy took a moment to get their bearings. The woman with the small children hurried past, pushing them out of her way, the smaller child beginning to wail as he was dragged faster than his short legs could carry him. A sun hat he was wearing fell off into the gutter as the woman hurried him on. Izette picked it up and started after her but the trio was soon lost in the crowd. At a loss, she stuffed the hat into her bag too.

'Come on,' said Izette, taking Nancy's hand, 'I don't think it'll take us long to walk home. Keep close, we don't want to get separated.'

They joined a group of people moving towards the centre of town, pushed along by the crowd's momentum. It was difficult to see ahead through the throng. Acrid smoke drifted across from the harbour area and their feet scrunched through broken glass. The crowd grew denser and the girls could see nothing but the backs of strangers.

'This is no good, Nancy. I can't see where we're going. Let's see if we can push our way out and head for the Parade.'

The girls forced a way through the general flow, pushing and shoving disgracefully, regardless of good manners and courtesy. Nancy would have tripped and fallen if Izette hadn't dragged her up and onwards. They found their way into a side street and eventually, after a few detours, they reached the open space of the Parade where the crowd was very much thinner.

They paused, trying to decide on the quickest way home, when Nancy cried out, 'Look, Izette! There's my dad and your dad...over there!'

Izette scanned the faces in the direction of Nancy's pointing arm and with relief recognised her own father hurrying alongside Mr Birrell.

'Dad! Dad!' she shouted as she pelted towards him.

He stopped mid-stride and turned towards her shout, opening his arms to gather her up. 'Oh my little love, thank God you're safe,' he gasped, 'and Nancy,' as his neighbour and old friend, Ted Birrell, wrapped his arms around his own daughter, Nancy.

He held Izette close, rocking her from side to side. She felt the rough cloth of his jacket against her face, smelt his familiar smell of pipe tobacco.

'I was so worried. When we heard those explosions I thought...' He broke off and Izette looked up into the face of this big, burly man who held her tight, a face down which now ran unaccustomed tears. 'Oh, thank God, thank God.' he moaned, his huge hand crushing her head back against his chest.

Izette pushed herself away to ask anxiously, 'Mum...and Edmund and Irene?'

'They're all safe, no need to worry. But your Mum's beside herself worrying about you and Nancy.' Remembering the state of mind in which he'd left his wife, he straightened up. 'Come on, we'd better get you home quick.' Wiping his face roughly with the back of his sleeve, he called to his friend. 'Ted, let's get these girls home to their mothers, shall we?'

'Aye,' nodded Ted, taking one of Nancy's hands.

As they hurried towards home, Izette's head was reeling. So much had happened in the space of an hour. She wished she were still small enough to be scooped up in her father's strong arms and carried home tucked inside his jacket, secure in the warm darkness. She gripped his hand even more tightly and pressed her cheek against his scratchy, tweed-clad arm.

He smiled down at her, 'Soon be home.'

*

On the way home they saw two or three ambulances tear by on their way from the harbour. The men watched them pass without comment. Izette didn't want to imagine what horrors lay inside the ambulances being rushed to the hospital. It was enough to be able to hold her father's hand and know that her mother and brother and sister were safe at home waiting for her. As they turned the corner of their avenue, Izette saw her mother standing anxiously by the gate with Nancy's mother. The women spotted them at once and flew down the pavement towards them. Then it was a barrage of hugs and questions and kisses and tears, Mum breaking off to say, 'I never should have let her go. I had a premonition something was going to happen. I told you, Bill, didn't I?'

Izette's father shrugged. 'They're safe now, Betty. That's all that matters.'

'Come inside, Izette. Look, Bill, she's shaking. She needs a hot drink; perhaps even a little tot of brandy might help. Let's all go in.'

Her husband shook his head. 'You go in. Ted and I are going back down to the harbour.'

Izette stopped abruptly when she heard this. 'No, Dad! They might come back again.'

Bill smiled at his daughter and, sounding as confident as he could he said,

'I don't think so. We wouldn't be going down there if we thought there was any danger. I want to go and find out what's going on. They might be making some announcements in town. You go in with your mother and stay put. Don't worry, I'll be very careful.' Kissing her briefly on the forehead he pushed her gently towards the door.

Once Izette was inside and out of earshot he caught his wife's arm, preventing her from following Izette inside. 'If they do come back, you know what to do, Betty? Get them all under the kitchen table and stay there until you hear the all clear. All right?'

His wife nodded.

Bill laid his hand briefly alongside her cheek then turned away. He jerked his head towards Ted and the two men hurried back down the avenue towards the centre of town, the sky above still dark with smoke.

Suddenly they heard Izette call out, 'Uncle Ted!'

Both men stopped in surprise and turned.

'Yes, my dear, what is it?'

'Tom? Is Tom all right?'

'Yes, he's fine. Look, there he is now,' and he pointed

to the front door, out of which Tom was emerging to hug his sister.

'Oh, yes,' said Izette, waving to Tom who smiled and returned her wave before disappearing back inside with his family.

'All right now, love?' said Izette's mother. 'The Birrells were having their tea when the bombers came. Everyone's safe and sound. Come on in now and I'll make you a hot drink.' She led her daughter inside and, after a moment's anxious scan of the sky, shut the door behind her.

CHAPTER 2

'There'll be no bloody white flag hung from this house!' Bill's roar could be heard all over the house and probably half way down the street as well, thought Betty.

'Dad, we've got to. The Bailiff announced it. Everyone's got to show a white flag.' insisted Izette.

'Over my dead body!' Bill slammed his fist down hard on the kitchen table then strode towards the back door. He turned to look at his family, daring anyone to challenge him. No one spoke. He felt their eyes upon him, disapprovingly, and his anger suddenly evaporated, leaving him feeling deflated. He lifted his hand as though to speak again then let it fall helplessly to his side. Who was he trying to kid? He shook his head and said quietly, 'I'll be in my greenhouse,' then turned and left.

The back door closed behind him, the slight impact dislodging flakes of paint that floated to the floor. Betty sighed and looked at her daughters with an exasperated expression. Edmund was, as usual, sitting quietly in a corner of the kitchen, his nose deep in a book. He gave no sign of having heard any of the argument.

'Well, we shall have to do something.' Betty ran a hand wearily through her hair. She didn't know which was worse. The prospect of invasion or the fear of what would happen when her husband first came face to face with the invaders. Bill would never knuckle down to the Nazis.

'Mrs Gibaut has put out a pair of her mother's old bloomers.' offered Irene.

'Hmph, that doesn't surprise me.'

'Personally, I think it's a splendid gesture.'

'It's a vulgar gesture, Irene. My mother never dreamed of hanging out her underwear even on washdays. It was put up above the range indoors and if anybody came to the door it all had to be taken down before they were allowed in the kitchen. I still don't like to see women's things flapping on the line for all to see.'

'Mum,' persisted Irene, 'this is 1940, not 1840.' She winked at Izette as she flopped down into a chair.

'Well, I'm sorry you think me old-fashioned, Irene, but it's the way I was brought up. Now, what are we going to do about this flag? Perhaps your father wouldn't mind if I used a small pillowcase.'

*

Bill stomped down to the bottom end of the garden, launching a kick at an old Brussels sprout stem as he marched down the central path. Vegetables to the right; fruit and flowers to the left, all laid out with military precision. That's how he liked it. Reaching the bottom of the garden, he paused for a moment to look out over the back wall. From here he had a clear view of the harbour. There was a small, gently sloping potato field on the other side of the wall, then the ground fell away steeply towards the town, chimneys and roofs stepping down in orderly terraces. The view from the back of the house was unobstructed. From her kitchen window, Betty could see the whole sweep of the bay, from the harbour right round to Noirmont Point.

Bill had been working in the garden when the bombers came over a couple of days earlier. Like most other people he thought it was just another reconnaissance flight until he heard the explosions. He watched in horror as the three planes streaked across the bay strafing the coast road before attacking St Aubins harbour and returning for a second assault on St Helier. It was all over in a few minutes. Looking down on the bay now, the sun shimmering down on an idyllic crescent of golden sand bordered by tranquil blue water, it was hard to believe the other evening was no more than the substance of a bad dream until he looked more closely at the burned out shells of warehouses alongside the old harbour.

Turning away, Bill stepped inside his greenhouse and slumped into the tattered old armchair he kept there. Despite his outburst of defiance in the kitchen he had to admit that there was little he or any other Islander could do to resist. Izette was right. The Bailiff himself had signed his name to the notice asking the Islanders to comply with German orders. Large white crosses were to be painted in Royal Square and at the new Airport, and all buildings had to fly a white flag. He'd heard it all with his own ears earlier that morning when, together with Ted, his next door neighbour and close friend, he'd joined the crowd waiting in Royal Square to hear the Bailiff speak. Silence had fallen when the Bailiff came out on to the balcony to read out the German ultimatum. They had no choice, he'd said, no alternative but surrender. Bill's heart had sunk when he heard those words. He'd known, since the possibility of invasion first occurred to the Islanders, that their position was indefensible. A couple of weeks ago, their spirits had been raised temporarily by the arrival of British troops and artillery but within a few days, the troops were withdrawn and the Islanders realised they were to be abandoned to their fate. Even so it was only now, hearing the word 'surrender' on the Bailiff's lips, that the sombre reality really hit him.

Bill and Ted had walked slowly home together after hearing the Bailiff's speech.

'Well,' said Bill bleakly, 'at least we know where we stand now.'

Ted was silent. He was thinking of his wife, Dorothy, and their daughter, Nancy,

'Ted?' Bill enquired anxiously.

'I could have sent them away, you know,' said Ted. 'I should have insisted Dorothy and Nancy went to her sister in Coventry when they sent the evacuation boats. They registered on the list for evacuation. Tom and me, we never had any intention of going but Dorothy would have gone if I'd insisted. I made the wrong decision, Bill. There's no telling what might happen to our womenfolk now.'

Bill sighed and shook his head, 'I've been thinking the same, Ted.' He placed his hand on the smaller man's shoulder. 'But on the other hand, there's no way of knowing whether they would be any safer in England than here. We've seen the squadrons of German bombers flying over, heading for England, and we've read the reports of the air raids in the 'Post'. Who's to say they would have been any safer over there? At least we're all together here.'

'Yes, but for how long?'

'Just let them try and lay a hand on my Betty or the girls. They'll have me to deal with first.'

*

Now, sitting in his greenhouse, thinking back on the things he'd said earlier to Ted, Bill wondered, if it came to it, how he'd go about defending his family. Would he be able to stand up to the Jerries or would his words be proved to be so much hot air? If the Bailiff had been forced to submit without a fight, what chance did the ordinary man in the street have?

From under the greenhouse staging, he took out the old tin in which he kept his pipe and tobacco. Following the example of his father, he never smoked in the house. He dipped the bowl into the tobacco pouch, thinking as he did so that he'd better go carefully with it from now on. Tobacco supplies were bound to run short, just as they had during the last war. He applied a match to his pipe and puffed away, drawing the flame deep into the bowl, settling back into his threadbare old armchair. This was his refuge in times of stress. What he needed, when he felt as he did now, was half an hour in there. It was the smell he loved as much as anything. Warm moist earth, the pungent smell of pelargonium leaves, the sweet tang of a rogue mint plant which, despite being confined in a bottomless bucket outside, had crept in under the greenhouse walls to establish itself by the door where his leg brushed against it as he went in and out.

Bill turned his mind once again to the matter of Betty and the white flag they were supposed to display. When I've finished this pipe, he thought, I'll go back in and tell Betty to do as she thinks fit. I don't want to add to her worries; she's frightened enough as it is. I suppose we must do as the Bailiff says, no matter how much we dislike it.

However, the following day, when the Germans actually set foot on Jersey for the first time, Bill was again roused to disgusted indignation by the apparently friendly reception they received from the Bailiff. He paced the kitchen angrily as he gave Betty his opinion of the description of the meeting as reported in the evening paper.

'He shook them by the hand, Betty! You wouldn't have caught me shaking their bloody hands. Some sort of official reception had to be organised, I suppose, but he needn't have made them feel welcome.'

He was all set to continue in this vein when he noticed the look of fear that had appeared on Betty's face. It stopped him short.

'Aye well,' Bill continued more quietly, 'I suppose he knows what he's up to. He doesn't tell me how to service motorcars so I reckon we'll have to leave that sort of thing to him and the Attorney General. Still, a little coldness wouldn't have gone amiss.'

Betty was relieved when Bill sat down again with the paper and she was able to carry on laying the table. She wouldn't dare admit it to Bill but she had found the account of the meeting reassuring. If the horrifying rumours of atrocities carried out by the advancing German troops in France were true, surely the Bailiff would not have greeted the invaders so cordially?

Izette, not usually interested in reading the evening paper, had also read the account of the meeting, studying the photograph showing the Bailiff greeting the German officers carefully.

'When can I go and see the Germans, Dad?'

'Not yet,' replied Bill.

'But Nancy's already been down to town with her father. I want to see if they have square heads and I want to hear what German sounds like.'

'They do not have square heads, that's just the shape of their helmets. And it's an ugly, harsh language; take my word for it. Besides, I'm sure you'll be hearing it soon enough, we all will,' said Bill grimly.

*

As it turned out, Izette had to wait a long time to see her first German at close hand. For the first week or so after the invasion, she wasn't allowed out of the house, except to go next door to see Nancy. So she spent a lot of time standing at the bottom of the garden watching the town. The harbour was filled to overflowing with ships of all kinds and bustling with activity. The German navy was there, of course, but also a seemingly endless convoy of supply boats of all sizes, many requisitioned from the French. She'd never seen so many ships standing off in the bay, waiting for the tide. The ships brought vehicles; lorries, armoured cars, even tanks. Her eyes followed their small grey shapes as they were driven up the piers then out along the Esplanade in long columns. Soldiers on motorcycles buzzed up and down the columns like fractious sheepdogs frustrated by the slowness of their charges. The sound of the engines droned on endlessly day after day.

Izette's curiosity was intensified when Irene, her elder sister, came home full of excitement one evening having herself encountered the Germans for the first time. She had gone over to Havre des Pas that morning, to the small sea front hotel where she worked as a receptionist. The manager had asked all the staff to come in to be told the hotel's future plans. The Germans had been requisitioning the larger hotels for accommodation but Irene wasn't optimistic about her chances of keeping her job. She expected to be told that the hotel would be closing down for the duration.

That evening over tea, Irene told the family what she had learned.

'They've taken over the Hotel Regent, all of it. They've requisitioned it for the officers, but Mr Grasett doesn't think they'll be interested in our hotel.'

Bill put down the paper he was reading. 'The Hotel Regent? That's the best hotel along there, isn't it? They obviously believe in making themselves comfortable.'

'Yes, it's directly opposite the swimming pool and they've their own tennis courts at the back. Some of them were out there playing hardly half an hour after they'd arrived.'

Her mother was laying the table for tea. 'Shouldn't be allowed,' she muttered indignantly. 'Do they think they're on holiday or something?'

'They certainly looked very happy. They were laughing and joking with one another,' replied Irene, 'then later lots of them came out in their swimming trunks with towels under their arms and ran into the sea. Marie and I watched them from one of the lounge windows.'

'You should have been attending to your work, girl,' said Bill gruffly, 'didn't you have anything better to do than stand gawping at a few daft Jerries?'

'They didn't look daft to me, Dad. They looked perfectly normal without their uniforms, just like anybody else,' replied Irene, remembering how she and Marie had giggled when the soldiers noticed them peering from around the curtains and waved invitingly towards the water. She leaned over and whispered in Izette's ear, 'Some of them were gorgeous.'

Izette's mouth dropped open in surprise. Weren't they supposed to be the enemy? Irene placed a finger beneath Izette's chin and pushed upwards.

'Don't sit like that. You'll catch a mouthful of flies!' she laughed.

Bill didn't miss this interchange. Putting down the paper he leaned forward over the table towards his eldest daughter.

'Irene, if I should ever hear that you were...involved with one of these men, these soldiers who are our enemy,

remember, who have deprived these islands of their liberty...'
As Bill counted off his points on his fingers, Irene's expression settled into one of sulky boredom. '...who have marched across Europe destroying any who dared stand against them in defence of their own freedom, taking whatever they want, forcing their own distorted ideology on the countries they have overrun and, if reports are to be believed, carried out appalling atrocities against innocent women and children...'

Here Irene shook her head and interrupted, 'I don't believe that for a minute. It's just propaganda.'

'Irene! How dare you interrupt your father.' Betty remonstrated.

Bill sat back in his chair. 'It's all right, Betty. Irene's entitled to her opinion. She's almost an adult now. I shan't say any more on the subject, but I think she understands me.'

Bill knew his first-born only too well, headstrong and impetuous from the day she was born. Now she was 19, and had grown into a shapely young woman, her dark hair cut fashionably short and teased into waves in the latest film star styles. Bill feared she would be an easy target for the predatory young Germans. The less she had to do with them the better.

Betty picked up the conversation. 'And what about your hotel, Irene? Did Mr Grasett say what was going to happen?'

'He said if he doesn't hear anything from the Germans authorities in the next couple of days, we'll be closing down.'

'Oh dear, and then you'll be out of a job?'

'Well obviously.'

'Irene! I'll not stand for impertinence, especially to your mother.' Bill dropped the Evening Post on the floor angrily. 'I think perhaps we'll have our tea now, Betty, since Irene doesn't seem capable of sustaining a civilised conversation.'

Betty went out into the kitchen, returning after a few

minutes with a tea tray, which she placed on the table and started to transfer plates to the table. Irene picked at her nails sulkily while this was going on.

'Come on, girls,' said Bill impatiently, 'give your Mum a hand.'

Irene stood up. 'I'm not hungry,' she announced.

'You've had nothing all day,' said Betty, 'You must...'

'You heard what she said, Betty.' Bill interrupted, then turned to his daughter, 'In that case, you can leave the room now, Irene.'

Irene glared at him for a moment before flouncing out. They heard her run upstairs and close her bedroom door with a slam. Bill looked at the remainder of his family gathered around the table.

'Well' he said, chucking Edmund under the chin and smiling wryly at Izette, 'I think that was the first battle of this family's war. The trouble is, and this goes for real war as well, nobody ever really wins.'

*

Izette was thoughtful as she ate her tea and, as soon as she could, she left the table and went upstairs to Irene's room. She stood outside the door and listened for a moment. Irene sometimes vented her feelings in a storm of tears and didn't take kindly to being interrupted, but this time there was no sound to be heard. She tapped on the door, hoping the clatter of dishes from the kitchen downstairs would mask the sound. She didn't want her dad to think she was taking sides. The door was opened quickly by Irene, looking completely composed.

'Brought me anything to eat?'

'No, but I could get you something later?'

Irene walked away from the open door and flopped down on her bed, leaving Izette to come in or not as she chose. Izette went in and sat down at Irene's dressing table. Her back was towards the bed but she could see Irene's reflection in the dressing table mirror.

'Haven't you got anything I could eat now? I'm starving.'

'I've got a few sweets, but they've been in my pocket.'

Irene came over to take the squashed paper bag and prised it open gingerly. She extracted a misshapen blob of sugared gum, holding it between two long tapering fingernails, varnished a vivid crimson, examined it closely for foreign matter, then transferred it to a mouth outlined in the same colour. Izette sighed, coveting the nails, the varnish and the lipstick but, most of all, the nails. The rest she could borrow, with or without Irene's permission.

'Tell me about the Germans,' said Izette, adding by way of encouragement, 'You can keep the sweets.'

Irene wrinkled her nose but took the bag anyway, resuming her position on the bed, stretching out her long legs elegantly.

'What do you want to know?'

'Everything! What they look like. What they said. Could you understand them?'

'Well, they look simply amazing! Not all of them, of course, but lots of them are tall, much taller than the sorry collection of men St Helier has to offer. Some of them have this wonderful white-blonde hair, and when they came out to swim they walked out of the hotel and straight across the road wearing just their swimming trunks!'

Irene smiled, remembering how she and Marie had hidden half-embarrassed behind the curtains to watch them.

'They had lovely sun-tans, and they looked so fit and

strong.'

Izette was puzzled. 'But we're not supposed to like them, are we?'

'We're not supposed to like having them here, being occupied and all that, but Marie says she thinks it could liven things up a bit. And anyway, they didn't choose to come here any more than our soldiers chose to go to wherever our soldiers are at the moment. They have to go where they're sent. It's not their fault they're here. While they are here, we might as well make the best of it.'

Izette considered this statement while her sister struggled to separate the last sweet from the paper. It sounded perfectly reasonable but if it was true, why was her father so angry?

'Did they speak to you?'

'No, not really. They shouted to us from outside. The windows were open.'

'In English?'

'Oh, yes. They speak very good English. They wanted us to go and swim with them. We refused of course.'

'But did you want to really?'

'No, of course we didn't,' replied Irene, suddenly all prim and proper, 'they're the enemy, remember?'

Irene got up and went out of the room to wash her sticky fingers.

Izette frowned. It was all very baffling. Getting up from the stool, she left Irene's room and wandered downstairs.

'I'm just going next door,' she shouted, intending to discuss what she'd heard with Nancy. She wasn't quite sure how it happened but instead of going into the Birrell's house, she turned in the opposite direction and found herself walking down the avenue towards the town. It wasn't premeditated; her legs just seemed to decide by themselves. It was only half past five. She wouldn't be long.

In town, most things looked much the same. She kept looking for signs of the invaders but there was nothing extraordinary, just some notices pasted up here and there. The white flags were all gone. It was a lovely evening and a few people were out walking, pushing prams or leading small children by the hand. She saw no-one walking a dog, however. Hundreds of pets had been put to sleep at the time of the evacuation. She thought that was terribly unfair for the dogs and cats.

The white cross was still to be seen in Royal Square though it was no longer very white. Dirty footprints criss-crossed it in all directions and someone had written something on it, which had later been scrubbed out. Izette stood at the edge of the cross and bent down to touch it with her fingers. She hadn't expected it to be so big. She'd overheard Mr Birrell telling her father he'd seen a German platoon drilling on it, 'walking all over our surrender' he had said sadly. Well she wasn't going to walk on it, out of respect for Mr Birrell.

She walked carefully around the outside then raised her eyes to look at the States Building. A huge red, black and white Nazi flag hung down the front of the building and, beneath it, a German soldier stood on guard by the entrance. He was not tall and blonde, however; he was short and rotund. He wore the square iron helmet about which there were many rude jokes circulating. His uniform was grey, a belted jacket over trousers and very shiny high black boots, like riding boots. They all had those, apparently. And he had a rifle.

Watching the young girl who was examining him closely, the soldier waited until he caught her eye then winked.

Embarrassed and confused, Izette turned quickly away and walked on towards the Weighbridge. Then she began to see them everywhere. Grey-uniformed soldiers in small groups, strolling along the pavements looking in shop windows or just standing around on corners, talking and smoking, just as though they lived here, thought Izette in surprise. They were joking and laughing, just as Irene had said. By contrast, the Islanders were hurrying along, ignoring the presence of the soldiers. On the corner of Broad Street the ice-cream seller had set up his cart and was doing a roaring trade with the soldiers. Mothers pulled their children past the ice cream cart disdainfully. It was clear the island children were not going to be permitted to share ice cream with the invaders.

But it was the harbour she really wanted to see. The burned-out buildings, the bomb craters, (if there were any), the German ships, the guns lined up along the quay waiting to be towed to their designated places....

'Izette!'

She turned. Running towards her was Tom. Her face broke into a smile.

'Hello, Tom.'

'What on earth do you think you're doing? Your Mum and Dad are furious. They sent me down to find you. You're not supposed to be down here by yourself. I shouldn't think they'll let you out for weeks after this.'

Her smile faded. Tom was obviously extremely annoyed at having to come looking for her. He took her roughly by the hand and started to hurry her back home.

'But I only wanted to see them for myself, Tom. I was on my way home actually,' she protested.

'Not walking in that direction you weren't.' He stopped and looked at her. 'You haven't changed, have you?' He shook his head and jerked her on towards home.

'It's not fair, Tom. I've been shut in for days. I only wanted to see what was going on.'

'Well, you'll have to learn to be a little more subtle. Why didn't you ask your Dad to take you down to town with him? He would have taken you eventually.'

'I got tired of waiting. And I wanted to stand and look properly...my way. I wanted to feel what it feels like...to be occupied, to see them right here in the town.' It was difficult to explain. 'Do you know what I mean?'

'I know you have a gift for landing yourself in trouble.'

Izette yanked her hand out of Tom's, not in order to run away, there would have been no point. She continued to walk, not alongside him, but a pace or so in front, her head held high in indignation. After a momentary pause, Tom shrugged his shoulders and followed her.

CHAPTER 3

Izette slept with her head four feet away from Tom's. No-one knew this, not even Tom. At night she rolled over to face the wall that divided her bedroom from Tom's, placed her fingers on the cold wallpaper and whispered good night. Her bed hadn't always been aligned with Tom's. In fact, it had been difficult persuading her father to push her bed up into the corner. Mum wanted her to have the bed away from the wall so that it could be made more easily. In the end, the only way Izette could get them to agree to let her have her bed in the corner was to promise to make her own bed every day. It was a small sacrifice.

The Vaubert family and the Birrell family lived in two identical, semi-detached Victorian villas. The houses rejoiced in the somewhat unimaginative name of 'Belle View Villas', number one and number two, which was certainly true if not very exciting, and had been home to Izette and Nancy for the whole of their young lives. The villas had once stood alone on a narrow, dusty farm lane, surrounded by small fields but the lane had long since been covered with cobbles and tar.

Over the years a rising tide of houses had gradually crept further and further up the hill out of town, eating away the little fields until they had consumed all but a narrow strip of green lawn on each side of the Villas. Behind each villa, however, remained a long ribbon of garden, stretching away down the hill, bounded by a low stone wall. On the other side of the wall a gently sloping field had survived intact, and on summer evenings Bill and Ted often smoked a companionable pipe, leaning on the wall, eyes scanning the broad sweep of St Aubin's Bay below. At potato planting time it was Izette and Nancy's turn to sit on the wall to watch the farmer wrestle the plough behind his draught horses.

Opposite the Villas and their neighbouring houses were more open fields, the Avenue marking the high tide line of brick and mortar. Izette's favourite view was from the highest point of the field opposite, from which she could enjoy the perfect symmetry of the villas. In the centre of each villa there was a front door with an overhanging porch, flanked by windows on either side. Above, on the first floor, there were three identical windows and a further two dormer windows popped prettily out of the roof to light the attic bedrooms. Old, painted wooden shutters were fixed to each window and only here did the houses differ. The Vaubert shutters were painted a soft green; the Birrell's a duck-egg blue. The rough rendered walls were whitewashed each spring. The name, 'Belle View Villas,' was incised in the plaster moulding that ran across the front wall between the upper and lower windows. Bill and Ted grumbled each year when they came to the final, finicky job of repainting the name. Bill did the 'Belle Vi' while Ted tackled 'ew Villas,' and their wives made sure the kettle was boiling on the hob as they started the last 'i' and 's'.

*

'Izette! Izette! Are you upstairs?'

Izette rolled lazily from her bed and opened her bedroom door to reply to her mother. It was bound to be an errand. 'Coming,' she called, jumping the stairs two at a time.

Downstairs her mother was in the back scullery, deep in the week's laundry. She straightened up when Izette appeared in the doorway, drying reddened hands on her apron.

'Can you go over to Aunt Margaret's for me? I need some eggs and I haven't the time to walk over myself. Whenever Margaret and I get together for a good chin-wag, the time seems to fly by and I really can't spare the time today. Tell her I'll be over on Tuesday. We can catch up with the news then.'

Betty reached down a stiff-handled basket from the scullery shelf, put a clean tea towel inside and handed it to Izette.

'Here, and don't swing it on the way back! I think it may still be too early but if the brambles are ready bring some home and I'll make a fruit pie. Take Edmund with you, he can help you pick. It's time he had some fresh air and exercise.'

Izette found Edmund in his attic bedroom. He was lying on the floor, hands behind his head, gazing at the ceiling.

'Hello, what are you doing?'

'Thinking.'

'You're always thinking. What are you thinking about this time?'

'I was thinking of painting the solar system on my ceiling – the sun and the planets in their correct relative positions. It's all in that book there.' He pointed to a large volume on his bed, his latest loan from the library. 'Do you think Dad would let me?'

Izette shrugged, 'I don't know, you'll have to ask him.

Anyway, forget that. I've got to go over to the farm for some eggs. Do you want to come?'

'Can we stay for tea?'

'I expect so.'

'All right then,' Edmund agreed, suddenly enthusiastic.

Betty tried her best but had never been able to match the glorious abundance of her sister's tea table. Perhaps, as she often said, it was having the best of home-grown ingredients that made the difference. Bill would nod loyally when she said this. Her children, however, didn't care about the whys and wherefores; they just made sure that their visits to the farm included the hours between five and six in the afternoon. This was when Uncle Jim and his men gathered in the big farm kitchen to swill tea in huge blue and white striped mugs and eat their way through mountains of bread, butter and jam, followed by fruit cake, apple cake, upside-down cake or whatever else Aunt Margaret had taken into her head to bake that morning.

*

It was hot when they set out for the farm. The weather had been so fine that summer it seemed to confirm their mother's oft repeated, 'the sun shines on the wicked.' There was no doubt in Izette's mind that the Germans were wicked, but it didn't seem very fair when you saw them off-duty, splashing happily in the sea.

'Come on, Edmund, keep up!'

Izette was already regretting bringing Edmund. All the way he had trailed slowly behind, stopping every few minutes to examine a plant in the hedgerow or point out a particular bird to her as though she didn't know what it was.

'We'd better pick the brambles on the way back at this

rate,' she grumbled.

'You didn't say anything about picking brambles.'

'Didn't I? Oh, I must have forgotten to mention it.'

Edmund was not taken in. 'I wouldn't have come if I'd known that,' he shouted indignantly, 'you cheated me, Izette. I hate picking brambles, they're all thorny and my fingers go purple. Well I shan't do it!' And he stopped and sat down in the middle of the lane.

Izette sighed and walked back to where he sat cross-legged and cross-armed in the dust, every bit of him cross in fact. He looked so ridiculously cross she might have laughed if she hadn't been so hot herself.

'Not even for Dad, Edmund?' she wheedled. 'Mum said if we find any, she'll make a fruit pie. You know that's his favourite.' She waited while Edmund thought about this. Eventually he grunted and got to his feet.

'Well, as long as you tell him I picked them,' he said, then added, 'in fact, you have to tell him I picked all of them. Do you promise?'

'If it will get you moving again, yes, I promise!'

Edmund smiled and set off along the lane at a brisk pace, Izette hurrying along behind him. She could always persuade Edmund to do something by suggesting it would please their father. Edmund adored his father. Izette wondered if Edmund sometimes sensed he was not quite the sort of son his father had expected. She had seen Bill sometimes listen to his son with a baffled expression on his face, clearly out of his depth when Edmund was relaying some new and exciting scientific fact he had discovered in one of his books, and wondered if Edmund felt a distance between them. This could perhaps account for Edmund's apparent need to please his father, as though by being the perfect son, Edmund could bridge the gulf. She wanted to tell Edmund that it wasn't necessary, that he was loved just as much as the rest of them, but she hadn't yet found the right moment to broach the subject.

Suddenly Izette's thoughts were scattered by a close burst of gunfire. Edmund ducked in alarm. Izette shouted at him to get down and they both dived for shelter into the ditch under the hedge. It was the first time they had heard gunfire at such close range and they had no idea what was going on. The firing continued for about ten minutes by which time they had worked out that it was not rifle fire but the steady pounding of much larger guns

'It must be coming from one of the new gun emplacements,' whispered Edmund knowledgeably, 'they've been building anti-aircraft batteries up here. It sounds like they're firing practice rounds.'

Izette looked at him in astonishment. 'How do you know?'

'I've been watching,' replied Edmund. 'I take notes of their positions and then I mark them up on my map back home. I have most of the defences in this area plotted.'

Izette was sceptical. 'But you hardly ever go out!'

'I do, you just don't see me.' He crawled closer to her, his voice dropping even lower, 'I carry out most of my surveillance...' he mouthed the word with intense pleasure, '...with binoculars, Grandpa's old binoculars, from the roof. I climb out of my bedroom window and get up on the ridge behind the chimney...'

Izette gasped. 'But Edmund, you might fall!'

Edmund ignored her interruption, '...and at night, when it's dark, I go out on reconnaissance.'

'Reconnaissance!'

'Shhh!' Edmund pressed a finger to his lips, 'we might be overheard.'

'Don't be silly, Edmund, there's no-one in sight. But

you mustn't go out at night. There's a curfew. You'd get into terrible trouble if you were caught. You might even be shot!'

Edmund glowed with pride. 'They never see me, I'm very careful. Besides, they make such a loud noise with their boots, I always have plenty of time to hide.'

'All the same, you shouldn't be doing it, Edmund, it's too risky. What would Mum and Dad say?'

Edmund looked alarmed. 'You won't tell them, will you?' he asked anxiously, 'I'm doing it for Dad, you see. I'm going to get together a plan of all the German defences and give it to Dad. He can send it to Mr Churchill and then they'll come and free us.'

'Oh Edmund,' said Izette, 'I don't think it's as simple as that.'

'Why not? I've heard Dad talking to Mr Birrell. He said one of the main problems was that the British Government didn't know what was going on here. We can't telephone or send letters to England any more, can we?'

'No, I know, but...I can't explain it properly. It's all much more complicated than you think it is.'

Edmund was quiet for a moment. When he looked up at Izette, she saw the beginnings of tears in his eyes. 'But you still won't tell?'

Izette put an arm round him, 'No, I won't tell Mum and Dad.'

'Do you promise?'

'Yes, I promise.'

'Cross your heart and hope to die?'

'For heaven's sake, Edmund. Yes, I promise. Now shake hands on it.'

They shook hands. As the firing appeared to have stopped they climbed cautiously out of the ditch and continued on their way to the farm. Edmund trotted along beside Izette cheerfully, delighted to have shared his spectacular secret.

*

Sweating and thirsty, their shoes whitened by the dust, they were relieved to turn the final corner and see the farm come into view. The old pump still stood in the yard and they rushed towards it to draw the pure cool water from deep below. Izette pumped the rusty handle while Edmund held his hands under the sparkling drops, splashing the water over his face and hair before bending under the spout for a long drink.

When they had each quenched their thirst and made a fuss of the farm dogs they went into the farmhouse to find Aunt Margaret. As always, she was working in the kitchen. It was cool and dark inside and the children flopped thankfully onto a couple of stools at the end of the table.

'Well, well, look who's here, Jim!'

Aunt Margaret was always pleased to see them. She had no children of her own. Uncle Jim came out of the dairy to join them and the children were subjected to a barrage of questions about the latest events in St Helier, though Uncle Jim also had plenty of news for the children to take back to town.

'They've been tramping all over my land as though they own it!' Jim muttered, 'and if I say anything they show me some papers written in German that I can't make head or tail of! They've dug up the fields overlooking the sea for their big guns and now they're driving up and down, ruining the bottom pasture, taking barbed wire and the like down to the beaches. Making a right mess they are. Tell your dad I'm going to write to the Bailiff about it.'

Izette told them about the fright they'd had when the guns suddenly started firing. Uncle Jim nodded, 'Well you can imagine what my cows thought about that noise when it first started. Regular stampede it was!'

The swapping of experiences continued throughout tea, Izette and Edmund taking note of every detail in order to be able to report it thoroughly at home. When the meal was over, Aunt Margaret placed a dozen eggs in the basket, together with tomatoes, lettuce, spring onions and a home-made cake, covering it all carefully with the tea towel.

'Now, you'll find the best brambles along the path down to the cove, but don't go down too far, the Germans are down there putting barbed wire and the like along the beach. Just stay at the top end of the path, you'll find enough there for a pie.' Aunt Margaret gave them a colander in which to collect the berries. 'Come back when you've picked enough and you can wash your hands before you go home.'

They were about to leave when Uncle Jim stopped them. 'Just a minute, I've a little job for young Edmund. You carry on Izette...' he winked at Edmund '...this is a man's job.'

Izette paused, hoping her uncle would give an explanation, but when it became clear he wasn't going to, she flounced out of the kitchen. She would make Edmund tell her later, one way or another.

'What are you up to now, Jim?' Margaret asked suspiciously.

'Never you mind, my dear. Like I said, this is man's business.' He took hold of Edmund's hand and led him out of the kitchen. Margaret overheard his question to the boy as they left, 'Now, young man, can you keep a secret, a very big secret?'

Jim took Edmund over to the cattle shed in which he over-wintered the cattle. In the summer his cows were free to graze the meadows so the shed was empty now save for a few bales of straw heaped up at one end and the house martins, which had temporarily moved in to bring up their young offspring.

'I've got something to hide from Jerry, you see, young Edmund. It's over here at the moment but I need to put it somewhere safer.' Jim walked over to the bales of straw and, thrusting his arm between them, drew out a long package wrapped up in sacking. Edmund watched as Jim carefully unwrapped the bundle to reveal his shotgun and several boxes of cartridges.

'It's your big gun, Uncle Jim.'

'Yes, you've seen it often enough, Edmund. The problem is, the Germans are saying we have to hand in all our guns. Well, they aren't getting this one. I've had this gun a good few years and I'm not parting with it, especially to the likes of them, so I'm going to hide it. That's where I need your help.'

'My help?' Edmund was very surprised.

'You see that hole up there?' Jim pointed to the roof of the cattle-shed where there was a very small opening in the rough ceiling, some of the plaster having broken away from the laths. Edmund nodded.

'I want you to wriggle up through that hole and hide my shotgun up there, resting between the beams. I can't do it. Even if I could get my belly through that hole, I'd likely bring the whole ceiling down with my weight. You'll have to be brave though, because there's likely to be big spiders up there. Do you think you could do that?'

Edmund looked up at his Uncle and nodded solemnly.

'And it will have to be a secret between you and me. No-one else is to know, no-one at all. Not even your Aunt Margaret knows what we're doing in here.'

'Can't I even tell my Dad?'

Jim shook his head, 'No-one at all.'

Edmund looked down at his feet and scuffed some wisps

of straw, saying very quietly into his chest, 'I'd really like to tell my dad.'

Jim smiled and ruffled Edmund's hair. 'When this is all over you can tell him. I'll tell him too. He'll be really proud then but, for now....'

'It's a secret!' interrupted Edmund, eyes shining again, 'cross my heart and hope to die!'

Jim winced. 'Well, we hope it won't come to that, young man. Now, you scramble up that stack of bales and see if you can squeeze through the hole.'

It was certainly a squeeze, a dusty, crumbly, cobwebby squeeze. Edmund closed his mind to the spiders and concentrated on his uncle's instructions. Once through the hole he could see a triangular space about three feet high that ran the length of the cowshed. Daylight filtered in through holes in the roof where tiles were missing. Edmund only just had enough room to turn himself around so that Uncle Jim could hand the gun up to him.

'See if you can wriggle a fair way along with it, then stuff it down between the beams so if anyone should shine a torch along, they won't see it. Can you manage that?'

'I think so.'

Edmund took hold of the heavy gun and dragged it through the hole till it lay alongside him. It was almost as long as he was. Then he edged his way along the beams on his stomach, pulling the gun along as he went. A cobweb stretched across his face and he clawed it off, spitting in revulsion. When he was a couple of yards along, he carefully laid the gun in its canvas wrapping behind one of the beams and turned to make the return journey for the cartridges.

'Well done, Edmund. Very well done indeed.' Jim congratulated him as he helped him down through the hole. 'My word, you're in a bit of a mess though. I shall have to clean you up before your Aunt Margaret sees you.'

Taking Edmund once more by the hand, Jim led him through into the stable where he took one of the grooming brushes and began to brush Edmund's clothes. Edmund beamed with achievement.

'There we are then, that's not too bad.' Jim knelt down to examine Edmund's face, took a grubby handkerchief out of his pocket and spat on it, then applied it to his face. 'Don't screw your face up like that...that's better. Your knees are a bit dirty too but I expect they were like that when you got here.'

Straightening up at last, Jim stuffed the handkerchief back into the depths of his corduroy trousers and released Edmund. 'Come on, my little hero, let's see if your sister is back yet.'

Edmund galloped back into the farmhouse kitchen happily, causing his aunt to raise her eyebrows.

'Looks to me like you 'men' have been up to some mischief.'

Seeing Edmund flush bright pink she nodded but didn't pursue the matter. Time enough for that when she had her husband alone later. Izette was sitting on a stool, swinging her legs, trying to look uninterested while her aunt packed the freshly picked berries into the basket.

'Off you go then, my dears,' Aunt Margaret said, 'straight home, no dawdling and don't go near the guns.'

Izette picked up the basket and led the way out of the kitchen without a word to Edmund. There would be time enough for questions on the way home and she was well versed in methods of extracting information from Edmund.

Aunt Margaret watched them out of sight, giving a last wave as they turned into the farm lane, then turned to her husband with much the same thoughts in mind as her niece.

CHAPTER 4

Bill was sorting through some papers in the small glassed-in cubicle that served as his office when the German officer walked in through the open workshop doors. At the other end of the workshop Donald, Bill's chief mechanic, was working on a van, head under the bonnet, hands deep in the engine compartment, so didn't see him. It was Tom who spotted the German first and walked over to Bill's office to tap lightly on the glass.

'Bill, we've got a visitor.'

Bill looked up and took off his glasses, peering through the glass at the stranger. The German was short and slightly built but immaculately turned out. He stood in the sunlight flooding through the open doors; feet planted slightly apart, his eyes scanning the workshop as he waited for attention. Bill came slowly out of his office and walked over to where he stood. He caught the faint smell of cologne.

The German smiled as Bill approached.

'You are the proprietor?'

At least six inches shorter than Bill, he had to tilt his head up to look Bill in the face but gave no sign of feeling at any disadvantage. Bill nodded. By now, Donald had emerged from under the van's bonnet and, like Tom, was standing watching. The German looked down at the clipboard he was holding.

'You are William Vaubert?'

Bill nodded again.

'Good. I am Captain Nebel, of the Purchasing Commission. We require your assistance in the matter of requisitioned vehicles. These men here,' he indicated Tom and Donald, 'these are your employees?'

'Yes, just the two of them now.'

'They are fully trained mechanics?'

Pointing to Donald, Bill said, 'This man is an experienced mechanic, but Tom here has only been working for me about a year. He still has quite a bit to learn.'

The German studied Tom, noting that, unlike the older men, he was lounging against the workbench, holding a tea mug; his manner obviously intended to convey contempt. A smile of amusement lifted the corners of the German's mouth.

'I agree, he still has quite a bit to learn - but can he drive?'

'Yes he can,' said Bill, 'now do you mind telling me what this is all about?'

'As I said, Mr Vaubert, we will require your assistance with vehicle requisitioning. Will you kindly report to me, with your papers, and those of your employees, tomorrow morning?' Handing Bill a card, he added, 'this is where you will report, please.'

Bill read the card then looked up, 'Do I have any choice?'

The German smiled patiently. 'I assume you read the

Evening Post, Mr Vaubert. You will therefore have read the communication to your Governor from the Commander of the German Forces, which said, 'In the case of peaceful surrender..."' he paused, 'which of course is the case here in Jersey, '...the lives, property and liberty of peaceful inhabitants are solemnly guaranteed.' So you see you are quite free to choose, Mr Vaubert. If you do not choose to assist us, there are many other garages on the island and, as you know, in times of war, fortunes may be made or lost. But, as an experienced man of business, I am sure I do not need to tell you this. I hope I shall see you tomorrow. Good morning.'

The German clicked his heels together and made a small bow, then turned and walked out. A staff car was waiting outside for him. The men watched silently as his driver opened the door for him, then got back in the car and drove away. Donald and Tom walked out to stand on the pavement, gazing in the direction the car had gone.

'Dapper little squirt, wasn't he?' commented Donald.

Tom grunted in response.

Donald continued, 'Nice motors they give them to drive around in, too.'

'They'll have an even nicer collection by the time they've finished helping themselves to ours.' replied Tom. 'Didn't you hear what he said, Donald? He's from the Purchasing Commission. They're taking all our cars and shipping them over to France. Only it's all fair and square because the Purchasing Commission is going to pay the owners compensation.' Tom dropped his cigarette end on the ground and ground it out in disgust.

By now, Bill had joined them outside.

'What are you going to do then, boss?' asked the older man.

'I know what I'd like to do,' growled Bill. He crumpled

the card the officer had given him in his fist. 'Can you two manage without me for the rest of the day?' Looking round the workshop, empty except for the van Donald was working on, he gave a short bitter laugh. 'Who am I kidding? There's precious little to keep even one of us busy here.'

Going back into his office, he took the bunch of garage keys off their hook on the wall.

'Here Donald,' he threw the keys towards him. 'I'm off. Lock up when you've finished, will you? Tom, can bring the keys home to me later.'

Donald caught the keys and slipped them in his overalls pocket, nodding towards Bill.

'See you tomorrow, then, Bill?'

'Aye, I expect so.'

They watched as Bill wheeled his old bicycle from the back of the workshop. Bill's own car was safely hidden somewhere on the island. As soon as they'd got wind that the Germans would be requisitioning Islanders' cars he'd driven it away, returning a few hours later on his old bike. So now he used his old bicycle for running to and fro between the garage and home.

As Bill left the garage, instead of taking his overalls off and hanging them on the hook by the door as usual, he just threw his old working jacket with the sagging pockets over the top. Once outside he didn't mount the bike but walked away slowly, pushing it along with one hand.

'The boss is taking it all very bad,' commented Donald placidly.

'Aren't we all?' said Tom sharply.

'Yes, of course, young Tom, but life goes on and a man's got to earn a living. Got to put the food on the table when you've a family, you know. You wouldn't understand that yet.' And taking an empty pipe from his pocket, Donald clamped it between his teeth and returned to his work on the van.

Tom looked at the older man with irritation. It was true of course but there were times when he'd like to ram his stoicism down his throat. Didn't he care what was happening in the Islands? But then he remembered Donald wasn't an Islander. He'd moved to the Island from England as a young man about 15 years ago and married an Island girl. Bill had taken him on soon after he arrived and trained him up as a motor mechanic. He was a hard-working, dependable sort, but his horizons were limited, at least that's how Tom saw it. As long as he could rely on his weekly pay packet, a bit of overtime now and then and a bonus at Christmas he was content.

'No, I don't,' agreed Tom, adding to himself, 'and I hope I never have to.'

He took another cigarette from the packet in his pocket and lit it, feeling the sunshine warm on his skin. He didn't want to be stuck in the workshop today. The few bits of jobs he had on could wait.

'I'm going to take a break, Don, get a breath of fresh air. There's not much on.'

'Aye, all right.'

*

Tom turned towards the harbour. He thought he'd go and do a bit of Jerry watching. Busy as a colony of ants they were. As he walked towards the Weighbridge he wondered what life had in store for him in the long term. This work with Bill was all right for the time being. His father had been anxious for him to learn a trade. His time at school had yielded no qualifications, though not due to any lack of ability. Tom was as bright, if not more so, than his classmates, but his school reports always said the same thing - he lacked application. He didn't see it that way, of course. All he knew was that the classroom had stifled and suffocated him with its pointless exercises and irritating discipline so, as soon as he could leave, he did. He drifted for a while, had a bit of fun, picking up odd jobs where he could to keep him in pocket money, but it didn't take him long to work out that it was getting him nowhere, so when Bill offered him an apprenticeship he thought he'd give it a try.

He'd always got on well with Bill, thought of him more as an uncle than just a neighbour, and he knew him to be honest and fair, good qualities to have in an employer. Besides, he was interested in cars. He particularly liked driving, always the one offering to pick up a car for service or deliver it back to its owner even if the return trip meant a long walk home. And it was satisfying to be able to lift a car bonnet with confidence, knowing he could probably find the source of a problem for a customer. Sometimes he saw himself with his own garage in a few years, not a general workshop like Bill's, but selling glossy new cars imported from the continent, sports models with drop-hoods, white-walled tyres and cream leather upholstery. At other times his mind filled with thoughts of the world outside the Island's shores that as yet he knew nothing about, and he longed for the day when he would be able to leave the island. When he reached the harbour, Tom lit another cigarette and leaned on the railings to watch the Germans unloading their ships. One thing was for certain, he thought grimly; he wouldn't be going anywhere while this lot were in control.

*

Betty was in the garden hanging out the washing when she

heard the gate hinges squeak and turned to see Bill wheeling his bicycle into the shed. She hurried over to ask if he was feeling all right. It was unlike Bill to come home in the middle of the morning.

'No, I'm fine,' Bill answered. 'We just had a visit from one of those Germans doing the requisitioning. They want us to "*help out*",' Bill snorted in disgust. 'Of course we don't have to co-operate, he said, we're perfectly free to choose. As if we had any real choice!'

He leaned his bike up against the shed wall, locked the door and walked slowly into the house. Betty followed him anxiously.

'What happens if you refuse?'

'Oh I don't expect they'll do anything to me but the business would go to another garage. I don't think there'll be any shortage of takers.'

'But you don't want to work for them, Bill?'

'No, I don't, but there's precious little work left to do at all. They're taking all our cars, petrol is rationed and it won't be long before the only cars on the road will be German cars. I can't keep the garage going on bike repairs!'

Betty didn't know what to say. Bill never involved her in the garage affairs. She very rarely went there. It wasn't a woman's place, Bill said.

'What about Tom and Donald?' she asked.

'I have to take their papers in as well as mine tomorrow, so it looks like they want all of us.'

'Oh…well, I suppose that's good in a way,' Betty commented tentatively, 'I mean, Donald has his family to think of.'

'Yes, as have I!' In a rare show of feeling, Bill put his arms around his wife and held her close.

'Don't you worry, Betty, we'll be all right. As long as I can keep us fed, eh? In fact, since I'm home early I think I'll give the vegetable patch a good going over today. We're going to need it. That's something I can do.'

'That's right, Bill Vaubert. Never say die! And I'll make you a nice mug of tea.'

They kissed, a homely smack on the lips. Then Bill walked down to his greenhouse to plan the day's labour while Betty busied herself in the kitchen, wondering which of them was more convincing when it came to putting on a brave face. No doubt they'd be getting a good deal of practice in the months ahead.

*

The bad news didn't end there that day. When Irene came home later and joined the rest of the family for tea she announced that they'd finished all that needed to be done at the hotel and it would close now for the duration, however long that might be. All the staff had been given a week's wages and their cards. Izette wondered why Irene didn't sound more disappointed. Hadn't she just lost her job? Betty looked across the tea table to see how Bill would take it but he said nothing, just nodded solemnly and reached across the table for another slice of bread. Irene was surprised at his silence. She caught her mother's eye and raised her eyebrows questioningly.

'Your father had a visit from the Germans today,' explained Betty, 'they want the garage to be involved in the requisitioning. Dad's not very happy about it.'

'Oh I see,' said Irene.

Edmund looked up quickly when he heard this. 'Really?' he asked excitedly, 'Can I come and watch?'

'Watch what, son?'

'What they're going to do,' replied Edmund.

'You'll be at school, my lad,' answered Bill, 'and anyway I don't think it will be all that interesting – just a lot of cars coming in for checking over. They're calling in all the fairly new models at the moment. Each one has to be checked and valued so that they can compensate the owner...or so they say.'

'You'll be fairly busy then, Bill?' said Betty.

'Mm, I suppose so.' Bill admitted grudgingly.

Irene showed nearly as much interest in her father's news as Edmund.

'In that case, Dad,' said Irene, 'could you use me down at the garage? I could do reception and keep the accounts. I've done wages at the hotel and....'

'No, Irene.' Bill interrupted her abruptly, then added more gently, 'no, I'm sorry, love. A garage is no place for a woman, as you've heard me say before, there's a lot of rough men's talk goes on, not for your ears. More to the point, since it looks like we'll be having Jerry in and out all day, I'd rather you were not there. I've seen them talking to some of our women in St Helier, those who'll give them the time of day, that is. They're a long way from home and....lads will be lads. You know what I mean?'

'Yes, Dad.' Irene was obviously disappointed.

Bill paused and, reaching across the table to pat her hand, added, 'besides, I pay terrible wages!'

She managed half a smile at this, and the conversation turned to other matters as the family finished their tea. Afterwards, Irene went up to her room and Izette followed her, leaping on to Irene's bed and settling down to hear the more intimate details of Irene's day.

'Move over, Izette, I'm exhausted. We've had to clean out every single room today.' Irene flopped down on the bed beside Izette and sighed a long, weary sigh.

'So what are you going to do now, Irene?' asked Izette.

'I don't know. There is a possibility of a job coming up but Dad won't like it.'

'What is it?'

'You know Marie, the girl I work with, or rather, used to work with?'

Izette nodded, though she had never actually seen her.

'Well she's been offered a job at the Hotel Regent and she says the manager there is looking for more staff.'

'But isn't that the hotel the Germans are using?'

'Yes, that's why he needs more staff, idiot. The thing is, if I want the job, I'll have to send in my references straight away. With all the hotels closing, there'll be hundreds of people out of work. I can't afford to wait. And it's a fabulous hotel – makes our place look like a run-down guesthouse.'

'So what are you going to do?' Izette asked again.

'Dad's the problem. I don't mind working with the Germans. Someone's got to do it and I need the money, but I know he'll be dead set against it. You heard what he said about me working at the garage. I can't even think how I'd tell him.'

'But you haven't got the job yet.'

'No,' said Irene, 'but I know Mr Meurs, the manager. He's friendly with our Mr Grasett, comes in for a quiet drink sometimes in the back office. I think he'll offer me a job if he knows I'm interested.'

Getting up from the bed. Irene went over to her dressing table and sat down. She looked at her own reflection in the mirror and turned her head first to one side and then to the other.

'I'm not sure I like these earrings any more. I think I would look better in something more sophisticated, perhaps just plain pearls. You can't go wrong with pearls.'

Realising that little else of interest would be forthcoming from Irene that evening, Izette got up and left Irene's room. She stood on the landing scuffing the carpet with her shoe, feeling at a loose end. Perhaps she would see if Edmund was doing anything interesting. She found him in his attic room scribbling away in a notebook. As she walked across the room towards him he covered over what he had been writing.

'You can't see. It's secret. Go away.'

Sighing, Izette walked away from him to the window where she stood looking out, wondering what to do with the rest of the evening. Edmund's dormer window faced inland. There was a good view of the cemetery where she and Nancy sometimes played. That would do. Turning quickly she ran out of the room and jumped down the two flights of stairs, shouting to her mother as she left the house, 'I'm going to the cemetery with Nancy.'

'Keep an eye on the time, Izette. You mustn't be out after curfew,' her mother called but she was already out of earshot. Bolting straight in through the Birrells' back door, she rushed from room to room until she found Nancy. They told Nancy's mother where they were going.

'What? The cemetery again? I don't know what you girls find to do there. Still, off you go then.'

*

It was a lovely evening but they passed no-one as they walked up the lane. Izette had overhead Mr Birrell telling her father that an evening stroll had lost its pleasure when you came across groups of off-duty Germans on every corner. Mrs Birrell had still not ventured into town. Her husband did what shopping she needed, not that much was available any more. The German troops had bought up almost everything they could find in the shops, clearing the shelves like locusts, and it was difficult to know when new stock would be brought in from France. There would certainly be nothing now from England.

'When do you go back to school, Nancy?' Izette asked.

The girls attended different schools. Nancy went to the States Intermediate but Izette had been sent to a private convent school, a decision that had caused some tension between the two families when the decision was first made, especially since the Vauberts had never previously had any dealings with the Catholic Church.

'Thursday, I think.'

'Me too.'

'Some schools are closing and joining up with others.'

'I know. I think we might be getting St Gregory's boys in with us,' said Izette, 'the Germans have taken over their buildings.'

'Golly!' said Nancy. 'What will the nuns make of that?'

'They probably won't know the difference!'

They turned into the Cemetery and wandered down the central avenue, branching off after a couple of hundred yards to the left along a path that led to the oldest graves. These were the gravestones they most liked to read. They liked to work out how old people had been when they died, sometimes trying to find the oldest, at other times searching for girls who had died at their own age. They would make up stories as to how their chosen victim had met her untimely end. Irene said it was ghoulish.

There was another purpose to their visits. Since no one visited these old graves, the high box tombs provided an ideally secluded area for their current interest. Sitting down on the springy turf, backs to a stone vault warmed by the afternoon sun, Izette would pull a squashy packet of Woodbines from her pocket. Nancy would produce the matches and together they would sit, puffing away. This evening, they followed the usual pattern. When each of them had a lit cigarette held casually between her fingers, Izette shared her startling news.

'Irene's going to work with the Germans.'

Nancy spluttered with astonishment, starting off a coughing fit. When she could speak again she looked at her friend in awe.

'Wow! So she'll be seeing them all the time, talking to them and… everything?'

Izette nodded.

'Won't she be frightened?' asked Nancy.

Remembering her sister's reactions to the German bathers, Izette shook her head slowly. 'Not at all. She's rather looking forward to it.'

'Golly!'

Izette flicked the ash from her cigarette rather expertly. Time to practice blowing smoke-rings, the ultimate sophistication. Pursing her mouth, she blew. It was a complete failure. Nancy watched then had a try herself, but it was no good, neither of them could produce anything resembling a ring.

'It's no good. I can't do it, 'Izette said eventually, stubbing out her cigarette irreverently on the tomb behind them. 'Come on, let's go and see if there are any new German graves.'

The girls made their way to the area of freshly turned earth set apart from the rest of the graveyard that had been designated for German use. Since the beginning of the occupation, the Germans had buried only a few casualties. The graves were marked with a simple German cross. Accustomed to seeing one new grave appear occasionally, the girls were surprised to see a whole row of fresh graves. They counted them up silently.

'Golly,' said Nancy, 'I make it 13. Something awful

must have happened.'

Izette bent down to touch the bare soil humped up over the nearest grave, pressing her palm to the earth. It was strange to think that someone lay down there as though they were sleeping; someone who presumably had been walking around a few days ago. The body wouldn't have started to decompose yet. She'd never seen a dead body.

'Izette!' whispered Nancy urgently, 'there's someone coming!'

They scuttled away quickly, ducking down to hide behind a large headstone.

'It's a German,' Nancy whispered, as the man came into clear view. He was on his own, in uniform but without a gun or helmet, just a sort of cap on his head. They watched him walk over to the German graves and stop at the one Izette had touched. He took off his cap and stood looking at the cross for a long time. Then he knelt down and bowed his head.

'It must be his friend.' whispered Nancy.

'Shh!' hissed Izette, 'have you no respect?'

Nancy was puzzled by this but accepted that Izette, as a convent schoolgirl, would know about such things.

After a few minutes, the German got up and replaced his cap. As he turned to leave he wiped roughly at his eyes with his sleeve and the girls got a clear sight of his face. He was very fair and very young; his face flushed a little. Replacing his cap, he walked away slowly. When they were sure he was out of sight, the girls emerged from their hiding place and Izette walked over to the grave again.

'Look, he's left something. It's a note, a card.'

It was a small hand-written card, folded into three and tucked down the side of the grave marker, almost out of sight. Izette stooped to pick it up.

'It's in German,' said Nancy.

'Of course it is, stupid! I wonder what it says. There's 'Werner', that's a name, isn't it?'

Nancy wasn't particularly interested. She looked at the sky. 'We'd better be going. It's getting late.'

'I know what I'm going to do. I'm going to borrow it and translate it.' said Izette.

'You can't do that,' protested Nancy, 'that would be...sacrilege,' anxious to demonstrate that she knew a few religious things too.

'No, it isn't. He just left it on the grave. It could easily have blown away in the wind. Anyway, I'll copy out the words and bring it back first thing tomorrow morning.'

'I can't see the point myself.'

'I want to know who he is, apart from just his name. I'd like to know something about him. Aren't you curious?'

Nancy just shrugged. Izette had funny ideas sometimes.

'Nancy! Izette!'

They looked up to see Tom striding up the path towards them. Izette quickly hid the note in her pocket.

'Come on, you two, time you were inside.'

'We were just coming, Tom.' said Nancy.

'If I had a pound for every time I've heard that, I'd be a rich man by now.'

Tom took hold of their collars, turned them towards the cemetery gates and frog-marched them a little way down the path before they managed to wriggle free. 'Off you go then, girls, I'll catch you up. I'm just going to have a quick cigarette,' he said, looking around the cemetery, 'it's nice and quiet here.'

Izette and Nancy looked at one another and burst into giggles. He didn't know the half.

CHAPTER 5

'So, will you tell him for me, Mum, please...pleeease?'

'Oh Irene, I don't know. You'll have to give me time to think...I'll have to wait until he's in a good mood.'

'There isn't any time for that,' said Irene, 'when he notices I'm not here today, he's going to wonder where I am.'

Betty brought the filled teapot over to the table and sat down heavily. 'All right then. Finish your breakfast and go,' she said resignedly, 'and that goes for you too, Izette,'

'But I'll be too early,' protested Izette.

'Then go to your room until it's time to go. I need to speak to your father alone.'

The sharp edge to Betty's voice told Izette she'd better not argue. The girls listened to their father's footsteps overhead as they finished their toast, following his progress from bathroom to bedroom. At the sound of the bedroom door opening, signalling Bill's imminent descent to the kitchen, both girls rapidly got up and left the room, Irene hurrying straight out of the front door. Izette squeezed past her father on the stairs on her way to her bedroom.

On the landing she paused outside her door, then decided to carry on up the attic stairs to Edmund's room. She wanted to be out of earshot of raised voices if there were to be any. Hurrying into Edmund's room and closing the door behind her, she found him packing his school satchel. Edmund was surprised to see her.

'What's the matter?'

'Mum's got to tell Dad about Irene getting a job at the German hotel.'

Edmund returned to packing his bag, carefully selecting his books and pencils as always. He understood fully the implications of what Izette had said. He was unlucky enough to have been in the kitchen during the last family argument about it. Bill had come home from town full of the news that the States were opening a factory in St Helier making clothing and shoes to provide employment for some of the many women who had lost their jobs. He thought this would be the answer for Irene.

'I'm not working in a factory, Dad,' Irene had said with disgust.

'Oh? And why not? I seem to remember you asking to work in the garage. Where's the difference between a garage and a factory?'

'The garage is different! It's ours. It's the family business.'

'Ah, I see, and you see yourself as the boss's daughter, I suppose?'

'Well, aren't I?'

Bill raised his hands in despair.

'Irene, you see factory work as demeaning. Fair enough. Ordinarily I would agree with you. I'd hope that any daughter of mine would be able to find better work than that, but we're in a war situation now and you'll have to learn to take what jobs are available.'

'But there are other jobs available, Dad,' protested Irene.

'And most of them seem to involve working with the Germans. I've no choice down at the garage. I either work with them on this requisitioning or they close me down. You have a choice...at least at the moment.'

'Well, I'm not working in any factory and that's that! You can't make me do anything I don't want to do!' And with that, Irene had flounced out of the kitchen and run upstairs to her room.

Since that altercation, Irene had been offered the job at the Hotel Regent and had accepted it. Now, and not for the first time, it was Betty who had the task of interceding between Bill and his elder daughter. As Bill descended the stairs, Betty decided that she would leave it until he returned from work later. That would give her more time to prepare herself and, if necessary, his favourite dinner.

Upstairs, Izette was mystified by the smile on Edmund's face as he handed her his satchel so that she could help him slide it on over his school blazer. Then she handed him his cap. He placed it on his head, buttoned up his blazer, adjusted his satchel and pulled up his grey knee socks, turning down the tops neatly.

'Do I look all right?' he asked as always.

'Fine,' Izette replied as always, 'I'll walk part of the way with you.'

'Right,' replied Edmund, 'come on, then.'

The reason for Edmund's smile was that he had been thinking. He had decided to put together his own plan of action against the enemy. No one would suspect a boy of his age, especially since he knew he was small and looked younger than he actually was. That in itself gave him an enormous advantage. And there were precedents. Joan of Arc had been only 12 when she started hearing voices telling her it was her divine mission to free her country from the English. Unfortunately he hadn't heard any voices but his dad and Mr Birrell were always saying someone needed to do something to let England know what was happening on the Islands. Well, he had already perfected a system of slipping out at night to collect information. When he had enough information collected about the German defences it would simply be a question of getting it to England. At the moment he was finding that a bit of a problem, but he was sure he would come up with an idea eventually.

This present family crisis could also turn out to be to his advantage. If Irene took the job at the hotel, that would bring her into daily contact with the Germans and she would possibly get to know some of the soldiers. He could then ask her to acquire information for him. She would be his spy. Yes, he thought, this could all turn out to be very useful.

On their way down into town, Edmund asked Izette if they could call in to the library on the way home.

'If you like. Mum asked me to pick up some shopping so you can choose your books while I'm doing that.'

Edmund and Izette had reached the point at which their ways parted.

'Meet me here at quarter to four, Edmund, and we'll go to the library. Don't be late.'

She watched him for a few minutes as he walked away in the direction of his school, wondering why she had said that when she knew that Edmund was never late for anything. His life was planned down to the last detail. Thinking what a peculiar brother he was, she turned and walked on.

*

'Boss is late,' said Donald

'Mmm,' agreed Tom.

'Didn't he have to go and report to the Germans with our papers today?'

'That's what he said.'

Tom walked over to the office and went in, closing the door behind him. He couldn't be bothered with Donald today. If he wasn't careful, he'd be subjected to one of Donald's homilies on making the best of a bad job. Fortunately for Tom, who couldn't find anything to keep him safely occupied in the office for any length of time, Bill walked in at that moment and straight over to the office where he threw down a sizeable bundle of papers.

'Cup of tea, Bill?' asked Tom.

'I could murder one, Tom.'

'What - the tea or a German?'

'At this moment, both! A German first, then a good cup of tea to celebrate!' Bill laughed.

Tom filled the kettle and put it on the gas ring, thinking things couldn't be too bad if Bill could crack a joke after an interview with the Germans. Donald came over to rinse out his mug for the fresh brew.

'So, how did it go then?'

'Well, I saw this supercilious bastard first. An officer - can't remember his name. Belly on him like a pregnant sow and he spoke to me as though I was some muck he'd found under his fingernails. I was beginning to get a bit hot under the collar when the little chap who was here the other day came in. Perhaps he'd overheard things getting a bit heated. Anyway, he said something to the fat one who then got up and left, and he took over the interview himself. Nice as pie, he was, you'd think he was delighted to see me.' Bill paused to take a long draught of his tea. 'The long and short of it is they want us to inspect all the cars they're requisitioning, check they're fully roadworthy, make a note of any faults and put a compensation value on them. Then we deliver them to the harbour.'

'And what happens to them then?'

'I've no idea, but the owners certainly won't see them again. That's why the Germans are paying compensation.'

'I'll believe that when I see it,' said Tom, 'you did well to hide yours when you had the chance, Bill.'

'Maybe, though if they start checking the records, they'll find out easily enough. Still, I think they're busy enough at the moment handling the cars they can see without worrying about the ones they can't.'

Suddenly Tom's temper snapped and he brought his clenched fist down hard on the workbench. 'Bastards! Who the hell do they think they are! Helping themselves to our cars and making themselves comfortable in our hotels. Well they might get a few surprises from the cars I check over. They might find the brakes are not as reliable as they expected!'

'Now, Tom, we're having none of that.' Bill put his hand on Tom's forearm. 'We can't risk it.'

'Why the hell not?'

'Just think about it. Firstly, we don't know who'll be driving those cars. It could be anyone, not just military. And secondly, I won't let you put yourself at risk, Tom. It isn't difficult to find out if a car's been tampered with and they'd soon trace it back to this garage. And you needn't think there'd be any point in you owning up to it. We'd all be for the high jump; you, me and Donald. I've seen how these Germans work. No, that's not the way.'

'Well what can I do, Bill? I can't just stand here and let them get on with it!'

'If I knew what we could do, don't you think I'd be

doing it?' Bill shouted. 'You're not the only one who feels useless, you know!'

At this point, Donald held up his hands to quieten the other two, jerking his head towards the door to remind them that anyone walking past the door could hear what was being said.

'Aye, you're right, Donald.' said Bill. 'Sorry, lad, no point in taking it out on each other.'

'No, Bill...I'm sorry.'

'Anyway, you may not be doing much in the mechanical line. They want you for a stand-by driver.'

'What?'

'That little captain put you down as a reserve driver. Seemed quite interested in you, don't know why. He described you as 'the young man with the angry eyes.' You see? You've already been noticed so, if they do send for you to do some driving, keep your head down and your mouth shut.'

'Do I have to do it?'

'Don't ask daft questions, lad. Have you been listening to what I've been saying or not? A few minutes ago you were asking what you could do. Well, if you bide your time and keep that temper of yours under control, there's no telling what you might learn in the company of your passengers. People tend to forget the chauffeur has ears.' Bill tapped the side of his nose.

Taking his overalls from the peg, Bill walked out into the workshop.

'Now, we've still got some work to do, haven't we? If you finish off that van, Donald, I'll take a look at the lorry. You can give me a hand, Tom.'

'Right, Bill.'

Tom slowly put on his overalls, his mind on what Bill had just said. Was Bill implying more than he'd actually said?

Did he mean there were already the beginnings of a resistance movement of some kind? Nothing had been mentioned in his own circle of friends but if there was, or if there was going to be, they would need men on the inside, local men whom the Germans trusted, perhaps whom they even regarded as friends. It was early days yet, the Islanders were still recovering from the shock of invasion but he knew the island spirit. They would never submit to German rule. Once the Islanders had caught their collective breath, despite the warnings of the Bailiff, someone was bound to get some sort of underground organised, and he'd make sure he was the first volunteer. This driving job might well put him in the ideal position to pick up information from the Germans. At the very least he'd probably be able to go into the many prohibited areas that were springing up all around the island.

'Come on, Tom, what are you doing?'

'Coming.'

'So's Christmas.'

Grabbing a few tools from the rack behind the workbench, Tom hurried over to help Bill, feeling more encouraged than since before the Germans first set foot on the island.

*

Later that afternoon, when Izette and Edmund arrived home, Betty was waiting anxiously at the front door.

'Where on earth have you been until this time?'

'We've been shopping, Mum, remember you asked me to go? And then Edmund wanted to go to the library.'

'Oh yes,' Betty seemed distracted, 'I'd forgotten that. Too much on my mind, I suppose.'

She turned and went into the house, Izette and Edmund

behind her. They dropped their bags and took off their coats.

Izette followed her into the warm kitchen. 'And then when we came out of the library, the Germans were having a parade so we had to come home the long way.'

'Did you manage to get those things on the list I gave you, Izette.'

'Not many of them. There was hardly anything left.'

'Oh dear,' said Betty, 'this rationing is getting bad already. Still at least there's Margaret and Jim at the farm. They'll help us out if things get really short. Where's Edmund? His tea's ready.'

'I think he took his books upstairs.'

'Can you go and give him a shout please, Izette?'

Izette got up and went upstairs to the first landing. He would hear her from there. She gave a shout and, satisfied that he had heard, turned to come downstairs. Before she reached the foot of the stairs however, the front door opened and Irene came in, shutting the door quietly behind her but instead of walking through to the kitchen she stopped and leant her back against it. She looked peculiar; all the colour had drained out of her face. Looking up, she saw Izette and pressed a finger to her lips to silence her. Then, taking off her shoes, she tiptoed up the stairs, taking Izette by the hand and pulling her along behind her. Once they were safely in her bedroom, she slumped on to the bed, her head in her hands.

'What on earth's the matter?' whispered Izette.

'Is Dad home yet?'

'No.'

'Good. Can you ask Mum to come up straight away, Izette?'

'Yes, but...'

'Please, Izette, just go will you!' and Irene burst into tears.

Izette flew down the stairs, nearly missing her footing,

and into the kitchen to fetch Betty. 'Mum, come quickly! It's Irene!'

They rushed upstairs, passing a puzzled Edmund on his way down, and into Irene's room. Irene was sobbing on her bed, her face buried in the eiderdown. Betty lifted her into her arms and soothed her as best she could. 'Pass me some hankies, Izette. There now, Irene, there.'

Izette sat on the dressing table stool watching her mother comfort Irene, hoping she would be allowed to stay and hear what had happened.

'There now, that's better.' Irene had reached the sniffling stage now.

'Now,' said Betty, 'tell me what all this is about.'

'Oh Mum, it was so awful...I can't....'

'Come on now, Irene,' then a little more briskly, 'blow your nose...here's another hankie. Now tell me what was so awful.'

Irene wiped her eyes again and, after a few false starts, was finally able to tell them what had happened.

'One of the German soldiers...he was drowned today....at Havre des Pas.'

Betty looked across at Izette. In that brief glance her relief was plain to see.

'Is that all....' she stopped. 'Is that why you're so upset?'

Irene looked sharply at her mother, 'He was only a boy, Mum! A child! He looked barely older than Izette.'

'But a German?'

'If you'd seen him, Mum...they brought him into the reception hall, you see. I was working on some papers at the desk when they carried him in. They had nowhere to put him so they laid him on one of the sofas...and the whole place was suddenly silent. No one said a word. No one moved. We all just looked at him lying there. There was seaweed in his hair...and around his ankles. Then water started to drip on to the floor making a big puddle. It was so...sad.'

'I see,' Betty was brusque, 'How did it happen?'

'I don't know. Pandemonium broke out when an officer arrived and started shouting orders. He was very angry but it was all in German so none of us could understand what was going on. I expect we'll hear tomorrow.'

'Well, Irene, I suppose I can understand you feeling upset. A young man has died accidentally and a young life has been wasted, which is always a tragedy but you must remember he was one of the enemy....'

'Mum!' protested Irene.

'I don't mean it doesn't matter because he was a German. But you have to remember that if circumstances had been different, that same lad could have been somewhere in the front line of the fighting, looking down his rifle at George Birrell. Poor Ted and Dorothy haven't had a word from George since the Germans arrived. They don't know where he is. They don't even know if he's alive.'

'I know, I know, Mum. And I've heard it said often enough – the only good German is a dead German – but that doesn't mean they aren't people with feelings just like us. He was some woman's son, Mum, little more than a child really.'

Betty was quiet for a moment. If she was honest, she had to admit that she couldn't feel any sympathy for the boy, or even for the boy's mother. The boy had no right to be here, swimming in the bay, enjoying the natural beauty of the island. It was as though the island itself had revenged itself on the invader and she could see a natural justice in that. Sighing, she got up.

'Tea's ready downstairs,' then, 'If you like, Irene, you can have yours on a tray up here. I can tell your father you've had a hard day and are feeling a little under the weather.' She paused. 'It might make it easier for him if he thinks your first day has been difficult.'

'You told him then?'

'Yes, he came home at lunch time.'

'How did he take it, Mum?'

'He wasn't surprised. He said he was getting used to you ignoring every piece of advice he gave you.'

Irene had the grace to look ashamed when she heard this.

'But you'd better keep things to yourself. He won't want to hear you prattling about the goings-on at the hotel like you used to. And watch yourself with those soldiers, my girl,' Betty warned, 'there are times when I could wish you were not so pretty, but I don't need to tell you what would happen if you became...involved with one of them. That would be the end for your father. He'd never forgive you.'

'I know, Mum,' said Irene solemnly. 'Don't worry, I know what I'm doing.'

Betty's glance at her daughter revealed her scepticism but she said no more. She went downstairs, leaving the two girls alone.

'So, you actually saw the dead body?' asked Izette.

The only dead bodies she had seen were those of her succession of pet hamsters. The lifespan of each of these had been about a year, at the end of which she buried their cold, little bodies with due ceremony. It was hard to imagine dead people looking stiff and flat in quite the same way.

'Yes, but it wasn't horrible, just terribly sad. They carried him in very gently. His head rolled to one side when he was put on the sofa and one of the Germans, an older man, lifted it and placed a cushion underneath, as if it mattered...' Irene paused, rerunning the scene in her mind. 'When they'd taken him away the imprint of his body was left on the sofa. A damp outline, darker where his head had rested on the cushion.

I went over to the cushion and picked off the strands of seaweed...I don't know why.'

'Did you know his name, Irene?'

'He was called Ernst. While I was standing there, with the piece of seaweed in my hand, another soldier rushed in. He looked at the seaweed in my hand and the water on the floor. He said 'Ernst?' as though he was asking me if it was true. Then he said a lot more that I couldn't understand but I got the impression he was hoping I could tell him it was all a mistake.'

Irene's eyes filled with tears again and Izette came over to sit beside her on the bed. She cleared her throat and continued, 'I just shook my head. I didn't know how to speak to him. The seaweed in my hand made me feel guilty in a way...'

Izette took Irene's hand in her own. He was only a boy, Irene had said. Like the boy in the cemetery, he had been young too, hardly much older than herself. Irene did not cry easily except when she was in a temper. Izette would have liked to ask her some more questions but it felt...unsavoury to pry. Perhaps this was what Irene had meant when she called their play in the cemetery 'ghoulish.'

'I'll go and bring you something to eat now, Irene, if you like?' Izette stood up. Irene nodded through her tears. 'You're not a bad little sister, you know.'

Izette smiled. That was a rare compliment indeed.

*

Downstairs, Izette noticed her school bag was still in the hall where she had left it when she came in. Before going through to the kitchen to ask her mother for something for Irene to eat, Izette picked up her bag and took it to her room. She opened it up and took out the German dictionary she had borrowed from the Library.

The Librarian had given her such a disapproving look when she took it to the loans desk that she had almost abandoned it and run out. However, she had stood her ground and the book was now in her possession. She hid it behind her other books on the bookshelf. Later, after everyone had gone to bed, she would see if she could translate the card from the grave.

CHAPTER 6

It was the 11th of January, 1941 and the Germans had been on the island for six months. The Vaubert's Christmas festivities were already a fading memory but it had been a good Christmas, all things considered. The entire family had gathered at Uncle Jim's and Aunt Margaret's, the old farm a natural focus for the family get-together, the putting aside of old rivalries or jealousies and, this year, a time of strengthening family bonds against the invaders, of whom there now seemed to be overwhelming numbers. The German garrison had increased steadily and private homes were requisitioned as billets when hotels and schools proved inadequate to house the growing population of soldiery. Grey uniforms blanketed every street corner in town, grey backs obscured the view in every queue, the clatter of boots on pavement separated soldier from civilian. The Islanders had settled reluctantly into second-class citizenship but, for this first Christmas of occupation, they celebrated as lavishly as possible to demonstrate the defiant Island spirit. The Feldcommandantur might rule their islands but their hearts remained unconquered.

The January day was bright but bitterly cold. An icy wind cut through Irene's thin old coat as she walked towards the sea. It was probably madness taking a walk along the beach in this freezing weather. Marilyn thought Irene was crazy when she announced that she was taking a walk in her lunch break but she wanted to get out into the open air to be able to think clearly.

She had the un-mined part of the beach all to herself. Not another living thing struggled across the desolate space. The wind lifted dried bracts of seaweed, tumbling them across the sand towards the sea wall and pressed cold probing fingers through her thin clothing. Her shoes sank into the sand, filling up with cold grains, chilling her toes to numbness. As though to compensate for the cold, the sea was magnificent. Richly foaming rolls cascaded over and over each other, spilling across the sand, wash and retreat, wash and retreat.

Irene found she was heading towards the pier, which led to the Swimming Club. A long time ago at the end of the pier, at the edge of the sea, a huge artificial pool had been constructed to trap and hold the seawater whatever the state of the tide. Around this pool there were refreshment and sunbathing areas, changing rooms and spectator stands for summer swimming galas. Now abandoned and empty, even by the hardiest among the German troops, it was only a few shorts months since it had thronged with splendidly tanned German torsos. Irene remembered the boy Ernst who had been amongst them.

Finding the wrought-iron gate to the Swimming Club open, Irene crossed the windswept terrace, climbing the steps to the upper viewing platform above the sea wall. The wind was so strong here, she had to grasp the ironing railings for support. She felt the roughness of rust breaking through last summer's fresh paint. The searing cold of the metal froze her fingers and she let go, plunging her hands into her pockets for warmth, leaning forward instead with her whole body on the rail to watch the winter waves smash themselves against the pool's concrete ramparts. She hadn't ventured out here in the summer, despite knowing many of the soldiers by name. Some local girls had, a handful careless of what people might think of them. The Islanders took to calling them 'Jerry-bags' and their names were noted and remembered. Irene was relieved now that she had resisted the frequent invitations to join them.

After watching the waves for a while, Irene retraced her way down green-slimed steps to the lower terrace, tucking herself into the shelter of a concrete wall. From here, she had a clear view of the row of houses bordering this stretch of coast. Most had been given over to tourism, the larger houses converted into hotels or guest houses but a few private dwellings remained, overshadowed by their commercial neighbours. Irene's hotel took pride of place on what might have been grandly entitled an 'esplanade' elsewhere. She thought about the soldiers she had come to know in her time at the hotel. It was difficult to think of them as the enemy when you knew them as individuals. They were men like any others. They showed her photographs of their wives and children and shared their worries about their safety. They could hardly believe their luck in landing such a safe posting in Jersey. As for the war itself, what could they do? Most of them had been conscripted.

The reality of Germany as enemy came home to her more forcibly when she heard the steady, deadly drone of squadrons of German bombers overhead on route for England, or when she overheard Mrs Birrell telling her mother that it was now six months since they had last heard from George and they had no idea where he might be. It came home to her even more personally when her bicycle was requisitioned and her last pair of shoes began to let in water and she saw her mother surreptitiously taking in the seams of her dresses while Bill was out at work so that he wouldn't realise how much weight she had lost.

Since the day of the drowning she had come to know the German soldier who had been so distraught and had discovered that the drowned boy was his younger brother. He was called Gunther and, after he had spoken to her on a number of occasions, she began to suspect that he was engineering at least some of their apparently accidental meetings. Gunther was keen to improve his English and this was one of the reasons he gave for wanting to talk to her whenever they met. He would often talk about his brother, their childhood together and their home back in Germany. These were the things most of the soldiers talked about if you could spare them a few minutes but, with Gunther, instinct told her there was more to their conversations than simply his need for a sympathetic ear.

And it wasn't one-sided. Irene told him about her own family and life on the island, even, once she got to know him a little better, what it felt like to live on the island under occupation. On these occasions he became quiet and thoughtful, shaking his head sometimes when she mentioned her fears. However, most of the time they found they laughed a great deal when they were together.

As the weeks went by, the friendship with Gunther persisted and Irene was at a loss to know what to do about it. She found she looked forward to the times when they met accidentally in the corridor, her spirits lifting when she saw his familiar face. Surely it could do no harm, this exchange of words with one of the enemy? And she knew she helped to fill the void left in his life by the death of his brother. More than once he expressed his appreciation. 'It is good to talk with a woman after so many months living with only men. They are good comrades but it is not the same. Women have the better understanding of how it feels inside…to lose someone.' Gradually however, Irene had to admit that the time she chose to spend with Gunther was no longer driven primarily by a feeling of sympathy. She simply liked to be with him.

She was also acutely aware that he could be gone at a moment's notice, sent to the Russian Front that all the soldiers dreaded. For all the soldiers on Jersey, the threat of transfer to one of the fighting fronts was ever present. Perhaps that would be the best solution for both of them, but she couldn't help hoping it wouldn't end that way.

She shivered in the cold wind. She wore no watch but could tell that it must almost be time for her to be back at work. She was no further forward in her thinking about Gunther. Her nose was running. She sniffed and, taking a handkerchief out of her pocket, blew her nose. Time to put this nonsense out of her mind, if that is what it was. Time would tell…perhaps. She turned back towards the hotel and set off at a brisk walk.

*

'We'll just finish checking that grey Citroen over there,' Bill jerked his head towards the car parked in a corner of the garage yard, '…and then call it a day, shall we, Donald?'

'Right, boss, I'll fetch it into the workshop.'

It was Friday afternoon and the end of a long week. The weather had been bitterly cold for a fortnight now and the old stove in the workshop provided only enough warmth if you could stand within a couple of feet of it. They kept an iron kettle on the top to boil water for their hoarded supply of tea, allowing themselves just one mug a day mid-morning, reusing the tea leaves once or even twice. Betty made vegetable soups that bubbled away on the stove all morning, whetting their appetites for the mid-day break. She knitted finger-less gloves for them to wear while they were working, unravelling old washed-up sweaters for the wool. Make do and mend was the order of the day.

Tom came into the workshop through the small access door in the big garage doors, muffled to the ears in a bright red woollen scarf of his mother's. The other two pulled his leg about the colour but he didn't care, saying there was altogether too much grey wool in the Island already and he wasn't going to add to it!

'We're just finishing this Citroen, Tom,' Bill said to him. 'This can be the last one for this week. Shouldn't take us long. You'll have time to deliver it to the depot before they shut shop. Make yourself a hot drink if you like, lad.'

Tom slid the kettle onto the hot plate of the stove. 'It's real brass-monkey weather out there. How's our stock of wood going?'

'It's going down fast, Tom. I'm going over to Jim's tomorrow with a cart to collect some more. Like to come along and give me a hand?'

'Yes, I don't mind. But don't forget, I've a few contacts now at the German depot. I'm sure I could arrange for some logs to be dropped off.'

Bill gave Tom a straight look. 'I know there's a fair bit of mutual back-scratching going on but I want nothing to do with it. We'll manage without any help from the Jerries.'

Tom cursed himself under his breath. He must be more circumspect in front of Bill. Since he started his driving duties for the Germans, he'd worked on building up friendly relationships where he sensed a warm response. After a few months he was accepted and trusted by many of the soldiers at the transport depot where he delivered the requisitioned cars and he was now trying to establish a similar reputation with the officers. To achieve this, he made sure he was always available, whatever time of day they requested a driver, never complaining if he had to wait late into the night when his passengers were attending a late dinner or party. Of course, he knew the island's roads intimately and was familiar with the large residences where parties were held. He even knew suitable secluded spots if his officers wanted him to stop on the way home. On these occasions he would step out of the car for a cigarette and stroll down the lane to stretch his legs while his officers entertained their lady friends. He was the very soul of discretion as far as they were concerned but every scrap of information that came his way was noted down in a thick notebook later.

However, it was proving a difficult balancing act and the last thing he wanted was for Bill to misinterpret his loyalties. He thought quickly and came up with a suggestion, which might set Bill's mind at ease.

'I'll come over in the morning then, Bill. I'll sharpen up Dad's axe and split a few logs.'

Bill's head came out from inside the car again, 'Right, thanks lad.'

'And it'll get me nicely limbered up for the dance.'

'The what?'

'The dance, tomorrow night.'

'Oh, you mean the Irish cultural evening.'

Tom grinned, 'Oh yes, my mistake. The Irish cultural evening, like it says on the permit!'

Bill shook his head. A few youngsters had come up with the idea of arranging a dance or series of dances if they could get away with it, under the guise of national cultural evenings and surprisingly had managed to obtain a permit from the authorities. It was to be held in the church hall for respectability, as though ecclesiastical bricks mystically exuded decorum and decency, and was declared a private gathering strictly by invitation only. This latter measure to ensure no Germans attended.

'And what happens if the Germans decide to check up on your cultural evening?'

'We've anticipated that. We'll have lookouts taking it in turns to watch out for patrols and if they raise the alarm, the band will hide their instruments and a young lady will commence a very long and tedious reading from Yeats.'

Bill shook his head again but smiled none-the-less. 'Come on then, Tom, the Citroen's finished. I'll lock up once you've driven her out.'

Tom drove the car away while the other two men put out the stove, wrapped themselves up and stepped outside into the cold evening. Bill had the long climb out of town ahead of him, reminding him, as it often did, that he wasn't getting any younger. He fixed his thoughts on the warm kitchen at the end of his long walk and his supper of vegetables and gravy, and possibly baked apples. Betty still had some dried fruit left with which to stuff them but there'd be no custard. What he wouldn't give for a tin of Birds Custard powder! Still they were luckier than some. Jim and Margaret kept them well provided with such produce as the farm could supply together with some 'extras', which came by way of barter. They'd killed a pig at Christmas, illicitly of course, but Jerry couldn't keep up with all the culinary goings-on around Christmas. Everybody seemed to be able to rustle up a treat of some sort. Perhaps Jerry had turned a blind eye. He didn't know or care particularly and he was damn sure they hadn't gone short of a Christmas roast in the officer's mess.

When he reached home he found one end of the kitchen table had been cleared to take Betty's sewing machine and the female members of his household were hard at work on one of Irene's old frocks.

'What's this creation for?' he asked.

'I'm cutting this dress down for Izette, for the dance tomorrow,' Betty answered. 'She didn't have anything suitable of her own and she wanted something a bit more grown-up.'

Izette whisked the dress out of the room to be tried on and was back in a couple of minutes to show off the finished result, parading up and down the room in a parody of the catwalk saunter. Bill was shocked when he saw her. Even in ankle socks, she looked at least three years older in the dress, bringing home to him how few years were left before she would fly the nest.

Irene studied her younger sister with surprise. The dress emphasized her slenderness, making her appear taller than she was. Her hair was loose, hanging well down her back in thick, dark, silky coils. Izette's skin was bare of make-up at the moment but Irene could see that a touch of mascara and lipstick would highlight her features, transforming her from pretty to downright attractive. With a small pang of jealousy, she recognised that in a couple of years her sister would probably turn out to be a real beauty.

'Gosh', Irene exclaimed, 'I don't think it ever looked that good on me. It's perfect, Izette. You'll have all the boys after you!'

Izette's cheeks flushed pink. 'But what can I wear on my feet?'

'You can borrow a pair of my shoes, silly. You can't go in your lace-ups and socks.'

'What? High heels?'

'As long as they're not too high, Irene,' Betty added.

'We don't want Izette spraining her ankle.'

'It's all right, Mum,' replied Irene. 'I have a pair of plain court shoes with a small heel which should be ideal. Come on, Izette, let's see if they fit you.'

*

While Betty cleared the table, Bill settled in his armchair with the Evening Post muttering that he didn't know why he bothered to read it since the Germans had started editing it.

'They're all going to this dance then?'

'Yes, Irene and Tom will be there to keep an eye on Izette and Nancy. They need a bit of fun. It's been such a long time since they had any sort of get together.'

'I suppose it is,' agreed Bill. 'That goes for all of us, you know. I can't remember the last time you and I went out anywhere together.'

Betty paused with her hands in the soapy water.

'Well, I suppose we could go along to the dance too, just for an hour or so. It might be nice to hear a bit of music again,' she ventured.

'No, I don't think so love. We wouldn't want to cramp the young one's style, would we?' replied Bill.

Betty remembered the dances of their youth when they were courting. Bill wouldn't miss a single dance then. He loved to swing her around the floor in a quickstep, quite a show-off he was. The other girls used to envy her; he was such a striking figure of a man.

'No, I suppose not, Bill,' she agreed wistfully.

Bill couldn't have heard the longing in her voice because a few minutes later he put down the paper and went out through the kitchen door into the garden, lifting his old coat off the hook as he went. When Irene and Izette burst into the kitchen a few minutes later to show off Izette's complete outfit, Betty was wiping her eyes, but in answer to their anxious questions she would say no more than that the war was getting her down.

*

That night, Izette heard the clock on the sideboard chime each quarter-hour until well into the early hours. She was much too excited to sleep. Each time she rolled over she could see her dress hanging from the wardrobe door, its satin bodice shimmering in the moonlight. What would Tom say when he saw her? Surely he couldn't go on thinking of her as a child once he'd seen her in the dress? Even Dad had been surprised, although he'd tried to hide it, burying himself in the paper. He would have to have at least one dance with her since he was escorting her and Nancy, and Irene of course, but Irene would know lots of people at the dance, whereas she and Nancy might not know anyone at all. She had to admit it was all a little frightening really but she wouldn't miss it at any cost.

She groaned as she heard the clock chime out the full Westminster two o'clock. I must go to sleep, she chanted to herself, I must go to sleep, I must go to sleep…

*

By four o'clock the following afternoon she was ready, much too early of course, although the dance was starting early so that everyone could be home before curfew. She sat impatiently watching Irene put on her make-up, having already scrounged some lipstick and powder for herself.

'Come on, Irene, you haven't even put your stockings on yet.'

'There's plenty of time. Tom and Nancy aren't due to

meet us for another three quarters of an hour.'

Izette groaned. Irene smiled, remembering her own first dance. She hoped Izette hadn't set her hopes too high. This was hardly going to be the social event of the year.

'For heaven's sake go and find something to do, Izette, instead of fidgeting on my bed.'

Izette sighed but got up from the bed and left, turning to climb the attic stairs to Edmund's room. She opened his door to find him studying a collection of small pieces of machinery on his table. He looked startled when she walked in, which Izette mistakenly attributed to her glamorous appearance.

'Hello, what do you think?' She gave a twirl.

'Mm?' Edmund responded absently.

'My new dress, of course. How do you think I look, Edmund.'

'Oh...all right, I suppose.'

Izette raised her eyes to the ceiling. 'I don't know why I bother!'

Walking over to his table she started to poke around among the pieces. 'What's this?'

'Um...it's my alarm clock. It wasn't working properly so I decided to take it to pieces. Careful! I don't want to lose any bits.'

Hearing the front door knocker downstairs, Izette spun round and shot out of the room. By the time she reached the top of the stairs Betty had already opened the door to Tom and Nancy. Much to her satisfaction, Tom watched her descend the stairs, sweeping his gaze admiringly upward from her toes to her hair as she came into view.

'Wow!' he grinned, then stepping into the hall he held out his right hand towards her. 'Won't you introduce us, Nancy? I don't think I've met this friend of yours.'

Izette laughed and slapped his hand away, but it was exactly the response she'd hoped for. Nancy, in her old-fashioned party frock with sash and bow and ankle socks, stood with her mouth drooping in dismay. Seeing her expression, Izette felt a twinge of guilt. Thinking rapidly, she caught Nancy by the arm and whisked her off up the stairs.

'Let's go and see if Irene has some lipstick you can wear.'

*

Nancy soon forgot her appearance once the dance was in full swing. Someone had made a fine job of decorating the bare church hall. Colourful paper streamers stretched around the walls, looped up to huge, green, cardboard shamrocks. There were tables at one end to hold the refreshments and chairs were arranged down the sides of the hall leaving the main area of the floor clear for dancing. In the corner, close to a door, through which they could make a quick escape if necessary, were the musicians. Izette recognised the father and brother of one of her school friends, each wielding a heavy accordion. A man with a violin and a young woman with long, dark hair and tambourine completed the quartet.

Izette and Nancy headed for the refreshments first. Clutching glasses of lemonade, they chose a couple of chairs near to the musicians and sat down to watch. It took about an hour for them to summon up courage to get up and dance with each other, since no one else had asked them. They found it excruciatingly embarrassing initially but, as the light faded outside and the room warmed to the huddle of energetic dancers, they found they were rarely off their feet, breaking off in between dances to gulp much-needed glasses of water.

Izette kept a close eye on Tom, noting that it was already eight-thirty and he hadn't yet had a dance with her. He'd spent most of the evening talking to a group of his friends. She'd seen him dance only once, choosing one of Irene's friends as his partner, a sophisticated looking girl who was almost as tall as he was, but afterwards they separated and returned to their own groups. In one of the refreshment breaks, Izette pulled Nancy to her feet and headed off up the room.

'Come on, Nancy, I think it's time Tom danced with us.'

Nancy wrinkled her nose. 'What on earth for?'

'Because he should, that's why. It's only polite.'

'Well, you can if you like. I'd rather sit down for a minute. I'm whacked.'

They found Tom near the refreshment table and Nancy helped herself to another drink, leaving Izette to cajole Tom into a dance.

'Enjoying yourself?' he asked.

'Yes but it's your turn now,' said Izette.

'My turn?'

'To dance with me.'

'I see. Well, how can I refuse?' He grinned, offering her his arm, but as they moved away he turned back to his friends and she overheard him say by way of explanation, 'My kid sister's friend.'

Izette's spirits fell immediately, her happy mood dispelled in a second. He's spoiled it all now, she thought. As the music started she moved into his arms but, instead of it being the delicious experience she'd imagined, she kept hearing the four demeaning words, '...my kid sister's friend.'

Unaware of his faux pas, Tom talked and joked as they swung round the room, calling out to friends as they passed within earshot. Izette forced a smile on her face, for appearance sake, but she was impatient for the music to stop. However, as the number came to a close, her disappointment found solace in a rather spiteful idea. With a final twirl at the end of the song and trying to make it look as accidental as possible she brought the heel of her borrowed shoe down hard on Tom's toes.

Tom yelped and hobbled off the floor to remove his shoe and examine the damage. Izette followed, her expression one of deep concern.

'I'm so sorry, Tom. I don't know how I could have been so clumsy.'

He peeled his sock off to reveal a large red weal.

'You great clumsy idiot,' Tom shouted, 'I've a lot of driving to do next week, Izette. This bruising is going to make it damned uncomfortable.'

'I'm sorry,' she repeated helplessly.

Tom replaced his shoe and sock with irritation. 'It's time we were getting home anyway,' adding roughly, 'get Nancy will you?'

Despondently, she started to trail up the room towards Nancy. It hadn't been nearly as satisfying a revenge as she had imagined and, as a result, he was taking them home early. And she only had herself to blame.

Before she reached Nancy, a scuffle by the entrance door caught her attention. The dancers paused and a ripple of anxiety passed through the room. The music stopped but before the musicians could make their planned escape through the back door, a German patrol burst into the room. The centre of the room cleared as the soldiers spread out. They were armed and seemed nervous. The leader of the patrol took up position in the centre of the room.

'Stand back! Stand back! All of you, please.'

Izette felt her arm grasped and she was pulled back against the wall. Turning around she saw it was Tom and he had hold of Nancy with his other hand. He pushed the girls behind him and indicated they should make their way slowly towards the small back door.

'You will all disperse, please,' the German continued, 'go home to your houses now, please. Do not stay outside. You are to go home and stay there.'

People started moving quickly towards the door without a word. Irene caught up with Izette and Nancy. In the delay to get out of the door, Izette turned round to see the German in charge preventing a woman from gathering up the remains of the refreshments.

'Leave this. You must go now.'

He was waving his rifle impatiently but the woman was still reluctant to leave the food and started to argue. He nodded towards another of the soldiers who started to move in her direction but suddenly Tom was at the woman's side, speaking quietly into her ear and guiding her towards the exit, nodding at the soldier as he did so. The German seemed satisfied and hurried his patrol out of the hall. The doors were locked and the soldiers stood outside until everyone had left. Tom found Irene and the girls again outside.

'What's going on, Tom?' whispered Irene.

'I don't know. You take the girls straight home. I'm going to see if I can find out.'

Tom walked back to where the German patrol was waiting and, before Irene hurried her around the corner, Izette was surprised to see him chatting with them affably and handing round a packet of cigarettes.

When they reached home, Irene pushed both girls into the Vaubert house and stepped into the hall behind them, closing the door quickly for the blackout. Edmund was sitting at the foot of the stairs.

'Hello,' he said.

Izette took off the high-heeled shoes and examined the

blisters that had been raised on the hurried journey home. 'I'm not going to bed yet, Irene, not until Tom gets back. I want to know what's happened.'

'What's that, young lady?' Betty shouted from the kitchen.

'Nancy's nearly asleep on her feet,' said Irene. 'I'll take her home while you tell Mum about the evening.'

She switched off the hall light then ushered Nancy out through the door again.

By the time Irene returned from next door – Mrs Birrell had demanded an account of the evening – Izette had been sent unwillingly to bed with the promise that, should Tom arrive with any news and she was not already asleep, she would be told. She tried and failed to remain awake but, as it turned out, it didn't matter. It was so late by the time Tom was dropped off by one of the German staff cars that he went straight into his own house. Bill was woken by the sound of the car's engine as it laboured up the hill and was the only person to see him arrive home. If Tom could have known the suspicions his mode of transport would arouse in his employer, he might well have thought twice before accepting the lift he was offered that night.

CHAPTER 7

'Betty, Betty, are you there? Where are you? In the kitchen?' It was Mrs Birrell from next door, rushing excitedly round the Vaubert house with a card in her hand, looking for Betty.

'What is it, Dorothy? Is everything all right?' Betty grasped her friend by the shoulders to calm her down, noticing with relief that her friend was smiling.

'Look!' she waved the card happily, 'I've had a Red Cross message from George and he's fine! He doesn't say much – well you can't in 25 words, can you? But here, you can read it.'

Betty read the card quickly. It was short and cryptic but she managed to gather that George was now back in England. He'd been in the fighting somewhere but couldn't say where. He sent his love to them all and was missing home.

'Oh, that's wonderful news, Betty! I'm so relieved. It's been such a long time since you heard from him.'

'Yes, Ted's over the moon. And Nancy is, of course. The card came after Tom had left for work this morning but I think Ted might walk down into town to let him know the news. I must go and write a letter to Ted's sister and her husband over in St Ouen's straight away.'

Betty smiled as her friend rushed out of the house again. It was wonderful to hear some good news. It seemed to have been nothing but bad news recently. For instance, a young man had been shot dead by a German patrol simply because he was walking in the Military Zone after curfew. And the Germans had been saying that the invasion of England was about to begin and the war would be over in three months. Bill didn't give much credence to that. He said they were just trying to keep the morale of the troops up but it was still very worrying. You couldn't ignore the huge numbers of troops and all the heavy equipment that was pouring into the island. Bill had counted 40 ships in the harbour last week, all unloading men, equipment or building materials.

'Well,' she said to herself, 'this isn't getting the housework done. I'll just put this bit of washing out on the line, then I might walk over to see Margaret and Jim. They'll be glad to hear the good news about George.'

*

Despite what Ted and Dorothy had assumed that morning when Tom left the house, he didn't turn up at the garage at all that day. Ted called in as intended later in the morning to give Tom the news about his brother and was surprised to discover he wasn't there.

'That's grand news about George,' said Bill, 'I'll tell Tom when he gets in but I've no idea where he is. I assume the Germans must have called him in for a driving job but he doesn't usually have to go off like this at a moment's notice. He usually has time to let me know first.'

'Well, it could be that they've got a flap on. I noticed

on the way down that they're buzzing about like a swarm of bees today.'

'I wonder if it's anything to do with last night.'

'Why? What happened last night, Bill?'

'I don't know exactly but a German patrol interrupted the dance at the Church hall and sent them all home long before curfew. They were edgy about something. Tom was going to find out what it was all about and let us know but, of course, I haven't seen him yet today.'

'Dorothy and I must have been fast asleep when he came in last night. It must have been very late.'

'It was,' confirmed Bill, adding when Ted looked curious, 'I happened to be looking out of our bedroom window when he came home.' He didn't mention the German car.

'Well, we shall just have to contain our curiosity until we see him,' said Ted. 'In the meantime, if that kettle is boiling for a purpose I'll have a cup of tea with you before I go.'

The tea was weak but welcome. The weather was still bleak with no promise of anything better coming along. Ted tightened the muffler around his neck and warmed his hands on the mug he'd been given.

'I feel sorry for those foreign workers they're bringing in now, Bill. Have you seen them? Some of them are dressed in rags and they have no boots, just sacking or more rags wrapped around their feet.'

'Yes, I've seen the poor wretches,' replied Bill. 'They're half-starved, too. Donald saw some of them being taken off one of the ships in the harbour. They were fighting over a few mouldy potatoes that had been dropped on the quay. Irene tells me they're nothing to do with the German army. It's some outfit called the Todt Organisation that's responsible for them. They're sent all over Europe, wherever the Germans can't get enough voluntary labour and treated worse than cattle.

The Todt don't care if they survive or not. They work them from dawn until dusk on heavy construction work, give them the barest minimum to eat and bury the bodies inside the camps at night so that we can't see how many are dying.'

Ted was shocked. 'How do know all this, Bill?'

'Mainly from your Tom, and Irene confirmed it when I asked her. She gets to know a lot working in that hotel.'

'I didn't know it was as bad as that. My God, they're inhuman bastards, these Germans.'

Bill nodded. 'And I think it'll get worse before it gets better,' he added grimly.

*

Later that same day, the Vaubert family were gathered around the table for tea when Bill interrupted the meal to read from the Evening Post.

'Well, well, well! Listen to this! "*The German authorities would be grateful to receive any information pertaining to the escape from the island last night by sea of two or more young men from the St Aubin's area. A reward will be paid for any information relating to the whereabouts of these persons*".'

'That might be why they stopped the dance last night. The soldiers looked to be in a bit of a flap,' said Izette.

'Yes, it could be. Well, I hope those lads make it. They must be brave young men.'

At that moment a tap sounded on the door and Tom walked in, dropping into an easy chair without being asked. He looked exhausted.

'Are you all right, lad?' Bill asked with concern.

'Yes, thanks. It's just been a very long day,' replied Tom.

'Your trousers are soaked, Tom,' said Izette.

'Yes, I know,' said Tom wearily, 'if you could spare a cup of tea I'll tell you why.'

Betty poured him a mug of tea and took it over to where he was sitting.

'Were you reading about the escape in the paper as I came in, Bill? Could I have a quick look, please? See how much the censor has allowed through.'

He scanned the article quickly.

'Mm, not very much there. But, as they say, there has been an escape from the island, the first one of many, I hope. That's why I've been out all day, Bill. The top brass are hopping mad about it. I've been driving them all over the island. I don't know if the lads will make it to England but nothing's been spotted yet. In fact, Jerry doesn't even know where they might be heading, though they're assuming it's England, of course. In their shoes, I think I might have headed for the French coast. It's much closer and the Germans can't keep an eye on every single bay. A small boat could slip in undetected at night.'

Izette interrupted, 'But who was it, Tom? How many of them? The paper says two or more.'

'There were three of them. Gerard Le Queree, Alfred Lucas and Herbert Syvret. I don't think you know any of them. They're all from St Aubin's. I met Gerard a couple of times because his father used to send his Wolseley over for service.'

'Yes, I remember his father,' said Bill, 'a tall man, solicitor, isn't he?'

'That's him.' Tom took a mouthful of tea before continuing. 'Well, they seem to have hidden a boat somewhere near the harbour in St Aubin's and last night, when the tide was right, they simply rowed out.'

'Without any of the Germans noticing?' asked Izette.

'Apparently. I reckon Jerry wasn't expecting anyone to try something like that under their very noses. The harbour patrol on duty last night at St Aubin's have been confined to their billet. It's usually so quiet there, I expect they were trying to catch up on a bit of sleep.'

Tom drank some more of his tea while the Vauberts digested this news. It was Izette who asked about his wet trousers again.

'Well, I'm afraid they didn't all make it. I helped the Germans pull Gerard's body out of the harbour this evening. It was floating face down and I wanted to see who it was.'

'Oh dear!' said Betty.

'I don't know what went wrong. He had some bad injuries to his head, the sort you would expect if he'd been washed up against a rock, but we'll only find out what happened if the other two are caught. It'll be hard for Gerard's parents though.'

'Yes, yes indeed,' agreed Bill.

'Well, if you'll excuse me, I must go and get changed out of these wet clothes. I'll be in tomorrow, Bill, all being well.' Tom rose to leave.

'Yes, thank you for coming to tell us, Tom. Let's hope we don't have any repercussions from this episode, eh?'

'Oh, I think we'll find Jerry tightening up after this. They were talking about calling in all small boats, seaworthy or not.'

'You'd better let Jim and Margaret know that, Betty. He's still got that old dinghy in the barn, hasn't he?' Bill asked.

'I don't know. I haven't seen it for years. It might have been chopped up for firewood by now but I'll let him know, just in case.'

*

That night in bed Izette tossed and turned, finding it difficult to go to sleep. Through the wall, she could faintly hear the sound of snoring proving that Tom obviously wasn't sharing her difficulty. No doubt hearing about the escape attempt added to her restlessness but it was primarily what she had seen that afternoon that was keeping her awake.

Her mother had sent her over to the farm on another errand and, on the lane, she'd come across a group of foreign labourers being herded along by two Todt guards. You could tell the Todt guards by their uniforms and the long truncheons they carried. The labourers had shuffled along in an assortment of filthy, dust-covered, ragged clothes, their faces grimy and haggard. They didn't speak. Perhaps this was not allowed or perhaps they were just too exhausted. Izette could not tell their nationality. There were said to be Russians, Poles, Czechs, Belgians, French, even Algerians and Moroccans on the island. Their eyes had passed silently over her as she'd walked by, causing a shiver to pass down her spine. And the stench that accompanied them turned her stomach.

After they had passed out of sight, she'd taken to her heels and run, ashamed of her squeamishness. It was horrible, she had said as she described them to Aunt Margaret and her aunt had shaken her head.

'The poor souls. Where will it all end, I wonder?' Margaret had murmured.

Finally giving up her attempt to sleep, Izette got out of bed and walked over to the window, drawing back the curtains. It was very dark outside except for a small rectangle of golden light visible on the field opposite. Izette was perplexed for a moment, then realised that it must be coming from Edmund's bedroom window, above hers in the attic. He's forgotten the blackout, she thought. Slipping on her slippers and dressing gown, she opened her bedroom door and tiptoed quietly outside on to the landing. Pausing to check that there was no light shining from beneath her parents' bedroom door or Irene's, she crept up the attic stairs to Edmund's room and went in. His bedside lamp was switched on and his curtains were wide open. He would be in trouble if the light was spotted. She closed the curtains quickly.

Izette crossed the room back to his bed. Pulling back the sheet gently expecting to see his blonde head on the pillow, she found instead his teddy bear neatly tucked up, a couple of knitted jerseys adding bulk to the body and a school scarf rolled up and pushed down the bed for legs. She replaced the sheets and looked around the room. There was no sign of Edmund anywhere. Although it seemed unlikely, she started towards the wardrobe. Then she remembered what he had been saying about his spying activities.

'Oh no,' she whispered, 'surely he can't have gone outside.'

She moved back to the window and pushed it gently. It swung open. She leaned out. There was no sign of Edmund but there was a flat area of roof in front of the dormer. Izette climbed carefully out on to it, closing the window behind her. Then she stood up and looked up towards the ridge of the roof and the chimney. Against the near black of the night sky, she could make out Edmund's darker silhouette.

'Edmund!' she whispered, trying not to startle him. He looked down and gestured to her to climb up.

'How?'

'Just to your right there's a hole where a slate is missing. Put your foot in there and you'll be able to reach the ridge. Then shuffle along to here.'

She followed his instructions and found herself astride the ridge without too much difficulty. Then, as he said, it was simply a matter of shuffling along to the chimneystack.

'What are you doing?' she asked when she reached him. Edmund thought it a silly question but allowances had to be made for the fact that Izette was a girl. Declining to answer, he handed her the binoculars and pointed up the hill. From their vantage point on the roof, they had a good view of a German anti-aircraft battery. The Germans seemed to be carrying out some kind of exercise. The big gun barrels swung round in response to shouted orders.

'They're doing one of their night exercises,' explained Edmund. 'They might fire off some live shells but they don't always. It depends.'

'Depends on what?' asked Izette.

'Whether they feel like it or not, silly.'

'Oh, I see.'

She didn't see, of course, but it was jolly interesting all the same. She had known the battery was there but she hadn't actually seen it before because it had been constructed in a slight hollow so that you couldn't see it from the lane.

'It's a bit cold up here,' she observed.

Edmund ignored her comment. 'If you turn around carefully, you can see the harbour from here as well. There's a great deal goes on down there. I've noted down the numbers of the ships that have been coming in and out and a description of each one: their size, the number of guns they're carrying, that sort of thing. The unloading goes on all through the night. Hundreds and hundreds of troops are pouring in. Did you know?'

'I know, Dad said so.' Izette had turned the binoculars on the harbour area and could see exactly what Edmund meant. Big arc lamps illuminated the whole dockside brilliantly. 'Isn't it an obvious target for English bombers, lit up like that?'

'They would have to get past the anti-aircraft batteries

first. The whole approach to the harbour is pretty well defended.'

Izette followed the line of the bay all the way round to St Aubin's with the binoculars, remembering that first day when she'd watched the German bombers follow the same course.

'What's that over there…?' she asked.

Edmund put a hand on her arm to silence her but it was too late.

'What the dickens is going on up here?' It was their father's voice. 'Get down here immediately, both of you…and be careful.'

He was standing on the flat area outside the dormer window, his striped pyjamas flapping in the slight breeze.

'I don't know what silly game you both think you're playing at but you, Izette, should know better at your age.'

Without a word, Izette and Edmund started their descent, Bill's big hands guiding them both down as soon as they came within his grasp. When they finally clambered back in through the window, they saw their mother standing in the middle of the room, hands on hips, waiting for an explanation while Irene sat on Edmund's bed with his teddy on her lap, trying to keep a straight face. Edmund sighed. The game was well and truly up.

*

Izette and Edmund were sent to stay at Uncle Jim and Aunt Margaret's farm after the roof incident. Mum had gone completely to pieces about it and Dad had said he was not prepared to have her worrying about their 'irresponsible behaviour' on top of everything else she had to cope with, so Izette was sent to help on the farm straight away and Edmund joined her as soon as his school closed for the summer holidays.

Izette had not minded leaving school at all, in fact, she considered that she was really too old to be there at all, despite the States Education Department encouraging young people to stay on even longer because there was no work for them to do if they left. On the contrary, she had found to her cost that there was plenty of work to be done here on the farm and it was all back-breakingly hard.

As now for instance. Izette groaned wearily; this had to be the most tedious job she had ever done in her life. Mounds of potato flour were spread out on plates around her, drying in the sun, but there was still a huge vat of potato pulp to be squeezed and sacks and sacks of potatoes to be peeled and pulped and the whole damn lot would only yield a few miserable pounds of flour. Her back ached, her hands were red and raw and it was no consolation to know that hundreds of farmer's wives all over the island were having to do exactly the same monotonous, exhausting job in order to have flour to bake with. There was no longer any wheat flour to be had in the shops; what little flour the Purchasing Commission were able to obtain went straight to the island's bakeries. So now the potato, the crop they had always produced on the island, had become their life-saver but that didn't make it any more appetising when it was the main component of every meal. Potato soup, baked potatoes, boiled potatoes, mashed potatoes, potato cakes, potato bread. Izette thought she must look like a potato by now.

The food rations went steadily down. There were occasional treats, depending on what the food purchasing commission was able to obtain from France or what was being offered on the Black Market but, for most of the time, their diet was dreary and repetitive. She should, she knew, be grateful that she had enough to eat here on the farm. Many others were not so fortunate.

Izette had to wait a few months before Edmund was free to join her. She had felt lonely in the evenings with just Uncle Jim and Aunt Margaret. They were very kind to her but it wasn't the same without her family around. Once Edmund arrived, the two of them were off into the fields after supper, leaving their Aunt and Uncle tuning in the wireless to listen to the latest developments on the BBC.

On the day Edmund arrived, as soon as Izette saw him walking down the lane in his best clothes with Mum, his small leatherette suitcase in his other hand, she ran out of the yard to greet them.

'Oooh, this is lovely!' she grinned, hugging him closely, much to his embarrassment.

Fighting free of her grasp, Edmund straightened his jacket and asked where he was to sleep. Leaving Betty and Aunt Margaret in the kitchen deep in conversation, Izette took Edmund upstairs to show him the bedroom she had prepared for him. After giving the room a cursory look he put his suitcase on the bed, opened it and proudly extracted his old surveillance notebook.

'Edmund! Dad said you were to stop all that,' said Izette.

'He said I was to stop all that larking about on the roof,' replied Edmund, 'and he screwed my window shut to make sure, but he didn't say anything about my notebook so here it is, and now I'm here, it's a completely different situation, isn't it?'

'Is it?'

'Yes,' he replied eagerly. 'This really is a tremendous opportunity, Izette. Now we can keep an eye on the German installations here on the farm at our leisure. We won't need to go out at night. The batteries here are designed to protect the Eastern approaches to the island...'

'We?' interrupted Izette.

'Well, I assumed you want to be involved?' he asked anxiously. 'It's much more fun if there are two of us.'

Izette considered for a moment. She didn't want to disappoint him. If he wanted to carry on with his surveillance game, there could be little harm in it here on the farm, provided he kept a safe distance from the German installations.

'All right,' she conceded, 'but you're in charge.'

*

So, for Izette and Edmund, the summer of 1941 passed in long days of hard physical labour, starting at six o'clock in the morning, helping with the milking of the few cows Uncle Jim still kept on the farm, followed by feeding the chickens and collecting the eggs. After that, there were the pigs to be fed, then they collected vegetable leaves and grasses for the rabbits that Aunt Margaret now kept in hutches in the barn, destined for the pot.

The heavier work was done by Uncle Jim, with the help of a man who had been sent over from England to replace his two farm labourers, Sidney and Albert, who had joined up in 1940. This man, Henry, was a conscientious objector. A hundred or so of them had been sent over from England just before the occupation to help on the farms. They weren't used to this kind of work. Many of them were professional men, teachers, solicitors and so on, but this was the work assigned to them. Some of the farmers were reluctant to take them, disapproving of their unwillingness to fight, but most, like Uncle Jim, had no choice. Henry was a good worker and Uncle Jim was one of those who respected a man who chose to stick to his principles, no matter how unpopular it made him. After work, when Henry tried to have a drink with his fellow conchies, as they were called, some publicans would refuse to serve them. Similarly some shopkeepers refused to serve them so, after a while, Henry and his friends used to meet instead in one of the houses allocated for their accommodation.

Izette and Edmund both liked Henry. If they came across him resting for few minutes he was always keen to talk to them. He'd been a schoolteacher in England and had left his wife and two children behind in Bristol. He would talk to them about his family and his home, and they would compare life on the island before the war with that in England. Of course, he worried about the safety of his family. Bristol was one of the main targets for the German bombers but his house was well out on the outskirts of the town, as near to the countryside as he could find, he said. He loved the countryside. That's what helped to make his time on the farm more bearable. He enjoyed the peace and beauty of the countryside - in between battery practices that is, he would joke.

It was in the evenings that Izette and Edmund were free to roam the headlands and valleys of the farm with, of course, strict instructions to stay away from the Germans and be back by curfew. During the long summer evenings, they liked to climb up to the highest point on Uncle Jim's land, a small rocky outcrop at the top of a sloping pasture that ran along the cliffs. From here, they could look out across the sea. Edmund called it the 'Observatory' and concealed his binoculars there in a tin biscuit box that he buried between two rocks. On evenings when there were ships to be seen, Edmund would take up position resting the binoculars on a convenient rock for stability and shout out their descriptions for Izette to write down in his notebook.

From their position, they also had a good view of the breakwater below. It ran out into the sea a long way. Before the war, one of their summer holiday activities had been to walk along to the end and fish for spider crabs with lines baited with bacon fat. There would usually be a few small boats tied alongside but it was no longer a working harbour. There was no point with St Helier just around the corner but occasionally boats used to put in for shelter or holidaymakers might hire a boat for an afternoon and tie up against the breakwater to go for a walk or a picnic.

Nowadays, they were forbidden access to the breakwater. The Germans had set up a guard post at the landward end, building a small concrete bunker for the guards and had fenced off all approaches, erecting tall flood-lights which illuminated the entire length of the breakwater. Edmund had made a sketch map of these defences in the notebook and the times when the guards were changed over.

Having completed their surveillance work for the evening, Izette and Edmund relaxed in their different ways. Edmund might scramble over the rocks, practising his mountaineering skills or do some birdwatching. (He carried a second, smaller notebook for this purpose.) Izette was more inclined, especially if it had been one of the back-breaking, flour-making days, to simply lie on her back on the grass, watching the clouds drift gently overhead. The evenings were beginning to draw in and the first coppery tones of autumn were starting to appear in the woods. This particular evening, she settled herself on a soft patch of grass and closed her eyes, wondering what she would find to do in the long winter evenings ahead. She heard Edmund's steps approaching. She would miss him when he returned to school in the autumn but perhaps he would be allowed to come and stay at the farm for some of the Christmas holidays. Something tickled her nose and she opened her eyes to see a feathery stalk of grass hovering above her face.

'Go away, Edmund, you little pest,' she said and closed her eyes again. After a few moments, the tickling resumed so she stretched her hands above her head to grab her tormentor.

Instead, her own wrists were grabbed and held and she opened her eyes to see a familiar face upside down above her own, grinning down at her.

'Tom!' she shrieked.

'Little pest am I?' he said while she scrambled into a sitting position, straightening her dress and attempting to smooth her unruly hair.

'What are you doing here? I haven't seen you for simply ages! How's Nancy and everyone? And how did you find us up here?'

'Steady on, one question at a time please. Where's Edmund? Your aunt said you were both up here.'

'Oh, he's gone wandering off but he'll be back. Now tell me all your news.'

Tom made himself comfortable, his back against a rock, and took a packet of cigarettes out of his pocket. While he was lighting one, he examined her critically.

'Well this country life certainly suits you. You've filled out.'

Izette flushed, embarrassed by his compliment. It was principally her breasts that had 'filled out' that summer.

'It's Aunt Margaret's baking,' she stammered, '...and all these wretched potatoes! I swear I'm turning into one,' she laughed.

Tom raised an eyebrow, 'I've never seen a potato that shape!' he said and then grinned.

Her flush deepened but she smiled back at him, taking her turn to look him up and down. She wasn't as happy with what she saw. He looked thinner in the face and had grey shadows under his eyes.

'How are you, Tom? You look tired.'

He nodded, confirming that he was very tired. It had been a very busy summer. The Germans had sent a seemingly unending stream of cars to the garage for checking. Having requisitioned all the newest cars, the Purchasing Commission had gradually extended their demands to include older cars. Soon there would be hardly any cars left on the island other than those used by the Germans. And more troops had been pouring into the island. Tom said it was thought more than ten thousand troops were now on the island together with the hundreds of foreign workers who had been brought over to strengthen the island's defences.

'You wouldn't believe the amount of building going on, Izette. I get to see it all when I'm driving the officers about.' He shook his head. 'There's a bad feeling of permanence about it all. These German engineers certainly know how to build defences.'

He seemed lost in thought for a few moments then looked up at Izette and smiled.

'But do you know what most people talk about all the time?'

'No?'

'Food! That's what dominates most conversations. Food and how to get enough of it! People pay ridiculous prices for it on the black market, trade anything for it; some even steal it. You'd better tell your Aunt to lock up her chickens and rabbits. In the town, some people keep their chickens in the house now, up in the loft if there's nowhere else. As for the crazy recipes some people come up with – I expect you've seen some of them in the Evening Post, haven't you?'

'Yes, like bramble leaf tea and parsnip coffee?'

'And dandelion coffee. Awful stuff.'

'Our parsnip coffee isn't too bad at all,' Izette protested. 'I made it with my own fair hand! I'll give you some to take home.'

'Well, it couldn't possibly be as bad as the dandelion coffee. And here's a riddle for you. What's grey, greasy, sludgy and comes in glass bottles?' Tom asked.

'I can't imagine,' laughed Izette. 'Is it something you use in a car engine?'

'No, it's the new bottled stew we can buy in St Helier! Actually it tastes rather better than it looks.'

'Oh dear, things are tough in the town. At least we have the chickens and the rabbits. Uncle Jim kills one or the other most weeks.'

Tom looked at her in some amusement. 'Are you telling me you eat rabbit now? Those sweet, fluffy creatures you used to cuddle and push around in a toy pram?'

Indignant, she pushed him hard on the shoulder, rolling him over in the grass. When he'd stopped laughing, she said, 'We all grow up sometime, you know.'

'Mmm,' he said, teasingly, casting an eye over her again, 'you certainly have!'

Tom was saved from further attack by the return of Edmund. By this time, it was getting late so the three of them walked back down to the farm, exchanging news and joking together. When they burst laughing into the farm kitchen, Aunt Margaret and Uncle Jim looked up in surprise but it was Aunt Margaret who hit the nail on the head.

'My, my, young Tom. You've brought a sparkle to her eyes. What on earth have you been up to?'

CHAPTER 8

1942

It was the relentless struggle that wore the women down. Every day the same difficulty: how to find enough to eat. How to stretch the steadily reducing rations even further; how to produce an appetising meal from the dreary selection of vegetables available; how to keep clothes and home clean without soap. As for the men, it was the lack of work and the helplessness they felt as the German garrison steadily increased and the island disappeared under a sea of concrete. Grey uniforms everywhere you turned, helping themselves to whatever they wanted and not a thing you could do about it. Most took comfort from the link with the outside world provided by their wirelesses. They could at least follow the progress of the war, though there was little to be heard that raised any hope of an end to it all. The war seemed set to run on and on.

As the year turned the corner into spring, and farm work demanded every minute of her time, Izette worked harder than she had ever imagined possible, but no less hard than Aunt Margaret and Uncle Jim. Most nights, she fell into bed exhausted. Her thoughts, on those nights when she could stay awake long enough to think, extended no further than simple gratitude for the few hour's comfort her bed would provide. Sometimes, by candlelight, she examined her red, work-roughened hands, remembering the days when she had coveted Irene's long, polished nails. Now it was her company she coveted. She hadn't seen her sister for months. Her mother said she spent nearly all of her time at the hotel, not even coming home to sleep at night. She missed Edmund, too. Edmund had returned to school after Christmas and the grey months of January and February and March dragged slowly by until his return in the Easter holidays. Aunt Margaret was for ever saying to Betty and Bill that she wanted him to have the freedom to play in the fields and woods, particularly since the German restrictions had put nearly all the beaches out of reach. No one was fooled and there was truth in what she said, but it was the comparative abundance of food on the farm that Aunt Margaret had in mind for Edmund. She knew Betty couldn't feed her family nearly as well as she could.

When it did arrive at last, the Easter holiday was a welcome relief from the daily drudgery. As a special treat, Aunt Margaret dyed chicken's eggs for breakfast on Easter Sunday and for lunch, Uncle Jim presented a joint of pork as though by magic, smiling and tapping his nose with one finger when Izette asked where it had come from.

'Ask no questions and you'll be told no lies, my dear.'

Edmund had rushed out of the kitchen with a worried expression on his face to return a few minutes later announcing with relief that it wasn't one of their pigs. He'd counted them and they were all still there.

'I take it that means you'll be prepared to eat it then,

young man?' Uncle Jim asked. 'You could have extra potatoes instead if you'd prefer?'

Edmund shook his head vigorously.

'That's good,' said Aunt Margaret, 'because your mum and dad are coming over for lunch and I'd hate them to think I was starving you!'

'Oooh wonderful!' Izette said, giving her Aunt and Uncle a hug in turn. 'You kept it a surprise for us.'

And it was a wonderful day, one that would remain in Izette's memory for a long time, one that she was to recall later that year when events on the island took a turn for the worse. The pork was moist and tender with delicious salty crackling. When Bill asked where they obtained their salt, Izette was proud to explain how she maintained their stock of salt by painstakingly boiling down buckets of seawater.

'And it isn't easy to get the seawater because most of the bays are mined,' she continued excitedly, 'but Edmund knows a safe place.'

Her father raised his eyebrows at this and Edmund kicked her shin under the table but, fortunately, Uncle Jim interceded at this point.

'Don't you worry, Bill. We don't let them do anything silly. I know every square inch of this farm and I know exactly what Jerry's been up to here. I showed Edmund which places to keep clear of. There's still quite a few places where you can get down to the sea safely.'

Later that afternoon, Bill, Jim, Izette and Edmund took a walk to help settle their lunch while Betty and Margaret settled down for a good talk together. Edmund wanted to show Bill where they went to fetch the seawater.

'It's our secret cove, Dad. The Germans don't know about it. We come down here all the time.' He danced about in front of them, delighted to be leading the little party.

'They do know about it, Edmund,' argued Izette, 'but I think it's too small for them to bother about. Nothing could land there.'

'It could so. A rubber dinghy could land there.'

'How would anyone be able to find the cove from the sea?' she continued. 'It looks as though the cliffs drop straight down into the sea, even when you're close to it.'

'That's what makes it so perfect, silly! Someone would need to signal with a torch to guide them in.'

'Well, that's pretty unlikely,' said Izette.

'Not if we could get a message to them. What do you think, Dad.'

'Sounds like a damn good scheme to me, Edmund.' Bill ruffled Edmund's hair fondly and Izette watched Edmund beam with pleasure. He didn't realise Dad was joking.

'Here we are then,' Edmund announced.

They had come to the edge of a field where the cultivated pasture stopped and scrubby undergrowth stretched for a few yards before the land fell away to the sea. There was a splendid view of the sea that Bill stopped to enjoy but Edmund hurried him on, pulling him into the undergrowth where a narrow path wound down through the bushes. It was a bit of a scramble to get down but within a few minutes they were standing on a small beach, no more than four yards across, with the cliff rearing out of the water to their left and a projecting spit of land, heavily overgrown, to their right.

'You see,' said Edmund, 'this is hidden by those bushes. You can't be seen from the sea.'

'Yes,' agreed Bill, 'it's certainly well hidden. A good place for you to play, Edmund, but I don't want you, either of you, swimming from here. That's too dangerous at the moment.'

Edmund was about to explain that 'playing' wasn't what

he had in mind when his father continued.

'Now, I've brought some of my precious baccy with me and Uncle Jim and I are going to enjoy a peaceful smoke, so you two can have a paddle if you like.'

The two men climbed back up the path, looking for a suitable place to sit for their smoke, leaving Izette and Edmund alone. Edmund put his hands on his hips. He was thoroughly disgusted. The significance of the cove seemed to be entirely lost on his father.

'Did you see that, Izette? He didn't understand, did he? Neither did Uncle Ted.'

Izette had taken off her shoes and socks and was dabbling a toe in the cold water.

'Well, it's only pretend, isn't it?' she answered carelessly.

'No it isn't! It isn't pretend at all. This is the perfect spot for a secret landing.' Edmund was kicking with frustration at the pebbles. One of them hit Izette's bare shin.

'Ouch! Stop that, you pest.' Annoyed, she came out of the water and stood in front of him. 'So what could we do exactly, Edmund? What great plan do you have in mind? How is Edmund Vaubert going to single-handedly arrange for an invasion party to land here and drive the Germans from this island then?'

Edmund scowled up at his sister. 'Just you wait and see. I will do something. I will. I promise.'

She looked at him. He was pink in the face and cross but with his feet planted squarely on the beach and his hands still on his hips he looked as determined as she had ever seen him.

Her annoyance evaporated and, giving him a smile, she said, 'Tell you what, Edmund, we'll show this place to Tom next time he's here. He'll understand.'

Edmund's face broke into a grin and, picking up a flat

pebble, he skimmed it across the smooth surface of the water.

'Wow! Seven bounces. Did you see? I must tell Dad.' Turning, he raced back up the path.

Izette sat down to pull her socks and shoes back on before following him.

*

That Easter Sunday, the BBC transmitted a message to the occupied peoples intended to encourage and renew hope. Like many others, the Vauberts gathered round the big old wireless set in the farm kitchen and were cheered by what they heard. So, when eight weeks later, the Germans issued instructions that all civilian radios were to be handed in, they greeted the news with understandable anger. Uncle Jim was outraged and Izette knew her father would be feeling much the same. She just hoped, for her mother's sake, he wouldn't be tempted to express his sentiments in person to the German admin-istration. They were rather less patient now with the Islanders than they had been at the beginning of the occupation. The Germans claimed the sets were being removed for military reasons and would be kept in safe custody but few of the Islanders believed that for a moment. Uncle Jim thought it was to keep their own troops in the dark.

'According to your dad, Izette, young Tom Birrell reckons there's a lot of Germans here who've had as much of this war as we have and just want to go home. He says Jerry's taking away our wirelesses because they don't want them to hear that things are not going their way. They're short of food as well, you know. A bunch of them came up to me in the field the other day asking if they could buy eggs. I told them what they could do with their Reich marks.'

Aunt Margaret and Izette looked up in alarm.

'It's all right,' Jim reassured them, 'they just shrugged

their shoulders and went about their business."

'All the same, Jim, 'Aunt Margaret said, 'you'd better watch that tongue of yours. It wouldn't be the first time it's got you into trouble. You and Bill have always spoken first and thought afterwards.'

'Aye, it's called freedom of expression, Margaret, and it's not something I shall give up without a fight, nor will most of us on this island. And I'll tell you something else. If I can get that old wireless set of your father's working, I'll be taking this set down to the depot and I'll hide the old set somewhere. No Jerry's going to tell me what I can and can't listen to.'

Izette wondered what her father would do about the radio set at home. She couldn't see him complying willingly. The mention of Tom stirred uneasy feelings. The last time she had seen her parents at Easter, her father had been concerned about Tom. Since it wasn't something he could talk to Ted Birrell about, he had discussed the situation with Uncle Jim. The day Edmund took them all down to the secret cove, Izette had overheard the two men discussing Tom as they walked. Edmund had run on ahead and they obviously thought Izette was out of hearing as well but she'd heard enough to cause her to wonder.

'It's not just the amount of time he spends driving for them, Jim, he seems to spend a lot of his time at their HQ, evenings included.'

'But doesn't he have to wait there until they need him for a job?'

'Yes he does but I've seen him in the evenings sometimes when he's come home and I've smelt drink on his breath. And he knows so much about what Jerry's up to. He says you hear a lot when you're driving them about but it makes me wonder. Jerry wouldn't be saying so much in his presence if they didn't trust him, would they?'

'Can he follow what they're saying then?'

'I think he's picked up enough German already to work out most of what's being said.'

'I see. Well, I shouldn't worry, Bill. You've known the lad since he was a baby. I should think you know him as well as his parents. He doesn't strike me as the sort who would feather his own nest at the expense of his principles.'

'No, that's what I used to think, Jim, but I used to believe no one on this island would inform on their neighbour either.'

'Yes, it is difficult to understand how anyone could stoop to that...'

Izette had heard enough. She ran on to catch up with Edmund. She wouldn't believe it of him. Tom would never collaborate with the Germans. It was just unthinkable. He had to work for them. He had no choice about that, as far as she knew, just as her father had to work on the requisitioning. They had ways of making you co-operate but collaboration was another matter altogether. Then she had an uncomfortable thought. She remembered the dance when he'd stood outside afterwards chatting to the soldiers but that was so that he could find out what was going on, wasn't it? And he came to tell them about the escape attempt later, didn't he? But a small inner voice reminded her that this was after the story had already been published in the Evening Post. She was surprised and ashamed that she could feel doubt. Perhaps the atmosphere of fear and mistrust was affecting her more than she realised. At any rate, she could see how easy it might be to misinterpret Tom's motives. The next time she saw him, if she had an opportunity, she would talk to him about it.

*

Uncle Jim took his wireless set down to the German depot and returned with a receipt for it, which he waved at Margaret in disgust.

'Here it is then! I'm supposed to feel confident that I'll get my wireless set back because I have this piece of paper with German gobble-de-gook written on it. All I can read is my name. Heaven knows what it says. It could just as well say, "*forget your wireless set. You'll never see it again, Islander, just as you'll never see the back of us,*" for all I know.'
He slammed the receipt down on the table and stumped off out of the door.

'Well, at least we have the old set hidden in the larder. Do you think it's worth the risk, Izette?' Aunt Margaret asked.

'I'm certain they'll never find it, Aunt Margaret. We must just be very careful when we use it. Edmund and I could stand guard outside while Uncle Jim tunes in.'

Izette picked up the receipt and looked at it.

'Have you got a German dictionary, Aunt Margaret?'

'Certainly not! Your uncle wouldn't have one in the house.'

Izette smiled. 'No, I suppose not. Sorry.'

Leaving the receipt on the table, Izette got up and went to her room. Going over to her chest of drawers, she pulled out a shoebox in which she kept papers she wanted to keep. Birthday cards, her best school reports, Sunday School attendance certificates, a snippet of Edmund's hair from his very first haircut. And...had she put it in here? Yes, down at the bottom of the box was the card she had taken from the German grave in the cemetery. She never had got around to translating it and had had to return the German dictionary to the library eventually. She looked at the card again but it made no more sense to her now than it had then. Propping it up against the wall on the top of the chest of drawers, she resolved to borrow another German dictionary from the library the next time she was in town. It might be quite interesting to find out what it said.

*

July the first was the second anniversary of the start of the occupation. Bill shut the garage for the day and announced that they would all go over to the farm. Edmund had been ill and away from school. He'd had a cough that had settled on his chest and Betty had decided he wasn't going back to school until after the summer holidays. There was so much tuberculosis about she didn't want to take any risks. They would take him over to the farm for the summer in the hope that the fresh air and good food would help him recover more quickly. Needless to say, Edmund was delighted. Irene also decided she would take a day off work in order to see Izette.

Betty was up in Edmund's bedroom, helping him to pack his clothes into a small cardboard suitcase.

'What on earth have you got in this box, Edmund? It's full of wires and things. You don't want to take all this rubbish, do you?'

'Mum! It's the parts for my things. You know, the things we can't mention.' Edmund hissed, quickly shutting the lid on the box.

'Oh, I see,' said Betty.

Since the confiscation of the wirelesses, Edmund had been making crystal sets. He'd started with one for themselves, then had made one for the Birrells and he'd been working on one for Uncle Jim, which he intended to give him today. Betty thought it was far too dangerous but Bill was full of admiration and had even helped Edmund assemble the parts he needed. He had also tried to reassure his wife.

'Don't worry, Betty. I make sure he keeps everything well hidden. If the worst came to the worst, I'd say I'd made them. No one would suspect a lad of his age. Anyway, anyone with a bit of technical know-how is making these things up. I wouldn't be surprised if every other family on the avenue has their own crystal set tucked away somewhere.'

'All the same, Bill, I'm not at all happy about it. I don't want you arrested and sent away to one of those camps.'

'It'll be all right, love.'

*

The day had a strangely Bank Holiday atmosphere. Many Islanders had closed their businesses or taken the day off. Some were wearing a rose for England and a black tie in mourning for freedom. The Vauberts decided a family get-together was enough for them. Izette hadn't seen her parents since Easter and Irene for considerably longer. She was so excited that she kept dancing around the kitchen until her aunt became quite irritated and sent her outside to wait for their guests. Izette was hoping Tom might have taken it into his head to invite himself along. He knew he was always welcome at the farm.

The weather had been swelteringly hot for the last few days and Izette had chosen to wear a sleeveless cotton print dress with a close fitting bodice down to the waist and a full skirt gathered at the waistband. Aunt Margaret had found a belt to match the colours of the print that finished it off perfectly and emphasized Izette's small waist. Izette had no stockings to wear so her legs were bare but the outdoor work had toasted them to a rich gold. Despite her limited diet, she glowed with health.

Edmund was the first to appear. By the time she'd caught him to her in a hug, in his case reluctantly as usual, the rest of the family were around her and Edmund was able to escape. Tom was not with them but she hid her disappointment. Irene was amazed to see the transformation in her little sister.

'Izette, I can't believe how you've grown up. You're as tall as me...and look at your figure!' Izette laughed and twirled around to show herself off to Irene.

'You look so well, doesn't she, Mum? This outdoor life certainly suits you.'

Izette's mother agreed wholeheartedly. She hoped the fresh air and better food would have the same effect on Edmund, whose poor health had been such a worry that year.

Jim and Margaret joined them and then drew them all inside the farmhouse, out of the blazing sun, to enjoy the big lunch Margaret and Izette had prepared. Margaret thought both Betty and Irene looked pale and more tired than when she last saw them. She kept offering them extra helpings of everything on the table and, although they ate adequately, they didn't eat nearly as much as Jim and Izette could manage.

After lunch, since Edmund had plans of his own and the others wanted to sit down quietly with a cup of tea and catch up with each other's news, Izette and Irene were able to have some time alone. Irene suggested they went up to Izette's room but Izette didn't want to be shut inside on such a glorious day.

'But it's so hot, Izette, I'll simply melt if I go out there.'

'Don't be silly! Anyway, I know a lovely cool place. You'll love it, Irene. Come on!'

In the end, Irene was persuaded to follow Izette. Her shoes were not ideal for walking but the place Izette had in mind was not very far from the farmhouse. There was a small spring at the edge of a birch copse where the water flowed throughout the year, forming a sandy-bottomed stream. Izette often came here on hot days to take advantage of the shade and cool water. Irene was enchanted when she saw it.

'Here we are. It's lovely, isn't it? Now take off your shoes and stockings and put your feet in the water. It's sheer heaven!'

They both dabbled their toes, squealing and giggling as they immersed their feet in the chilly, sparkling stream. They splashed around, paddling up and down, even jumping in and out, behaving like children, almost managing to forget the outside world. Almost but not quite. Eventually, breathless and satiated, they climbed out and lay down on the bank, letting their feet and legs dry in the sun.

'Ooh', groaned Irene, 'I have a pain in my side from laughing and look at my dress. It's soaked! Oh, well, who cares?'

Izette was just as wet and cared just as little. On the contrary, she felt blissfully happy. 'It's good to be together again, Irene. I've really missed you.'

Irene took her hand as they lay side by side and squeezed it. She hadn't had much time to think about Izette in recent months but now they were back together again, she realised the strength of the bond between them. They lay quietly together, enjoying the moment of closeness.

'I wasn't joking earlier, Izette, when I said you'd grown up. I meant it, you're not the little girl you were last time I saw you.'

'It's a pity not everyone seems to think so.'

Irene sat up in surprise to look at Izette. 'Everyone? Who do you mean?' then, as realisation dawned, 'You don't mean Tom, do you? You're surely not still carrying a candle for Tom?'

Izette's silence confirmed she'd guessed correctly.

'I thought he might come with you today,' she admitted eventually.

'Oh, Izette.' Irene sighed. 'Don't...' she paused, trying

to find the right words. 'I know you've known him all your life and he's always been kind to you but I really don't think he sees you in that way. I'm sorry if that hurts but it's the way things happen sometimes. I'm sure he's very fond of you but you must try to accept that he thinks of you as another sister.'

Izette sat up crossly, 'I know that! But I thought when I grew up things might change. It does happen, you know. I read a novel where...'

'Exactly,' Irene interrupted, 'you read a novel. That was a story. Real life isn't like that.'

'It can be!' insisted Izette.

Irene could see there was little point in arguing with Izette. She had nurtured her fantasy for too many years. She could only hope that a real lover would come along in due time for her sister to take the place of the fairy tale she'd spun for herself. She lay back down on the grass and closed her eyes. 'You're right, it can be,' she sighed.

Puzzled, Izette waited.

'I'll tell you a story, something you could never imagine happening in a thousand years if you like. Do you want to hear it?'

'Is it a true story?'

'You'll have to decide that for yourself.'

Mystified, Izette agreed to listen. Irene reached into her pocket and drew out a folded sheet of paper, creased from much handling, and began to read.

'*Once upon a time but not so long ago, a blacksmith fell in love with a lovely young girl who brought her horse to be shoed. The girl was beautiful and fair, and her father was rich and owned lots of land. The blacksmith was a humble man, not very tall, certainly not at all handsome and he despaired of the young girl ever really noticing him. However, as time went by, the young girl and the blacksmith came to know each other well and the young girl did fall in love with him. They promised themselves to each other but before they could ask permission to marry, a terrible thing happened. The king of the land decreed that all young men must join his army to fight a great war and the blacksmith, together with his younger brother, was forced to leave his love and travel far, far away to fight an enemy he did not know.*

They came to a strange land across the sea, a beautiful land of flowers, rolling green meadows and endless sunshine and they took this land from its people because the people were few and could not defend themselves. The blacksmith and his brother loved this strange land but one day an accident happened and the blacksmith's brother was drowned. After that, the blacksmith came to hate the land which had taken his brother and longed to return home but that was not possible. The blacksmith looked at the sea that had taken his brother and decided to throw himself in too, since his suffering was so great but someone stopped him. A serving maid took his hand and led him away from the water. She talked to him and soothed him. She eased the pain in his heart and gave him a reason to live again. For this, she asked nothing of him but he gave her his friendship. As he watched her and spoke with her, the picture of his first love faded from his memory and he gave his heart to the serving maid.

He asked her to marry him but she said she could not. Her people would despise her. He asked her again and again she said she could not. Her father's house would be closed to her forever. He said to her "I will take you away from this land to my land where you will be welcomed by my people and by my father. My home will be your home and you will be loved for ever".'

Irene paused before reading the last sentence.
*'And now is the moment when **you** must choose.'*

Irene folded the paper and replaced it in her pocket. There was silence, except for the low drone of insects. Izette lay on the grass, not knowing what to make of the strange story. After a moment, Irene stood up and brushed the grass from her skirt. She looked down at her sister, who still hadn't moved or said a word.

'Not a word of this to anyone, Izette.'

Then she turned and walked slowly back to the farmhouse, alone.

CHAPTER 9

Tom leaned back against the wing of the car and blew out a long plume of cigarette smoke. He checked his watch. Erich had been inside the barracks for an nearly an hour. With any luck, this could be the last trip of the day, in which case he might send Tom home for the evening. He was certainly due an evening off. He'd had to collect Erich late in the evening for the last four days on the trot and it was mostly from meetings at the various HQs, not social events. There seemed to be a bit of pressure coming through from Berlin, if Erich's mood was anything to go by. Last time Tom had collected him, Erich had come stony-faced out of the HQ doors and walked straight past the sentries without comment, which was uncharacteristic. Erich usually made time for a few words with the guards as he came and went. Unlike a lot of his snooty fellow officers, he liked to encourage them if he could. He was that kind of man. If circumstances had been different, thought Tom, he and Erich might well have found enough common ground to strike up a friendship. As it was, they'd developed a good working relationship, good enough for Erich to let Tom know when he wasn't happy about the orders that were coming through, which he certainly didn't seem to be at the moment.

Tom heard a door slam and saw Erich hurrying down the steps towards the car. He squeezed the lit tip from his cigarette, pushed the remaining end into his pocket and opened the rear door for Erich, who shook his head, indicating he'd sit in the front passenger seat. Erich pulled the front door open himself and got in without a word. Another bad session then, thought Tom, as he walked round to his side of the car and got in.

'Back to the Mess, sir?' Tom had adopted the 'sir' in preference to Erich's long-winded military title. He thought it conveyed the right amount of deference without making him feel as though he was on the German staff. Bit of a fine distinction, perhaps, but Erich didn't object.

'God, no; not this evening; I need to 'unwind', as you say. Take me somewhere where I can look out over the sea. I need to remind myself that there is still beauty in the world and a God in heaven.'

Tom raised his eyebrows but said nothing and started the engine. He would take him up past the Mackesey's farm. They could park right on the headland half a mile or so beyond the farmhouse. There was a good moon that night. Could have been romantic if you'd had the right company.

When they got there, Erich got straight out of the car, lit a cigarette and walked over to the cliff edge. Tom stayed in the car. His watch now said eight-thirty. His hand moved to his pocket as he thought about lighting up but he checked himself. Better save that half for later. He wound down the window. It was quite still outside, no wind at all and silent except for the occasional tick from the engine as it cooled down. Erich sat himself down on a rock, and gazed out to sea. Tom leaned back in his seat and relaxed. He knew from past experience that Erich's 'unwinding' could take some time. Still, it was peaceful up here. Better than waiting outside some busy barracks for him.

Eventually Erich stood up, walked back to the car and got in beside Tom, startling him out of a light doze.

'Tired, my English friend?' He didn't wait for Tom to reply. 'I expect you are. Tired of me keeping you out every evening, eh? I know, I see you look at your watch.' He laughed. 'Or are you, like me, tired of stupid orders, tired of being away from home, tired of this whole bloody mess?' He paused and offered Tom a cigarette. 'I suppose I should be grateful. I could be over there on the Eastern front but here I am on your beautiful island, helping to cover your beaches with mines and build concrete eyesores on your loveliest headlands. Do you hate me, my friend Tom, eh?'

Tom was caught off-guard. It wasn't unusual for Erich to talk and complain about the war but Tom wasn't usually invited to comment.

'Well, I can't honestly say I hate you personally. You seem a decent sort of chap, just following orders like anyone else. But I do hate the process of war and I hate the perpetrators of war. I hate the way it's the innocent who suffer most for the expansionist greed of a few evil men.' He looked across at Erich, trying to gauge his mood. 'But perhaps I'd better not say too much about that?'

Erich waved his hand dismissively. 'Don't worry, Tom. This is strictly 'off the record'. You know I'm no Nazi. And you're right. How do they do it, these few evil men? How do they persuade us all to leave our families and homes and go out and kill one another? It's not as if we haven't done it all before and what did we achieve then? Hundreds of thousands of widows and fatherless children. My own father was killed in the First War and my mother was never truly alive again after that.'

Tom nodded in agreement. Erich reached into his tunic pocket and brought out a hip flask. He offered it to Tom. 'Here, my friend, drink with me to the end of all this madness.'

Tom was surprised but took a swig from the flask. It was whisky, very good whisky if he wasn't mistaken, as he commented to Erich.

'Yes, it is indeed. As you know, the glorious German army leaves no wine cellar un-violated.' He sighed. 'If only that was the worst of our violations.' He took a hefty swig himself and passed it back to Tom again. 'Drink; that's an order; it's the only way to get through this hell.'

The flask passed between them until it was empty, Erich having downed the lion's share. By this time, Erich had moved on to reminiscences about his home and his fiancée and the plans he'd had for their future together before the war intervened. While Erich talked, Tom wondered if he was in a sufficiently convivial mood to risk showing him the card Izette had given him when he last saw her. She told him she'd tried to translate it herself but found it too difficult, so she gave it to Tom for him to have a go. Noticing that Tom had been quiet for a few moments, Erich slapped him on the thigh like an old chum and grinned.

'You say nothing, Tom. What are you thinking, Jerseyman? Note that I do not call you English like some of my compatriots. You are British and proud of it but never English, eh?' He started to laugh. 'Do you know that when we first arrived on the island, some of our troops thought this was the Isle of Wight and we had started the invasion of England? But I shouldn't laugh; many of them are simple, uneducated peasants who have probably never seen a map of

Europe. But wouldn't you have thought their officers would have told them where they were?'

When Erich was silent again, Tom decided to take the plunge and pulled the piece of card from his pocket, handing it to the other man.

'I came across this the other day. I've no idea what it says, the German's way beyond me.'

Erich struggled to focus on the card. It was just legible in the moonlight. He read it through then looked at Tom cautiously.

'Where did you get this?'

'I picked it up at the main transport depot. It was just lying on the ground between two staff cars. What is it then?' He managed to sound casually curious.

'I suppose I shouldn't expect you to tell me where you really got it. You're too intelligent for that, my friend, or perhaps too calculating? I know what I would be doing if our positions were reversed. Do you make notes of our conversations, eh? Do you take advantage of my indiscretion? Come on, tell me; I thought we were friends.'

Tom floundered for a reply. Erich suddenly appeared absolutely sober. Had he been stringing him along all evening, drawing him into a trap?

Then Erich's expression changed and he upended the flask once more, disgusted to find it empty. 'Don't worry, Tom. I'm only teasing you. What do I care any more! You write whatever you like about me but don't let it fall into the wrong hands. You would be signing my death warrant.' He threw the empty flask out of the car window. 'Come on, drive me home; it's time I was in bed.'

Tom started the engine and put the car into reverse gear. 'So what does the card say?' he asked cautiously.

'It's an anti-Nazi propaganda poem. Quite well written

actually' it has some literary merit. However it would not do you or me any good to be found carrying it so...' He set light to the card with his cigarette lighter and threw it out of the window when it was nearly burned through. 'I'm not altogether surprised you found it. There's a growing feeling of disenchantment among the men. I expect, despite the fact that you have, of course, handed in your wireless set, you hear how the war is going? You've heard how the RAF is bombing not just military targets but German cities now? So you must be able to imagine how they feel.'

The car turned into the long drive of the large manor house in which Erich was stationed with his fellow officers. Erich yawned. 'So, are you going to tell me who gave it to you, Tom?'

Tom pulled on the handbrake and looked across at Erich. 'I did...sir.'

Erich shrugged, 'As you like,' and got out of the car before Tom could get round to open the door for him. As he reached the passenger door, the two men came face to face. Keeping his voice low, Erich said, 'You won't like what you hear in the next few days. I'm sorry, my friend.' Then he turned and walked up the steps to the entrance door, calling, 'Goodnight, driver,' as he saluted the sentries on the way in.

Tom took the car round to the garages at the rear of the house and locked it up for the night, then began the walk home. He was angry with himself. It had been a mistake to show Erich the card and let himself be drawn into that cat and mouse game. You couldn't be too careful, even with a German who appeared as open and friendly as Erich. The Germans had all the cards stacked in their favour. Erich knew he could disclose his personal feelings to Tom because no one would subsequently believe Tom's words if Erich denied them. It was every man for himself in the end. Still, it was a bloody good job the card had nothing more significant on it than a piece of propaganda. He thought of the source of the card, Izette, and shook his head. As long as I've known her, that girl has been trouble. I've lost count of the times I've had to get her out of scrapes and here she is, still causing me problems. I should know better by now.

He turned the last corner into the avenue wondering how long he could carry on this game. He was getting a reputation for being 'well in' with Jerry and, while it served his purposes for the moment; it left a nasty taste in his mouth. As his key turned in the lock, he remembered Erich's last words to him and a chill of fear suddenly shot through him. At the time, he'd thought Erich meant more unpopular measures were on the way for the Islanders but was the warning for him personally this time?

*

It was September already. Where had the summer gone? Izette could hardly believe it when Aunt Margaret said they would need to be setting a little something aside for the Harvest Festival. It couldn't be very much that year, of course, but it was important to have a small thanks-giving just the same. After all, they were all managing to keep body and soul together and they had the Good Lord to thank for that. Izette was clearing the tea plates from the table and, as she passed the half-glazed kitchen door into the scullery, caught sight of her reflection in the glass. She seemed to have been wearing the same faded and slightly threadbare blouse and dull, brown, hand-me-down skirt of her aunt's for months.

'I wish the Good Lord could see his way to providing a new frock for me,' she said wistfully.

Aunt Margaret looked up. It was rare for Izette to

complain about anything.

'Dearie me, I was forgetting how hard it is at your age. You want pretty things like Irene had and to be able to show yourself off to your best. Why don't you ask Irene if she has anything tucked away in her wardrobe that you could have?'

'I already have, but she says she can't spare anything. She needs to look as smart as she can while she's working for the Germans at the hotel. She can't afford to lose her job.'

'No, I suppose that's true, but still I would have thought...'

Aunt Margaret left the matter there but Izette knew what she was thinking. She no more approved of Irene working for the Germans than her father did. Even Uncle Jim had said he'd scrape together a little wage for her if she were willing to come and work on the farm for him. Izette smiled as she remembered the look of absolute horror on Irene's face. The shock of his offer rendered Irene speechless for a couple of minutes but she did eventually pull herself together sufficiently to thank Uncle Jim for his kindness. As soon as she could escape from the scene to her room, Izette had the best laugh she'd had in weeks about that.

Hearing running footsteps in the yard, Izette came out of the scullery to see Uncle Jim hurry in through the kitchen door, having just got back from St Helier.

'Margaret! Izette! Where are you both? Come and take a look at this. I can't believe it. They can't do this.'

'What on earth's the matter, Jim?'

'Read that!'

He handed them a copy of a notice that had been issued that day by the German authorities, stating that all men between the ages of 16 and 70 who had not been born on the Islands, together with their families, were to be evacuated to Germany. These families were to be report to the Weighbridge by 4.00

PM the following day.

Jim stormed up and down the kitchen while Margaret and Izette read the details of what these unfortunate families were allowed to take with them, which amounted to little more than the clothes they were wearing and a blanket each.

'But surely they can't do this, Jim! And why? What have they done?'

'As far as anybody knows, absolutely nothing, Margaret! No one's any idea what it's all about. The town's absolutely seething with it. The Bailiff has objected of course. It's against the Hague Convention and it's also a direct contradiction of that statement they made when they first invaded, that they would guarantee the livelihood, liberty and so on of the Islanders. I tell you, it's absolutely outrageous.'

'And they have to be ready by tomorrow! That's terrible, the poor souls! They can't expect people to pack up and leave their homes in a few hours.'

'You can if you're Jerry! Scum! I tell you, Margaret, these bastards...oh, pardon me, Izette, I didn't mean to use strong language in front of you...they're completely ruthless. You've seen the poor Russian and Polish slave workers they're using to build their blasted fortifications; they treat them worse than animals. I tell you, this whole occupation by co-operation with the Ruling Council with guarantees about the rights of the Islanders is a complete sham! A pack of lies! 'Evacuation' they're calling it! It's deportation, not evacuation, and if we don't do something about it, we could all find ourselves being shipped over to Germany. Not a bloody Islander left!'

'Jim, that's enough,' Margaret nodded her head towards Izette. 'You're frightening Izette. Look at her; she's white as a sheet. Anyway, I expect as soon as Britain gets to know what's going on, they'll send troops to stop it. They wouldn't let innocent British families be taken like this.'

Jim was sceptical. Britain had failed them in 1940 and he didn't see why this situation would be regarded any differently but he could see that Izette was shaken. He would hold his tongue for the time being. More quietly he continued, 'We'll lose Henry, of course. He'll be on the list for deportation.'

'Oh dear, the poor man. Can't we hide him?'

'No, they've already got a list of everyone on the Island. They know where they all are. Heaven knows how we'll manage without him.'

The mention of Henry brought the matter home even more painfully for Izette and, bursting into tears, she fled up to her bedroom. Margaret started to follow her but Jim stopped her.

'Leave her be for now. A good cry is probably the best thing for her in the circumstances. She's grown quite fond of Henry. This'll be her first experience of loss.'

'And ours,' replied Margaret.

'Yes, indeed,' agreed Jim after a moment.

*

The next day, the day scheduled for the deportations, Izette accompanied her Uncle down to St Helier. The Bailiff's objections were ignored since the evacuation order had come, apparently, directly from Hitler. The only reason suggested for such a measure was thought to be pure spite for the recent RAF bombing campaigns on Germany. Izette and her Uncle went to the Vaubert house first to meet up with the rest of the family before going down to the harbour to help give the deportees a good send-off. Donald, who worked for Bill at the garage, and his family, were amongst those selected to go on the first ship that day. Izette was glad to see her parents and Mr and Mrs Birrell and Nancy from next door but disappointed that Tom was not there. Mr Birrell told her he was out working, he didn't know where.

They joined many other groups of people making their way down to the harbour around two o'clock in the afternoon. Everyone seemed to be of the same mind. If they couldn't prevent the deportations they would jolly well show Jerry how much they were against it. Many of the women were red-eyed and tearful but, as the numbers swelled the closer they came to the harbour, they held their heads high and looked scornfully in the direction of any Germans they passed. Amongst the crowd of supporters, the deportees had dressed up in their best clothes and joked and sang patriotic songs on the way down. Many hands helped carry their pitiably small bundles of possessions. The pace of the crowd slowed as they neared the harbour where they found their way blocked by German soldiers who would only allow the deportees through on to the Weighbridge. As a result, the final tearful farewells had to be said there in front of the German guards. Bill insisted on walking to the checkpoint with Donald and his family. They shook hands at the point of parting.

'All the best then, Donald. You can be sure we'll be thinking of you often. And you can be sure your job will be waiting for you as soon as you get back.'

'Thank you very much indeed, Bill. I know I can rely on you. Might be back sooner than you think, eh?' Donald was working hard to keep his voice steady.

'Indeed you might, Donald. I very much hope so.'

Bill squeezed Donald's shoulder, then shook his wife's hand and bent down to say goodbye to Donald's two little girls, then the family were ushered through to wait in a long queue to be checked by a panel of doctors. Those not considered fit enough to travel were being turned back. Unfortunately, Donald's family was not among them.

Henry, Uncle Jim's labourer, had also walked down with

them. Neither Jim nor Bill agreed with Henry's principles as a Conscientious Objector but they did agree that he had a right to hold them and they gave him as warm a send off as they would a member of their own families. Aunt Margaret promised to try to get a Red Cross message to his wife in Bristol.

Having said their good-byes, the Vauberts pushed their way back through the crowd to find a place from which they could see the transit boats at the quayside. German troops lined all the approaches to the harbour and nearby roads but eventually they managed to find a spot. Then they settled down to wait. The crowd was noisy and emboldened by their numbers to risk shouting some abuse at the Germans, who were looking distinctly uncomfortable. The demonstration could easily have erupted into an ugly riot but the Germans seemed aware of this and were anxious to keep the situation as calm as possible. They had allowed the authorities to provide refreshments for the deportees. The waiting crowd was not so fortunate, unless they'd had the foresight to bring some provisions with them, for it was to be a very long wait.

Izette wriggled through the crowd to her father. 'How long do you think it'll be, Dad, before they go?'

'Difficult to say, love, but looking at the length of that queue, I don't think they'll all be embarked before this evening. You and Edmund don't have to stay until the end though. You could go back home if you like.'

'No, I'd like to stay,' and, checking with Edmund first, 'and Edmund would too, but I think we'll have a bit of a walk round while we're waiting.'

Izette asked Nancy if she'd like to join them but she preferred to stay with her father so the two of them pushed their way out of the crowd and climbed to the rocky headland that rose up behind the harbour. Edmund said he'd like to take notes about the ships at anchor and thought he might do a few sketches of them as well so they found themselves a place to sit. Edmund happily chatted about gun turrets, firing ranges, and observation posts unaware that Izette was barely listening. She gazed out to sea where a number of German ships could be seen anchored well out, she listened to the crowd as they broke into song from time to time, she watched the regular shuttle of buses carrying the deportees from the Weighbridge to the waiting ships and thought how unreal it all seemed. People were chatting and laughing as though they were waiting for the start of a regatta. But then she remembered Henry coming to say goodbye to her before they'd left the farm. Everything he had brought with him from England fitted easily in the canvas holdall slung over his shoulder. He'd cleared his room, stripping the bed himself to save work for Aunt Margaret, and soon there would be no sign that he had ever been there. Would it be the same for these families? Would their houses now stand empty and silent, dust settling on their abandoned possessions?

As she brooded over these things, she noticed a familiar figure making its way up Pier Road. Immediately she stood up and waved, 'Tom, Tom, over here!' He looked up and smiled and started scrambling up the bank to join them.

'Hello there, you two. I saw your dad and the others further down the road. They said you'd walked up in this direction.'

Tom sat down beside them and ruffled Edmund's hair, who ducked out of reach and moved to sit a few paces away. Tom shrugged his shoulders and took a packet of cigarettes out of his pocket. Absentmindedly, he offered one to Izette, who shook her head.

'Oh sorry, I wasn't thinking,' he said. When he'd lit one for himself he asked Izette how she was managing.

'Oh, fine, I suppose,' she replied, 'the farm work is hard and dull, though I don't mind the hard work, it's the monotony that gets me down, especially making the wretched potato flour.'

She paused to laugh but there was no answering response from Tom.

'And we've lost Henry now, of course. He's down there with the others. I don't know how Uncle Jim will manage without him.'

She paused but again there was no comment forthcoming from Tom.

'How about you, Tom?'

Tom had been sitting with his elbows resting on his raised knees and now he bent his head, pressing his thumbs into his eye-sockets.

'If you want the truth, Izette, I feel like giving up. I feel like throwing in the job with Jerry and getting out of St Helier altogether. I thought I might be able to get a job on a farm, perhaps on the other side of the island, where I could just keep my head down, get on with the work and sit it out until this war comes to an end, one way or the other. I'm sick and tired of being at the beck and call of this lot, having to turn out any time of the day or night, then waiting for hours on end until they're finished doing whatever it is they're doing.'

He took another drag from his cigarette.

'And don't think I don't know what people are saying about me, including your Dad. They think I'm a damn sight too familiar with Jerry. Which is hardly surprising since they see me driving around in the staff cars, they hear them call me 'Tom', they notice I never seem to be short of a packet of cigarettes. I'm seen out and about after curfew so folk put two and two together and come up with five. I'm right, aren't I? That is what they're saying?'

Izette couldn't deny it. 'Well, yes, I suppose...'

'Yes! You see?' He turned to face her. 'Do you know, Izette, after my own father, I trust and respect your Dad more than anyone else and to see that uncertainty in his eyes sometimes when he speaks to me…just breaks my heart. It makes me think this has all been a complete waste of time. I've managed to pick up a lot of information about what's going on in these islands but what's the point if your own family and friends think you're betraying them?'

'But isn't what you're doing vital? I mean, if you could get this information…'

He interrupted her. 'Exactly! *If* I could get the information off the Island! Any suggestions? I haven't come up with any ideas in the last two years except take it off myself and you know what's happened to the poor chaps who've tried to get away.'

Izette couldn't think of anything to say.

In the short silence, Edmund piped up. 'I've got information as well, Tom. I've been doing surveillance since the very beginning and I've got everything written down in my notebooks. Would you like to see this one?'

Tom winked at Izette but took the proffered notebook from Edmund. He flicked through the pages casually at first, then stopped to study it in more detail.

'Good Heavens, Edmund. You've got all the duty rotas here…and plans of the batteries and what's this?' Tom pulled out a folded sheet.

'That's a map of the mined beaches on Uncle Jim's farm. I watched them do it.'

'Have you shown this to anyone else, Edmund?'

'No, only Izette.'

Tom looked at Izette in astonishment. 'This is astounding. The amount of detail he's got here…it must have taken ages for him to put all this together. I wish there was a way of getting this to the UK. It's invaluable.'

Privately, Izette had dismissed Edmund's notebooks as just another of his hobbies, useful in providing him with something to do, so she was surprised by Tom's reaction. Edmund was positively glowing with pride. Tom handed the book back.

'Now look, Edmund, I think what you have here is very important indeed. It is also very dangerous. If the Germans were to find your notebooks you'd be in very serious trouble and they probably wouldn't believe you collected all this information by yourself, so the whole family might be in danger. I don't know where you're keeping the notebooks at the moment but I want you to find a very secure hiding place for them somewhere on the farm. Can you do that?'

'Oh yes,' beamed Edmund, 'that's no problem at all.'

'Right. I want you to do that as soon as you get home today. Next, I'd very much like to look through the rest of them myself so I'll try to come over to the farm in the next few days. Is that all right?'

'Yes,' said Edmund, 'I'll be ready. Shall we have a password? Then, if Uncle Jim and Aunt Margaret are there, you can say it and I'll know it means you want me to take you to see the notebooks.'

Tom grinned. 'If you think it's necessary, choose one and let me know what it is. Very well done, Edmund, I'm proud of you.'

Tom stood up and beckoned to Izette to walk with him a little further up the hill. Eagerly, she stood up and brushed the grass off her skirt, wishing she'd had something a little prettier to wear that day. They walked a little way side by side then Tom stopped and turned. He placed his hands on her shoulders and smiled down into her eyes.

'I'm so glad I've seen you today, this has really raised

my spirits!'

Izette was about to confess that she'd enjoyed seeing him too when he went on.

'Seeing that notebook of Edmund's has really encouraged me. He's put all that work in, day by day, even though he has no idea how anyone might be able to make use of it. A lad of 11! It makes me feel ashamed of even considering giving up.'

Izette smiled and nodded in agreement, relieved she hadn't spoken, thinking what a fool she was to raise her hopes every time she saw him.

'So what are you going to do?'

'I don't know yet but this so-called 'passive resistance' is getting us nowhere. It's time I started stirring up a bit of bother for old Jerry.'

Tom paused to check his watch. 'Is it that time already? I shall have to go. I'm supposed to be meeting someone in a minute. She won't be very amused if I'm late.' He grinned. 'Bye, love, I'll be seeing you.' And he loped off down the hill, saluting Edmund as he passed.

Izette watched him out of sight, feeling utterly stupid. Why should he think of her as anything other than the girl next door, a playmate of his childhood? The four years between them yawned wide and seemingly insurmountable for Izette. He'd probably had dozens of girlfriends by now and he was obviously off to meet another one now. She hadn't a chance of competing. Why on earth did she waste her time dreaming about him? She walked back to where Edmund was still sitting.

'Come on, I'm getting cold. Let's go back down.'

*

The long afternoon dragged on into a long evening and it wasn't until nine o'clock that the transport ships finally cast off and started to pull away from the quay. The crowd was quieter by this time, no doubt feeling the strain of the long vigil but, as they heard the deportees raise their voices in 'There'll always be an England' from the boats, they roused themselves to join in and the sound of their voices resounded round the harbour. The singing and shouts of encouragement continued until both ships were out of sight. Only then did the Islanders turn sadly for home. It was past curfew as the people walked home that night but they went unchallenged. Edmund and Izette returned to Belle View Villas, it was too far to walk all the way to the farm at that time of night. All the family except Betty went straight up to bed, exhausted by the day's emotional toll. Izette was curled up under the eiderdown when a soft tap sounded at the door and her mother came in.

'I've brought you a hot water bottle. You looked cold.'

'Oh, Mum, you shouldn't have. How did you manage to heat the water?'

'I put a little a little pan on the fire. We had a few bits of stick to burn.'

Izette took the bottle gratefully. Her mother was right. She had been chilled through by the time they had reached home. On top of everything else that had happened that day, the discomfort of getting into the cold bed had brought her close to tears. She put her hand out to her mother and pulled her down to sit on the bed.

'This means you and Dad won't be able to heat water for breakfast in the morning, doesn't it?'

Her mother denied it, saying they had a bit of firewood stored up in the shed, but Izette was unconvinced. The house had felt more than ordinarily cold when she came in. It felt and smelled like the empty houses. It had that same damp coldness that comes from absence of heating over a long period.

'Anyway, there's only your dad and myself here most of the time. Irene often works late and has to stay over at the hotel because of the curfew. And it's warmer there and she gets plenty to eat.'

Which is more than you do, thought Izette. 'Mum, you've lost some more weight. I'll see if Aunt Margaret can spare any more food and I'll bring it down myself.'

'You'll do no such thing, Izette. Margaret and Jim have been more than generous already. Your father spends every spare minute in the garden and we've done very well with the vegetables this year. If I have lost a bit of weight, it's probably because I'm on my feet more than usual. You know how much queuing has to be done to buy the rations.'

There was no point in arguing with her mother. But she would ask her aunt if they could spare a freshly killed rabbit each week for her parents.

'Good night then, my dear, sleep tight.' Betty kissed her daughter and blew out the stub of candle on the dressing table. Izette was grateful for the dark. At last she could press her face into the pillow and let the tears fall.

CHAPTER 10

The deportations continued during September but Izette didn't go down to St Helier again. She told herself that since she didn't know any of the later deportees her absence wouldn't matter. Nonetheless, a sense of betrayal tormented her. She told herself it was a question of personal survival. If she didn't see it, she could persuade herself it wasn't happening. Like the Russian Todt workers, it was only when she came across them accidentally that their plight became unavoidably real. Perhaps refusing to face up to suffering could be described as cowardly but, in a position of complete helplessness, there's only so much the conscience can bear. So it was with a great sense of relief she read the German announcement that the evacuations were over for the time being.

Izette attacked her work on the farm with reckless determination, so much so that Uncle Jim had to restrain her from tackling jobs that really were beyond her strength. He could see she was trying to make up for the loss of Henry but he was not going to stand by and let her work herself to a standstill, as he told her one morning.

'Now look here, Izette. I know what you're trying to do and I appreciate your effort but there is only so much that one body can do. If you carry on like this you will make yourself ill. You're a plucky lass but I won't have you ruining your health. This is my farm and, from now on, you will start work and stop work when I say so. If I have to, I'll lock you in your room to stop you getting up before dawn! If things get really difficult with harvesting, I might be able to get some casual labour to tide us over.'

'But I'm fine, honestly. I'm tired at night but that's natural, isn't it? I've never felt better in my life.'

Jim looked to Margaret for support. She sat down and placed the teapot firmly on its stand. 'Izette, you're not a slave worker like one of those poor Russians up at the camp. I won't have your Mum and Dad see us wear you out. So young lady, if you're not prepared to abide by your uncle's decision, you'll just have to go home.'

Izette looked up, astonished. 'You wouldn't send me away?' She looked from one to the other.

They each nodded gravely.

'I was only trying to help,' she said.

Uncle Jim put his huge hand over hers where it rested on the table. 'We know that, you silly girl. So, do we have an agreement?'

'Yes, all right.'

'Good.' He rubbed his hands together. 'Now what do you think you're doing still sitting here? There's work to do. Go on, get off out of it!'

Izette grinned and jumped to her feet.

*

One sunny morning in October, Izette had finished mucking out the pigs and was standing in their pen watching them snuffle through their feed in the trough, day-dreaming. A shadow fell across the floor of the pig pen and she looked up to see Tom standing there, looking amused. Delighted, she started to move towards him but he backed off, his hands raised.

'Keep your distance!' he laughed. 'Have you any idea what you look like...and the smell! Phew!'

As she clambered out of the pen he took to his heels across the farmyard, with Izette close behind. She cornered him by the cowshed where he pressed himself against the wall, cowering in mock terror.

'Lock me up! Shoot me! Anything, but don't make me suffer that pong, please!'

'Well, it's good to see you, too, Tom Birrell.'

He pulled himself away from the wall laughing.

'That's quite close enough, honestly, Izette. Any chance of a cup of coffee?'

'Substitute?'

'That'll do.'

'Aunt Margaret's in the house. She'll put the kettle on for you. I'll just clean myself up a bit and see you in the kitchen.'

'Don't rush,' he said. 'Make a good job of it, please!'

She pulled a face at him and walked off towards the pump.

When she got to the kitchen, Uncle Jim had decided to take a break too, and he and Aunt Margaret were sitting round the table discussing the latest news with Tom. A few nights earlier, they'd heard a terrific amount of gunfire that had culminated in a huge explosion that appeared to come from north of the Island. Since then, the Germans had appeared twitchy and Jim noticed the troops had been kept busy reinforcing the defences nearby the farm. Tom was explaining what had been going on.

'British E-boats intercepted a German convoy off Guernsey. The explosion you heard was a German ammunition ship being blown up.'

'Ah, that accounts for the size of the blast,' said Jim. 'But what's Jerry so fidgety about lately? They're scuttling about like blue-arsed flies.'

'Jim! Watch your language,' remonstrated Aunt Margaret, nodding at Izette.

'Grey-arsed actually,' corrected Izette.

'Izette!'

They talked some more, then Tom announced that the intention of his visit was to offer his help with the heavy farm work should it be needed.

'My driving duties are a bit irregular. I never know much in advance when I'll be needed, but there are quite a few days when I'm at a loose end. And now the car requisitioning is coming to an end, Bill doesn't need me much at the garage.'

Jim accepted Tom's offer gratefully. 'I can't pay you much but we can let you have eggs and such-like.'

Tom indicated he didn't need payment. Being out in the countryside would be a welcome change for him. He got up to leave.

'Where's young Edmund today?'

Jim and Margaret shrugged their shoulders. He often took off for the day with his bird-spotting books and a couple of hard-boiled eggs with a twist of salt in paper and a wrinkled apple in his pockets.

'I can probably find him,' said Izette.

*

She led Tom out of the farmyard and up through a deeply cut lane to an unploughed field bounded by woodland on one side. 'He's usually up here, somewhere.' Putting two fingers in her mouth, Izette gave a piercing whistle.

Tom, standing close to her, winced. Out of the wood in reply came a whooping sound, Edmund's impression of an owl's call, followed a few moments later by Edmund himself.

When he saw Tom, he looked annoyed. 'I haven't decided on the password yet,' he said crossly.

'Sorry. Operational necessity for me to see the notebooks immediately. I can't say any more. Trees have ears!' Tom tapped the side of his nose.

'Ha, ha. Very funny.'

'Edmund!' Izette glared at him. 'Sorry, Tom, he can be a bit prickly sometimes.'

'Mark of a rare genius,' declared Tom. 'Come on, old chap. Let's have a look at them.'

Mollified, Edmund led them to one of the outhouses and went inside. They followed him and watched as he prised a plank off a wooden partition dividing what had once been stock holding pens from the rest of the outhouse. Inside the framework of the partition was a large space where Edmund had placed his notebooks.

Tom spent about an hour going through the notebooks with Edmund. Izette left them alone, using the time to check the chickens and bring down some more feed for them from the loft. One broody hen had recently hatched a clutch of eggs and Izette moved her and her babies to a more secure corner of the barn and made sure that her coop was securely fastened. The barn was always locked at night and Uncle Jim's old sheepdog slept in there now. Most nights, the Evening

Post carried accounts of burglaries of food from farms. Izette had no intention of losing her precious chickens or rabbits that way.

Tom found her on her knees playing with the day old chicks and watched her for a few minutes before he spoke.

'I hope you haven't given them names,' he said. 'You'll never be able to put them in the pot if they have names.'

She smiled and put them away, then stood up. 'I'm not the sentimental little girl you used to know, Tom Birrell.'

'Hm,' he said sceptically.

'Having said that, I can't wring their necks myself, yet. I have to leave that to Uncle Jim.'

'I'm surprised you're even considering it. That's not a woman's job.'

'Plenty of farmers' wives do it.'

'But you're not a farmer's wife. You're just a girl.'

She gave him a straight look, then pushed past him towards the door of the barn.

'Have you seen all you need to see?' she asked him over her shoulder.

Tom was puzzled. It felt like he was being dismissed. 'Yes, I think the information could be very useful indeed. He's a very resourceful lad.' He was following her, obliged to speak to her back. 'Oh, and there's one other thing.'

She paused and turned.

'You remember the note you gave me, the one written in German? I showed it to someone, a German officer.' Izette looked alarmed. 'It's all right. I can trust him. He's a friend.'

He continued, 'It was an anti-Nazi propaganda poem. Things like that are beginning to appear because the troops are losing confidence. Many of them just want the war to end so that they can go home to their families, just like our lads, I imagine.'

'I see,' said Izette. 'Wasn't it risky showing it to a German?'

'Not really, Erich's always complaining to me about how stupid he finds his orders. He has no sympathy with the Nazi cause.'

'So you know this Erich quite well?'

'I'm his preferred driver. We spend a lot of time together and he likes to talk, to let off steam sometimes. He likes me to tell him about life on the Island, before the Germans arrived that is, and there's no doubt he likes the Island girls.' He laughed, remembering some of Erich's amorous exploits, but when he looked at Izette, her smile was cool. He changed tack rapidly. 'I do have to be careful though. He can be moody. Most of the time he talks and I listen.'

Izette nodded but made no comment.

'Well, I'd better be on my way. Tell Edmund to keep up the good work. I don't know when I'll see you next but it won't be long.' Tom stepped uncertainly towards her, then raised his hand and squeezed her shoulder. 'Take care.'

She watched him get on to his bike and cycle off down the lane. When he turned round she waved. It gave her an uncomfortable feeling to hear Tom talk familiarly about this Erich. Yet she was absolutely certain that if he'd been old enough in 1939, he would have enlisted along with George. As it was, she knew he was bitterly frustrated by his imprisonment on the Island. She concluded that he needed to be on close terms with some the Germans if he wanted to pick up information. It was just such a pity it was open to misinterpretation.

Izette went back into the outhouse to find Edmund. The outhouse was empty. He was supposed to be helping her today but could make himself scarce when it suited him. She checked Edmund's hiding place. He'd replaced the plank and there was no sign that it had ever been removed. She stepped outside and whistled again. This time there was no response.

'Lazy little monkey,' she muttered. She went back to the field where she'd found him earlier and whistled and shouted but he was clearly out of earshot, probably by design. 'Well, I'm jolly well not going to move all those bales of straw by myself,' she said to herself.

She walked up through the woodland to search for him. There were leaves underfoot but many more yet to fall, the ones still attached making a pleasing mixture of autumnal rusts. She scuffed through them in her wellingtons, enjoying the cool breeze off the sea below. At the top of the field, she squeezed through the gorse and brambles to the edge of the cliff-top. The fresher wind here took her hair and whipped it into a tangle as she stood looking out to sea. She counted the grey ships standing off, waiting for the tide. Seven today.

Looking along the coast, she had a clear view of the cliffs and coves that formed the eastern boundary of her Uncle's farm. Here and there, the barrels of anti-aircraft guns poked out aggressively and the small beaches had been desecrated with anti-tank spiders and barbed wire. Surprisingly, the seabirds had adjusted to all the noise and activity. They continued to launch themselves off their nests, catch the updraft and soar away over the water to return a little later to dispute boundaries with neighbouring birds just as they always had.

Just as she was turning away to go back to the farmhouse, she caught sight of Edmund. He was down on the edge of one of the coves, directly beneath one of the emplacements but out of their line of sight.

'Oh Lord,' said Izette, 'what is he doing now?'

She whistled but he didn't appear to hear her above the sound of the sea. Slowly she started to climb down the cliff hanging on to tussocks of grass and gorse stems. It was hard going. Her wellingtons couldn't get a grip on the shaley surface and more than once she slithered a few yards on her backside. By the time she reached the bottom she was dusty and irritable. Climbing over the rocks at the bottom towards Edmund was easier but she glanced nervously upwards every few minutes, aware all the time of the gun emplacement a short distance above.

Eventually she came within earshot and hissed his name. He looked around startled and immediately put out a hand to stop her.

'Don't step on to the sand, Izette. This beach is mined!'

There were barbed wire entanglements preventing access to the beach. Edmund was on the other side of them, lying on his stomach on the sand. Up against the cliff Izette could see where Edmund had thrown a bundle of sacks and some driftwood over the barbed wire to enable him to climb over. She crept closer.

'Edmund, what on earth are you doing?'

'Shh!,' he gestured upwards towards the guns and turned back to what he was doing. She couldn't see whatever it was because his body was in the way. She had no choice but to wait. After a few anxious minutes, Edmund got up and turned round slowly. He had a canvas bag slung round his chest. Cautiously, he walked back towards the cliff and climbed over the barbed wire.

'Here, give me a hand with this.' He pulled the driftwood and sacking off the wire, passing it back to Izette who bundled it up. 'This last one's always the most difficult,' he said matter-of-factly, struggling to unhook the last piece of sacking from the barbs.

'But what....' Izette started to ask.

'Quiet!' Edmund hissed. 'I'll tell you later. Stuff that wood in the gap between the rocks over there. We'll take the sacking with us.'

With a quick glance upwards, Edmund led the way back, staying close to the bottom of the cliff. He continued past the point where Izette had scrambled down to a place where the rocks became submerged at the base of the cliff. He looked back at Izette.

'What have you got on your feet? Wellies? You'd better make sure you have good handholds then. This bit can be slippery.'

Horrified, Izette said, 'You mean we have to wade over the rocks? It's much too deep.'

Edmund checked his watch. 'No, at the moment we can do it, but if we wait for the tide to come in any further we won't be able to. Come on, once round the corner we're home and dry.'

'We may be home but I don't think we'll be dry, Edmund!' complained Izette, as she edged into the water. It was tricky finding firm footholds and Izette skinned her knuckles on the sharp rock but they did eventually make it round to the next sandy cove. Edmund sat down on the sand, took off his shoes and socks and squeezed the seawater out of them.

'Did it come over the tops of your wellies?'

'Yes,' she replied irritably. She hauled them off and tipped them upside down.

'Now, Edmund, tell me what you're up to…and it had better be good. Uncle Jim will skin you alive if he finds out you've been on the mined beach.'

In reply, Edmund took the canvas bag from around his neck, reached inside and pulled out a round grey object.

'Edmund, that's a landmine!' stammered Izette, 'for heaven's sake put it down, very gently.'

'It's perfectly safe. I've defused it. Watch!' and, picking

up one of his shoes, he hit the mine on the top. Izette instinctively threw herself backwards, hitting a rock hard and crying out in pain. However, there was no explosion. She opened her eyes and winced as she picked herself up from the sand. Her shoulder hurt, adding to the discomfort of her frozen feet and skinned knuckles. Anger boiled up inside her as she thought about the recklessness and sheer stupidity of what Edmund had done. With slow deliberation, she returned to where Edmund sat and, raising her arm, slapped him across the ear as hard as she could. The force of the blow sent him rolling over.

'How could you?' she screamed, 'how could you terrify me like that? You could have killed yourself! You stupid, selfish…stupid, stupid boy,' and burst into tears. Edmund got to his knees, holding the side of his face and groping for his glasses, which had flown off. Retrieving them, relieved to see they were unbroken, he shamefacedly came over to where his sister knelt on the sand, sobbing. He sat down, close to her but not quite touching. He drew a grubby handkerchief from his pocket and pushed it towards her. Snuffling she picked it up, shook it and blew her nose loudly on it.

'Sorry,' he mumbled. She sniffed and wiped her eyes. 'I'm really sorry, Izette. I didn't think,' he repeated.

Izette stood up and brushed the sand off herself, wincing as she touched her sore shoulder.

'Shall I take a look at that for you?' asked Edmund solicitously.

'If you like.'

Izette unfastened her shirt sufficiently to pull it off the shoulder. Edmund eased the fabric gently away from her skin.

'That's quite a bad graze and there's a bruise…but it's clean, your shirt protected it. A bit of Germolene should sort it out.' He carefully pulled the shirt back up over her shoulder.

She turned to look at him. 'What are you going to do with the landmine?'

'What I did with the others.'

'What others?'

'Um...could I tell you about it later?'

'No, Edmund. You will tell me right now.'

So they sat down again and he told her everything. He'd been lucky enough, in his words, to come across the Germans laying mines on the beach so he had watched them carefully and made a detailed diagram of exactly where the mines were placed.

'Although even if you don't know where they are, you can find them easily enough by probing the sand with a stick, carefully of course.' Izette put her head in her hands and groaned. He paused uncertainly, 'Shall I go on?'

She nodded.

'I watched the Germans setting the fuses, I knew they could be defused, so I read up everything I could find about the landmines used in the First World War. I guessed they wouldn't be very different. Then I came back and dug one up.'

'And I suppose you worked out how to defuse it.'

'Yes. It's not difficult actually.'

'It probably isn't for you,' she sighed, 'but didn't it cross your mind what might have happened?'

Edmund shrugged his shoulders. 'But it didn't.'

Izette shook her head and stood up.

'So how many of them have you defused?'

'Three.'

'And where are they now?'

'I put them back where I find them, in case Jerry checks, but I keep the detonators. I only brought this one away to show you. I'll put it back later. Then, when we need to use one I can just go and dig it up again.'

Izette turned on him furiously. 'What do you mean, "when we need to use one"…are you mad, Edmund? Making notes is one thing but this is…crazy! Listen to me, Edmund,' she pointed at the landmine, 'get rid of that, straight away. Throw it into the sea or something.'

She looked him straight in the eye, emphasizing each word, 'I absolutely forbid you to go anywhere near that mined beach again. Never. Ever. Do you understand?'

Edmund started to argue but Izette cut him off abruptly.

'This is so serious I might have to tell Dad about it. I haven't decided yet. And you know what that would mean?'

Edmund nodded glumly. 'Back to school.'

'Right.' Izette forced her feet into her uncomfortably wet wellies. 'Ugh! I'm going back now to get some dry socks and clothes. I'm frozen, thanks to you.' She started to walk away then paused and added, 'Don't think this is the end of the matter. I want to speak to you later when I've had a chance to think this over properly.'

When she had gone, Edmund pulled on his own wet shoes and put his socks in the canvas bag. He looked at the landmine. He simply couldn't comply with Izette's instruction to get rid of it so he picked it up and put it in the bag as well. He rubbed the side of his face, which was still burning from Izette's blow, then set off up the track towards home. He was very fond of Izette, very fond indeed, but when it came to matters like this well…you had to remember she was just a girl. You couldn't really expect her to understand what needed to be done. It was most unfortunate that she'd discovered what he was doing. She could sabotage the whole plan now, not deliberately of course but just by fussing as women do. Perhaps he would talk it over with Tom when he next saw him.

CHAPTER 11

The new year, 1943, came in with bad news. It was Izette's father who brought it, pedalling furiously into the farmyard on his bicycle, his face red and flushed. He dropped his bike carelessly on the ground to hurry into the farmhouse. Izette saw him arrive from the barn where she was working. She threw her brush down and ran across the yard to the house.

'Dad, what is it? What's happened?' she said, as soon as she was in the door.

Aunt Margaret was standing by the cooker, a look of alarm on her face. 'Izette, shout for your Uncle Jim, he's outside somewhere.'

Izette looked at them both, confused for a moment, then ran outside again to find Uncle Jim. He came running when he heard her shout. When they were all together in the kitchen, Bill broke the news.

'Let me put your minds at rest first; it's none of our family. Every one is fine.' A wave of relief passed around the room and Aunt Margaret sat down heavily. Bill beckoned

Izette to him and put his arm around her, holding her close.

'The Birrells have had some bad news though, some very bad news.'

Aunt Margaret brought her hands to her face, 'Oh no,' she said, 'not George?'

Bill nodded. 'Yes, I'm afraid so. They heard this morning. He's been killed in action.'

'Oh no, oh dear, poor Mrs Birrell.' Aunt Margaret started to cry, covering her eyes with her apron. Uncle Jim moved to stand by her, his hand squeezing her shoulder.

Bill looked down at Izette. She was dry-eyed, stunned. 'Are you all right, love,' he asked quietly.

'I don't know,' she whispered. Aunt Margaret was crying. Should she be crying too?

'It's all right,' said Bill gently, 'it takes time for these things to sink in.'

Jim then asked Bill for more details and the men discussed the tragedy in low tones, while Aunt Margaret wept quietly. Izette couldn't seem to take in what they were saying. 'Killed in action' repeated over and over in her head. Meaningless words. How could George be dead?

'I think...I need to go outside...' Izette waved vaguely in the direction of the door and pulled away from her father's grasp. He tightened his grip.

'Steady now, Izette. Wouldn't you rather stay here with your Aunt Margaret?'

Aunt Margaret looked up, concerned.

Izette shook her head. 'No, I'm fine. I just...need to be on my own, you know...'

Bill let her go. They watched as she walked very carefully out of the door. For some reason, she felt fragile. Cracked, like an old plate. Not whole any more. She went back into the barn and over to where her chickens were cooped. She sat down on a bale of straw and watched the birds pace up and down with slow, tentative steps, heads cocked on one side to watch her. When they realised she wasn't going to feed them, they resumed pecking the floor.

She remembered George as she'd last seen him, boarding the boat for England along with the other recruits, waving happily, excited to be going off to play his part in putting Hitler in his place. He had not been afraid. She had been puzzled by that. People died in wartime. So why had he not been afraid? Tom was at her side as they waved off the ship. Tom smiled and waved energetically but she knew he was in turmoil inside. He'd wanted to go with George. They had always done everything together. This would be the first time in their lives they had been separated.

Tom! Something akin to pain shot through her as it suddenly dawned on her how he would be feeling. And Nancy and Mr and Mrs Birrell. How would they bear it? She stood up suddenly, clutching herself tightly around the middle as though to suppress the pain. Then she ran out of the barn, away from the house and out into the fields, running wildly up towards the cliffs, forcing herself to keep going even when a stitch started to stab in her side. On and on she ran until she reached the cliff edge and there she stopped, gasping for air.

George. She saw his dark, stocky figure, his thick curly hair, heard his voice, always on the edge of laughter. He would not be coming home. She would not hear his voice or his laugh again. She thought of the games they used to play when they were younger, the four of them, Tom, George, Nancy and herself. It didn't seem long ago though it must be six, seven years. She wondered how he had died. They don't tell you that. Was he blown to pieces by a shell, his body so torn apart that there was nothing left to bury, or was he lying still and cold somewhere with hardly a mark to show where the fatal bullet had entered? She shivered. Some looked as though they had just fallen asleep. Please let George look like that.

Spinning on her heel, she started to run again, back towards the farm, hoping her father would still be there but when she reached the yard she saw his bicycle had gone. She burst into the kitchen.

'Has Dad gone already?'

'Yes, he had to…'

'I must go home, Aunt Margaret. I must see Tom and the others.'

She didn't give her aunt a chance to reply, just ran upstairs to her room to change out of her working clothes. She stuffed a few things in a bag and was back downstairs again in five minutes.

'Tell Uncle Jim I'm sorry but I have to be there with them.' Izette hugged and kissed her aunt then hurried out of the kitchen. Jim came in a few minutes later to find Margaret still gazing thoughtfully out into the yard.

'Izette's gone. Barely two minutes ago. I was going to talk to her, give her a little comfort you know, but she rushed off. She's gone home.'

'Aye, well she grew up with those two Birrell lads. It's a hard blow for her. But she'll be back, don't worry.' Jim sat down heavily. 'How about a cup of tea, Margaret? I could do with one.'

Margaret sighed and lifted the big iron kettle on to the stove. She never thought the day would come when she would count it a blessing that she and Jim never had any sons.

*

It was Nancy who opened the door to Izette's timid knock. Without a word, they put their arms around each other. Nancy's tears opened the way for Izette to cry and the two friends stood in the hall, weeping quietly on each other's shoulders. Nancy's father came to see who their visitor was and, when he saw it was Izette, he drew the two girls into the living room where Mrs Birrell was sitting, white-faced, a handkerchief crushed to her mouth. The girls went over to sit one on either side of her and she opened her arms to draw them to herself. They laid their heads on her chest just as they had when they were little girls and she held them close. Mr Birrell sat on an upright chair at the table, his head in his hands. Mrs Birrell started talking.

'Do you remember, girls, that day when George chopped down the wrong tree? Dad had said the old pear tree had to come down before it fell down of it's own accord and George decided he was going to surprise us by chopping it down himself while we were out. But he chose the wrong tree. He was only 13 at the time. I suppose one tree looks much like another at that age.' She laughed to herself. 'Didn't he catch it when his father came home!'

And on she went, relating tale after tale of George's achievements and follies, hardly pausing for breath. She looked out of the window as she talked, words pouring from her mouth, holding the girls tightly, looking but not seeing what was there, only the images in her mind. After a while, her voice started to falter, her sentences trailed away unfinished and a puzzled look came over her face.

Ted got up from the table and came over to her. 'Come on now, Dorothy, I think it's time you had a little rest.' He took her hands, releasing the girls from her embrace, and gently pulled her to her feet. She looked alarmed.

'No, I can't go yet! I have to be here, in case they come. We don't know when they'll come,' she said.

'It's all right, Dorothy. I'll wait for them,' replied Ted. 'You have a lie down upstairs and if anyone comes, I'll wake you up. But you need to sleep now.'

He led her from the room. Izette could hear his gentle reassurances as he guided her upstairs.

'Who's coming?' she asked Nancy.

'She thinks they're going to bring George home,' said Nancy flatly.

'Oh, but surely...'

Nancy shook her head.

'Sorry,' she said.

'The doctor says she'll be back to normal in a few days. It's the shock, you see,' explained Nancy, 'she's in a little world of her own but it's hard on Dad. He has to pretend to agree with her, he can't try to bring her to her senses. She just couldn't take it at the moment.'

Nancy seemed to Izette to have grown-up in the weeks since she'd last seen her. It was hard to believe she was still at school. Or was this what a death could do to someone?

'I'm going to make a hot cup of tea for Mum. It seems to help settle her. Your Mum gave us some proper tea that she had been saving. It tastes strange after all the substitutes but very good. Would you like one?' asked Nancy.

'No...thank you,' replied Izette. Then she asked where Tom was.

'I don't know,' said Nancy. 'He was here earlier, thank goodness, when Mum was worse. He was the one who fetched the doctor in his car. And he was good with Dad as well. Dad was all shaky and confused; he didn't know what to do until Tom took over. He produced some brandy from somewhere and made Mum drink some and then he just held her until she was quiet.'

Nancy turned away to lift the kettle off the stove.

'He said he'd be back later. I'll tell him you're home, Izette.'

'Yes, thank you. I'd like to see him to say...well, you know,' her voice trailed away.

'I know,' said Nancy, 'there's nothing you can say.'

Izette stood up to leave, tears spilling down her cheeks. Nancy came over to her and they held each other again.

'Oh Nancy, how can you bear it? I can't bear it.'

'Don't,' murmured Nancy, 'you'll set me off again.'

'I'm sorry,' snuffled Izette, 'I'd better go now.'

Nancy walked with her to the door, saw her out and closed the door gently after her. Izette took the few paces to her own front door and let herself in. In the hall, she turned towards the kitchen door but her courage failed and she ran instead up the stairs to her own bedroom where she threw herself face down on to the bed. Downstairs, her parents had heard her come in and go straight to her room. When Betty heard her crying, she got up to go to her but Bill stopped her and, after a little while, Izette was quiet.

*

Rolling over on to her back on the bed in the darkness, Izette realised she must have fallen asleep. She sat up and groped in her bedside cabinet for a handkerchief. Her nose was blocked and her eyes felt puffy and sore. She wondered what time it was. She felt around for a candle, which she found on her dressing table but could find no matches. As she stumbled round her room, she heard a car pull up outside. Looking out of the window she saw Tom get out of the car and go into his house. There was a brief flash of light as he slipped in through the front door. She watched for a moment then picked up her shoes and tiptoed down the stairs. There was no light under the kitchen door. Her parents must already be in bed. She opened the front door and stepped outside. It was crisp and cold. Her toes flinched from the chill of the paving stones and she crouched down to pull on her shoes. There was enough light from the moon to see a little. She walked over to the Birrell's front door and stood looking at it. She wanted to go in but this was not one of those times when she could burst in without knocking. The loss of George encircled and enclosed the family like an impenetrable wall of grief. So she stood and waited outside the house, for how long she had no idea. Thoughts and memories raced through her mind but her claim on George was not one of blood. George's blood, the spilt blood they didn't tell you about, the blood they must have cleaned off him, covering the horrors done to the rest of his body with a sheet, was not her blood.

Then the door opened and someone came out, almost colliding with Izette.

'Who's that? Good heavens, Izette. What are you doing?' It was Tom.

'I...I was just waiting,' she answered.

'Waiting? For what?'

'To see you.'

'Well, why didn't you...' He stopped, realising she was standing there in the bitter cold without a coat. Tom took hold of her hands. They were frozen. He turned back to open the door again, then seemed to change his mind and bundled her towards his car.

'Come on, I need to get you warmed up. Get in the car, Izette.'

The car smelled of oil and leather. It was still slightly warm inside. He sat her in the front passenger seat and leaned over to reach a travelling rug from the back seat. He smelled of tobacco and warm kitchens. He tucked the rug over her knees, then took off his own jacket and put it round her shoulders. She protested but he insisted, wrapping it firmly around her so that her arms were pinned inside.

'I feel like a helpless little girl,' she said.

'Aren't you?' he smiled, then shut her door and walked round the driver's door, got in and started the engine.

'Where are we going?'

'Wherever you like. The engine will be warm in a few minutes. I'll put the heater on and get you really warm.'

She snuggled down, content to watch him drive in silence. They could talk later. His profile was faintly visible in the light from the car's instrument panel. His left hand moved smoothly from steering wheel to gear change and back as the car wound through the lanes. Warm air rolled over her feet. He glanced across at her.

'How's that now? Feeling better?'

She nodded. 'But I came to comfort you. You shouldn't be looking after me.'

He shrugged his shoulders. 'You were frozen.'

He drove on. They were on the outskirts of St Helier. Suddenly he turned the car in to a large imposing entrance. Izette sat up in alarm. A German sentry approached the car.

'Don't say anything. Just smile if he looks in the car,' Tom muttered.

He wound the window down to speak to the German. They exchanged greetings. The sentry obviously knew Tom by sight. Then he peered curiously across to look at Izette. She managed a half smile. He said something further, which Tom agreed with and laughed, before walking back to the gate and raising the barrier. Tom drove through.

As soon as they were clear of the gate, Izette said, 'Tom! Where are we?'

'German Military HQ.'

'What! I can't come in here! What on earth are you doing?'

'Ssh! Just relax. It's all right. He thinks you're just one of the French prostitutes.'

'What!' Izette was speechless for the few moments it took to reach the large old house that had been requisitioned by the Germans. Tom swung the car around the side of the house to the back into a courtyard which evidently housed the garages and stables. He switched off the engine.

'Here we are then.'

'I'm not getting out, if that's what you think, Tom.'

'In that case, you'll be jolly cold by the morning,' and with that, he got out of the car and slammed his door shut. He walked round to her side and opened the door. Izette glared at him but got out, throwing the travel rug back on to her seat. He took her arm and walked towards the stable block. 'Look friendly,' he whispered in her ear, and put his arm round her shoulders.

A couple of German soldiers stumbled out of a door and stopped to light up cigarettes. They shouted goodnight to Tom and added a comment, which Izette was glad she couldn't understand. He opened a door that gave immediately on to a narrow wooden staircase, flicking on his cigarette lighter so that Izette could see where to step.

'These are the old grooms' quarters over the stables. Let me go up first to show you the way.' Tom took her hand and led her up the stairs and along a dim corridor to a door, which he unlocked. He stepped back to let her enter the room, which was in darkness. 'Stay there a minute while I check the blackout.'

Izette heard him cross the room, then a light came on and she was able to see the room. Tom came back to where she stood and closed the door, dropping the catch.

'Sit down. I'll get the fire going.' He opened the ash drawer on the old cast-iron stove and poked inside with a steel poker. 'Good, the embers are still alight.'

While he added some logs to the fire, Izette looked

around the room. It was a simple soldier's billet. Narrow iron bed covered with a grey blanket, a wooden locker, a small wooden table set against the wall and two upright chairs. A naked light bulb hung from the centre of the ceiling but Tom had switched on a small reading lamp on the table. Its light gave the room a cosy glow. The stove stood in one corner. The walls were wooden tongue-and-groove panelling, painted cream. The floor was plain, varnished floorboards. Someone had added a small rug by the bed.

Tom shut the stove doors, satisfied with the orange glow that now flickered inside. He stood up and turned round, rubbing his hands together. Izette had not moved.

'Sorry, it's a bit bare in here, I know, but the stove keeps it cosy. Here, sit on the bed, it's a bit more comfortable than those two chairs.'

Izette crossed to the bed and perched on the edge. She still had Tom's jacket around her shoulders and she hadn't yet said a word. Taking her silence for continued disapproval, Tom explained that he'd been given a room because lately the Germans he chauffeured had been meeting late into the night, all night on some occasions. 'So this is a lot more comfortable than hanging around in a cold car waiting for them to finish.'

'Yes, I see,' said Izette but it was clear that she was uncomfortable.

'Look, it's not what you think, Izette. I know it looks as though I'm pretty 'well in' with them but this is really no different to what Irene is doing. She stays overnight at the hotel sometimes, doesn't she? And I expect she knows most of the men's names by now. Probably has a joke with them, too. It's impossible to work alongside the Germans and not pass the time of day with them at the very least.'

'My father seems to manage it.'

'Yes, but he doesn't have the day-to-day contact with

them that Irene and I have. His is a very different situation.'

Izette thought this was probably true but wasn't going to admit to Tom.

Tom went over to the locker and took out a bottle of brandy and a glass. Turning towards Izette, he raised the bottle to ask if she would like a drink. Without thinking, she nodded. Taking out a second glass, he poured a good measure into each, brought them over to the bed and sat down beside her, handing her a glass. She took it from him but didn't drink. Tom, on the other hand, drained his in one, then sat looking at the empty glass in his hand. He had been in a strange mood since he put her in the car and bringing her here was crazy. While she wondered why he had brought her there, Tom got up, refilled his glass and brought the bottle back, putting it on the floor by the bed when he sat down.

'My brother is dead,' he said slowly and carefully, as though he was trying the words for the first time. 'George is dead,' he repeated, 'another victim of this bloody war. He's no longer a person you know, Izette. He's become just another statistic. Someone will write a report saying something like, "*Estimated casualties in this action: 49 dead, 236 injured.*' That's all. The report won't say, '*One of the 49 who died in this action was George Birrell, eldest son of Ted and Dorothy, brother of Tom and Nancy."* Nor will it say Ted and Dorothy's lives will never be the same again, that Dorothy weeps for the loss of the first baby she held in her arms, that his brother, Tom, has lost his closest friend, his childhood hero, that Nancy...' his words failed and he put his hand over his eyes.

Izette placed her hand on his arm.

'They won't even say they're sorry,' he finished quietly. He dropped his hand and took another gulp from his glass. He looked directly at Izette. 'What makes it even more unbearable is that I'm not trusted any longer. Even you don't trust me, do you? Admit it.'

Izette tried to protest but he raised a hand to silence her. Taking another swig from his glass, he continued, 'Your father has doubts about me and I've even seen my father look puzzled. If my own family can't trust me, what about all my other friends and acquaintances? Are they all saying the same things?'

He got up abruptly and refilled his glass once more.

'You know, Izette, I've just remembered something. I popped into a bar a couple of days ago, one over at St Aubin's that I've been going into for years. There were no Germans in that day, just locals. I knew most of them by sight but, when I walked over to order my drink, they stopped talking. I ordered my drink and looked around and they were all looking at me. I nodded but no one nodded back. So I took my drink outside and finished it up smartish.'

'I'm sure they didn't…'

'Yes, they did, Izette. I feel like a leper, a pariah. What's the male equivalent of a Jerry-bag?'

He sat back down on the bed. Izette put her untouched drink down on the floor. She wanted to put her arms around him as she had round Nancy. In the silence, she could hear the logs crackling in the stove.

He looked at her. 'You haven't touched your brandy.'

'I don't like it very much,' she admitted.

'You soon get used to it, believe me.' Tom refilled his glass and handed hers back to her.

'Go on, try it. It'll warm you up.'

Izette sipped it, trying not to screw up her face when the spirit burned her throat. She coughed slightly, 'I think it might be wasted on me.'

Tom looked at her again. 'How old are you now, Izette?'

'I'll be 17 in July.'

She watched his face as he studied her critically.

'I shouldn't have brought you here. I'm sorry; it was a

crazy thing to do. I'd better get you home.'

'No,' she said sharply. 'It's all right, Tom. I was just surprised when you brought me here. But I did want to talk with you. I thought it might help, you know, after all those years together, the four of us. I thought we could talk about the good times.' She paused, struggling to explain how she felt. 'I wanted to be with you,' then, taking the plunge, she added very quietly, 'I wanted to hold you.'

She didn't dare look at him but she knew he had turned to look at her again. She heard him put his glass down on the floor.

His voice, when he eventually spoke, faltered. 'Hold me then, Izette. Hold me...please.'

CHAPTER 12

The arrival of spring in 1943 brought decreased food rations and a proliferation of German regulations extending into every part of Island life. Food supplies were low because German supply boats were failing to get through the British blockade around the islands and, while the Islanders greeted this news with satisfaction, it also meant that they had to tighten their belts another notch.

Large numbers of German troops were brought from the Eastern front to recuperate on Jersey. Some of them were billeted in Irene's hotel and she soon noticed a change of mood amongst the men. The evening sing-songs had stopped some time ago. There was no longer the patriotic enthusiasm for them but with the arrival of survivors of the Russian front, the atmosphere changed from disenchanted to mutinous, many soldiers openly saying that they hoped Britain would win the war. They just wanted it over and done with so that they could go home.

One of Izette's trips home coincided with Irene's

weekend off so they were able to catch up on each other's news. After tea on Saturday, the sisters went upstairs to Irene's room. Although it was April and the weather had been bright, the room felt chilly. Irene shivered, accustomed to the warmer temperature maintained in the hotel.

'It's so cold in here. Let's get into bed under the eiderdown.'

Taking off their shoes, they climbed into Irene's narrow bed, propped themselves up against the pillows and pulled the eiderdown up to their chins. Irene laughed.

'We used to do this when we were little. Do you remember?'

'Yes. When it was really cold, we'd sit like this, blowing clouds of hot breath, pretending we were smoking cigarettes.'

It seemed a long time since they had shared a room. Their lives had moved on fast since the Germans arrived.

'How do you think Mum and Dad are coping, Izette?'

'They've both lost weight, Mum especially. I bring what I can from the farm but I can't come home every week, there's just too much work to do.'

'No-one's getting enough to eat now. Even the Germans are complaining about their rations. I used to be able to smuggle food out of the kitchens to bring home, but not any more. Everything is kept locked up so that the men can't help themselves to it. Have you had any food taken from the farm? The Evening Post says most farms have been burgled. The Germans say it's the foreign workers but I'm not so sure.'

Izette had seen a ragged squad of foreign workers being herded past the farm only a few days ago. They didn't look as though they would have the energy to go raiding farms for food. It was as much as they could do to put one shuffling foot in front of the other.

'We've only lost a few vegetables from the fields. Uncle Jim keeps Danny in the barn where we store everything. He makes an enormous fuss if he hears anyone creeping around.'

'I didn't know Danny was still alive,' said Irene. 'He must be ancient by now.'

'He is,' laughed Izette, 'but a prospective burglar wouldn't know that. He'd just hear him barking. Anyway, it's worked so far.'

'Some of the foreign workers were machine-gunned by the Todt guards. Did you hear about it?'

'No!' Izette was shocked.

'The German censor kept it out of the Evening Post but I heard about it. A group of them attacked their Todt guards so the Germans simply turned the machine guns on them. About 30 of them were killed.'

Izette shuddered. Many of the foreign workers were young boys, barely more than children. And they were so weakened by malnourishment and overwork, the guards could easily have overpowered them without resorting to such brutality.

'How will it all end?' asked Izette.

Irene shrugged. 'I just take one day at a time. What else can you do?'

Izette was quiet for a while, wondering if she dared ask Irene about the strange story she had read to her last summer. Since then, on the few occasions they had met, Irene hadn't mentioned it again and Izette wondered if she'd misunderstood.

'Um, Irene,' she paused, uncertain.

Irene looked at her queryingly.

'I don't mean to pry...but last year, you remember you read a story to me?'

Irene nodded and sighed.

'You'd like to know what all that was about?' she asked.

'Well yes, if...'

'I shouldn't have done that. I don't know what came over me that afternoon. I was so happy I think I almost felt drunk. All that splashing about in the water and the lovely hot sun on my skin.' Irene paused, considering whether she should tell Izette. 'I'll tell you...but you mustn't say anything to anyone.'

'Of course I won't,' said Izette, 'you know you can trust me.'

'Right. Well, where to start? Do you remember the boy who drowned on my first day at the hotel?'

'Yes, you were so upset about it.'

'Well, you remember there was another soldier, one who was distraught?' Izette nodded.

'That was his brother. His name is Gunther.' Irene stopped, struggling to find the right words to continue. 'And the awful thing is that I think I'm in love with him.'

'No!' Izette looked at her sister in amazement.

Irene couldn't meet her eyes. 'In fact, I know I'm in love with him.'

Izette was stunned. She didn't know what to say. 'Oh Irene!'

'I know,' said Irene miserably, 'Dad will throw me out. I don't know what I'm going to do.'

'But how did it happen?'

'The way these things always happen. We started talking. He was very upset about his brother and wanted to talk to someone...and I was there. Then we began talking about all sorts of things and I suppose we gradually became friends. And over the months the friendship grew stronger until we realised it had become something much more than that. By that time it was too late. I go round in round in circles wondering what to do. We've talked about ending it, for both our sakes, but we can't do it. I only need to catch a glimpse of him and my whole spirit seems to lift. You can't imagine what it feels like.'

I think I can, thought Izette. Then she said, 'but how does that strange story fit into this?'

'I was helping Gunther with his English. He had found a book in English that he was trying to read. It was 'Pilgrim's Progress' of all things.' Irene laughed. 'He wanted to talk about it and I explained to him that it was an allegory, a story written to convey another story or meaning. He must have found that an interesting idea because a few days later he wrote that story for me. It was his way of making a proposal.'

'I see,' said Izette, 'and now?'

'Well, now I live in constant dread that Gunther will be sent to the Eastern front or somewhere awful like that and in constant fear that Dad will find out about us. There doesn't seem to be a happy ending either way.'

'I did wonder about talking to Mum about him this visit,' Irene went on, 'but I've changed my mind. I don't think she would feel it was right to keep it from Dad. Anyway, she looks so tired I really don't think she could take any more bad news. Not after George.'

Izette agreed. The aftermath of George's death still hung heavily over the two adjoining households. It had been a terrible blow for both families.

'So there it is...and heavens knows how it will all end! But don't think it's all bad news, Izette. When Gunther and I are together, it's wonderful. I've never felt so happy. I just hope we can find a way to be together eventually. Now, tell me your news. What's been going on here? How are the Birrells, for example?'

Izette was disappointed by the change of subject. There was so much more she wanted to ask, but she restrained her impatience. There would be other opportunities.

'Mrs Birrell is more or less back to normal. Nancy says they feel they can talk about George now. She doesn't get as upset as at the beginning. So, they're managing I suppose.'

'And Tom?' Irene looked at Izette carefully as she asked the question.

Izette frowned. 'I've hardly seen him since January,' she replied truthfully.

Since that night in his room over the stable block, he had paid only one brief visit to the farm. When she saw him drive into the farmyard, she had hurried across to meet him, expecting a friendly reception but he had seemed preoccupied, withdrawn even. After the briefest of greetings, he excused himself by saying that he needed to speak to Uncle Jim and left her standing by his car, puzzled.

'I saw him a couple of weeks ago,' said Irene. 'He dropped a couple of officers off at the hotel when I was on duty in the foyer, so I nipped out to have a word with him. He seemed very surprised to see me, as though he'd forgotten I worked there. Anyway, I chatted to him for a few minutes but he didn't have much to say. Actually, I think he was relieved when I said goodbye. He drove off pretty smartish.'

Izette felt somewhat comforted. It was a relief to know she wasn't the only one Tom had virtually ignored. But she wondered if it just George's death that was troubling him or was there something else?

Irene yawned and stretched. 'It's a pity to leave this bed now that we've warmed it up but if I don't get up, I shall fall asleep. Move over, Izette. I haven't talked to my little brother yet. Is he in his room?'

'I think so,' replied Izette, getting out of the bed herself. She left Irene's room and went downstairs to the kitchen to talk to her mother. She would see if her mother had noticed anything odd about Tom's behaviour

*

At that moment, Tom lay stretched out on his bed over the stables, fast asleep. An empty brandy bottle lay on its side under the bed and the stove had gone out. Daylight was failing fast outside, the rectangle of sky visible through his window a dirty grey. The temperature in the room fell steadily but Tom slept on, enough spirit inside him to guarantee a lengthy respite from his thoughts.

He was off duty that weekend but couldn't face going home, so he'd lied when his mother asked if he'd be there for Sunday dinner, such as she could scrape together. She'd recovered enough to reinstate family dinners on Sundays. She liked the family together for Sunday dinner but there were now only four dining chairs around the table. George's chair had remained at the table all the time he was away with the army but his father had decided to remove it, leaving a space that spoke far more poignantly than the empty seat ever had.

So Tom had chickened out and retreated to his room with a couple of bottles. Some might say it was the coward's way out but he didn't care. All he wanted was the oblivion of sleep and this was fast becoming his only way of achieving it. He thanked whatever star he was born under that he was on excellent terms with the corporal in charge of the wine cellar at German HQ.

Around midnight, however, Tom was woken by a torch shining in his face. He struggled to claw his way out of a deep sleep and, at the same time, understand what the German who'd woken him was jabbering about. He swung himself into a sitting position on the bed, waiting for his head to clear.

Meanwhile the German pulled down the blackout blind and switched on the harsh overhead light. Tom closed his eyes and groaned. When he opened them again, he peered at the young man's face but didn't recognise him. Whatever Tom was wanted for, he was wanted urgently, according to this soldier. He staggered to his feet, took his coat off the nail on the back of the door and followed the man out of the room. At the end of the corridor was a small washroom. Tom opened the door and went in, smiling to himself at the little dance of impatience the German gave as Tom took his time to empty his bladder and swill his face in cold water. When he'd finished, he went down the stairs in front of the young soldier and across to the main house.

There was obviously a major panic on. Lights were burning in all the main rooms and soldiers rushed about with papers while senior officers shouted into telephones.

'Ah, there you are, Tom.' Erich came over to him. 'I'm sorry to take you from your beauty sleep but we have an urgent job for you.'

Without thinking, Tom glanced at his watch to see what time it was. Noticing the movement, Erich slapped him on the back and said, 'Never mind, my friend. It could have been worse. At least tonight you were alone.'

Tom looked sharply at him but Erich's smile gave nothing away. Drawing Tom over to a table on which a map of the Island was laid out, Erich pointed at a stretch of the northern coastline.

'Do you know this area?'

Tom nodded to indicate that he did. Erich glanced around the room to make sure there was no one in earshot then continued in a low voice, 'Look, I shouldn't tell you this but you'll probably work it out yourself anyway. We think the British might try an invasion soon and one of our batteries up there on the north coast sent in a report tonight of lights spotted offshore. I'm sending some units over to investigate but I want an officer up there quickly to assess the situation. I'd like you to drive him. His own German driver doesn't know the area and you know how confusing your little lanes are in the dark?'

Tom nodded, 'Who is it?'

'Von Nebel. He's waiting downstairs.'

Tom knew the man by reputation. A committed Nazi and no friend of Erich's. Erich had probably enjoyed having him dragged out of bed, too.

'Go carefully, my friend,' said Erich, smiling, 'he's not in a very happy mood.'

Tom smiled back at Erich then left the room, hurrying down the stairs to collect his passenger. He knocked at the door of an office near the front entrance and entered when he heard a shout. Von Nebel was pacing the room impatiently. He was short and stout with a coarse pig-like face and clearly in a foul temper.

'About time, driver,' he said, when Tom announced himself, 'I don't care to be kept waiting.'

I'll bet you don't, porky, thought Tom to himself. Without a word, Tom opened the door for him and led him outside to the car in the yard. The officer refused the back seat, choosing to sit in the front passenger seat next to Tom. The engine started on first press of the starter button and Tom guided it smoothly out of the yard and down the drive. Once through the gates Tom put his foot down, pushing the car as fast as he dared along the narrow roads.

Fortunately Von Nebel was not inclined to talk. Tom noticed with some satisfaction that his passenger braced his legs and hung on to the strap handle as the car hurtled into the night.

'I hope this is not too fast for you, sir? I was told it was urgent.'

'No,' said Von Nebel abruptly.

Tom smirked to himself and swung the car round the next corner a little too fast, losing the back wheels momentarily in a squeal of rubber. Recovering control he glanced sideways at the German. Von Nebel said nothing, staring fixedly ahead through the windscreen. So, thought Tom, little porky is made of quite stern stuff. This could be the one I've been waiting for.

They pressed on through the darkness, the shielded headlamps casting a mere sliver of light on the road ahead. Although Tom knew the road well, he drove recklessly, pushing the car beyond what was safe, once or twice scraping the car against the high banks on each side. Von Nebel remained silent even when Tom spun the car through 90 degrees on a particularly sharp bend. If they'd met anything coming the other way Tom wouldn't have been able to avoid a collision but he didn't care. Only Germans would be on the road at this time of night, so what did it matter?

By the time they arrived at the coastal village Erich had shown him on the map, Tom had decided on his plan of action. The basic plan was one he'd worked out some time ago, going over the possibilities in his mind during the long nights in his room, waiting to be called on duty. He'd just been waiting for the right location and opportunity and this was it. All he needed now was speed and a bit of luck. He must get Von Nebel to the right spot before the rest of the German units arrived. Thank you, Erich, he thought, you've given me just the right man.

When Von Nebel got out of the car to consult with the sentries on duty, Tom got out as well, ostensibly to stretch his legs and light up a cigarette. He followed Von Nebel at a slight distance, close enough to hear what was being said. He couldn't understand it all but he could tell from their gestures that the soldiers were indicating the general direction in which they'd spotted the lights. Von Nebel was scanning the sea with binoculars and shaking his head. He rattled off some abuse at the soldiers that Tom didn't catch but he could see the men were worried. Probably threatening them with the Eastern front for getting him out of bed on a wild goose chase, thought Tom. When Von Nebel turned round in disgust to walk away, Tom took a deep breath and stepped in.

'Your line of sight is obstructed at this point, sir,' said Tom, 'but, if I take you further to the east, you'll have a clear view of the entire bay and coastline.'

Von Nebel looked at Tom suspiciously. 'Do you know why I'm here then?'

'No,' Tom shrugged his shoulders, 'but you were using binoculars. I assume you're looking for something out there.' He waved his cigarette casually in the direction of the sea.

Von Nebel continued to study him.

'Just trying to be helpful, but you're in charge...sir.' Tom dropped his cigarette end on the ground and crushed it with his shoe, turning to walk back to the car.

'Wait,' said Von Nebel, 'I don't like your tone, Islander, but I'm told you know the Island very well. Where is this place you mean?'

Von Nebel shouted to the soldiers and one of them brought over a map, which they spread on the bonnet of the car. In the light of a torch, Tom pointed out the place he had in mind.

'The cliff here is very high,' he said, which means you can see from here in the west,' he pointed to the map, 'all the way to here.' He traced a line to the most easterly promontory.

Von Nebel studied the map for a minute or two, interrogating the soldiers again about their sighting. Tom heard tides mentioned. He didn't think they would know the tidal pattern around the Island but he couldn't be sure.

Deciding to risk it, he looked at his watch and said, 'The tide will be running strong about now. Anything out there is likely to be carried east, anything not under power that is.' He hoped he hadn't gone too far.

Von Nebel looked suspicious again then barked a question at the men. They shrugged their shoulders.

'Your German is quite good, Islander.'

'I've done this job for over two years. You pick it up,' he replied casually.

Von Nebel thought for a moment or two, then said, 'Very well. Take me there and I will see for myself.' He gave the men some orders then strode towards the car.

Tom's heart was beating hard as he opened the passenger door for Von Nebel. No going back now. He got in on his own side and closed the door, then started the engine. Fortunately, Von Nebel had not ordered any of the soldiers to accompany them. Tom drove some way back along the road then turned off on to a farm track. It was rough but passable. After half a mile or so, a farmhouse loomed up out of the gloom but Tom drove on, taking a right fork on to a track which started to climb steeply. He had to increase the engine revs to keep the car moving. Over on their left, some distance below, the sea came into view. In another minute the track petered out by a field gate.

'One moment, sir,' said Tom, 'we're nearly there. I'll open the gate.'

After opening the gate, Tom swung the car into the field, which was rough pasture and reasonably firm for the car's wheels. He took it carefully at first, then accelerated hard until they were being bounced around. Von Nebel looked at him angrily,

'What are you doing, you idiot? Slow down.'

'Certainly, sir,' said Tom then, stamping his foot down even harder on the accelerator, he swung the car straight towards the cliff edge.

Von Nebel lunged for the wheel. Tom swung his elbow hard into Von Nebel's face. As the German fumbled for his pistol the car sailed over the edge. It wasn't a sheer drop but it was steep enough. As they went over, Tom flung open his door and jumped. He gasped in pain as he smashed into a rock and started to fall. He rolled over and over, clawing at the earth, trying to halt his fall until his back slammed agonisingly into something hard and all movement stopped. Pain was shooting through his head and arm and a darkness was creeping steadily over his vision but not quickly enough to prevent him seeing a huge flash of flame as the car exploded further down the cliff. Tom raised one arm in salute.

'Here's to you, George,' he gasped before the darkness overtook him.

*

When the German staff car drew up outside the Birrell's house the following morning, Betty assumed it was Tom at the wheel as usual but she stopped what she was doing when an officer and two soldiers got out and knocked on the Birrell's door. Bill was still at home. He was intending to go down to the garage later in the morning.

'Bill,' she shouted, 'come here quick1 There's some Germans gone into next door.'

Bill hurried downstairs in his vest, shaving soap still smudged around his chin. Together they peered through the lace nets covering the front window. After a few minutes, the Germans came out again with Ted, who got into the back seat of the car and they drove away. Once the car had disappeared round the corner, Bill and Betty hurried into next door.

Dorothy and Nancy were still standing in the kitchen, shocked. They hadn't moved since the Germans left.

'What's going on, Dorothy? Why have they taken Ted?' Bill asked.

'They said a German officer has been killed in a car...a car our Tom was driving,' stammered Dorothy.

Betty pulled a chair out. 'Sit down, Dorothy.'

'Do you mean there was an accident?' asked Bill.

'I don't know,' replied Dorothy, 'they didn't say.'

Bill frowned across at Betty who was guiding Dorothy to the chair.

'What about Tom? Is he all right?'

'I don't know that, either,' Dorothy said, her mouth beginning to tremble.

'Right,' said Bill, 'you stay here, Betty love. I'll see what I can find out.'

Bill hurried back into his own back garden, unlocked the shed to take out his bike and pedalled off fast down the road. God knows what the lad had got himself involved in but if it meant he'd got Ted and family into trouble as well, he'd have something to say to him all right. As if they hadn't got enough on their plate this year with the sad business of George. Tom was a good lad basically but he was prone to jump first and think about the consequences later. And since he started this driving, he seemed to be so chummy with Jerry that there was no shortage of gossip about what he was up to. Well, perhaps he'd gone too far this time. Bill thought about Tom's mother, Dorothy. She certainly couldn't bear to lose her other son, if matters were serious enough for him to be imprisoned in France or worse. It didn't occur to Bill until he was in the centre of St Helier that it might already be too late. If there had been a crash, had Tom survived it?

*

Two days later Tom finally came round in the prison hospital. His first thought was that he was waking up with one hell of a hangover. His vision was blurred, his head throbbed and his mouth felt like an old floor cloth. However, when he tried to pull himself into a sitting position, a sharp pain shot through his chest and he fell back. He shut his eyes, trying to remember what had happened. Blank. His right arm felt very heavy and his chest felt tight. Tentatively he felt his chest with his left hand. It was bandaged. He continued his explorations, discovering that his right arm was in plaster and his head was bandaged too. Strangely exhausted by these discoveries, he let his hand drop back by his side and drifted off into sleep.

The next time he woke, someone was trying to get him to drink some water. He felt the cool moisture on his lips and struggled to gulp it down, suddenly desperately thirsty. He tried to grasp the cup but couldn't seem to locate it. A woman's voice said something soothing. His thirst partly relieved, he lay back on the pillow and tried to bring his eyes into focus. A nurse stood by his bed. So, he was in hospital. He turned his head slightly to look around the room causing a spasm of pain to shoot up his neck into his skull. He gasped.

'I think you'll find it more comfortable if you stay as still as possible,' the nurse said.

Tom tried to speak but only a croak emerged. He tried again and managed to get out, 'What happened?'

'You were in a car accident. You've broken your arm and several of your ribs and your head got a nasty crack but you're going to be fine. You were very lucky. Now, don't go trying to remember it. Just go back to sleep and the next time you wake up you'll feel a little better.'

Tom was puzzled. What does she mean? How was I lucky? He couldn't even remember where he'd been. What car? He closed his eyes and withdrew again into the shadows.

*

A week later, he was able to sit up with assistance and his first visitor or, at least, the first he could remember, stood by his bed.

'Good morning, Tom,' said Erich, 'you are awake at last. Have they told you where you are?'

Tom nodded, very carefully. He knew now he was in the prison hospital in St Helier. No one would be bringing him any flowers or grapes.

'And do you remember what happened?' Erich asked.

Tom couldn't remember anything after opening the gate to the field but he knew what his plan had been. He had to assume he'd carried it out. He shook his head.

'Well, I suppose that could be regarded as very convenient for you,' said Erich. 'I have, however, spoken to your doctor, who assures me your concussion is likely to prevent you from remembering anything, so I suppose I must take your word.' Erich pulled a straight-backed chair up to the bed and sat down. 'You know you are under arrest?'

Tom looked at him blankly. 'What for?'

'Von Nebel died,' explained Erich.

'Von Nebel?'

Erich looked sideways at Tom. 'Very convincing, my friend. Do you really not remember anything?'

Tom didn't reply.

Erich took off his fine black leather gloves and placed them on the bed. Then he leaned forward, his face close to Tom's. 'You drove the car straight over the cliff with Von Nebel inside. You jumped clear. Von Nebel didn't. He died.'

Tom thought about it. Yes, that was what he had intended to do. He could remember that much. Looking Erich straight in the eye, he said, 'I must have lost control.'

Erich snorted and sat back. 'I'm in charge of the investigation so you'd better prepare your story carefully. At the moment, the car is being recovered. So we'll see if there was anything wrong with the brakes or the steering.'

Erich stood up and replaced the chair against the wall.

'We will talk again soon, my friend.' He turned to go, but after a couple of paces, stopped and turned to Tom again. 'Oh, I nearly forgot. There was no invasion.'

Tom watched him go, his boots clicking sharply on the linoleum floor. He heaved as big a sigh as his ribs would allow and wondered how he was going to get out of this one.

*

It was a long and very tedious recuperation. Tom was not allowed visitors. The only people he saw were Erich and whichever nurse was on duty. The bed alongside his remained empty for the whole of the time he was in the prison hospital, whether by accident or design he never discovered.

The car yielded no clues, one way or the other. Fire had damaged it so badly that it was impossible for the German engineers to say whether any of the controls were faulty. Erich returned several times to question Tom, who stuck to his story.

'Why would I risk my own life?' he asked Erich. 'I'm not one of the patriotic types who won't have anything to do with the Germans. They might be prepared to sacrifice themselves but not me. I've been working for you for nearly three years. I hadn't even met Von Nebel before.'

*

When Tom was well enough, a court martial was arranged. He was taken from the prison under armed guard to the German HQ. They insisted on placing him in handcuffs, which made him smile since he could hardly walk without assistance. They were put to wait in a small ante-room with hard-backed chairs ranged against the walls and the handcuffs were taken off. After about half an hour, Tom was called in for his hearing. The court was formally arranged in what had once been an elegant drawing room. Three senior German officers sat behind a table in front of which there was a chair for Tom. Erich has his own small table on one side. There were no civilians present.

Erich started by addressing the senior officers in German. Tom could understand enough to know that he was giving them an account of the known facts about the accident. Then Erich questioned Tom in English. Tom was quite truthfully able to say that he remembered nothing about the accident and repeated his claim that he had no reason to stage the accident; on the contrary, he had far too much to lose, starting with his own life.

After a discussion in German between Erich and the officers, Tom was escorted outside while the panel decided the verdict. Although it was not warm in the ante-room, Tom could feel sweat running from his armpits. There was no telling how it might go. He wondered what he might get if the verdict went against him. If the worst came to the worst and it was the death penalty, at least he had the satisfaction of knowing he had squared it for George.

The doors opened and he was summoned back to stand before the panel. He noticed the chair had been removed and he would have to stand. He hoped they wouldn't take long. The officer in the centre read out his name, together with the charge, then looked up from the paper he was holding. His English was impeccable.

'Mr Birrell, due to insufficient evidence, this court martial finds you not guilty of deliberately causing the death of a member of the German Military Forces. You are, however, forbidden from working for the German Military Forces in any capacity whatsoever. In addition, should your name come to this court's attention on any future occasion, you may be assured that you will be dealt with most severely.'

Tom remained standing while the officers gathered up their papers and left the room. Then Erich motioned to the guards to escort Tom out of the room. He walked painfully and shakily towards the door. The guards took him all the way downstairs and out through the huge double doors then simply walked away. He stood baffled for a moment, then one of the sentries jerked his head towards the gates. Tom walked uncertainly towards them. Once outside on the street, he stumbled on until he found somewhere to sit down before his legs gave out on him. There was a bench a short distance down the street on to which he lowered himself carefully. He couldn't say how long he had been sitting there, amazed that he wasn't on his way to a German prison, when a car drew up opposite him. A German chauffeur opened the rear door and Erich got out and walked across, sitting down beside him. He offered Tom a cigarette. Tom took one gratefully.

'Your hands are shaking, Tom,' observed Erich.

'Wouldn't yours be?'

'Probably,' admitted Erich. 'Well, you were very lucky.'

'Was I?' asked Tom.

'Yes indeed. It is very fortunate for you that Von Nebel was a man with many enemies. He was a thorn in everyone's side, always causing trouble. No-one was sorry to see him go. So, you see, you have done us a favour, accidentally of course.'

'That wasn't enough to get me off,' said Tom, 'you

swung it for me, didn't you?'

Erich didn't reply. He stubbed out his half-smoked cigarette and stood up.

'I must return to my duties.' He gestured towards the car. 'You see, I have a new driver? A German, unfortunately. He is not nearly as interesting or... accommodating as you were, Tom.' He paused then added, 'Please accept my condolences for the loss of your brother.'

Tom jerked his head up. Had Erich known about George's death all along and kept it out of the court martial?

Erich looked him straight in the eye. 'We understand each other, I think,' said Erich, 'but I can't guarantee being able to do you any more favours in future so "keep your nose clean" is the phrase I think you use?'

Erich got into his car. He looked back at Tom as he was driven away and Tom thought he saw him touch his cap brim in a salute but he couldn't be sure. He let out a deep, shuddering sigh of relief. He could hardly grasp that it was all over and he was free. During those long empty days and nights in the hospital, he'd gone over and over the possible outcomes, none of them at all encouraging but he'd never dared dream of release. Erich had done an extraordinary thing. Tom wondered if he would ever know why.

CHAPTER 13

By the autumn, Tom was more or less fully recovered from his injuries and back working in the garage for Bill. Only the Birrells and the Vauberts knew what had really happened and it wasn't something they could share, even with close friends and neighbours but the fact that Bill had offered Tom his old job back spoke volumes. Bill was known to be a man who didn't place his trust lightly. Those who had gossiped about Tom's allegiances fell silent, even going so far as to slap him on the back and congratulate him on his miraculous escape.

On one of the weekends when all the Vaubert family were at home, Bill gathered them around the kitchen table to discuss what Tom had done. Although they already knew the danger of the secret getting out, Bill wanted to stress the importance of keeping the matter to themselves, particularly to Edmund.

'Don't you go boasting about it to any of your friends, my lad,' said Bill, 'and I don't want you thinking you can get away with any of your foolhardy schemes either.'

Edmund was extremely irritated to be singled out as a risk, particularly after the success of his cat's whisker radio sets. Seeing his face flush red with annoyance, Izette kicked his shin hard under the table and frowned across at him to prevent an indignant outburst.

The discussion over, Betty got up from the table to put the kettle on. As she stood up, she appeared to lose her balance and staggered sideways. Bill, sitting beside her, managed to catch her before she could fall to the floor.

'Betty! Steady now.' He supported her across the kitchen to the old easy chair and gently lowered her into it. The rest of the family gathered round anxiously.

'I'm all right now,' said Betty, 'just a touch of giddiness.'

'Irene, bring some of that brandy from the top shelf,' said Bill. He knelt in front of his wife, holding her hands in his. 'I think you've been overdoing it, Betty. Here, drink this, then I'll make you a nice cup of tea.'

'No, I'm saving that last bit of tea for a special occasion,' protested Betty.

'No arguing, Betty. Anyway, I know where I can buy some more.'

'No, Bill. We can't buy on the black market; it's too expensive,' argued Betty.

Bill wagged his finger at her. 'If you've got the strength to argue, you must be feeling better already. And Irene's already put it in the pot, so you just sit there quietly and do as you're told.'

Irene made the tea, just enough for two cups and filled a hot water bottle with the remaining hot water. Betty drank the tea obediently, conscious of all their eyes on her.

She smiled weakly when she'd finished. 'That was lovely but I object to being a floor show you know. Are you all waiting for me to give you a song?'

They laughed, relieved to hear Betty make a joke. When Bill announced that her bed was warm and he would help her upstairs, she didn't object.

'But I'm not having the doctor,' she said as she went up the stairs, 'I'm just a bit tired, that's all.'

'Mm,' grunted Bill, not committing himself either way.

When Betty had left the kitchen, Irene and Izette looked anxiously at each other.

'I think she should see the doctor,' said Irene, 'she doesn't seem to have got over that chesty cold she had a couple of months ago.'

'We'll see if Dad can persuade her to see him,' agreed Izette. 'Did you hear her coughing in the night?'

'Yes, I did. But you know how difficult she can be about seeing the doctor.'

'Well if Dad makes his mind up he'll fetch the doctor no matter what she says.'

When she reached the bedroom, Betty said she wouldn't bother getting undressed. She would just take off her shoes and lie down under the covers as she was.

'No, Betty,' Bill said gently but firmly, 'you're not just having a short nap. I want you to stay here until the morning. So you'd better put your nightie on. I'll just put it in the bed to warm for a few minutes on the hot water bottle while we get you undressed.'

'I can manage that myself, Bill Vaubert, I'm not in my dotage yet.'

Bill said nothing to this and busied himself turning down the covers and plumping up the pillows. Betty unbuttoned her blouse, then stood up to unfasten her skirt. As she stepped out of it, she lost her balance and fell back on the bed.

'Betty!'

'I'm fine, Bill. I just lost my balance,' she reassured him, 'but if you like, you can help me off with these stockings.'

He helped her take off the rest of her clothes and eased the warmed nightdress over her head and shoulders, noticing with a shock how her shoulder bones protruded sharply through her skin. He knew she'd lost weight, they both had, but Betty was usually tucked up in bed by the time he got upstairs at night after locking up and he hadn't seen her undressed for a long time. He helped her into bed and when she was comfortably settled, he came downstairs and told Izette and Irene that he was off to fetch the doctor. Saying no more, he buttoned up his coat and went out, closing the door quietly behind him. Betty had settled down to sleep as soon as she got into bed and he didn't want to wake her.

As he walked briskly down the road, Bill felt an unaccustomed twinge of fear in the pit of his stomach. Betty was seldom ill. In fact, he couldn't remember when she'd last had to spend some time in bed on account of illness but only last week the Evening Post had carried an article about the poor state of the Islanders' health. It said the restricted diet they had to put up with under rationing was beginning to effect people's health. They were less able to fight infection. That's probably why Betty hasn't been able to shake off that chesty cough, thought Bill. Well, we'll see what the doctor has to say about it

*

The doctor arrived at the Vaubert house later that day and gave Betty a thorough examination while Bill waited anxiously at the bedside. When he'd finished, he sat on the end of the bed and smiled at her.

'Well, Mrs Vaubert, under normal circumstances, I would be recommending plenty of rest and good food but I realise the latter is not going to be easy to find.'

'Don't you worry, doctor,' said Bill, 'I'll be making sure she eats as well as she can if I have to sell the coat off my back to manage it.'

The doctor smiled. At this stage of the occupation, probably half his patients were troubled by the kind of ailments that didn't use to be a problem when people had a balanced, nourishing diet.

'Mrs Vaubert's lungs are slightly congested. I'll prescribe something for that which should also help that troublesome cough. I'd like you to keep a close eye on your wife and let me know immediately if she appears to get any worse.'

Bill nodded his agreement. Betty had been serving herself small portions for far too long, claiming she wasn't very hungry and heaping the rest on to his plate. He should have spotted it before. Well, he'd make sure she ate plenty from now on. He'd spoon feed her if necessary.

When Margaret got to know, she suggested to Bill that Betty should come and stay at the farm until she got her strength back but Betty would have none of it. She refused point blank to leave Bill on his own and so, as a compromise, Bill announced that he would be finishing work early from now on. There was precious little work to keep him and Tom occupied, any-way. He would be home at three o'clock each day to prepare a meal and do whatever chores were needed. Betty was horrified by this but she'd been married to Bill long enough to know when he could be talked round and when he couldn't. This was one of those occasions when she would be wasting her breath and she had to admit she didn't really have the energy to argue this time.

So, by the time Christmas came around, Betty was resigned to being a spectator to the preparations. Nevertheless she enjoyed it, especially her mode of transport to the farm. Assuming, probably correctly although it was never put to the test, that she would not have the energy to walk to the farm, Jim brought his tractor down to fetch her. He put some straw bales in the trailer to provide seating and collected all the Vaubert family early on Christmas morning. The day went off very well and, there being an extension to curfew for the Christmas holiday and the weather being very mild, at the end of the day they all rode home again in the trailer under the night stars, each clasping a jam jar containing a stub of candle and singing carols softly.

*

Izette stayed at home with her parents for the next few days. Uncle Jim refused to allow her back on the farm until the New Year celebrations were over, insisting she needed a good rest from farm-work but, more importantly, a bit of fun. He'd heard there were several New Year's Eve dances due to be held in the town and he threatened her with the sack if she didn't go to one. A quick conversation with Nancy settled which one they would be going to and the rest of the intervening time was taken up with frantic attempts to assemble new dance frocks out of old cast-offs.

By seven o'clock on New Year's Eve, Izette was fully dressed and had finished putting on her make-up and arranging her hair. She sat in her bedroom, in front of the dressing table, looking at her reflection in the mirror. She was pleased enough with her outfit. It wasn't bad in the circumstances. She'd scrounged an old crepe de Chine dress in soft aquamarine that Irene could no longer get into. It was an old-fashioned style but that hardly mattered these days. Looking for something with which to brighten it up, she had found an old hat of her mothers, decorated around the crown with silk flowers in purples and blues. She took these off and arranged them into a corsage that she then sewed on to the plain neckline of the dress. As there were a couple of flowers left over, she sewed these on to a hair slide and pinned back a sweep of her long, dark hair.

Izette didn't know if Tom would be at the dance or not. He'd been vague about it when Nancy asked him, saying he might drop in for a couple of turns around the floor. However, she didn't see how she could fail to enjoy herself, regardless of whether he was there or not. At about half-past-seven she put on her coat and hat, shouted goodbye to her parents and went next door to collect Nancy. Together, they walked down into the town, giggling in anticipation.

The dance hall was already packed when they arrived. Leaving their coats in the cloakroom they squeezed through the press of people around the door to find some seats, greeting old friends as they passed. At the end of the room, near to the stage, they found a small table with two chairs and claimed it for the evening. The hall was brightly decorated, the band was warming up with a medley of tunes and the mood was festive. Izette felt herself grinning from ear to ear.

'Gosh, I must look like an idiot grinning to myself,' she confessed to Nancy, 'but I'm really looking forward to this.'

'Me too,' said Nancy, 'and if Peter turns up you'll probably have to remind me to stop drooling.'

Peter Guignard was Nancy's current idol. He had been in Izette's class at school where she remembered him as gangling and weedy. According to Nancy, a transformation had taken place and he was now absolutely 'dishy'.

'I'll get us something to drink, Nancy.'

Izette got up and made her way across the room. The choice was beer or a strange looking sort of lemonade that someone had concocted. Deciding to risk the lemonade, Izette asked for two and carefully carried the glasses back to their table. On the way back, Izette caught sight of Irene with a couple of girl friends and motioned with her head to show her where they were sitting. Irene waved and nodded but carried on talking to her friends. Izette had just reached the table when the compere announced the first dance and the band swung into action. As usual, people were reluctant to take the floor for the first dance but, after a few brave couples stood up, others quickly followed. Izette sipped her drink and sat tapping her feet, enjoying the music and the bright, swirling spectacle. It was good to be able to forget what was going on in the world outside for a few hours.

After a couple of dances had gone by and no-one had asked them to dance, Izette pulled Nancy to her feet. 'Come on, Nancy, we're not going to be wallflowers. We have to make the most of this evening.'

The girls whirled each other round the floor. Izette caught sight of Irene again, this time dancing with an older man Izette did not recognise. She didn't look as though she was enjoying herself.

Halfway round their next circuit, Nancy nudged Izette and announced she'd spotted Peter. Grabbing Izette's hand, Nancy dragged her off the dance floor. 'We have to sit down...so that he can ask me to dance,' explained Nancy.

Izette was disappointed but understood Nancy's tactic. She returned to her drink and foot tapping. Within a couple of minutes, Peter was at their table, smiling at Nancy and asking to be introduced to Izette.

'Don't you remember Izette, Peter? Izette Vaubert?'

'Ah, of course. I remember you now, Izette. My goodness, you've changed.' He ran his eyes over her smoothly, much to her amusement. The last time she'd seen him, he'd been wearing short trousers.

'Well, so have you, Peter. I don't think I would have known you either.' They shook hands formally and Peter offered to fetch them another drink, which they accepted. When he'd gone, Nancy said, 'Well, what do you think?'

'He's certainly looks different in long trousers,' said Izette, 'not bad, not bad at all, Nancy. Are you and he actually going out?'

'Not exactly, not yet. But I've got my fingers crossed.' Izette grinned.

Peter was soon back with the drinks and, finding a spare chair, pulled it up to their table. The three of them talked through the next dance and Izette warmed to him. He had a good stock of humorous anecdotes to keep them entertained. Nancy was hanging on his every word. Then, when the band started a new number, to Izette's surprise, Peter stood up and invited her to dance with him. In the few moments of uncomfortable silence that followed his invitation, Izette glanced over at Nancy. She was studying the band intently, a fixed smile on her face.

Izette stood up. 'No thank you, Peter. It's very hot in here. I was just going to pop outside for a bit of fresh air, but I'm sure Nancy would love to.' She gave him a hard look as she left the table but the response she got was a challenging wink.

At the door, she looked back and was relieved to see Peter and Nancy join the dancing. She pushed her way out into the cool night air and walked a short distance away from the hall.

'What a cheek!' she said to herself indignantly and shivered a little in her thin dress. It hadn't been particularly hot in there but what else could she have said? She hoped Nancy had not been too offended. She would do her best to avoid him for the rest of the evening.

'Cold?' a voice said close to her ear, making her jump. A warm jacket landed around her shoulders and she turned round to see Tom smiling at her.

'Tom!' she couldn't hide the delight in her voice. 'I didn't expect to see you here. I was just getting...'

'...a little cold?' He finished her sentence, 'I saw you shivering. What are you doing out here? Had a lover's tiff in there?'

'No, but I did nearly have a tiff with Nancy's boyfriend.'

'Oh, do you mean young Peter the Charming? What did he do?'

'He asked me to dance, in front of Nancy.'

'Well, that sounds like an excellent idea. Why didn't I think of that first? Come on, Izette, let's show them how it's done.'

Grasping her wrist, Tom pulled her unceremoniously back into the hall, retrieved his jacket from her shoulders and led her on to the dance floor which, at that moment, was bouncing under the onslaught of several hundred stamping feet. They threw themselves into it, laughing at each other's attempts to co-ordinate hands and feet. Nearing the end of the dance, they bumped shoulders with Nancy and a rather surprised Peter. As the music stopped they staggered, exhausted, towards each other and Tom put his arm around Izette's shoulders and held her close. He extended his free hand to Peter.

'Hello, Peter. Nice to see you again. Take care of my little sister, won't you?' he grinned at them both.

'Er...yes, of course, Tom,' Peter replied uncertainly.

Tom punched him playfully on the shoulder then turned away, guiding a giggling Izette towards the bar.

'What would you like to drink?'

'Lemonade, please.'

He looked at her in mock horror. 'Lemonade? Is this the woman who shared my brandy?'

'If you remember, I didn't actually. It's horrible stuff.'

'I have to admit,' he said shamefacedly, 'that I don't remember very much of that evening. So, lemonade it is for the lady.'

He waited at the bar to order their drinks, buying a beer for himself. Izette watched him joking with the barman. He was in high spirits tonight. Had he already had a few drinks or was it just the festive season? Whatever the reason, he was fun to be with when he was like this.

They carried their drinks away from the bar, looking for a couple of chairs. Just as they reached a vacant pair, the band started a slow melody.

'Oh, I love this song,' said Izette dreamily.

'In that case,' Tom paused to take a quick drink then stood up, 'we'd better take to the floor again.'

Izette laughed and stood up, casually taking his hand. They walked on to the floor, hand in hand, then he turned and drew her close. She relaxed into the music. As they moved round slowly, she was intensely aware of every point at which their bodies made contact. His hand on her back, his shoulder under her hand, their bodies touching lightly as they moved. Tom hummed along with the song. She could feel his warm breath on her cheek.

'You're right. It is a lovely song,' he murmured and smiled down at her.

Did she dare lean her cheek on his shoulder? It felt the natural thing to do. Looking around the room she saw other couples doing it. Oh well, she thought, nothing ventured…and laid her head against him, dreading a mocking comment. To her surprise, he turned and kissed her lightly on the forehead then drew her closer. She closed her eyes.

Sadly, the song had to come to an end and, as the evening was approaching midnight, the compere announced the hokey-cokey. The noise level in the hall soared as everyone joined in the singing and surged in and out of the centre of the room. This was followed by a rumba, then the compere called for silence to hear the church bells ring in the New Year. As the last peal faded and people started wishing each other Happy New Year, Izette looked at Tom. He was still, his thoughts far away. She put out a hand to touch him.

'You're thinking about George, aren't you?' she said quietly.

His eyes were moist. He couldn't answer her.

The band played the opening bars to 'Auld Lang Syne'. Izette pulled him away from the crowd and out into the night, searching for a spot where they could be alone. Several couples were already outside, locked together. She found a shadowy corner near a wall and put her arms around him. He lowered his head to her shoulder and started to cry silently. She could feel his whole body shaking. She made soothing noises and stroked his hair, looking up into the clear night sky filled with stars. His change of mood had been sudden and dramatic. In a strange way, she felt privileged to be entrusted with his distress. He had turned to her for comfort a second time and she wouldn't fail him. He could rely on her...always.

She shivered in the thin dress and Tom raised his head immediately. 'You're freezing, Izette. Here, put this round you again,' and, taking off his jacket again, he draped it around her shoulders. His arms were around her, pinning hers to her sides beneath the jacket. He looked into her face and suddenly bent to kiss her. His lips tasted of salt tears. She returned his kiss and he pulled back, startled. They looked at each other for a moment in surprise.

'Again,' whispered Izette and he kissed her again.

This time she felt a thrill of excitement in the pit of her stomach. When it was over, his face still had that look of surprise. Tenderly, she wiped away the tears from his cheeks with her fingers. Then, not knowing why, she gently drew her finger along his lower lip.

He jerked away. 'What am I doing?' Tom ran his hand through his hair roughly. 'I'm sorry, Izette. I shouldn't have done that. I'm not...' he stopped in agitation. 'Look, I can't do this to you. It isn't fair.'

Why? What isn't fair?'

Tom had taken a step away from her but, catching sight of her distraught face, he pulled her to him again and held her tightly.

'Oh God,' he groaned into her hair, 'I'm so sorry, Izette. Please forget it happened. Please. Do you think you could do that?'

Izette shook her head. He held her at arm's length and looked into her face.

'Look, I know you'll find this difficult to understand but I can't get involved now. Not now. Not with you, Izette. There are things I have to do. I have plans...' Then, taking her face between his hands, he said, 'Look at me, Izette. I don't want to hurt you. You're very special to me, you always have been but I don't want you to have any false expectations. When this is all over, there might come a time when it might be possible but just now I can't commit myself. Everything is too uncertain.'

'I can wait.'

'No, I don't want that. I wouldn't ask you to do that. Who knows where you or I will be next New Year's Eve? I want you to leave me out of your life. Have boyfriends. Have fun. God knows we all need a bit of fun now and then to help get us through this. Please understand.' He paused.

Izette lowered her eyes.

'Izette?...I'm sorry. I don't know what else I can say.' He let go of her.

She turned and walked away. After a moment, he followed her to the door of the hall. The revellers were beginning to tumble out. She stopped, waiting for Irene and Nancy to appear. Tom waited by her side. Irene came out alone but Nancy was hand in hand with Peter. Forcing a smile to her face, Izette exchanged New Year's greetings with the others, then they formed into a group for the walk home. Irene had collected Izette's coat from the cloakroom for her and she now put it on, returning Tom's jacket to him. Izette walked between Irene and Tom, with Peter and Nancy following behind.

'Not a bad evening,' Irene commented without much enthusiasm.

'No, it was all right,' replied Izette flatly.

Irene looked at Izette, then across to Tom, wondering what had happened to dampen Izette's spirits. She took hold of Izette's arm, drawing it through her own.

'It sounds like you and I need to exchange some sisterly confidences when we get home,' she whispered softly.

Izette didn't immediately reply to Irene's suggestion. She didn't feel she wanted to talk about it, not yet at least. She needed time to think things over. 'I don't think so. Not this time,' said Izette eventually, 'I'm not sure I can.'

Izette's voice wobbled on the last sentence and Irene knew better than to pursue the matter further. Izette would probably tell her what had happened eventually. In the meantime, she might have to have a word with Tom. If he was playing some silly game with Izette, she would remind him that Izette was still only 17 and very vulnerable. Tom already had something of a reputation as a ladies man and he needn't think he could add her sister to his list of conquests.

Tom had completed the walk home deep in thought, without saying a word to anyone. Izette and Irene went straight into their house, leaving him alone in the avenue. Nancy and Peter were nowhere in sight yet, having dawdled behind the others. Tom realised, with some irritation, that he would have to wait for them. He sighed and took out a cigarette, settling himself on the low wall at the front of the house. He thought about Izette. The kiss hadn't been planned, it had just happened spontaneously and he was totally unprepared for the surge of emotion he felt when her lips responded to his. It reminded him of something that happened a long time ago. What was it? He took a pull on his cigarette and cast his mind back.

*

They had all been children at the time. He was about 14 so Izette must have been around ten. He remembered he was still wearing shorts. The four of them, George, Nancy, Izette and himself had been playing one of their games in the woods. It was summer, one of those long, hot days in the school holidays. They had been out all day. The game was a simple one they had often played. The girls had to hide in the woods and the boys had to find and capture them. Sometimes they were cowboys and Indians, at other times they were white explorers in the jungle and the girls were the natives. The characters changed but the plot was always the same and the game was over when both girls had been caught and tied up. On this particular day, Nancy had been found quite quickly but Izette was proving elusive. As he and George followed one of their routes through the wood, he suddenly had an idea about where she might be hiding. Wanting all the honour of the capture for himself, he sent George off in another direction and headed on alone. He came to a place where a large tree had uprooted from the valley side and fallen across a stream. At the base of the tree, there was now a cavity where the rootball had been dragged from the earth. The network of exposed roots effectively concealed this cavity, making it an ideal hiding place.

He passed close by the tree, making a lot of noise with his feet, walking straight past as though he meant to continue, then a few yards further on darted behind a mound of earth and crouched down to wait. After a couple of minutes there was a rustling and Izette crawled out on her hands and knees. He gave a whoop of delight and pounced on her.

'Hah! Got you at last. I thought you might be hiding in here. You never had a chance of escaping me. I know this valley like the back of my hand.'

'Well, it certainly took you long enough, Tom Birrell.' Izette flounced out of his grasp and began to dust herself down.

'Shut up. You're my prisoner now. I'm going to take you back to our camp. You'll have to be tied up. Hold out your hands.' Tom had put down his wooden rifle and was pulling some grubby twine from the pocket of his shorts.

'Not likely,' said Izette, hiding her hands behind her back.

'Oh, come on,' said Tom, 'You've got to.'

'Who say so?'

'It's the rules, Izette. You've got to keep to the rules. Otherwise it isn't fair.'

'Whose rules?'

'Our rules. You asked to join in so you have to abide by our rules.'

'Huh. Boy's rules,' scoffed Izette, 'Stupid rules! Nearly as stupid as you, Tom Birrell!'

Stung, and at a loss how to reply, Tom grabbed Izette's arms and tried to force the twine round her wrists but she easily twisted her wrists from his grasp. He couldn't both hold her arms still and tie the twine single-handed and, to make matters worse, she started to laugh at his frustration. She was stronger than he expected and he began to wish he hadn't sent George off on a wild goose chase. His face grew red in the heat and the effort of fighting with her. Then she changed tactics and kicked him, a really hard kick to the shin.

He gasped in shock and pain. 'You bitch! What a dirty, rotten trick! That really hurt.'

Even in their most violent of battles he and George never really hurt one another deliberately. He felt a furious anger rise in him at the injustice of it. His dad said you weren't ever supposed to hit girls but there were limits. He took hold of her shoulders and shook her hard, his fingers pressing viciously into her flesh.

'Ow! Tom, stop it,' she cried but he'd really lost his temper and he carried on shaking her. Izette struggled to break out of his grip, braced her hands against his chest and pushed away backwards. As she stepped back her feet caught in a bramble root and she fell, pulling Tom over on top of her. He landed heavily on top of her on the hard ground.

She lay very still, winded by the weight of Tom landing on her chest. His anger suddenly extinguished, Tom looked down at her anxiously. Her eyes were closed.

'Izette, are you all right? Izette? Izette?'

He rolled partly off her to one side, mindful that she could still try to escape, and poked her face tentatively with one finger. Her eyes snapped open and she gulped a great lungful of air.

'You squashed me,' she gasped. Their faces were a few inches apart. His had been daubed with the burnt end of a cork for camouflage. Hers, though not treated similarly, was scarcely any cleaner.

'Are you hurt?' He tried to brush some strands of hair from her face.

'No,' she whispered. But she made no attempt to get up, just lay there passively. His leg lay across hers, an insurance against further kicks and her right arm was pinned beneath him. His eyes moved down from her face, noticing the whiter skin of her neck where the sun did not reach, or was it just cleaner than her face? Her thin cotton blouse was all askew from their fight, the fabric stretched tight across her chest. His sister, Nancy, had the beginnings of two swellings there, but Izette was still quite flat. She was taller than Nancy, almost as tall as himself, but straight up and down, like a beanpole his mum said. He leaned over and took hold of her free wrist, just in case.

She watched his gaze travelling over at her, feeling the boniness of his body alongside hers. They examined each other warily. She could smell his sweat. Against the artificial darkness of his skin, his eyes looked startlingly blue.

'Promise you won't try to get away?' he asked.

She nodded her assent.

'And no more kicking?'

'I suppose that's in the rules too? Thou shalt not kick....'

Releasing her wrist, he shifted so that both his hands were free and encircled her throat with them.

'You know I could kill you now ever so easily,' he said slowly. 'I just need to press here...and here...' He pressed gently to demonstrate, '...and the blood flow to your brain would stop and you would die.'

He was leaning over her, his weight on one elbow. She looked up at the untidy fringe of his hair, flopping down over his forehead into his eyes, eyes that now looked into hers with a curious intensity.

'Go on, then. Do it.' She paused. 'I dare you.'

His eyes narrowed. She thought he was bluffing. Well, she was in for a surprise. He moved so that he was kneeling over her, one leg on each side and leaned forward to grasp her neck more firmly.

'Are you sure, Izette? This is your last chance.'

'What's the matter? Scared? Scaredy-cat, scaredy-cat.'

That did it. He probed with his thumbs until he found the pulse in her throat. Looking up from her neck he met her eyes, disconcertingly challenging. He began to press, gently at first, watching her face. Then she closed her eyes. He increased the pressure, feeling the throbbing under his thumbs, waiting for her to cry out or struggle. She did neither. He watched as the skin of her face darkened. Why didn't she struggle, for heaven's sake? His thumbnails were digging deep into her neck. It must be hurting. Panic began to rise in his chest but he couldn't stop now. She would laugh at him. He wished he'd never started this. Desperately he looked around, hoping to see George crashing through the wood, giving him an excuse to get up.

Izette's head rolled to the side and her eyelids fluttered partly open, revealing the whites of her eyes. Tom's eyes opened wide in horror. Was she unconscious? She wasn't dead yet; he could tell from the pulse under his thumbs but what should he do now? She'd dared him. It was her fault. Her mouth fell open and saliva started to run from the corner of her mouth. Suddenly her eyes flew open and her whole body jerked. Yelping with fright, Tom released his hold and leapt back.

Then she laughed at him. Tom blinked. She had the nerve to laugh at him. He hated her then as she laughed up at him. She'd made a fool of him.

'Right,' he said, kneeling over her again before she could get up, 'now I am going to tie you up. You're nothing but a mean little cheat, Izette Vaubert.'

He wound the twine roughly round one wrist and pulled it tight but she didn't even wince. In fact, she was still giggling. He straddled her to reach the other arm.

'What's that?' she asked

'What's what?'

'That...in your pocket.'

'There's nothing in my pocket. What are you on about?'

'This thing, here,' and she grasped his crotch of his shorts where either the excitement or terror of the past moments had wrought a physical reaction. He leapt up as though he had been stung, hot and terribly embarrassed.

'God, you're...you're the very limit, Izette,' he stammered out.

Izette was puzzled. What had she done? He looked at her with a look of disgust then turned his back on her and busied himself sorting the tangles from the twine.

'Get up, will you?' His voice was funny, peculiar. He turned his head and looked at her angrily. He was very red in the face. Getting to her feet and brushing off her skirt, she meekly offered both her hands to him to be tied together. Tom stepped forward and wound the twine around his prisoner's wrists without a word.

*

Tom smiled and ground out his cigarette underfoot. So there was something about Izette that had fascinated him even then. Perhaps she was a challenge. He'd wanted to capture her, to subdue her yet even when he had her pinned to the ground she still taunted him. She had the upper hand all those years ago despite the difference in their ages. And now? Well, he could no longer think of her as a child, this evening had proved that. But to think of her as a woman…a woman whose touch could stir his very depths…

'Hey, Tom, what are you doing?'

He started. It was Nancy, pushing open the gate. Peter was nowhere to be seen.

'Sorry, I was miles away then.' Tom got up from the wall and walked with her to the front door. 'Where's your beau?'

'Gone home. He saw you sitting on the wall and decided not to walk me to the door.'

'Charming! Am I that frightening?'

'Actually yes,' Nancy giggled, and ducked in through the door before he could catch her.

Taking a last thoughtful look at the night sky, Tom turned and followed her inside. It was the first day of a new year. Where might he be by the end of it?

CHAPTER 14

1944

Irene doubled over, clutching her stomach. She felt sick but she couldn't be sick. Her forehead was glazed with sweat. She shivered in the freezing bathroom. Grey February light filtered through the frosted glass of the window. She sat down on a small stool by the bath and let her gaze rest on the rust stains on the old enamel. Somehow, she would have to summon the courage to tell them. People were saying that this year would see the end of the war. Only a few days ago, an American pilot had made a forced landing on the island due to engine failure. The Germans found and arrested him but, before they took him away, he had talked to some of the local people and told them that everything was in place and the Allies were about to embark on a momentous action. The news had travelled round the Island in a matter of hours.

Irene stood up to look at herself in the pocked mirror. This nausea must be caused by anxiety. It had started after her last desperate conversation with Gunther, when they realised that there was now a very strong possibility that they would soon be separated. German troops were on the move, more divisions being shipped out to France every day. Those remaining were being drilled in anti-invasion manoeuvres. Gunther himself had been assigned to the division given the task of erecting pylons in fields all over the island to prevent allied aircraft landings.

'I tell you, Irene,' he had said, when they'd managed to get a few minutes alone in the hotel gardens, 'I have not seen the officers so worried before. They are running round like chickens with no heads. I am lucky so far to be given the job of the pylons but I could still be sent to France at any time.'

Gunther took Irene's hand and held it between both his.

'I want us to be married, Irene. You know this. I have to speak to your father for permission soon. Before I am sent away. I have to know if he will give his permission. Then, I can be happy even if I am sent to France because I know I will have you here, waiting for me. I will even be very careful not to get shot so that I can come back to you, I promise,' he joked, trying to lift her spirits.

'But what if he doesn't give his permission, Gunther?'

'Well,' Gunther shrugged, 'I guess we will be together anyway, one way or the other, but I know you love your father and I would like to do this the correct way, if we can. Cheer up, my little Jersey flower, he might even like me!'

Irene closed her eyes, struggling to imagine such an unlikely outcome. Poor Gunther. He didn't know her father.

They set a day when Gunther would speak to her father: Irene's next weekend off duty at the hotel. Irene had wanted to wait for an opportune time but Gunther suspected it might never come, so he insisted on a decision. Since then, Irene had been ill with anxiety. She was the one who would have to broach the matter with her father. Gunther couldn't simply turn up one day and knock on their door. Bill had to know why a German soldier was asking to see him. So, on her next half day, when it could be put off no longer, Irene went home.

Bill and Betty were in the kitchen when she arrived and were surprised to see her. The kitchen was cold as they didn't usually light the fire until the evening to conserve their firewood but Bill immediately put a match to the ready-laid grate. Betty thought she was looking a bit peaky.

'You're looking pale, Irene. Come and sit down and I'll make you a hot drink of something. It'll soon be warm in here,' said Betty.

'Thanks Mum, I'll just have hot water in a cup. I've stopped drinking the substitutes, they taste awful.'

Irene sat down but kept her coat on until the fire had burned up a little more.

'How are you, Mum? Is that medicine helping?' Irene asked.

'Not too bad. I think I'm getting better. You have to expect to catch coughs and colds in this weather. Everybody seems to be sniffling at the moment.'

'She'd be a lot better if she would do as she's told,' said Bill. 'I've told her to take it easy. I'll look after the washing and cleaning and cooking but she will keep interfering.'

Betty laughed. 'Can you imagine what a mess your father can make of ironing a shirt, Irene?'

Irene smiled, 'I can…but I could do the ironing on my weekends off. You should leave that for me to do.'

'If you can get your Mum to agree to that, you deserve a medal,' said Bill. 'Short of putting her in handcuffs, I don't know what else I can do.'

Betty chuckled and looked fondly at her husband. 'You do exaggerate, Bill Vaubert!'

By the time Irene had finished her cup of hot water, she knew she could delay her announcement no longer.

'Dad...and Mum. I have something to tell you.' In the moment of silence that followed, they looked at her anxiously. She could read what was in their minds and it made her smile, even at that moment. 'It's not what you're thinking, I'm not pregnant!'

Of course they protested. It hadn't entered their minds at all.

'In a way, you might think it's worse than that,' she continued. 'You see, I have fallen in love with someone, a man I really want to marry...and he wants to marry me. He isn't a married man or anything like that...but he is a German.'

There, it was out and the shock on their faces was awful. Neither said a word for a few minutes. Bill looked baffled as though he couldn't take it in. Betty's face crumpled and her whole body seemed to fold in upon itself. Irene crossed the room and knelt before her mother, grasping her hands, the tears pouring down her face.

'I'm sorry, Mum. I'm so sorry. We didn't mean it to happen. It started as a simple friendship. His brother had drowned you see, and I felt sorry for him so we used to talk. It seemed to help him come to terms with it. He was terribly upset at the time and I could understand a little of what he must be feeling. Then later...well, you know how these things develop. I tried not to care about him. I told him it was absolutely impossible and, for a time, we stopped talking to one another but it was like trying to hold back the tide. And now, with the war nearly being over, we want to plan our future, so...' her words faltered.

'Oh Irene,' her mother whispered, 'I never thought...'

'I'm sorry, I'm sorry,' Irene cried again, 'but I'm also happier than I've ever been.'

Mother and daughter cried together, arms around one another. Bill had yet to speak. He could feel anger boiling deep inside and he feared what he might say if he lost control of it. He buried his face in his hands.

'I can't take it in,' he said eventually, 'I keep asking myself what your mother and I have done wrong for you to be able to do this. You know how we feel about the Germans. I warned you what could happen if you went to work at that damned hotel. How could you do this? You were right when you said we might think it worse than if you were pregnant. At least then, you could marry the man if he was an Islander. But a German...'

'He's not like other Germans,' interrupted Irene desperately, 'he's a good, kind man and he hates the war.'

Bill held up his hand to silence her. He shook his head and, for the first time in her life, Irene saw her father look defeated. Then, with a hopeless gesture of his hands, he said, 'You'd better send him to speak to me.'

Turning away, Bill went out into the back garden to his greenhouse, leaving Betty and Irene together.

*

A few days later Gunther stood nervously on the doorstep of the Vaubert house. The knowledge that Irene was inside did little to calm him. He noticed the lace curtains of the house next-door move slightly and decided he'd better get inside as quickly as possible. He didn't want to cause any trouble for the Vauberts with their neighbours. His knock on the door was answered immediately by Irene. They smiled weakly at each other. Gunther removed his forage cap and straightened his hair before stepping inside.

'You look very smart,' she commented.

'Thank you. I thought I had better look my best…you know.'

Irene led him straight into the little used parlour. A fire had not been lit in this room since Christmas and the air was chilly. Bill was sitting in a high-backed chair by the window but stood up when Gunther entered. Irene introduced them and the men shook hands formally. Bill did not invite Gunther to sit down.

'You may stay, Irene,' Bill said, 'but I would appreciate it if you would not interrupt.' Bill motioned to her to sit on the sofa. Gunther stood in front of Bill, fingering his cap nervously in his hands. Bill looked him up and down. He was presentable enough, not one of the tall, athletic Germans they used to see showing off on the beaches but he had a pleasant face. If Bill had been interviewing him for a job at the garage, he would have described him as open and honest-looking. The sort of lad you wouldn't have to worry about sloping off early when the boss wasn't about. Gunther waited for Bill to speak first.

'I expect Irene's warned you what to expect from me. I'm not at all happy about this situation and, to put things plainly, if you were to be posted to the battle-front in France tomorrow, I wouldn't be at all disappointed.'

Irene made as though to object but a warning look from her father made her hold her tongue.

'I understand that, sir. If our situations were reversed, I'm sure my own father would agree with you completely,' replied Gunther.

'Are your mother and father alive?'

'I don't know. There has been a lot of bombing near my home town. I have not had news for some time.'

'I see,' said Bill, 'and I understand you have lost your brother?'

'Yes, he died in an unfortunate drowning accident, here on the island.'

'Irene told us about it at the time.' Bill cleared his throat, 'I'm sorry. He was very young.'

'Yes. Thank you.'

'Now, to get to the business in hand. I understand that you and Irene have formed a serious attachment. As you can imagine, this is very distressing to her mother and myself.'

Gunther shuffled uncomfortably. 'Yes, sir.'

'So would you like to tell me what you intend to do about it, given the circumstances?'

Gunther was surprised by the directness of the question. 'Well, sir, we would like to marry,' he stammered.

'I know that, young man. My daughter has already informed me but, in the present circumstances, how do you propose to go about it?'

'We have no plans as yet, sir. It is all so uncertain. We do not know what will happen.'

Bill stepped closer to Gunther.

'Well I know what's going to happen, and I'm sure you do, if you care to admit it.' Bill was a couple of inches taller than Gunther but Gunther managed to stand his ground in the face of the older man's rising anger.

'You and your damned Third Reich are going to be driven out of Europe with your tails between your legs and good riddance to the lot of you. So start getting used to the idea. And where will you be then? Back in the homeland or in some prisoner of war camp? You won't be much use to my daughter there.'

'You're probably correct, sir. But please understand. It is not *my* Third Reich. I am not a Nazi. I am here because I was conscripted into the German army. I had no choice. I will be just as happy as you when this war is over. And I thank God every day that I was sent to this island instead of to one of the battle fronts. But even more than that I thank God I was sent here because it is here that I met your daughter. If I have to go to a prisoner of war camp, I will wait until the time I am free and then I will return for Irene. And she will wait for me, I know this for sure, sir.'

After this long speech, he glanced anxiously across at Irene, who smiled in support. Bill shook his head.

'I think you'll agree that, to me, that doesn't seem to be a very promising prospect. I care deeply for my daughter and when she marries, I hope to be able to hand her to a young man who I like and respect and who I know will be able to provide a secure and happy future for her. You're simply not in a position to do that.'

'But in a couple of years, when this is all over, I might be able …'

'In a couple of weeks you could be dead! What are your chances? Have you any idea?'

Gunther shook his head. He couldn't deny it was possible. Aware of his distress, Irene reached out and touched his sleeve.

'Look, I realise my daughter may refuse to speak to me after this but, as things stand at the moment, I'm afraid I can't give my support to your intention to marry when circumstances permit. I believe it would be best for both of you to end the relationship now. It will be painful for a time but….'

'No!' Irene stood to face her father, 'I won't do that. We will wait as long as it takes, won't we, Gunther?'

Gunther held Irene's hand and looked at her for a long moment before facing Bill again.

'Sir, I was brought up to respect the wishes of my father. My family, if they are still alive, are very important to me. I will not marry Irene without your permission.'

Irene snapped her head round to look at Gunther in surprise.

Bill shrugged his shoulders. 'Then you won't marry her.'

As far as Bill was concerned, the interview was at an end. He left the parlour and turned to climb the stairs to their bedroom where he knew Betty was waiting anxiously to hear what had been said.

Once Bill had left the room, Irene flopped down on the sofa.

'How could you say that, Gunther? He'll never agree. I know him. He's the most stubborn man on this earth.'

'It is a question of honour, of trust,' replied Gunther. 'I understand how your father must feel. I am not much of a prospect, am I? He's a good man and he loves you. Did you notice he did not say I couldn't marry you because I am German? He was entitled to say that. Has not all this suffering been caused by my nation? I did not want to go to war but none of us is completely innocent. There were things we could have done to stop it perhaps. I don't know.'

'Well,' said Irene, 'what do we do now?'

'We must abide by your father's wishes…and wait. And perhaps pray. I know you do not have the faith I do but I can recommend it.'

Gunther put his arms around Irene, believing that this would be the last time he would do so for a while.

'Don't give up hope, Irene. There may be a way. We just have to wait.'

Gunther was right when he said Irene did not have his faith but what he may not have realised was that she had inherited her father's stubbornness. She was not going to give him up without a fight.

CHAPTER 15

All through the spring of 1944, heavy bombing could be heard from the Cherbourg Peninsula and, day after day, Allied planes flew over the Island.

Nor was the Island quiet. German troops were kept busy with gun practice and manoeuvres and defences around the coast were strengthened even further. The requisitioning of cars and lorries was stepped up. Almost any road-worthy vehicle, regardless of age, was seized to be shipped to France. Bill's garage buzzed with activity. Bill had Tom working for him again but, even so, he had to take on a young lad to help them cope with the work.

Tom had mixed feelings about his return to the garage. He was glad Bill accepted and trusted him again and, working together day by day, the two men grew steadily closer. On a practical level, Tom also learned the business side of the job. Since Bill actively disliked dealing with the Germans, Tom gradually took over that aspect of the business. His knowledge of German was useful in handling the mountain of paperwork imposed on them by the Germans. Nevertheless, he resented having to work for the Germans as much as Bill and the two of them never missed an opportunity to cause delays or disruption if they felt they could get away with it.

Whenever he could get away, Tom took off to the farm. He'd promised Jim that he would help with the heavy work and he intended to fulfil that promise. He didn't care if it sometimes meant he worked seven days a week. It was a joy to be out in the open fields working on the land, away from constant reminders of the German presence. He could lose himself in the tasks Jim gave him. Though the work was physically hard, at the end of a day ploughing with the horses, Tom felt refreshed, cleansed in his soul. It was a good feeling.

Naturally he saw a lot of Izette. When he first started going over to the farm regularly she kept her distance. In the middle of the day, they had to eat dinner in the farmhouse kitchen with the rest of the family. No-one detected the undercurrent of tension when they were in each other's company except perhaps Aunt Margaret, whose female intuition sometimes picked up a note of strain in their behaviour. But as the weeks passed, they settled into a kind of neutrality and there was some return to the relationship they used to have before the occupation.

At the end of March, the sound of a tremendous bombing attack carried across the water from the French coast. It was so heavy that Izette stopped what she was doing and walked up to the cliffs to see if any of the activity was visible. Jim and Tom were working in one of the fields by the cliffs and they too were drawn to gaze across the few miles of water separating the Island from the French mainland. Izette joined them.

'Someone's getting a hammering, poor devils,' commented Jim.

'They're building up for the invasion, I reckon,' replied Tom. 'They haven't said so directly on the wireless but it seems obvious now. The American Air Force and our boys have been pounding away for weeks on France and Germany.'

'Aye, I think it's only a matter of time now. The German spirit is broken. Look at that mutiny over at Portelet. The Germans tried to hush it up but they had to turf some Jerseymen out of Fort Regent to be able to lock up their own men.'

'How long do you think it will be?' asked Izette.

'Can't say, Izette love,' said Jim. 'Each New Year since this all started, we've thought we'd see the end before the year was out but here we are still crossing our fingers and counting off the days.' A jingle of harness reminded Jim that the horses were standing idle. 'Well, this won't get the field ploughed before dark. We'd better get on, eh?'

That evening, Tom and Izette returned to the cliff top with a pair of binoculars. The night sky above the French coast glowed from end to end, a continuous inferno. Yet wave after wave of aircraft continued to drone overhead. Izette shuddered.

'Oh Tom, it's dreadful. Do you think there are still French people mixed up in all that?'

'I don't know. I imagine most of them will have left the bombing zones but you know how it is. There are always civilian casualties.'

Tom lowered the binoculars and beckoned Izette away from the cliff edge.

'Come and sit down with me, Izette. I have something to tell you.'

Izette's stomach lurched uncomfortably, fearful of what was coming. She sat down on the grass where he'd spread his coat.

'You know there have been a number of escape

attempts?' he asked.

'Yes, Denis Vibert made it to England, didn't he?'

'Yes, and a few others since then, though a lot more have failed. Well, I've decided to try it myself.'

'Oh no,' she whispered.

'The way things are moving, I think the Allies will push Jerry out of France before the end of the year. When they do, that will make escape much easier because I'll only need get to the French coast. Then it should be simple to get to England overland and, with any luck, I could be in uniform fighting Jerry in a few weeks.'

Izette's heart sank.

'But is it worth the risk now? Surely the war will be over soon. You could just wait.'

'That's partly the point, Izette. The war will soon be over and I still have a debt to settle. I don't care about the risk. I missed enlisting because I'd been born just a little too late but, if I could get away now, I might get a few month's fighting in before it's all over. And it's not just about George; there's everything that's happened here on the Island. I have a score to settle for Jersey too.'

Izette sighed heavily.

'I knew you wouldn't understand,' he said.

'No, I do understand,' said Izette, 'I just hoped, after the car incident, you'd perhaps sit it out quietly.'

'I think you know me better than that, Izette Vaubert!'

Yes, thought Izette, unfortunately I do. She knew there was no point in trying to dissuade him if he'd made up his mind. She picked at the grass disconsolately. Tom waited for some response from her, growing increasingly exasperated.

'So will you help me?' he said at last.

'Help you?'

'I can't manage it all on my own. I'm going to need help. I'll probably have to ask your uncle as well because I'll need somewhere to store things. One of the farm buildings would be ideal.'

Izette flashed an angry look at him.

'You realise you'll be putting everyone at risk if you involve them? And you know very well Uncle Jim will agree to help you. He's hardly going to refuse.'

'Izette, please believe me, I'm not going to take advantage of your uncle's friendship. But this is something I have to do, with or without his help...or yours.'

'And what if it all goes wrong?'

Tom shrugged. 'If I'm captured, I suppose I'll end up in one of the German prisons. That's what they've done with the others who failed.'

'But some of them, quite a few in fact, have drowned! You don't know the tides, Tom. They're dangerous.'

'I know the dangers. It doesn't make any difference. I'm sorry, Izette.'

Izette sighed heavily again. 'Then there's nothing more to say,' she said resignedly.

They sat in silence for a while, each preoccupied with their own thoughts. Then Tom stood up and helped Izette to her feet. He kept hold of her hands.

'Your hands are cold. I must get you back to the farm, but, before we go, there's something I'd like to say. If I do this and the gods are merciful and I make it, I promise that I will come back for you. For you, Izette,' he repeated. 'Do you understand what I'm saying?'

She looked into his eyes and he could see the fear in hers.

'Hold on to that, Izette. Remember, it's a promise.'

'I daren't,' she whispered.

'You have to. It's all I can offer you...but it's also everything. Can you trust me?'

She nodded.

'That's my girl,' said Tom, placing a light kiss on her lips, 'come on, we'd better get back before you freeze.'

They walked slowly back hand in hand. Izette didn't care that she was cold. There were too many thoughts and fears spinning in her head to worry about a little discomfort.

By the time they reached the kitchen door she had reached a decision. 'Just a minute, Tom,' she stopped at the doorstep. 'I don't know how much use I could be but I will help you…if you want me to.'

Tom smiled at her and cupped her cheek with his hand. 'Just knowing you're with me in this will make all the difference. Thank you, Izette.'

'I have to admit for me it's more a question of making the best of a bad job.'

'That's good enough for me. I don't have the right to ask any more.'

They looked at each other, trying to gauge where they now stood.

'So, it's a deal then?' Tom said eventually, breaking into a grin.

'I suppose so,' replied Izette, 'you always did like to get your own way, Tom Birrell.'

'And I seem to remember you were never far behind me,' he retorted.

Izette laughed and pushed open the kitchen door. Aunt Margaret looked up as they came in, noticing the smiles on their faces. You never know, she thought, something good might come out of this war in the end.

*

Late one Friday evening, Irene was on her way home from the

hotel. It was her weekend off and she was looking forward to seeing her parents again. She was allowed only one weekend off each month. Her heels clicked out a brisk rhythm on the pavement as she walked quickly through the darkened streets of St Helier. She passed a group of men and girls standing outside a tobacconist shop, talking and smoking. Since she didn't know any of them she didn't stop to talk and simply stepped off the pavement on to the road to pass them by. As she did so, she heard a hiss. Surprised, she turned to look at the group. One of the girls, a skinny common looking type, took the cigarette out of her month to sneer at Irene.

'What are you looking at, Jerrybag?'

She was confused at first. Did they mean her? Then, as the rest of the group struck up the sinister chant, she began to panic.

'Jerrybag, Jerrybag, Jerrybag....'

Irene turned and ran. The group gave chase, howling like a pack of hounds. The men paused to pick up stones as they ran. Irene didn't dare turn round. A few stones hit her on the back, bouncing off harmlessly. Then one caught her painfully on the leg and she cried out. It was only a few yards to the next corner. She turned it with relief and, once out of sight of her pursuers, stopped for a moment. She looked around desperately but could see nowhere to hide. She ran on, then thankfully spotted a German patrol of three soldiers at the end of the street. Her pursuers rounded the corner and a well-aimed stone caught her sharply on the cheekbone. Irene stumbled and fell to the ground. The Germans shouted and ran down the street. Her pursuers stopped abruptly. One soldier went to where Irene was crouched, holding a handkerchief to her face, while the other two confronted the group. After a short discussion with the Germans, the group turned round and went back the way they had come. Irene's soldier took a quick look at her face then waved her on her way with his rifle.

*

That was the end of Irene's job at the hotel. Bill was livid when he saw the state she was in. Despite all Betty's efforts to stop him, he rushed out of the house to see if he could find any of her tormentors, threatening to kill them if he could lay hands on them. Fortunately for everyone, there was no sign of them and Bill returned home still raging. By that time however, Betty had cleaned and dressed the cut on Irene's face and she no longer looked as awful as she had when she first burst into the kitchen with blood pouring down her face.

Bill looked at Irene anxiously. 'How are you now, love?'

Irene said she was fine, just a bit shaken.

'I couldn't find the buggers. They must have cleared off after that patrol spoke to them. I never thought I'd have a reason to be thankful for Jerries on the streets, eh Betty?'

Bill guided Irene to a chair and pulled up another for himself, sitting down to face her. 'You know what this means, don't you?'

Irene nodded, 'I suppose someone must have seen me with Gunther...but I don't know how, we've always been very careful.'

Bill made a disgusted noise. 'Unfortunately, there's always someone who gets a weird kind of pleasure by getting other folk into trouble. Look how many people have been turned in by their neighbours for keeping their wireless sets. I can't understand it. Perhaps it's jealousy or settling old scores but you'd think at a time like this everyone would close ranks, not the opposite.'

'I'm sorry, Dad,' said Irene.

'There's no need for you to apologise, Irene,' said Bill,

'we know you're not one of those Jerrybag women, just out for a good time and everything they can get from the Germans. However, this is one of the things I was worried about when you first told us about Gunther. This is a small island and it's almost impossible to keep anything secret. You've got yourself into a dangerous situation and we're going to have to work out how to keep you safe from now on.'

'We've agreed not to see each other…for a while, at least,' admitted Irene.

'I think it's too late for that,' Bill said gently, 'though I appreciate you making that decision. No, I'm afraid we're going to have to get you right away from the situation. You'll have to give up your job, Irene, and go to stay on the farm. You'll be safe there.'

Irene gasped. 'Do you think that's really necessary, Dad?'

Bill nodded. 'I know no-one would try anything while you're at the hotel but I can't walk you over there and back every time. And you don't want to be looking over your shoulder every time you're alone.'

Betty got up and opened a drawer, took out a piece of paper and handed it to Bill. He looked at it grimly then spoke to Irene again.

'Irene, we weren't going to show you this but I think we have to now. This letter was pushed through our door a week ago.'

He handed the letter to Irene who took it reluctantly, already suspecting what it contained. It was from an '*anonymous well-wisher*' and informed Bill and Betty that they ought to be aware that their daughter was '*consorting*' with a member of the occupying forces. The well-wisher hoped they would see fit to take appropriate action. Irene flushed red as she read it, crushing it into a ball in her fist when she had finished.

'How dare they!' she muttered, 'it makes me sound like…one of those French tarts they brought over.'

'Unfortunately, that's the way some people see it,' said Bill, 'and bear in mind my garage has kept going solely on the work the Germans put my way. Some people might think this family is doing quite very nicely out of the occupation.'

'But you had no choice, Dad! The Germans made you do the work.'

'No, Irene. I had a choice,' said Bill quietly. 'You and I have both been offered choices and we've made our decisions. Now we have to live with the consequences of those decisions.'

'But Dad, everyone knows you. They know how you feel about the Germans. You don't keep it a secret!'

Bill shrugged his shoulders. 'Well, I hope that's so, but actions have a habit of speaking louder than words and you and I will be judged on our actions.'

Irene wanted to argue further but Bill held up his hand.

'There's no point, Irene. When this is all over, let's see how we stand then, shall we? Now, getting back to the point, will you go and stay at the farm?'

Irene nodded her agreement. 'I don't want to cause you any more trouble, Dad.'

Bill's relief was evident. 'Good. I don't think we'd better waste any time getting you over there. Would you go and pack what you need tonight and I'll take you over first thing in the morning.'

Irene got up immediately. Before leaving the kitchen, she hugged both her parents in turn.

When she had gone, Bill turned to his wife. 'Well, Betty, it's been a tough lesson for her.'

'Yes,' agreed Betty, 'and it's not finished yet. Far from it!'

CHAPTER 16

Izette had never been very good at waiting. 'Don't be so impatient, child,' often rang in her ears when she was younger. Now it seemed even harder because there was so much at stake. Repressed excitement fizzed at the back of everyone's mind but no-one dared put a date to the anticipated invasion, that would be tempting providence. Uncle Jim was glued to his wireless set. Aunt Margaret complained about him being forever under her feet.

'You'd think he had no work to do,' she muttered. 'The invasion won't come any faster for you listening in to every word from the BBC, Jim.'

But Jim only shushed her and turned up the volume.

Then suddenly it was upon them. One night in June, in the early hours of the morning, Izette was woken by the sound of anti-aircraft fire. She hurried over to her bedroom window. There was a steady drone of aircraft overhead and the German batteries were letting rip. Bright flashes lit up the night sky. Izette quickly put on her dressing gown and slippers and opened her bedroom door. Uncle Jim was already on the landing, a lit candle stub flickering in his hand. Behind him, Aunt Margaret was emerging from the bedroom.

'Do you think this is it?' whispered Izette.

'It could well be,' answered Jim, 'I haven't heard this much of a racket before. I'm going down to tune in the wireless. I don't think we'll be getting much sleep tonight.'

'I'll come down as well,' said Izette.

'Might as well make a cup of something,' commented Aunt Margaret, as she followed the other two down the stairs. 'Is Irene still asleep? I expect she'll come down too if she wakes up.'

Downstairs in the kitchen, Jim checked the blackout before switching on the light then fetched the wireless set from its hiding place in the potato sack in the larder. Aunt Margaret had sewn a kind of false bottom in one of the sacks so that if anyone looked inside the sack, they would only see potatoes. He was tuning in to the station when the women came down.

*

Over in St Helier, Bill and Betty were also awake.

'You stay in bed in the warm, Betty,' said Bill, 'I'll take a look from the bottom of the garden. I might be able to see what's going on.'

Betty pulled herself into a sitting position, the effort bringing on a spasm of coughing. Bill fetched her dressing gown from the back of the door and put it round her shoulders. She nodded her thanks, unable to speak until she had got her breath back.

'I don't care what you say, Betty, I'm asking the doctor to come and take another look at you in the morning.'

He didn't give Betty a chance to argue, just left the bedroom and went downstairs in the dark. Bill was worried. Betty had seemed to be getting better, then suddenly the coughing started all over again. Margaret sent over eggs and vegetables from the farm, and the occasional chicken or rabbit but Betty had little appetite for any of it. She seemed to be tired all the time which, he supposed, was hardly surprising if she wasn't eating properly but he would see what the doctor had to say about it. She couldn't go on like this.

Bill unlocked the back door and made his way to the bottom of the garden from where he had a clear view over the town and bay. There was plenty of activity going on. Squadrons of planes were passing overhead through a storm of anti-aircraft fire from the island. Down in the town, although he could not see much in the blackout, he heard the sound of heavy vehicles on the move.

'What do you reckon, Bill? There's something big going on tonight.'

Bill turned in the direction of the voice. Ted and Tom were standing on the other side of the wall, watching the night activity.

'Aye, this could be the start of the invasion,' replied Bill, 'let's hope so, anyway. We've waited long enough.'

The three men stood quietly, watching the night sky as they had done on many previous nights. Anti-aircraft tracer sliced into the darkness above, eclipsed momentarily by the crash of gunfire from the batteries. Just a few miles away on the French mainland, all hell was breaking loose. Tom lit up the stub of a cigarette. Was it on a night like this that George had been killed, in a maelstrom of fierce fighting, or had a lucky sniper simply picked him off as he scrambled back to his dugout for a brew of tea? Bill turned to go back inside.

'See you in the morning, Tom.'

Ted watched his neighbour shuffle back up the garden path in his carpet slippers.

'Bill's quiet tonight,' he observed.

Tom grunted, disinclined to conversation.

'Well, I think I'll go in myself,' said Ted finally, 'might as well try to get some sleep.'

'Me, too. See you in the morning,' said Tom.

*

As it turned out, not much work was done in the garage the following day. News of the Allied invasion of France was out and no-one was in the mood to carry on as normal. The Germans put a proclamation in the Evening Post. As soon as the evening edition was out, Bill and Tom took a copy over to the farm. They burst into the farm kitchen waving the newspaper.

'Look at this! Look at this!' shouted Tom. 'Let me read this out to you. You won't believe this. Jerry must think we're deaf, blind and stupid.'

Tom waited until everyone was settled.

'*Proclamation to the population of the Island of Jersey. Germany's enemy is on the point of attacking French soil,*' Tom broke off. 'On the point of...! What do they think was going on last night then? Perhaps they thought we were all tucked up in bed fast asleep and didn't hear anything?'

'Come on, Tom, read the rest of it,' said Aunt Margaret, impatient to hear the whole thing.

'*I expect the population of Jersey to keep its head, to remain calm and to refrain from any acts of sabotage and from hostile acts against the German Forces, even should the fighting spread to Jersey.'* Tom paused again. 'Then there's the usual threats of what will happen if we don't behave ourselves. Here, Jim, have a look for yourself.'

Tom passed the newspaper over to Jim. Aunt Margaret and Irene strained to read it over his shoulder. Tom grabbed Izette by both hands and danced around the kitchen with her.

'This is it, Izette! This is the beginning of the end. I'm willing to bet we'll be eating our next Christmas dinner in peace time!'

'Oh, that would be wonderful!' agreed Aunt Margaret.

'What about this though?' said Jim, from behind the newspaper, 'he says, *'should the fighting spread to Jersey.'* Do you think that could happen?'

'It's possible, I suppose,' answered Tom. 'And if it did, the fighting could go on for a long time. We all know how well defended the island is. The Germans could hang on here for months.'

'No, I don't think so,' said Bill, 'the Allies don't need to attack these islands. If they can push Jerry out of France and topple the German High Command, the whole shooting match will be over in a matter of weeks. The German troops here have had enough. The only reason they don't give up is because they're afraid of being shot by the officers. And the troops here are the lucky ones. This is like a holiday camp for them compared with what's happening on the battle fronts.'

'Well, however things go in the next few months, I think this news calls for a celebration, announced Aunt Margaret. 'We'll sacrifice that big chicken I've been saving for a special occasion. What do you say, Jim?'

'That sounds grand to me. The chicken might not be too enthusiastic though. Shall I go and ask her how she feels about it, my dear?'

Aunt Margaret threw the dishcloth at him. 'Get on with

you. I need time to get her stuffed and roasted.'

Laughing, Jim left the kitchen to prepare the poor victim.

'You'll all stay for supper, I hope?' asked Margaret.

'Thank you, but I can't,' said Bill, 'Betty isn't too well again. I must get back to make her some supper.'

'Well, I'll save some chicken for her and I'll make some of my special chicken broth. Izette can bring it over.'

'Thank you, Margaret; she'll appreciate that.'

Their eyes met for a moment. Margaret knew him well enough to see that he was worried. When he got up to leave, Margaret went with him, hoping they could have a few words in private. Margaret walked with Bill as far as the gate out of the yard, then placed her hand on his arm.

'You'd better tell me the worst, Bill.' She waited and when he didn't reply she said, 'it's TB, isn't it?'

Bill didn't answer her for a moment. He looked down at his feet, struggling to speak. 'The doctor didn't actually say as much but he wants her in hospital straight away. He's sending an ambulance for her in the morning.'

'Overdale Hospital?'

Bill nodded. He didn't need to say any more. Overdale was the isolation hospital. All cases of tuberculosis were sent there.

'Shall I tell the girls for you?' asked Margaret.

Bill looked up at her gratefully. 'I suppose I should do it myself but...'

'But nothing, Bill. You've enough to cope with and you know how close I am to your girls. They won't mind it coming from me instead of you.'

'No, you're right. Bless you, Margaret.'

She pulled him into her arms and he leaned on her for a moment.

'Let me know as soon as she's settled in and I'll be

down there to see her,' said Margaret.

'I don't know if they'll allow that. They're very strict on visiting.'

'Just let them try to stop me, Bill Vaubert! Off you go, now, and give her my love.'

Bill nodded, looking at his sister-in-law with real fondness. He kissed her quickly on the cheek and whispered, 'Thank you.'

Margaret watched him walk down the lane until he faded into the darkness, before turning back to the house. Two tasks lay ahead that evening; the first, the preparation of the dinner, would be easy; the other would be far more difficult.

*

Jim came back into the kitchen with the unfortunate chicken hanging limply from his hand.

'I'll pluck it,' announced Izette. 'Come on, Tom, you can give me a hand.'

She took the bird from her uncle and led Tom down the passageway into the scullery. Sitting herself on an old wooden stool, she put the chicken on her lap and started plucking. Tom leaned against the sink, his hands in his pockets.

'This puts a rather different complexion on things, doesn't it?' she said.

'How do you mean?'

'Now the invasion has started, surely there's no need for you to carry on with your escape plans. How long can it be before the war's over?'

Tom held up his hands in disbelief. 'This doesn't change anything! Have you been listening to me at all? It could be months and months before the fighting is finally over and I want a chance to play my part. I have a duty, don't you understand? Being trapped here for the last four years under

Jerry control, having to work for them makes it even more important. I have to redress the balance. What will I say to my children when they say, "What did you do in the war, Daddy?" "Oh well actually, I worked for the Germans." Sounds great, doesn't it?'

Izette ripped out a handful of feathers carelessly, taking the skin off with them.

'Blast it! That's nonsense and you know it, Tom. You worked with them for a purpose. You were collecting information to supply to the Allies.'

'And have I?' interrupted Tom

'What?'

'Have I supplied this information to the Allies?'

'Well, not yet...' admitted Izette.

'Exactly. And if I don't get it to them soon, it isn't going to be much use, is it? So that's another reason to carry on with the plan.'

Izette carried on stripping the bird in silence, her lips clamped together. Tom went over to her stool and squatted down in front of her, placing his hands over hers to stop the frenetic plucking.

'Izette, I need you to support me in this. I don't just mean your practical help. I want you to be prepared to take the risk with me. I want you to let me go.'

'How can I stop you?'

'Oh believe me, you can,' he smiled. 'If I thought you were absolutely against the idea, I wouldn't attempt it. But you're not, are you? You don't like it but you do understand why I have to go.'

Izette scowled. 'I wish you didn't know me so well, Tom Birrell.'

Tom grinned and stood up. 'For heaven's sake, hurry up with that bird. I'm starving.'

*

Following that night, the routine of Izette and Irene's lives changed dramatically. They decided they would take it in turns to return to St Helier to visit their mother and do the housework or anything else that needed to be done at Belle View Villas, each staying one week in St Helier and one week on the farm. Bill objected of course, saying he knew what they were up to and that he was perfectly capable of looking after himself. However, when Margaret took him on one side and suggested that perhaps they needed to be with him while Betty was in hospital, he accepted the arrangement. In truth, of course, he needed them just as much.

During one of the weeks when it was Izette's turn to be in St Helier, Tom had come over to the farm to give Jim a hand and Margaret insisted he stay for some supper. After they had finished eating, Tom said he was going to take a stroll outside before he had to leave to go home. A couple of weeks earlier, with Tom's agreement, Izette had told Edmund about Tom's intention to make an escape attempt.

'You know Edmund,' she had said, 'we won't be able to keep this from him. He misses nothing.'

'You're right,' Tom agreed, 'anyway, I intend to take those notebooks of his with me. They would be invaluable to an invasion force.'

So, when Tom got up to go outside, Edmund followed him, anxious to ask him how far his plans had progressed.

'Well, not very far yet, I suppose,' confessed Tom when asked. 'I've been out a few times at night to check on possible embarkation points but I haven't started getting together the equipment I'll need.'

Edmund launched in enthusiastically, 'I've been giving it a lot of thought since Izette told me about your plans. And

I've done a bit of scouting about. For a start, I found this.'

He handed Tom what looked like a battered old map.

'This is a chart of the sea area off the coast of the farm. Did you know Uncle Jim used to do quite a bit of sailing in his younger days?'

Tom shook his head.

'Do you know anything about navigation?'

Tom admitted he didn't. 'I was hoping to find someone who'd give me some advice about that, someone I could trust of course.'

'Well you won't need to look far. Uncle Jim can explain all that to you. I expect he'd help you plan a route. Does he know about your plans yet, Tom?'

'No, I'm trying to involve as few people as possible. I won't tell him unless I have to.'

'Well, have you decided where you'll be leaving from?'

Tom showed Edmund a sketch of the small harbour and breakwater he was thinking of using. Edmund knew where it was. He examined Tom's sketch. The Germans had built a guard hut at the landward end of the breakwater and erected a perimeter wire fence.

'I can see you would be able to launch easily from the far side of the harbour but that spotlight near the guard hut is a real problem. You couldn't put it out of action without getting inside the perimeter wire fence,' said Edmund.

'I know. I would have to hope the guards stayed inside their hut. When I watched them the other night, they didn't stir outside until their relief arrived. It's a very quiet spot.'

'Mm, sounds risky,' Edmund said doubtfully. 'Has Izette ever shown you the cove where we used to swim?'

'No, I don't think so.'

Edmund looked at the sky. 'We've just about got time to get down there before the light fades. Come on, I'll show you the place. You might not think it's any good but it's worth taking a look.'

*

They were back at the farm within an hour. Tom had been impressed by the seclusion the cove offered. It was well away from any German installations and well hidden from coastal lookout points on either side and from the sea. It had never been mined, probably because it was too small to be considered a significant risk. The drawback was the access. To get down to the beach you had to scramble down a near vertical path. It would clearly be very difficult, if not impossible, to get a boat down there.

'We'd need some sort of trailer to get a boat from wherever it was hidden to the top of cliff. We couldn't carry a boat for that distance,' said Tom as they walked back.

Edmund agreed. 'And then we would need some way of getting the boat down the cliff. Could we lower it down on pulleys or some sort of winch?'

'Jim has a winch on his tractor but the noise it would make might rule it out. Engine noise carries a long way at night,' said Tom.

It was clear they would need to plan very carefully and possibly experiment with a few trial runs.

Tom laughed suddenly. 'Aren't we forgetting a rather important point? I don't have a boat yet.'

They were back in the farmyard by now. 'Come with me,' said Edmund, and led Tom around the back of the barn to a low wooden shed. Edmund untied the piece of twine that held the old door shut and dragged it open enough for them to squeeze through. It was dark inside and smelled of musty old straw.

'I didn't bring a torch,' said Edmund, 'do you have a lighter, Tom?'

Tom flicked open his lighter and, in the feeble light, Edmund pulled some loose straw away from the broken bales at the back of the shed.

'Come and take a look at this.'

Tom lowered his lighter to the place Edmund was indicating and whistled when he saw what had been revealed.

'It's Uncle Jim's old dinghy. I've no idea what condition it's in. It's been in here for years. Uncle Jim dumped all this straw on top of it when the Germans first invaded, just in case they came snooping around.'

'Edmund,' said Tom, 'You're a marvel.'

'It could be completely rotten,' warned Edmund, 'and you'll need an outboard. Uncle Jim never had an engine for it.'

Tom slapped Edmund on the shoulder. 'Even so, it's a bloody good start. I better start brushing up on my French,' Tom joked.

Edmund grinned back at him in the darkness.

'Come on, Edmund, I think I need to have a long talk with your uncle.'

CHAPTER 17

On one of her stays at Belle View Villas, Izette decided to go down to St Helier early in the day to see if she could buy any food. It had been quite a while since she was last in the town and she was surprised by how things had changed. There were no German soldiers to be seen off-duty in the street. Since the invasion started in France, they had all been put on maximum alert. Postings to the various defensive positions around the perimeter of the island had been doubled, the military hospitals were in full operation and the harbour was bustling with activity. All the soldiers she saw were fully armed, even to having grenades strung around their necks. In contrast, the Islanders were cheerful and optimistic even in the face of more ration cuts.

After trailing fruitlessly round the shops, Izette was coming to the conclusion that it had been a wasted journey.

Few food convoys were attempting the trip from St Malo to the Island. Allied air attacks and naval activity were making it impossible. Then, just as she was about to give up on her shopping, Izette noticed a lively queue outside a small shop on Market Street. Hopefully she pushed her way inside. To her disappointment she found that the source of interest was a box of Union Jack flags for sale. She picked one up half-heartedly, then her eye was caught by a small boy waving his flag vigorously and making the V-sign with his other hand. His clothes were long out-grown, his jacket sleeves finishing well up his scrawny arms. His skinny legs were clad in darned socks and his battered old shoes had had the toes cut out of them to allow his own toes to stick through, yet a huge grin stretched from ear to ear. On an impulse, Izette took out her purse and bought a flag. There was more to survival than the daily struggle of finding enough to eat.

Back home she found her father having a doze in the armchair. It had been another noisy night so neither of them had slept well. The Island was well and truly in the thick of things now with bombing raids on Elizabeth Castle and the airport. A gun emplacement at La Roque had been bombed, the shells destroying several houses, fortunately with no civilian casualties. Night after night, Allied planes flew overhead as their advance continued over the Cherbourg Peninsula. By the middle of June, the Allies had reached Barneville and Carteret, a mere 15 miles away.

Izette didn't wake her father but put some potatoes in a pan to boil. She had brought an onion from the farm that she could fry with some tomatoes. Together, they would make quite a tasty meal. There was still a little salt left in the larder but she would need to be making some more soon. While she was working at the sink, a tap on the kitchen window startled her. Looking up, she saw Tom outside and gestured to him to come in through the back door. The sound of the door opening woke Bill from his snooze.

'Is the evening paper here yet, Izette?' he asked.

'No, not yet Dad, but Tom is.'

Her father hadn't noticed Tom come in through the back door. He looked up and beckoned Tom to a chair. Tom greeted them both then asked about Betty.

'She's doing all right, Tom. There isn't much change yet but it's a slow business. I just hope we can keep her spirits up. It isn't very cheerful in that hospital. And she can hear gunfire most of the time but can't see where it's coming from, so she worries. The Island fair bounces sometimes, doesn't it?'

Tom grunted in agreement.

'Well now, Tom,' asked Bill, 'how are your preparations progressing?'

Tom had taken Bill into his confidence. Tom told Bill about the discovery of Jim's old dinghy.

'Yes, I remember that boat but I thought it had gone for firewood years ago. Do you think you can make it watertight again?'

'Jim seems to think so. We're planning to move it into his workshop at the weekend so that we can make a start on it.'

'And does it have an engine?'

'No, but I think I know where I can lay my hands on an old outboard. It'll need completely stripping down though. That's partly why I came in to see you, Bill. I know it could be risky, but I wondered if I could work on it in the garage? I need the use of some of your machinery and tools.'

Bill didn't pause for a moment. 'Of course you can. We've got so much junk down there it won't be difficult to hide a small outboard. Anyway, even if Jerry were to catch you working on it, there's no reason why you shouldn't be stripping down an engine for a customer, is there?'

Tom smiled. 'I suppose not but I have got a bit of a reputation now, you know.'

Bill dismissed this. 'The Germans have other things on their minds right now. They won't be doing many inspections. And you won't need to go looking for fuel for it, either. I've been siphoning small amounts from the German cars we've been working on for the last few months. Just a little from each, not enough to be noticed. I thought it might come in useful for something.'

'That's marvellous, Bill. I never saw you do any siphoning!'

'Well, the fewer people who know about that sort of thing, the better.'

'I know,' replied Tom, 'that's what worries me about my plans. I seem to have involved most of your family and mine already.'

'You couldn't do it alone, Tom, and you know you can rely on us all.'

'Yes, of course I know that. I've never doubted it. It's what might happen to you all afterwards, when I've gone. They're bound to investigate.'

'You'll have to leave that to us, lad. You concentrate on getting yourself away safely.'

Bill stood up and stretched himself. 'How's that tea coming on, Izette? It smells good.'

Tom got up to leave. 'I'll leave you to enjoy your meal in peace. I'll see you at the garage in the morning, Bill. And thanks again.'

Bill acknowledged him with a nod and Tom let himself out through the back door.

*

Izette's life settled into the new rhythm of one week at home running the house and visiting her mother whenever she could, alternating with a week of farm work. Common to both existences was the daily struggle to find something nourishing and palatable to eat and the daily vigil by the wireless set. However, behind the tedium of the daily routines the families shared ran a current of excitement, fuelled by each completed stage in the preparations for Tom's escape. Unfortunately, as Tom's excitement grew, Izette's dread increased. She was hard pressed to show any enthusiasm when he proudly started up the outboard motor in the garage after days of reconditioning work.

'There she goes, purring like an angel,' Tom said, stroking the outer casing fondly.

'Aye,' agreed Bill, 'who'd have thought it could sound like that. You've done a good job there, Tom. That motor must be 20 years old at least.'

'If it's that old, how do you know it won't break down on the way,' Izette asked doubtfully.

The men turned and smiled at her in that smug way men adopt when their mechanical ability is questioned.

'Tom's checked through every part of this motor with a fine tooth-comb,' replied her father. 'You don't need to worry about it breaking down.'

Reading between the lines, Izette heard 'don't bother your pretty little head with things you don't understand.'

Izette returned home to prepare the evening meal. Despite the BBC reports of the steady advance of the American army through France, Izette was feeling despondent. She knew it was partly to do with not getting enough to eat. The rations were so small and their diet so dreary, she now hated preparing food and had to force herself into the kitchen. As the US army ploughed southwards, reaching Avranches by the end of July and on into Brittany, taking Brest a month later, the French ports from which their meagre food supplies had been brought were cut off one by one and the Island entered a state of siege.

She tried to ignore the way her father's clothes hung on his skinny frame. As far back as she could remember, he'd always been broad and well fleshed. Many times, she had hidden in the generous expanse of his embracing arms. Nowadays, the best items of food were saved for Betty but even this didn't amount to much. Their carefully hoarded tinned food was almost at an end. The top shelf of the larder now boasted one tin of corned beef, some mustard powder and a small jar of pickled onions, held in reserve against some unknown emergency. Well, the emergency was upon them. As Izette walked home, she knew she would open the last tin of corned beef that night and make a corned beef hash, spiced up with some mustard. Then she and her father would both say they were not very hungry and save the major portion for Betty. The following day she would take the hash in a pudding basin as hot as she could hold with a clean tea towel tied around the rim and try to persuade her mother to finish at least a quarter of it. 'Just one more tiny mouthful, please,' she would say, to which her mother would reply, 'I'm absolutely full, Izette, I couldn't manage another crumb.' Then Izette would set aside the basin and shake up her mother's pillows, saying, 'you've done very well today. I can see I'll have to bring larger portions for you soon.' And they would smile and agree with each other. Neither was fooled but it was that or cry.

The other dark cloud on Izette's horizon, one that drifted steadily closer, was Tom's impending departure. Nothing, short of betrayal, would prevent him from making the attempt. In her worst moments, she was ashamed to admit that she had considered a note to the German authorities hinting about the whereabouts of the boat. But she had to accept that the French ports were open, the boat was nearly ready and Tom could see just a few miles of water between himself and the opportunity he'd waited four years for.

*

By the beginning of September, Tom's preparations were in their final stages. The outboard motor had been smuggled out to the farm underneath a load of fertilizer. The men now had to fix up a framework to hold the outboard on to the back of the boat. All the repairs to the boat's structure were complete and Jim was pretty confident that she was watertight. The oars had turned up in the rafters of the barn, with a scattering of wormholes but Jim had treated them and replaced the most badly damaged wood. After three coats of varnish, they looked good as new. Tom's supplies - the chart, a compass, a baler, a spare can of fuel, waterproof clothing, a torch, a couple of coils of rope and Jim's shotgun - were concealed in an outhouse. Edmund's precious notebooks had been wrapped in oilskin with the chart. If the worst came to the worst and Tom was picked up by the Germans, he would put the heavy torch in the oilskin and throw the lot overboard. If the Germans suspected he was a spy he would be shot.

Jim advised Tom that the best tide conditions for his escape occurred twice a month but the final decision would depend on the weather conditions on the night in question.

*

The night agreed for the fixing of the outboard fell on a Tuesday, during a week in which Izette was in St Helier and Irene was working on the farm. During tea, Bill announced to

Izette that he was going over to the farm that evening to 'finish off a job.' After so long, the habit of speaking with caution was hard to shake off, even in your own home.

'Be careful about the curfew, Dad, you don't want to be picked up on the way back.'

'If it gets late and we still haven't finished, I'll probably stay the night. So don't worry if I don't come back tonight.'

Bill arrived at the farm at around seven o'clock. It was still light. Margaret told him that Jim and Tom were already in the workshop and Edmund was around somewhere. He made his way across the farmyard and around the back of the barn to the workshop. As he approached, he shouted a greeting to the two inside to let them know he was there. He didn't want them to jump out of their skins when he opened the door.

'Hello there, how's it all going tonight?'

After greeting Bill, the others explained the problems they were having fixing the frame for the outboard.

'Tom can't be struggling with this on the night in question,' commented Jim. 'He needs everything to slip into place smooth and silent as a whistle.'

'Mm, I see what you mean,' said Bill, peering closely at the fixing, 'perhaps we could re-drill that hole to allow a little more movement. Let's get the frame off again on to the workbench so that we can experiment.'

Under Bill's direction, the men took the frame apart, re-drilled some of the holes and reassembled it before fixing it back on to the boat. It took several attempts before Bill was satisfied. Edmund looked in a couple of times during the evening to see how they were progressing. On his last trip, he carried a message from Margaret.

'Uncle Jim, Aunt Margaret says the BBC bulletin will be on shortly and do you want to come in for it?'

'Yes, I will,' answered Jim, 'that is, if the others can manage without me for a few minutes?'

Jim wiped his oily hands on a rag and left the workshop with Edmund. It was dark as they crossed the yard. Halfway across, Jim stopped and laid a hand on Edmund's arm, listening. After a moment he released Edmund's arm and carried on.

'Sorry if I gave you a fright, lad. I thought I heard something then but it must have been my imagination.'

When they reached the kitchen door, Edmund went straight in but Jim stood on the doorstep for a moment, listening again. Eventually, shaking his head, he stepped inside and closed the door.

After the bulletin was finished, Jim said he'd take a mug of what passed for tea nowadays out to Bill and Tom so Margaret got up to put the kettle on. Since Edmund didn't want any, he left the kitchen and walked back across the yard. As he rounded the corner of the barn, he stopped dead. In the light coming from the small workshop window he saw a figure. The man had his eye to the window, obviously trying to see what was going on inside. The figure was wearing a German forage cap. Edmund withdrew back round the corner. Moving as quietly as he could, he retraced his steps to the farmhouse.

'Uncle Jim!' he whispered urgently as soon as he got inside, 'there's a German outside the workshop! He's peering through the window!'

'Bloody hell!' Jim put down the mugs he was carrying and crossed the kitchen.

'Oh my goodness!' said Margaret, 'what shall...'

'You hide the wireless, Margaret,' barked Jim, 'how many of them are there?'

'I only saw one,' replied Edmund.

'Are you sure?'

'I think so.'

'Right, come with me, Edmund.'

'No, the lad would be safer...' protested Margaret, but she was too late. They were already outside, closing the kitchen door quietly after them. Hurrying across the kitchen, she grabbed the wireless, yanking the plug out of the wall by the flex, and ran with it to the larder.

Outside, Jim and Edmund crept stealthily across the yard, stopping when they reached the corner of the barn. Jim peered very slowly round the corner. There was no one there but the workshop door was now open. Jim picked up a shovel that was leaning against the barn. He signalled to Edmund that he should stay where he was and slowly crept around the corner towards the open door. There were short bursts of conversation coming from inside. It sounded like Bill and Tom were being questioned. Jim manoeuvred himself into a position where he could see what was going on inside. There was indeed a German soldier in there with his rifle levelled at Bill and Tom, his back to the door. Jim glanced quickly around. No sign of any others with him. That's strange, Jim thought, and stupid. Raising the shovel, he slipped silently through the open door and brought the flat of the blade down heavily on the back of the German's head. The man staggered and collapsed forwards on to the floor. Tom was on top of him in a second, grabbing the rifle.

'He's out cold.'

Edmund stumbled into the workshop, stopping abruptly when he saw the German lying face down on the floor.

'Crikey! Is he dead?'

Tom felt for a pulse in the German's neck. 'No, but that isn't to say he won't be soon. There's a lot of blood.'

Tom stood up and handed the rifle to Edmund, thinking fast.

'Right. This is what we've got to do. We either finish him off here and get rid of the body by burying it...or we get to get him up to the cliffs now, while he's still unconscious and chuck him over.'

Jim was shocked. 'Finish him off?'

'Well, you're the one who just clouted him with a shovel, Jim. He might not make it anyway. What's the difference?'

'He was pointing a gun at you. I didn't have any choice. But killing him...in cold blood...that's different.'

'It's him or us, Jim,' Tom said grimly, 'and the quicker we get on with it, the better. He might come round. It would be even harder then.'

Jim looked across to Bill, 'What do you reckon, Bill?'

'I think we'd better make absolutely sure he's on his own first. Edmund, go on outside and take a look around. See if you can see anything...and for God's sake hide that rifle somewhere.'

Edmund dashed out of the workshop, glad to have something positive to do.

'Now,' said Bill, 'since we can't let him go, we have to get rid of him. I don't like the idea of killing him any more than you do, Jim, but we don't have any choice. As for killing him in cold blood as you put it, I don't think I could do that, so I say he goes over the cliff and the sea will take care of him.'

Tom nodded. Jim was still unhappy about it.

'But what if he comes round once he's in the water? It's only a slight chance but he could still survive. If he made it back...'

'How's the tide now, Jim?' asked Tom.

Jim looked at his watch. 'Going out, I think. I'd need to check the tables to be sure.'

Tom thought for a moment. 'Does that mean the water's cleared the foot of the cliff?'

'Probably,' answered Jim, 'in which case we couldn't

just chuck him over. He'd land on the rocks, not in the water.'

'But the tide would eventually take him out?' pursued Tom.

'Yes but not until the next high water. He could lie there for hours.'

'Aye,' agreed Bill, 'and if they came looking for him and found him there, we'd still be buggered.'

'Right then,' said Tom, 'we'll take him down to the cove and float him off in the water face down. That way we can be sure he drowns. We'd better get his rifle back and strap it on his back, it could help to take him under. Then, if the body does wash up, it might look more like an accident.'

'Or a suicide,' commented Jim.

'Maybe,' replied Tom, 'but at least he won't be found with a bullet hole or a stab wound in him.'

Jim reluctantly agreed it seemed the best plan.

'Should we find out who he is?' suggested Jim. 'He'll have papers on him.' Jim started to bend down over the body.

'Not much point, Jim,' said Tom, 'we'll have to leave his papers on him, in case he's found. It would look suspicious if they weren't there.'

'Anyway,' said Bill, 'do we really want to know?'

Bill was right. Knowing the man's name would turn him into a person instead of just something that needed to be disposed of.

'Right,' said Bill, 'we'd better improvise a stretcher of some sort to carry him on. Where's that boy Edmund got to?'

Edmund returned to the workshop and said there was no sign of any more Germans. Nor had he found any sort of transport, so the assumption must be that the German had walked to the farm.

'That's odd, you know,' said Bill, 'they don't usually come out snooping on their own. There's usually at least two of them.'

'Unless he was out on his own scrounging for food,' suggested Tom. 'He could have been trying to pinch a chicken or something.'

This was a reasonable suggestion. The Germans were as badly off for food as the Islanders. They had been caught breaking into houses to steal food and also been seen scouring the rocks for limpets.

'Well, I suppose we should be grateful he won't be too heavy to carry then,' Bill added grimly. 'Edmund, go and bring that rifle back. It's going with him.'

The men threaded the boat's oars through some sacking to make a rough sort of stretcher. By the time Edmund returned with the rifle, they were ready to roll the body on to it. They laid the stretcher alongside the body. Tom checked for a pulse again while the others waited.

'He's still alive,' Tom announced finally, 'let's get him on the stretcher.'

They positioned themselves on either side of the body, Jim and Bill on the stretcher side, Tom opposite them.

'Push that oar as far underneath him as you can,' suggested Tom, 'then I'll roll him over on to it.'

Jim straightened up the man's limbs so that he was lying flat on his stomach, then Tom rolled him over on to his back on the stretcher.

'Bloody hell!' said Bill. 'I know him! It's Gunther, Irene's young man.'

CHAPTER 18

When it became clear that Bill was not going to come home that night, Izette decided to pop next door to see Nancy and her mother rather than spend the whole evening on her own. Leaving her own house she tapped on the Birrell's door knocker lightly, calling through the letterbox at the same time so as not to alarm them. Nancy let her in and they went into the kitchen. The Birrells were pleased to see Izette and asked about her mother. Izette tried to sound positive but there was nothing much she could say except what the doctor had told her a couple of days ago, that her mother was 'satisfactory for the moment'. Izette had actually thought her mother looked weaker when she last saw her but she couldn't bring herself to admit this to anyone else.

Mrs Birrell took a covered bowl from her larder and gave it to Izette.

'Here's some rice pudding I made for Betty. It isn't

very sweet because I only had a tiny bit of sugar but it might tempt her appetite. I thought it would be easy for her to digest.'

Izette took the bowl reluctantly, knowing the sacrifice this represented for the Birrells. They didn't have any means of supplementing their rations beyond their own vegetable garden, although recently, since Tom had been up at the farm so often, she had seen her Aunt Margaret giving him food to take back to his family. She thanked Mrs Birrell profusely, hoping she would be able to persuade her mother to eat some of the precious pudding.

The conversation drifted naturally to the latest news on the war front, then what was going on in St Helier and how that affected the work at the garage and it eventually came around to Tom.

'I've hardly seen him recently, Izette,' Mrs Birrell said, 'he spends all his spare time up at your uncle's farm. Don't misunderstand me. I'm very pleased about it. While he's over there working for your uncle, it keeps him out of trouble. How he managed to get away with that car accident when the German officer died I'll never know but he's a marked man now. The less he's seen around St Helier the better.'

Izette was surprised. Either Mrs Birrell was being extraordinarily careful about what she said or she genuinely didn't know about Tom's escape plans. She decided to probe a little further.

'So you don't mind him being away a lot of the time?'

'Good gracious no! It was much worse when he was doing that driving job for the Germans. I never knew where he was then or what he was doing. After a while, when people had seen him around town so much with the Jerries, they started being a bit off-hand with us. It got quite uncomfortable. No, I feel much easier in my mind when I know he's over at the farm. He must be a good help to your uncle since he lost his labourers?'

Izette nodded her agreement.

'And your aunt is very kind. She often sends something back with him.'

While Mrs Birrell had been talking, Izette had watched Nancy and her father. Mr Birrell was barely listening to the conversation, absorbed in his newspaper. Nancy was listening and adding a few comments of her own. None of the Birrell family had given the slightest hint that they knew what Tom was really up to. So he hasn't told them, concluded Izette. She was surprised, then relieved that she hadn't accidentally let anything slip. Tom must have his reasons for keeping them in the dark. Perhaps he was thinking of what happened on the previous occasion when Mr Birrell was hauled off to the German Headquarters to be questioned about the car accident. If he knew nothing about Tom's plans this time, he would find it easier to plead ignorance...if it should come to that.

'Still, it can't be much longer now, can it?' Mrs Birrell was saying, 'if we can just get through the next few months, I think we'll see the Germans leaving the Islands with their tails between their legs and then we'll all be able to get back to normal. Tom can go back to working in the garage with your father, Edmund can go back at school and you girls will have to decide what you're going to do. I suppose you could go on to college or you might start work, a proper job I mean. Yes, all back to normal...' she paused, '...though it won't ever be quite the same again.'

Mrs Birrell's chatter tailed away and she fell silent. Nancy looked at her anxiously. Mr Birrell folded his newspaper and announced he thought it must be getting close to bedtime. Izette took the hint and got up to leave, noticing how tenderly Mr Birrell helped his wife out of her chair and started to guide her towards the door to the stairs.

'I hope I haven't upset your mum,' Izette whispered to Nancy.

'No, she'll be fine,' said Nancy, 'she's getting better. It will just take time.'

Nancy opened the door for Izette and she crept back to her own house. Once inside, she checked the blackout and switched all the lights on. The house was so empty. She shivered, though not with cold.

*

The first indication Margaret had that anything was wrong was when the kitchen door was flung wide open, crashing into the sideboard. Startled, she turned to look at the door where she saw the men carrying someone in. At first she thought one of them had had an accident in the workshop but when all four of them struggled inside with their burden she realised that couldn't be so.

'What's happened? Who's this?' she asked, then, catching sight of the German uniform, she stepped back with a gasp. 'Oh my lord! What on earth's going on?'

'I'll tell you later,' grunted Jim, 'we need to get this young lad out of sight first. Put some hot water on, Margaret, and see if you can find any bandages. He's hurt.'

They put the stretcher down on the kitchen floor in order to catch their breath. While they were discussing what to do, a groan came from the prone figure on the stretcher.

'He must be coming round, thank God,' said Bill. 'Let's get him upstairs where we can take a proper look at that wound.'

Margaret looked at the men in astonishment.

'Be quick, Margaret,' said Jim, 'bring up that water and some towels…and some antiseptic if we have any.'

Margaret hurried over to hold open the door leading to the stairs, taking a good look at the German as the men squeezed past her. His eyes flickered open for a moment then closed again, his head rolling to the side. When the men had disappeared upstairs, she returned to the stove to put some hot water on to heat. On the floor where the stretcher had lain was a pool of blood. Margaret quickly looked away and reached for a pan to use. A few minutes later, Irene came downstairs into the kitchen.

'What's going on, Aunt Margaret? I can hear a lot of bumping going on in the attic.' Then she, too, saw the blood on the floor. 'Oh heavens! Has there been an accident?'

'I've no idea what's going on yet, Irene. The men have just brought an injured German in. They've taken him upstairs.'

'An injured German?' Irene turned and ran back up the stairs. Margaret took a cloth, moistened it and started mopping up the blood from the kitchen floor. The next thing she knew, Irene flew into the kitchen again and started ransacking the cupboard where Margaret kept their first aid supplies, carelessly dragging everything out on to the floor.

'Just a minute, Irene!' shouted Margaret. 'You won't find what you're looking for like that!'

Irene stood up and Margaret saw her panic stricken face.

'I know him, Aunt Margaret! He's a friend,' Irene burst out, 'and he's very badly hurt.'

Margaret was dumbfounded. He must be someone Irene had got to know while she was working at the hotel but to describe him as a friend! What was she thinking of? Jim clumped down the stairs next, asking for the water and towels. She poured some water from the pan into an enamel basin and took some clean towels off the rack over the stove.

'I'll bring this up myself,' she announced, 'Irene, sort

some bandages and whatever you think we might need from that mess you've made on the floor and bring them up,' adding, 'now, girl, not next week!'

They had put Gunther in the spare bedroom in the attic. Fortunately, Margaret noticed, they'd had the common sense to put a pad of something under his head, which was where the blood was coming from. He was groaning and trying to get up. Tom was holding him down. Margaret came over to the bed and looked the man up and down.

'Is it just his head that's hurt or has he any other injuries?' she demanded of Tom.

'Just his head. Jim hit him with a shovel.'

Margaret looked at her husband in amazement, then turned her attention to the man on the bed. He'd stopped struggling to get up but he was obviously confused. She put the basin and towels on the floor, motioned to Tom to move out of the way and sat down on the side of the bed.

'Now, I need to look at your head,' she said slowly and clearly, pointing at the same time to the back of his head. 'Can you turn your head for me?' She made a turning movement with her hand.

'Yes, thank you,' said the young man.

'Ah, you speak English?' asked Margaret.

'Yes, he bloody does,' answered Bill. At this moment Irene reappeared in the attic carrying a number of dressings.

'Ask Irene,' continued Bill, 'she can tell you all about him.'

Ignoring her father, Irene hurried to the bedside, dropping to her knees on the floor.

'Gunther! It's me, Irene. Can you hear me?'

Gunther's eyes kept opening and closing. It wasn't clear whether he was fully conscious or not. After a pause, he managed to say her name.

'Well!' said Margaret. 'I'll have the full story later, once we've cleaned him up and made him comfortable. You men can leave us to it now. Irene, go and get some clean sheets for the bed and a pair of scissors please.'

Dismissed, the men trooped downstairs and slumped into chairs around the kitchen table. They reached for the mugs of cold tea that Jim had prepared earlier and drank in stunned silence. When the mugs were empty, Jim turned to Bill.

'Ok, Bill, who the hell's this Gunther and what's he doing here?'

*

By the time Bill had finished explaining, Margaret was coming back down the stairs. She took the basin over to the sink, where she threw away the blood-stained water. She wiped her hands dry on her apron then turned around to find the men looking at her.

'He'll live,' she said, in reply to their unspoken question. 'He must have a hard head.'

The men exchanged relieved glances.

'And,' continued Margaret, 'in case you were wondering what he was doing here, he wasn't spying on you lot. He'd come to see if he could catch a glimpse of Irene. He wanted to speak to her.'

'So he wasn't checking up on us?' asked Jim.

'No, no-one's tipped off the Germans. They don't know anything.'

Jim gave a huge sigh of relief.

'Don't think we're out of trouble yet though,' warned Tom. 'Margaret, is he well enough to go back to his billet?'

'No, certainly not tonight. He keeps passing out and coming to again. I think he'll be badly concussed for a few days. Anyway, we've settled him down for the night now.

You can't drag him out of his bed.'

'What happens when he's missed?' asked Jim, 'Won't they come looking for him?'

'He says he told no-one where he was going and slipped out of his billet without anyone seeing him, so they won't notice he's missing right away and when they do, they won't know where to start looking. He's told no-one about Irene.'

'That's good,' said Tom, 'so they might think he's a deserter. Let's hope they're too busy with the Allied advance to worry about another soldier who's disappeared.'

There was a general murmur of agreement.

'Well,' said Bill, 'it looks like we might come out of this much better that we could have hoped.' He stood up stiffly. 'I don't know about the rest of you but I feel exhausted so, if I can borrow a blanket again, Margaret, I'm going to settle down on your sofa for the night.'

Margaret went out of the room to fetch blankets and pillows for both Bill and Tom, since neither could risk walking home after curfew.

Pausing by the door, Bill said quietly, 'We've had a close escape but there's no reason for Tom's plans to be abandoned. However, you might like to give some thought as to what exactly we are going to do with this young man.'

*

The following morning, for the first time since she'd arrived at the farm, Irene didn't have to force herself out of bed. She was already in the kitchen preparing breakfast when Margaret got downstairs.

'Good morning, Irene. Have you looked in on him yet?'
'Yes but he's still sleeping,' replied Irene.
'Don't go waking him too early. He needs to rest,'

warned Aunt Margaret.

Irene was heating a kind of potato porridge on the stove. It tasted quite awful but it filled the stomach. She would boil Gunther an egg to go with it. While the porridge was simmering, Irene laid a breakfast tray, taking a white linen tray-cloth from the dresser.

'Good heavens, Irene! This is not a hotel,' snapped Aunt Margaret.

'I just thought…'stammered Irene.

'It's a bit late for that. You should have thought before you got involved with that young man in the first place. Have you any idea of the danger we're all in now?'

Irene felt as though she had been slapped in the face. She hadn't known Aunt Margaret speak so harshly before.

'I'm sure Gunther won't say anything, Aunt Margaret. We can trust him.'

'That may be so but what is Gunther going to do when he's well enough to get out of bed? Will he stroll back in saying he felt like taking a few days leave to visit his girlfriend? How is he going to account for his absence?'

'I don't know,' murmured Irene.

'Well he'd better start thinking up a good story.'

'Do you think we could keep him here?'

'I don't know yet. It's very difficult to know what is going to be the safest thing to do. The men discussed it a little last night but decided to sleep on it.' Margaret walked towards the door to go out into the yard, adding, 'Don't forget, Irene, they were all set to finish him off last night before they realised who he was.'

Irene returned to the stove to stir the porridge, chilled by her aunt's words. If they wouldn't agree to let him stay, she would have to find a way of hiding him herself, though heaven knows how she would go about it.

Irene waited about half an hour before taking the tray up to Gunther. He was still asleep when she entered the room but woke quickly when she spoke his name. She sat down on the side of the bed.

'How are you feeling?'

'A bit dizzy, I think. And I have a bad pain in my head,' Gunther replied.

'Well, it could have been worse,' said Irene, thinking she might one day tell him how much worse it would have been if Bill hadn't recognised him. She helped him sit up, which made him wince and gave him his breakfast, saying she'd check his wound when he'd eaten.

'I'm sorry for all this trouble, Irene. I just wanted to see you. It has been so long and I thought, now that the war is nearly over for us Germans, I must speak to you to make our plans. Also they were talking about taking my unit off the island next week, so I had to come now.'

Gunther paused to finish off his porridge hungrily and took a sip from the mug of home-made coffee Irene had brought.

'This is good. Thank you. Already I am feeling better.'

He smiled and Irene smiled back sadly, pushing the hard-boiled egg towards him.

'There's a little bit of salt to go with that but no bread until later I'm afraid.'

'I haven't had an egg for weeks. This is wonderful.'

He did look thinner than when she had last seen him and his face was badly bruised from his fall on the hard workshop floor. She traced the hollow of his cheek with one finger.

'You look terrible,' she smiled, 'but I'll soon have you looking handsome again.'

'But I can't stay here. It's too dangerous for you all.'

'You can't go anywhere at the moment. You're not well enough.'

'I must go,' he declared, 'look, I am all right now.' Flinging back the blanket, he tried to swing his legs out of bed but soon discovered movement was out of the question. Everything in the room was spinning. Clutching his head and moaning, he sank back on to the pillow.

'Oh,' he groaned, 'I feel terrible.'

'I did warn you.'

Irene carried the tray away, putting it down on a chest of drawers. She returned to the bed and asked Gunther to roll over so that she could check his head wound. When she had finished, she smoothed his pillows and settled him down again.

'The gash in your head is looking all right. It should really have been stitched but it's holding together at the moment, so don't go exerting yourself. You might make it open up again,' she added sternly.

'Ok, nurse! I will do as I am told,' Gunther replied, with closed eyes. Irene smiled and sat quietly beside him on the bed, thinking.

'Gunther?' she said tentatively, after several minutes silence. He grunted but didn't open his eyes.

'Gunther,' she repeated, 'do you remember what you saw in the workshop?'

Gunther opened his eyes and frowned as he cast his mind back.

'Um, no, I don't. I remember creeping around in the darkness. I was hoping you might come out of the house to see to the chickens or something like that. I waited for quite a long time but nothing happened. Then I saw two men come from behind the barn and go into the house. When they were inside, I crept around to see where they had come from and I could see light coming from a shed.' He paused, thinking. 'I suppose I must have gone to take a look inside, but I really can't remember. The last thing I can remember seeing is the light shining through the door.'

He closed his eyes again.

'I would like to sleep now, Irene.'

'That's good, Gunther. You go to sleep now. I won't be far away.'

Irene kissed him gently on the forehead. There was no response. He was already asleep. She sat on beside him for a while, holding his hand, until she heard her aunt call her name from downstairs. Then, picking up the tray, she left the room, closing the door silently behind her.

*

That same evening, the family reassembled in the farmhouse kitchen to decide on a course of action. Bill had been home during the day to tell Izette what had happened and had then brought her back to the farm with him. After supper, they all gathered round the kitchen table; Bill, Irene, Izette and Edmund, Jim and Margaret, and Tom. Bill started the discussion.

'Right, we all know what needs to be decided tonight. The only person involved who is not here at the table to speak for himself is Gunther. That doesn't mean that we won't be taking his views into account but our first priority must be the safety of everyone here and our families. We have to decide what we are going to do about Gunther and how that might affect Tom's plan to escape to France.'

Bill paused and looked at the familiar faces around the table. No-one appeared to have anything to add at this point so he continued.

'So, the first decision to be made is whether he goes

back to his unit when he's well enough or not?'

'I don't see how he can,' started Tom, 'how is he going to explain his absence convincingly? They'll investigate whatever story he comes up with. They're also bound to notice his head injury. And if he did get away with it somehow, can we trust him not to say anything?'

'Of course we can trust him,' interrupted Irene indignantly.

'No need to get uppity, Irene,' said Bill, 'you might think you know Gunther well but the rest of us don't. He's a stranger to us and he's a German. We have to be sensible about this.'

'Well Gunther doesn't want to go back to his unit,' said Irene. 'He can't think of any explanation his captain would accept. He says they'd most likely assume he was trying to desert but had to go back when he couldn't find anywhere to hide.'

'So what would happen to him if he did go back?' asked Aunt Margaret.

'Court martial and execution probably,' replied Tom briefly.

'What? Even at this late stage of the war?'

'Yes,' confirmed Tom. 'The Germans are very strict on military discipline, especially now the troops are so disillusioned. They don't want another mutiny.'

'That's what Gunther said too,' agreed Irene. 'He said they're so twitchy at the moment they seize on any opportunity to enforce discipline.'

There was silence around the table as this information was considered. Then Jim cleared his throat and spoke up.

'Here's my two-penny-worth. It strikes me that if we do send him back against his will, his most convincing story, one that could save his own skin, would be to claim that we'd knocked him on the head when we caught him snooping round, then held him here but he managed to escape. He's got the head injury as proof. To protect Irene, he could simply say he'd never seen her.'

Irene looked angrily at her uncle. 'Gunther would never do that. He'd know there would be reprisals against us.'

'Be realistic, Irene,' Jim said. 'If you had to choose between almost certain execution and turning in a few Islanders, what would you do? Anyway, it's the truth, isn't it?'

There were murmurs of agreement.

'So that would seem to confirm that he can't go back. Whether we trust Gunther or not, it's just too risky. Are we all decided then?' asked Bill.

When no objections were raised, Bill placed the next decision in front of them.

'So what are we going to do with him?'

At that moment, they heard a sound from the stairs and turned to see Gunther stagger into the room, holding on to the doorframe for support. Irene and Izette immediately hurried over to help him. While Irene scolded him for getting out of bed, they half carried him to the armchair and lowered him into it. It was the first opportunity Bill had had to look at him closely. He'd lost a good deal of weight since Bill last saw him. Jim's old pyjamas hung loosely on him and every part of the lad's body looked thin and scrawny. The white bandage around his head contrasted sharply with the bruised, grey skin of his face.

When Gunther spoke his voice was a little breathless but his words were determined.

'Thank you, all of you. I was listening on the stairs. What you have done for me is dangerous for you. I understand your fears but I tell you that, even if you turn me out of your house, I will not return to my unit. I am finished with all that now. I am no longer a soldier. I take no more orders from the Fuehrer. I am a free man. I will die rather than go back.'

'Well, young man,' said Bill, 'you don't know how close you came to that.'

The others smiled and nodded at Bill's comment, relieved they had been spared that ordeal.

Bill continued, 'I suppose we must take what you say on trust, just as you have to trust us. You overheard what Jim suggested your story might be to your officers but we could just as easily say you came to us as a deserter, begging for shelter.'

'Indeed so,' agreed Gunther amiably.

'So, since you're obviously not going back, we'll have to decide whether we can hide you here or perhaps find a safe house for you on the island. Either option is dangerous. They'll be looking for you, though Irene tells us they won't know where to start since you said nothing to anyone when you left. But, if you are found, here or elsewhere, you're not the only one who'll be in trouble. There is another option. When you're stronger we could simply give you some clothes and food, wish you luck and show you the door.'

Irene opened her mouth to object but Bill raised his hand to silence her.

'Let's hear what Gunther has to say, Irene.'

'You are a good man, Mr Vaubert. This...' – Gunther used his hands to include everyone in the room – '...is a good and courageous family. You have been more than kind to me and now I tell you that as soon as I am well again, I will go. I will not put you in any more danger. I will be grateful for the clothes and food but I am happy to take my chances out there.'

'But Gunther,' said Irene anxiously, 'if you are caught you will be shot.'

Gunther shrugged his shoulders. 'Then I will have to

be very careful not to get caught.'

Irene stood up from her place at the table in frustration, looking at each one of her family in turn, horrified that no-one else seemed to object to him going.

'You can't let him do this!' she said. 'How is he going to survive?'

No-one answered her. Edmund shuffled on his seat then piped up.

'There are a lot of empty houses. I could show…'

'Shut up, Edmund!' said Irene.

'Only trying to be helpful,' he muttered.

Tom had been studying Gunther thoughtfully during the discussion. Now he spoke up.

'He could come with me.'

Everyone turned to look at Tom in surprise.

'Where are you going?' asked Gunther.

'To France,' replied Tom, 'like to come along?'

Gunther looked baffled for a moment then, as he realised what Tom was saying, his face broke into a big smile.

'I would be delighted to accompany you.'

CHAPTER 19

A couple of days after Gunther's unexpected arrival, when the family was seated around the kitchen table at midday, Edmund hurried in from outside, breathless and looking worried.

'I think we've got trouble,' he announced.

Everyone looked up anxiously and Tom half rose to go outside to check what was happening.

Edmund held a hand up to stop him. 'No, there's nothing happening here, not yet,' he paused to catch his breath, 'but I've just come back along the lane and there's a party of Jerries being marched up this way. There's about 20 of them.'

'How far away are they?' asked Tom.

'Down at the turning to the old mill. I ran back as soon as I saw them. They won't be here for ten minutes or so.'

'Right,' said Tom. 'Irene and Izette, go up to Gunther and hide him somehow. Make sure his uniform is out of sight.

Jim, you hang about the yard, look as though you're working. You, Edmund, go upstairs and watch the yard from the landing window. If you see them come towards the house to search it, warn Irene and Izette to be ready. I'll see to the boat.'

Tom and Jim hurried outside and the others disappeared upstairs, leaving Margaret alone in the kitchen. Tom ran to the workshop. Fortunately, they'd made a point of removing the outboard from the boat and storing it out of sight every time they finished working on it and Tom's other items of equipment were kept hidden, so all Jerry would find if they searched the outbuildings would be the boat itself. Tom scanned the workshop quickly in case they'd overlooked anything. Picking up a handful of dust from the floor, he scattered it over the tarpaulin covering the boat. Since he couldn't hope to hide the boat, it might give the impression it had been standing there untouched for some time. Satisfied, he shut the door to the workshop and joined Jim who was squatting down beside the old baling machine in the yard.

Upstairs in the house, Irene and Izette hurried in to Gunther's attic bedroom and hustled him out of bed. Irene told him to get under the bed while she herself stripped off her outer clothes.

'This room looks like a sick room,' she said to Izette, pointing at the bedside tray bearing a bowl and antiseptic, and the towels draped over the end of the bed, 'so, if they come upstairs, I'll be the one who's sick and you can be looking after me.' Stripped down to her underslip, she climbed into the bed while Izette made sure the bedcovers overhung sufficiently to conceal Gunther underneath.

'What's wrong with you, if they ask?'

'I don't know! It had better be something horribly infectious. What do you think?'

The girls pondered a moment then Irene said, 'no, on

second thoughts, pass me that spare pillow.' Izette handed her the pillow, which Irene stuffed under the blankets. 'I'll just draw up my knees. There, I'm in the middle of having a baby! That should frighten them off if they come in here.'

This provoked a muffled exclamation from beneath the bed. Izette would have laughed if she hadn't been so terrified.

In the yard, Tom and Jim waited tensely by the machine. Jim had a screwdriver ready. Tom held a hammer. His palms were sweating. Neither man spoke. Within a few minutes they heard the rhythmic crunch of boots on gravel and turned to look in the direction of the gate. The soldiers were brought to a halt outside the yard and the commanding officer walked forward alone. Tom and Jim straightened up as he approached them, drawing some papers out of his pocket. Reaching them, the officer wished them a good day and introduced himself, then asked to see their identification cards. Tom and Jim handed them over. After inspecting and returning them, he turned his attention to the papers he carried.

'Under the present emergency, you may be aware that it has been necessary to increase the number of coastal patrols to safeguard the island from enemy attack.' Here he smiled briefly. 'I refer, of course, to enemies of the Third Reich.'

Tom and Jim nodded to confirm their understanding.

'This property includes an area of coastline. As you know, two of the larger beaches are already mined. There are, however, other areas that are not protected from approach from the sea. I have orders to inspect these areas and station patrols if I think it necessary. My men and I will commence the inspection now. I'm sure I don't need to remind you that it is an offence to obstruct these men from carrying out their duties.'

Bowing smartly, the officer turned and walked back to the waiting men. After a brief discussion, the men split up into two groups, each of which marched through the farmyard and on to the lane leading to the fields bounding the coast. Once they were out of sight, Jim and Tom returned to the house where Margaret was waiting for them. Tom went straight upstairs. As he burst into the attic bedroom, both Irene and Izette stared at him with terrified faces.

'It's all right,' Tom said immediately to reassure them, 'they won't be coming inside the house.'

Irene flopped back on the pillow, her eyes closed in relief. Izette crumpled where she stood. Tom moved quickly to catch her.

'Sorry, my legs are suddenly like jelly.'

He helped her sit down on the edge of the bed. She leaned forward, head close to her knees as though she might faint. Tom held her firmly in case she toppled and after a minute or so she straightened up.

'Gosh, I'm not much use, am I?' she said, trying to laugh it off. 'I was never very good at amateur dramatics either. I couldn't act to save my life.' Her face fell as she realised what she'd said.

'Oh, I think you could,' said Tom, 'but let's hope we don't have to put it to the test, eh?'

'But I was so terrified, Tom.'

'Don't worry about it. It's the first time you've been that close to a dangerous situation, that's all. You'll find it easier the next time.'

'The next time?' she exclaimed in horror.

Tom grinned at her in what she considered was a most unsympathetic way.

'Whatever happened to that fearless little girl I used to know who dared me to swing across the river on a rotten piece of old rope she'd found and when I refused, because I was in my Sunday clothes and I knew my mother would kill me if I got dirty, proceeded to show me how to do it herself?'

'That was different,' Izette argued, but smiled all the same.

'Is it? I seem to remember you couldn't swim then.'

'Ah, but I knew you would rescue me if I fell in.'

'Well, that was a lot of faith to place in a young lad, Izette, but if you could do it then, do it again now.'

She looked at him quizzically. He smiled at her and placing a finger under her chin, gave her a quick kiss on the lips.

'Come on, let's help poor Gunther out from under the bed!'

*

Initially, the relief that no searches had been carried out produced a false sense of security. But later that day, as they watched the soldiers reassemble in the farmyard before being marched back to their barracks, the implications of the German presence on the farm began to worry everyone. On his return that evening, Bill was very concerned when he heard what had happened and called everyone together to discuss what they should do.

'Well Tom,' started Bill, 'this turn of events could put paid to your escape plan altogether. For a start, I don't see how we're going to get the boat down to the cove without being seen.'

'I don't think we should be too hasty, Bill,' replied Tom. 'Let's see exactly what Jerry proposes to do in terms of extra patrols first. Edmund is going to watch them for the next few days to see what their routine is going to be. Once we know where they're going to station men, and the times of the patrols, we can work out whether we can still get away with it.'

'I don't want the lad putting himself in any danger,' interrupted Bill.

Edmund wriggled impatiently, 'I can take care of myself, Dad.'

'There's also Gunther to be taken into account,' continued Tom. 'As long as he stays here in the house, he's putting everyone at risk. They haven't come here looking for him yet but there's still a chance that they might. Someone might remember seeing him with Irene and put two and two together. If they think he's deserted, she's the obvious one he would run to and it wouldn't take them long to trace her here.'

Gunther was sitting next to Irene, looking distressed by what Tom had just said. Noticing his discomfort, Tom added, 'In another sense though, Gunther's appearance is a blessing in disguise for me. I haven't mentioned it before but I have to admit I was very worried about managing the boat by myself. I know there will be plenty of help to get the boat down to the cove and into the water but after that – well, I'm not an experienced sailor. I'm not sure I could have managed the sailing part by myself. We all know how many of the failed escape attempts have ended in someone drowning. As it is, there'll now be two of us to share the rowing and helming and that's a great relief to me.'

Tom knew Bill and Jim had been baffled by his offer to take Gunther along. They probably thought he was taking Gunther simply in order to get him away from the farm and reduce the danger to them all. Well, that was certainly an important factor but they should also have understood that he needed Gunther's help. Tom had talked at length with Gunther that afternoon and decided he liked him. Gunther had courage. If they were caught trying to escape, Tom might get away with deportation to one of the camps but Gunther would certainly be shot. Yet Gunther was still determined to try. For him the war was over, he would take no further part in it. All he wanted to do now was to find a way of surviving until it was all over and he could return to Irene. That was good enough for Tom.

'Well, you've got a point there, Tom,' conceded Bill, 'and there's no-one else who could go with you.'

'That's right,' agreed Tom, 'so the important thing now is speed. As soon as we have enough information about the new patrols here to finalise the details, I think we should make the attempt on the first favourable tide. How do we stand on the tides now, Jim?'

'The tide'll be at its highest in four days. That would make it Friday night but I don't know about the weather forecast.'

'We may not be able to wait for perfect weather. Will you be up to it, Gunther?'

'I make sure I am.'

'And do you think that's enough time for you to work out the patrols, Edmund?'

'It should be but I can't be sure. They might change their minds about something.'

'Right,' said Tom, 'Well, depending on what Edmund finds out, it's Friday.'

*

No-one saw Edmund for the next few days. Every so, often, he returned to the farmhouse to pick up supplies of food, looking as though he'd spent the night in a hedge, which was probably true. Fortunately the nights were mild and it was clear that, despite the seriousness of the situation, he was loving every minute of it. He reported back to Tom each evening, the two of them going into a private huddle that infuriated Izette. Eventually, the evening before the proposed day of the escape, she intercepted Edmund on his way back across the yard from one of his meetings with Tom.

'Edmund, how is it going? Will they be making the attempt tomorrow?'

'Um, not sure yet, Izette. We're going to make a final decision in the morning. There's a complication.'

'What sort of complication?' asked Izette.

'It's to do with the patrols,' Edmund offered unhelpfully.

'What about the patrols?' insisted Izette.

'Look, sis,' said Edmund, 'I'm absolutely starving. Couldn't this wait? I need to get some food.'

'No, it can't,' she said, grabbing his jacket sleeve to stop him pushing past her.

'Go and talk to Tom then. He's still in the barn. He'll explain.'

Izette let go his sleeve and Edmund continued on his way to the kitchen. She went into the barn where she found Tom finishing a cigarette. She sat down casually beside him.

'So,' she said.

'So?'

'Don't be so infuriating, Tom Birrell. You know why I'm here. I want to know what's going on!'

'Oh, and there's me thinking you wanted to be alone with me,' he grinned.

She blushed, which made him laugh out loud.

'Well, that as well, I suppose,' she stammered, 'but what I mean is…'

'Ah, she admits it - but not with much enthusiasm.' He put on a mock hurt expression.

'Be serious, Tom. I want to talk about the escape plan. I want to know if…'

'Well I don't. Not at this moment. I've thought of nothing else for weeks and now I'd like to think about something completely different.'

He stood up and ground the cigarette end out under his foot.

'Come here, Izette.' He pulled her to her feet and into his arms. 'Let's think about us, shall we?'

She was startled for a moment but when he bent to kiss her, her urgent need to know about escape suddenly became unimportant. It was a long kiss, long and fierce and it aroused feelings in her for which she was not prepared. When it was over, she stood stunned in his arms, eyes closed. Tom watched her without a word until she opened her eyes and looked into his. He wasn't joking now. He could see she was his for the taking if that was what he wanted.

He led her away from the door through which the early evening light was spilling to the far end of the barn where the straw was stored and pulled her down into it's prickly softness beside him. It was what he'd wanted to do for so long. Bending over her, he smoothed the hair from her face and brushed some wisps of straw from her neck. Then he kissed her again. This time she responded eagerly, her hands grasping his hair, his neck, his shoulders. He felt her body move against his in a way that made him want to groan aloud. Breaking away from her lips he kissed her face, then her eyes and her neck, inflamed by her gasps of pleasure.

'Oh Izette, I want you so much,' he murmured.

'Don't stop,' she whispered, 'I love you.'

His hand moved to the buttons on her blouse and he unfastened them one by one, pausing to kiss the flesh revealed as each button slipped free. Her skin was pale and smooth. She wore no perfume but she smelled clean and sweet. He licked her skin and tasted the slight saltiness on his tongue. Izette closed her eyes and moved languidly against him. She was wearing a slip and brassiere beneath the blouse. Sliding his hand under the straps, he slipped them down over her shoulder and pulled the fabric down to expose one breast. He paused to look before allowing his hands the exquisite pleasure of cupping the silky softness. The aureole was small and pink, innocent. He stroked it gently, eliciting another gasp from Izette, then lowered his head to take her nipple between his lips.

She arched her back and groaned softly while he played his tongue over her breast. Then, placing her hands on either side of his face, she drew him back to her lips. She kissed him hungrily, moving her lips over his face as though she needed to touch every part of him. Then suddenly she turned her head away from him.

'Izette? My love, what's wrong?'

'Nothing.' She squeezed her eyes tight shut and shook her head.

Tom put his hand on her cheek and turned her face back towards him. There were tears in her eyes and streaming down her face.

'There is. Why are you crying?'

'I don't know...I don't know,' she cried. Then she rolled away from him, curling herself into a foetal position began to sob uncontrollably. He moved close to her, curling his body around hers and stroked her hair gently while she wept.

Eventually she quietened and started fumbling for a handkerchief. Tom already had one ready and handed it to her with a smile. Izette sat up looking terribly woebegone and blew her nose. Tom sat beside her patiently until she'd finished then started refastening the buttons on her blouse.

'I'm sorry, Tom,' she said, 'I don't know what's the matter.'

'It doesn't matter...'

'But I wanted to...you know.'

'I know you did,' laughed Tom, 'and so did I but perhaps it's just as well we didn't.'

He started picking strands of straw from her hair.

'I'm so frightened, Tom.'

'There's no need to be. I know you haven't done this before but...'

'No, not of that! I'm frightened for you. I'm frightened you'll be caught or shot. I'm frightened the boat might capsize and you'll drown. I'm frightened I'll never see you again. You seem to see it as an adventure but all I see is terrible danger.'

Tom sighed and took her hands in his. 'What would you have me do then, Izette? Tell me what it is that you want.'

Izette looked into his face again. What could she say? That what she really wanted was for him to sit quietly at home twiddling his thumbs until peace was declared? That she didn't care if he honoured the debt he felt he owed to the Island or not? That she didn't care what happened to Gunther as long as he left the farm? That, on top of all this, she was terrified her mother was dying and she needed him to be with her?

But what she said was, 'You must do what you think is right, Tom. I won't stand in your way but you'll have to understand if I get upset now and then.'

Tom kissed her lips gently. They were puffy, either from weeping or from arousal. Deliciously soft and moist. Reluctantly, he dragged his lips away and stood up before he could be tempted to continue what they had started. He helped Izette up out of the straw and they spent a few minutes brushing themselves down. Suddenly he laughed out loud.

'We've done this a few times before,' he said.

'What?'

'Had to tidy ourselves up before going home. Don't you remember when we used to play in the woods?'

Of course she did. She remembered always carrying a large hankie so that she could wet it to wash their faces and knees before their mothers saw them.

'Well, you look fine. How about me?' she asked.

He held her at arms length. 'A little pink around the eyes but you'll pass muster.'

'One last kiss?'

'Of course.'

*

No-one paid much attention to them when they strolled back into the kitchen together because Bill and Jim had been hearing from Edmund what he had discovered about the patrols so far and they hadn't liked what they had heard.

While Tom and Izette had been outside, the others had been discussing the situation.

'It doesn't sound too good, Tom.' Bill commented, as soon as they entered. 'Edmund's been telling us there'll be a lot of Germans around on the night. There's too much risk of you being spotted for my liking.'

'That's right but it's not impossible,' replied Tom.

Bill waited for him to go on but Tom seemed to be weighing up an idea. Catching Edmund's eye across the table, Tom raised his eyebrows as though asking a question. Edmund shrugged his shoulders. Tom drew out a chair and sat down.

'There is one idea that Edmund's come up with which might work,' he began.

CHAPTER 20

Izette went to bed at her usual time, around ten o'clock. Despite brushing herself down earlier, she was itchy from the straw. Small fibres must have penetrated her clothing and were irritating her skin. She took a jug of hot water upstairs to her bedroom so that she could wash herself. What she really wanted was a bath but that was out of the question. They had no fuel to spare to heat that amount of water. This would be pleasant though, she told herself. Perhaps she could imagine herself in a relaxing bath if she closed her eyes as she bathed herself limb by limb.

There was an old-fashioned washstand with china bowl in her room. Covering the jug of hot water with a towel to keep it warm, she took off her clothes, shaking them to dislodge any remaining straw fibres. When she was completely naked, she poured the water into the bowl and added rose geranium bath salts. A pleasant summery fragrance spiralled upwards with the steam. She inhaled deeply, dreaming of the future. When the war was over, she would have a bath whenever she felt like it and the water would always be perfumed.

She took a hoarded fragment of lavender soap from her drawer. She'd offered it to Aunt Margaret to help with the weekly washing but she had refused it.

'You hang on to that, my dear. It won't make much difference to the laundry whether it goes in or not but you might like to treat yourself one evening with it.'

This felt like the right evening. Rubbing it carefully between her palms she smoothed the lather over her face and neck, then rinsed it off with clear water from the bowl. Her skin felt wonderfully fresh. She repeated the process with each part of her body, taking her time, indulging herself, patting herself dry lightly. This was not washing; this was bathing, the sort of personal pampering she used to watch Irene enjoy a few years ago, wondering why she was bothering to waste so much time on such a simple task. She smiled to herself, thinking how naïve she was then.

When she had finished, she took a clean nightdress from the drawer. It smelled of cotton soaked in sunshine. She buried her face in it, breathing in the freshness. As she raised her arms to slip it over her head, she changed her mind and instead laid it across the foot of her bed. Pulling back the bedclothes, she got into her bed and lay back slowly against the pillows. She ran her hands down her body experimentally. It was pleasant but not at all like the sensations Tom's hands had aroused. And she remembered the way her body had moved against his, of its own accord. It was as though she had been an onlooker. Her body had moved in a way that was entirely new to her but it had felt right. More than that, it had felt wonderful. She closed her eyes, happily allowing herself to drift through the sensations again.

She must have fallen asleep because when next she opened her eyes, the house was quiet with that intense quietness that only comes when everyone is in bed. She lay waiting for the clock in the hall to chime so that she would know what time it was. There was moonlight filtering through the curtains but it was too dark to see the hands of her alarm clock. Then she jumped as she heard a rattle of stones on her window. Throwing off the bedclothes she hurried to the window and drew back one side of the curtain stealthily. Below her in the moonlight stood Tom. He waved when he saw the curtain twitch and gestured to her to open the window. She pulled on her dressing gown and opened the casement quietly.

'What on earth are you doing, Tom Birrell?' she whispered.

'I couldn't sleep. I realised I'd forgotten to tell you something.'

'Couldn't it have waited until the morning, you idiot? My Dad's asleep downstairs in the parlour.'

'It's all right. I can hear his snores from here.'

Izette giggled. 'What is it then?'

Tom spread his arms wide. 'I love you, Izette. I love you.'

'Shhh,' she warned. 'I love you too.'

Tom clasped his hands to his heart theatrically.

'Now you'd better get inside before anyone hears you,' she whispered.

'What do I care? My love loves me and I love my love.'

A thought occurred to Izette. 'Have you been drinking?

'Just a drop,' Tom replied honestly

'Go to bed, Tom Birrell...now or I shan't speak to you in the morning!'

'Harsh words, my darling, but I will do as I am told...just

this once.'

He blew her a kiss. She watched him as he walked a little unsteadily towards the barn. All the bedrooms were occupied and her father was on the sofa in the parlour so Tom had been consigned to a night in the barn. She returned his wave as he turned the corner out of sight then closed the window and climbed back into her bed.

She lay there smiling, suddenly feeling happier than she could ever remember. It was ridiculous. He would be gone in a few hours. How could she feel so elated? The clock downstairs chimed midnight reminding her that she needed to be up before seven. She closed her eyes and willed herself to go to sleep.

*

The clock chimed one o'clock then two o'clock and still Izette lay awake. Eventually, she got out of bed and walked over to the window, drawing back the curtains to look at the moon. It was cool and she wrapped her arms around herself, covering her breasts. It was then that she saw him come round the corner, walking towards the farmhouse. He glanced up at her window but gave no sign that he had seen her though he must have done. Izette shivered and crept back into her bed. Had she known he would come?

She didn't hear him come up the stairs but she knew it was him when the door opened. She saw him as a dark shadow against the wall as he closed the door silently. He must have removed his shoes because the next moment he was by the bed and she hadn't heard a sound. He placed a finger on her lips and kissed her forehead gently then withdrew, and she guessed that he was removing his clothes. Her heart beat faster and her lips felt dry. He hadn't said a word yet.

Tom slipped into the bed beside her and it was as though she received an electric shock. To feel his skin touching hers set her nerve ends tingling. His skin was cold in parts, warm in others. She tentatively touched his chest with her fingers and his hand folded around hers. He lifted her hand to his mouth and kissed her fingertips one by one, then ran his tongue down the inside of her palm. She drew in her breath sharply.

'Izette?' he murmured. 'Can I stay?'

'How can you ask that? Can't you tell?'

She spoke sluggishly as though she was in a dream, or drugged, which in a sense, she was. Her consciousness extended to their two bodies, no further. The room, the house around them had ceased to exist. All that mattered to her was the touch of his skin.

Pulling her nearer, he kissed her lips and she began to tremble. Putting her hands on his shoulders she felt the tension in his muscles. One of his legs lay heavily across her, between her legs, pressing against her. She couldn't remember parting her legs, nor did she care. She wanted him with a desire that frightened her.

Shifting his weight, Tom began to stroke her breasts, then she felt him kiss them and tease her nipples between his teeth as he had done earlier. She pressed the back of her hand to her mouth knowing she mustn't make a sound but gasped when he nipped a little too hard, startled by the shock this generated between her legs. She writhed against him and he responded by pressing himself more heavily against her. He was breathing faster now, whispering her name in between the kisses he planted all over her body. Izette urged him on, knowing he could satisfy the urgent need growing in her body.

In the midst of it all he paused. Lifting himself away from her he threw the bedclothes off the bed, then kneeled above her. She could see him vaguely in the faint light from the window. He was looking down at her, her own body faintly discernible, a series of pale mounds and shadowy troughs. Taking her hand, he placed it on himself, closing her fingers around his penis. Then, easing himself down again beside her, he slipped his hand over her stomach and between her legs. The exquisite thrill of his touch brought a moan to her lips that he stifled with a kiss. His fingers caressed and explored her tenderly and she found herself echoing his movements with her own hand. The firmness of it surprised and excited her and she was pleased when his hips started to move in time with her strokes. But as her own excitement grew her whole mind was brought to focus on that one part of her body where the intense feeling was centred and her hand fell away from him to grasp at his arm, to pull him towards herself. Tom could hear her breathing coming in rapid pants. He lifted himself on to her, resting his weight on his knees between her legs, hardly able to restrain himself.

'You mustn't cry out, my love,' he whispered into her hair, then eased himself into her as gently as he could. He felt her resist a moment and placed his hand over her mouth.

'Don't struggle. Just relax.'

Then he was inside and the compulsive rhythm started. He moved his hand from Izette's mouth and she took a great gulp of air as though she was drowning. Her legs were shaking but after a few moments he felt her relax and her hips begin to move in time with his, meeting his urgency. Her breath came in shorter and shorter gasps and she released her hold on his shoulders to fling her arms above her head. He held himself back until she arched violently against him, bracing herself against the bed head, moaning words he was beyond hearing into his ear. Then he let go and allowed the wave of sensation to overwhelm him.

When it had passed he rolled on to his side, drawing

her with him, but when he started to withdraw she pressed on his buttocks.

'No. Not yet…not ever,' she whispered.

He nuzzled into her hair. 'All right, if you insist.'

They lay face to face, their lips barely an inch apart, dazed by passion until their bodies separated. Then they moved so that Izette lay in Tom's arms and they were each as comfortable as it was possible to be in Izette's narrow bed.

'I didn't know,' she murmured. 'I had no idea.'

'I didn't hurt you too much?'

'No, only a little…then I forgot about it.'

Izette lay quietly in Tom's embrace, thinking about what had just happened until she realised by his breathing that Tom had fallen asleep. She smiled to herself. All these years, she thought, it's as though I have been waiting for this. I knew that this was how it would be between us in the end. And I know this is not the end. Tomorrow he'll leave me for a while, but he'll be back. I feel it.

Izette fell asleep herself eventually and slept deeply for the few hours that were left before sunrise. When she awoke she was alone in her bed once more.

*

The prospect of joining everyone in the kitchen for breakfast the following morning was daunting. Surely the effect of the night's activities was written plain on her face for all to read? Her changed condition must be obvious. Stepping into the kitchen quietly, Izette kept her eyes away from the table where everyone was already seated.

'About time, Izette,' said her father. 'Hurry up and sit down. We've been waiting for you.'

Izette squeezed herself in next to Aunt Margaret so that

she wouldn't have to look her in the eye. If anyone would be able to tell, it would be Aunt Margaret.

The men were discussing the weather forecast. It wasn't good nor was it particularly bad but it was sufficiently unsettled to make them think about delaying the attempt. Jim was counselling caution, suggesting that timing was not critical and the next favourable tide could as easily coincide with good weather as not, while Tom argued that the chances of good weather then were the same as now, fifty-fifty. September was that kind of month, weather-wise. Izette stole a cautious glance at Tom, not wanting to meet his eye. She needn't have worried. He was fired up, ready to go, his attention totally focussed on the matter they were discussing. He probably hadn't even noticed her come into the room.

'Well I'm willing to give it a go tonight,' he was saying. 'a strong wind would be to our advantage wouldn't it, Jim?'

'It'll be blowing the right way certainly but you don't want to have to tackle a big sea. The boat's too small to handle that safely.'

'How do you feel about it, Gunther?' asked Bill. Gunther was surprised to be consulted and took a moment to answer.

'I will accept Tom's decision...and I believe the sooner I am gone, the safer you will all be.'

'But it won't help anyone if the boat capsizes,' joined in Irene, 'if the two of you are caught together...or worse...I wish you would be more patient.'

Gunther squeezed Irene's hand. 'For you, the conditions will never be favourable enough for us to sail. I am sorry, Irene, but I must go with Tom when he decides.'

Edmund reported what he had found out about the timings of the patrols. He had discovered that the patrol stationed nearest to the cove, from which they hoped to launch the boat, was relieved at midnight. Since the Germans were now very short of fuel, the relief guards came up on foot from St Helier, arriving at the farm shortly before midnight. They then split up into smaller groups and continued to the various patrol points. By about 12:30, the off-duty Germans had usually reassembled just outside the farmyard for their return march.

'We will need to count them in because they come in from different points and the unit is so keen to get back they don't always wait for the stragglers. They have to catch up as best they can. There's no officer with them, you see,' explained Edmund. 'There are 18 Jerries in all. Once we've counted the 18 and seen them all go off down the lane, we can move the boat.'

'Good work, Edmund,' said Tom. 'So, as soon as Jerry is well out of sight and earshot, Bill, Jim, Gunther and I will get the boat and equipment down to the cove. I estimate that will take us at least an hour. Meanwhile, Edmund and Izette will be setting off to the old mill to carry out their part of the plan.'

For the first time that morning Tom turned to look at Izette. He smiled at her quite innocently but she flushed a bright pink. Bill noticed her colour with alarm. Misunderstanding it as a sign of anxiety he said, 'Now look here, Izette, you don't have to do this. You know my feelings on the matter. I'm not at all happy about it. I said Jim or I could go with Edmund but you insisted you wanted to play your part. Are you having second thoughts?'

'No Dad,' Izette stammered, 'I'll go with Edmund. I'm just…excited, I expect.'

Tom kept his eyes on the table, his face expressionless, not daring to look at her again.

'How about putting the kettle on, Izette,' he said, 'we'll need another drink when we're through.'

Seizing the lifeline, Izette rose from the table with relief. The discussion continued. She listened with half an ear as she filled the kettle and put it on the stove, then washed and dried the dishes in the sink.

Eventually it was agreed that Tom and Gunther would make the attempt that night. Although she had dreaded the moment of Tom's departure arriving, it was also a kind of relief to have the uncertainty end. Since he had first told her his plans, a black cloud of suspense had hung over her. Now the moment had actually arrived, she could no longer pretend it might never happen. The decision was made and now she had to concentrate on carrying out her part of the plan as effectively as she could.

*

By nine o'clock, it was dark and Edmund and Izette had assembled everything they needed in the barn. Tom made a final check of the contents of their rucksacks against Edmund's list. Edmund and Izette wore dark clothing and soft-soled shoes. Bill and Jim watched grim-faced as the final preparations were carried out.

'Now,' said Tom, 'you've plenty of time to put them in position, so take it slowly and carefully. We don't want any accidents.'

Tom then lifted the heavier of the rucksacks on to Edmund's shoulders. It contained a defused German anti-tank mine. The lighter rucksack contained four defused anti-personnel mines, a coil of wire, a torch and some tools. Izette lifted the lighter one herself and slipped the straps over her shoulders.

'Don't worry,' grinned Edmund, 'I've practiced this dozens of times.'

'Don't you be getting overconfident, my lad,' rumbled

Bill. Then he put his arms around Edmund and hugged him. 'Take care, lad. You're the only son and heir, you know.'

'I'll be fine, Dad.'

Turning to Izette, Bill repeated his embrace.

'The same goes for you, Izette. Don't take any risks.'

Tom checked his watch.

'Right. Nine-fifteen. You'd better be on your way. If you're not back here by eleven, we'll come down to see what the problem is. All right?'

Edmund and Izette both nodded. Tom's eyes met Izette's for a moment and he winked. Returning a brief smile, she turned to follow Edmund out of the barn. The men accompanied them as far as the gate out of the farmyard, then waited there until they could no longer see their shadowy figures.

'I think I'll go back inside now, Bill,' said Jim, 'are you coming in?'

'No, I'll stay here. I'd rather wait until they're back safely.'

Tom hurried off to check everything was in order in the boat, even though he'd already checked it twice earlier in the day. Jim returned to the farmhouse. Bill made himself comfortable on the stone wall by the gate and settled down to wait. He hadn't told Betty anything about the escape attempt. No point in her worrying. If all went well, he'd tell her afterwards, perhaps when she was feeling a bit better. If not, well…no point in thinking along those lines.

Edmund and Izette hurried down the lane towards the old mill as quietly as possible. Edmund's rucksack dug into his shoulders. He was glad he wouldn't be carrying it very far. The anti-personnel mines were a fraction of the weight of this one. The fuses were separately packed for safety in the outer pocket of Izette's rucksack. He and Izette had practiced and timed the assembly several times and he had already selected and prepared positions in the mill, so he was confident they could do it and get back easily by eleven o'clock, as long as nothing untoward happened.

The track leading to the old mill lay about half a mile down the lane. There was little of the old mill left standing, just a few crumbling stone walls, but the ruin stood immediately above a German anti-aircraft gun emplacement. The plan was to detonate the mines in the old mill when Tom was ready to launch the boat, drawing the attention of the German patrols in the area away from the cove. Hopefully they would assume the explosions were coming from the gun emplacement.

They reached the mill without meeting anyone. Fortunately, the ruin was heavily overgrown and provided them with plenty of cover but they had to move quietly because they were now very close to the gun emplacement. They took off the rucksacks, then, on Edmund's signal, Izette crawled on hands and knees to a position from which she had a clear view of the emplacement. She signalled back to Edmund that she could see four Germans, then gave him a thumbs-up sign to indicate that there was no activity to worry about.

Edmund quickly placed the mines in the pre-selected positions and laid a length of wire between them. That was the easy part. Then he returned to the rucksacks to take out the fuses and additional clips and wire to connect the mines together. His fingers were shaking as he undid the buckles on the rucksack. Taking out the fuses, he laid one by each mine, ready to be fitted. He glanced back at Izette and gave a low whistle. He needed her help for the next part.

Izette crawled back to where Edmund was waiting.
'All right?' she whispered.
'Yes, I'm ready to connect now.'
'Right, I'll get the tools.'

While she was doing this, Edmund wiped his palms on his trousers to remove the sweat. In less than a minute, she was back at his side with a torch, pliers and a screwdriver. When he didn't take them immediately she shone the torch on his face. His skin was pallid and sweaty and for the first time she saw fright in his eyes. She groped for his hand and found it.

'Take a deep breath, hold it, then let it out slowly,' she ordered.

He complied. She made him do it twice more.

'Better?'

Edmund nodded.

'Come on then, Edmund. You know you can do this. Dad will be so proud of you.'

Edmund moved towards the first mine. As they had practiced, Izette shone the torch on the mine and passed him the tools and clips as he asked for them. In five minutes, the mine was armed and connected to the main wire. Edmund sat back on his heels and wiped the sweat from his face, releasing a long breath.

'Well done,' said Izette, 'one down, four more to go.'

They repeated the process, one by one, until all the mines were armed. In the reflected light from the torch, Izette watched her brother as he worked, a small frown creasing his forehead. Sweat continued to bead his forehead but his hands were steady now and every movement was confident.

'That's it,' he said with relief, when the last mine was connected. Standing up in the shelter of the ruin, Edmund stretched his cramped legs. 'Now it's the detonation cable.'

Izette returned to the rucksacks and took out a long coil of cable, giving it to Edmund.

'Check the gun emplacement again, Izette, while I connect this.'

Nothing had changed since she had last looked. By the time she returned, Edmund had completed the connection. Now they had to run the length of cable through the undergrowth for about 200 yards. First, they each strapped on one of the rucksacks again, making sure they had left nothing on the ground. It had been decided that they would run the cable in the opposite direction to the farm so that, when the Germans found it, as they almost certainly would, they wouldn't automatically associate the explosions with the farm. Unfortunately, this involved laying the cable very close to the gun emplacement but there was no alternative.

Edmund led the way, crawling backwards on his hands and knees, slowly uncoiling the cable while Izette followed, untangling it where it became caught up in the undergrowth, pushing it down to ground level and drawing grass and leaves over the top to conceal it. As they approached the emplacement, they had to work in complete silence. They were so close they could hear the murmur of conversation from the soldiers. The trickiest part would be taking the cable across the dusty access track to the emplacement. They would need to excavate a narrow trench across the track in which to bury the cable.

When they reached the track, Edmund and Izette lay flat on their bellies in the undergrowth, watching for any sign of movement from the guards. Apart from the sound of conversation, all was quiet. Izette passed a half-inch chisel to Edmund who, from his prone position, began to gouge out a narrow trench in the sandy surface. It was not an ideal position from which to work and Edmund had to stop to rest his arm several times. When the trench reached halfway across the track, he dropped the cable into it and covered it over with sand, throwing the rest of the coil to the far side of the track.

'Ready?' he whispered to Izette.

She nodded and prepared herself to get up. As she

started to rise, Edmund suddenly grabbed her arm and pulled her down again. One of the guards had stood up and was walking down the track towards them. They wriggled backwards into the undergrowth and flattened themselves to the ground, watching him approach. He stopped a few yards from where they lay. If the guard looked along the track he might see the coiled loops of cable. He might even trip over it if he walked a few steps further. Then the guard stepped off the track to one side and, after a second or two, they heard the sound of trickling water. Turning to face Izette, who lay a few inches away, Edmund held his crossed fingers between their faces. She nodded. They lay there for what seemed like ages until the guard had re-buttoned his trousers, turned and walked back to the others.

'Phew, that was close,' breathed Edmund. 'Come on, let's get across the track.'

Keeping a cautious eye on the soldiers, Edmund and Izette crept across the track and resumed their prone position on the opposite side so that Edmund could dig out the second half of the trench. It didn't take him long. Once the cable was buried in the track, they continued laying the rest of it through the undergrowth.

'Right, that's it,' said Edmund; 'I just have to connect the detonator now.'

Izette held the torch again while he made the final connection. She checked her watch in the torchlight: it was twenty-five past ten. Edmund dragged long grass round the detonator to conceal it, then sat back on his heels. He handed the tools back to Izette who replaced them in the rucksack.

'All done. Let's go.'

They were quickly back on the lane and made good time to the farmhouse, hurrying into the yard at ten thirty-five. Izette saw the glow of her father's pipe in the darkness beside the gate before his big shadow lumbered towards them, chuckling and seizing them both.

'Eeh, that was the longest hour-and-a-half of my life! Thank God you're both all right.'

He led them towards the house.

'Any problems?'

'No,' replied Edmund airily, 'it all went like a dream.'

Izette raised her eyebrows. She wouldn't have put it quite so positively but she kept her thoughts to herself. Let Edmund bask in his moment of glory. He certainly deserved it.

As they entered the kitchen, the expression on their faces immediately told the others what they had been anxiously waiting for and, within minutes, Aunt Margaret had poured scalding water on some preciously conserved tea to celebrate.

When the tea had been drunk and a full account of the mine-laying exercise had been given, Tom stood up from the table.

'Well,' said Tom, 'there's two hours to kill before the next stage, so if anyone thinks they might be able to snatch a bit of sleep, do it now.'

CHAPTER 21

Although Tom's suggestion that they try to get a little sleep was sensible and practical, no-one felt able to take him up on it. Jim wanted to go over the course they had to steer one more time with Tom and Gunther to make sure they understood it fully and would know what to do if they found themselves off-course. The chart was laid out on the kitchen table. On it, Jim had marked their course in black indelible ink and was pointing along the line with his finger.

'So, for the first hour and half, you row due east, zero-nine-zero on the compass. The tide will be coming up to high water and the current will be pushing you north, so you'll actually be travelling north-east.' Jim straightened up. 'All right so far?'

Tom and Gunther nodded. They knew the course off by heart in theory. In practice they knew it would not be so easy.

'When you look back at the island, it will look as though you haven't come very far but don't worry. At three o'clock you can start the engine. Then you motor for about another one-and-a-half hours, still steering due east. The further you get from the island, the stronger the current will become and it'll be pushing you north at about eight knots, so you'll be making good speed. Around four-thirty you need to keep your eyes peeled for the Ecrehous rocks coming up on your port bow.' Jim stabbed his finger at the rock symbol on the chart. 'Once you spot them, get in as close as you safely can and drop the warp anchor. That's the halfway point. Rest up there while you wait for the tide to turn again, otherwise it'll be pushing you backwards faster than you're moving forward.'

Jim paused. He was not happy about the weather. The wind was a little too strong at the moment for the little boat but he knew he wouldn't be able to persuade them to delay. They would just have to pray the wind dropped at the night wore on.

He continued. 'Now the final stage. The sun rises at about half-past six. I suggest you wait until at least ten o'clock before setting off again. Then steer due east again and the tide should help you towards the French coast. If all goes well, you'll reach the coast in three to four hours.'

'Right, thank you, Jim,' Tom said, folding up the chart and placing it in the oilskin bag. 'Don't worry. We'll remember the course. It's down to good luck and good weather now.'

Jim's face was solemn. The weather had put paid to many previous escape attempts, sometimes with tragic result.

'Why not take two bailers instead of one,' suggested Jim, 'I know where there's another. The water's going to be a bit choppy until this wind drops.'

Jim went off to find the second bailer. Tom gathered up the items on the table to take them out to the workshop. When he went outside, Izette followed him. Tom paused to wait for her and they walked side by side across the yard.

'No second thoughts?' asked Izette.

Tom smiled at her. 'No, sorry, Izette. I'm really going but thanks for trying. How about you? Any second thoughts?'

'About what?'

'About last night.'

Izette looked round to make sure they were alone. 'None…except I keep feeling everyone knows, that it shows somehow.'

Tom laughed. They went into the workshop and Tom struck a match and lit the oil-lamp. By its soft light he stowed the oilskin in the boat then took Izette in his arms.

'Quick, before anyone comes,' he murmured, 'we may not get another chance.'

They kissed and held each other tightly, all the time listening for the sound of approaching footsteps. She wished he didn't have to do this. She wished he could be content to wait just a little longer.

'Will you wait for me, Izette?' he asked. 'I'll be back, you know, as soon as I can.'

'I've been waiting for you, Tom Birrell, since I was 12-years old!'

'No, I'm not joking now, Izette.'

'Neither am I. I've been waiting for you to come to your senses about me for the last six years.'

Tom looked at her in disbelief.

'What? You mean…'

'Yes,' continued Izette, 'and you had no idea how I felt about you. I was just your kid sister's friend, the girl next door, your playmate.'

'Well yes,' agreed Tom, 'you'd been there all my life. I suppose I didn't realise until now how important you were to me…are to me.'

He held her close, kissing her hair. They heard the kitchen door open and close. Izette lifted her face to his for a last kiss.

'I'll be here waiting for you, Tom.'

The next hour passed very quickly. Tom and Gunther changed into warm, dark-coloured clothing, including a knitted woollen hat each that Aunt Margaret had quickly run up for them. She had also packed some food into a tin box and filled an old lemonade bottle with tea. 'It'll be cold by the time you drink it but I think you'll be glad of it.'

The boat was ready to be moved, mounted on a trolley Jim had assembled. All the essential items of equipment were carefully stowed inside. All they had to wait for now was the German guards to be changed over at midnight. Edmund volunteered to wait outside to count the Germans through.

'I'll keep you company, lad,' offered Bill, and the two of them slipped quietly out into the darkness.

Once they had gone out, conversation in the kitchen ceased. The steady tick of the kitchen clock counted down the remaining seconds.

Outside, Bill and Edmund hid themselves in the corner of the yard that offered a clear view of the gate and lane beyond. It was five minutes to midnight. Almost at once, they heard the sound of the Germans approaching. At the gate, the soldiers split up to continue to their posts. There was a little conversation but not much. Those coming off duty would be more cheerful than this batch. The soldiers dispersed and silence fell again.

'All present and correct,' commented Edmund.

In about 15 minutes the off-duty soldiers began to drift in. When they reached the gate, they lit up cigarettes and stood around chatting in their greatcoats, waiting for the others.

The rest arrived in twos and threes. One of the guards did a cursory check then crushed out his cigarette and began to move off down the lane, followed by the others.

'I counted all 18. How about you, Dad?'

'Yes, so did I,' confirmed Bill, 'Let's go and give the all clear.'

According to the plan, Bill, Jim, Tom and Gunther would get the boat down to the cove while Edmund and Izette returned to the mill to detonate the mines.

'Right,' said Tom, rising from his seat, 'it's now twelve thirty-five. Edmund will detonate the mines at one-thirty and we'll launch five minutes later.'

Everyone stood. Tom and Gunther made their farewells. When he came to Izette, Tom pressed something small into her hand as he hugged her.

'Take care,' she said.

'I'll be back,' he replied, looking into her eyes, 'that's a promise.'

They filed out of the kitchen, leaving Aunt Margaret and Irene standing forlornly by the stove.

Jim had fitted the boat trolley with four large wheels taken off an old trailer with the result that it ran easily and quietly over the rough ground. Tom and Gunther pulled it from in front with Jim and Bill on either side to lend their weight through any difficult patches. It took them only 15 minutes to drag the boat across the fields to the cliff edge. Once there, they waited a moment, listening for any sound from the German patrol positions.

'All right so far,' whispered Jim, 'now let's get it down the cliff.'

Jim had rigged up a hand-winch on the cliff edge, concealing it amongst bushes. They pulled the boat around in front of it, stern to the cliff edge and secured a rope from the boat trolley to the winch. At a signal from Jim, Tom and Gunther pushed the boat towards the edge until the rope took up the strain and the winch started to turn. Then Tom and Gunther clambered over the edge and began to guide the boat down the steep slope, hanging on to the sides. Bill stood on the edge observing their progress, ready to signal to Jim to stop the winch if necessary.

It was slow going. Tom and Gunther had to guide the trolley around obstacles and found it difficult to keep their footing on the loose ground. Near the bottom, Gunther slipped and his foot went under the trolley. Bill signalled to Jim to stop the winch immediately. Tom hurried round to Gunther's side of the boat.

'Are you all right?'

Tom grasped Gunther's arm and helped him scramble out from under the trolley.

'Yes,' he answered breathlessly, 'just a few scrapes and bruises.'

Tom gave Gunther a couple of minutes to get his breath back, then they resumed their positions and signalled to Bill to continue lowering. Five more minutes and the boat was on the sand. Tom disconnected the winch rope and they pushed the boat into the cover of the rocks. Tom checked his watch.

'I make it one-fifteen. Better get it ready to launch.'

By the time Tom and Gunther had released the ropes holding the boat on the trolley, and made sure everything was safely stowed inside, Bill and Jim had joined them at the foot of the cliff.

'All set?' asked Bill.

Tom nodded. The men found places to sit on the rocks. Tom lit two cigarettes for himself and Gunther.

'Wind's still a bit strong,' said Jim, 'you'll have to take it steady.'

Tom looked at the waves crashing on to the small beach and, for the first time since the idea of escape had first entered his mind, knew a moment of doubt. He was an Islander. He knew the power of the sea posed a far greater threat than anything in the Germans' arsenal. Should they have called it off and waited for better weather conditions? He shivered and looked at Gunther.

'How's that leg?'

Gunther pulled up his trouser leg. The area around the ankle was very badly bruised and swollen. Tom frowned.

'Are you going to be able to row?'

'Tom, I could row with a broken leg...two broken legs even. You watch me,' Gunther grinned.

Tom smiled. Gunther was a good man to have by your side. He hoped he would still be as positive when he felt the strength of the tides that ripped between the island and the French mainland. He checked his watch again – one-thirty.

One thirty-five – the explosions thundered into the night, lighting up the sky, jolting the ground. The men stood up, waiting for the rumblings to subside. In the hush that fell afterwards shouts could be heard from the cliff-top.

'That's it,' said Bill, 'that's woken the buggers up. Give them a few minutes to get on the move.'

Tom got into the boat and slipped the oars into the rowlocks. He would be rowing for the first hour. Bill and Jim stationed themselves one on each side, and Gunther positioned himself at the stern.

'Right! Let's go!'

The trolley rolled easily across the firm sand and into the water. As soon as Tom felt the boat lift clear of the trolley he shouted to Gunther to jump in. The waves lifted the boat like a dry, dead leaf, threatening to throw it back on to the sand but Jim and Bill pushed it on through the surf. It wasn't until the water was nearly to their shoulders that they gave one last shove and let go. Tom flailed the oars, struggling to get a good purchase in the choppy water. He'd forgotten how difficult it was to get a boat past the surf. Straining on the oars, he gradually began to make headway. Gunther took the compass and torch out of the oilskin bag and dropped the compass in the hollow Jim had prepared for it. He was soaked to the thigh but at least the cold helped numb his painful ankle. Tom looked back to the cove. Bill and Jim were shadowy figures on the sand, fading fast as he pulled away from the shore. Over to the left and higher up on the cliff, flames from the mill illuminated the gun emplacement and the scurrying figures of German soldiers. He thought for a moment of Izette, hoping she and Edmund were now on their way back to the farmhouse. A wave slopped into the boat soaking his legs and bringing Tom's concentration back to his rowing.

'God, that's cold!'

Gunther grinned and got out the bailer. It had been a long time since Tom had done any rowing and his arms were already starting to ache. He would have to pace himself, take more strain on his legs and back if he was going to last the first hour.

'How's our course, Gunther?'

'It's OK at the moment. Trouble is, if I bring us more square on to the waves to keep the water out of the boat, we will be off course on the compass, so I guess we have to put up with the wet.'

Tom turned to see how the waves were running. Gunther was right. The priority was to stay on course; otherwise they would miss the Ecrehous rocks.

'Keep us on course, whatever happens,' Tom said, resigned to getting even wetter. It was going to be a long, cold night. Gritting his teeth, Tom settled into his rhythm.

Two hundred yards from the gun emplacement, Izette and Edmund were crouched in the undergrowth, waiting for an opportunity to creep away. The flames from the explosions were still burning fiercely, casting a lot of light which meant that it was too risky for them to move, a problem that they hadn't envisaged.

'We can't stay here, Edmund. If they find the cable and follow it, we've had it.'

'Give it another few minutes. Look, they're trying to beat out the flames. I guess they don't want them to be seen from the air by any Allied planes.'

They watched as the soldiers beat and stamped at the flames ineffectually. Then, from behind them, they heard the sound of vehicles approaching.

'Looks like reinforcements arriving,' said Edmund grimly, 'we'd better get moving when they've passed.'

A staff car hurtled up the lane, followed by two lorries carrying troops. As soon as the vehicles were past the point where they were hiding, Edmund and Izette rose and began to make their way carefully away from the scene, intending to make a long circular detour across the fields before returning to the farm. Crouching low, they crept through the undergrowth towards the lane, which they would have to cross to get to the fields beyond. The lorries had come to a halt further up the lane and troops were clambering out. Izette and Edmund paused on the edge of the lane.

'I don't like this, Edmund. We're too close to them. They'll see us cross if they happen to look this way.'

Edmund glanced down the lane in the opposite direction. It ran straight without a bend for some distance and the undergrowth alongside thinned to tussocky grass.

'There's no cover if we try to cross further down the lane,' whispered Edmund, 'and we're running out of time.

We'll have to risk it. You go first.'

Izette crawled slowly forward. The soldiers were milling around, waiting for orders. It was impossible to tell if any were looking in her direction. Taking a deep breath, she launched herself across the lane, plunging into the bushes on the opposite side. She crouched, heart thudding fast in her chest, waiting for the clatter of boots.

Nothing happened. Now it was Edmund's turn. As he stepped on to the lane, Izette felt a sudden dread. She whispered a hoarse, 'wait!' but it was too late. He was already in the middle. The next moment they heard a shout. Edmund dived into the undergrowth beside her as a second shout rang out, followed by a rifle shot.

'Run!' he yelled.

The ground was very rough, hampering their progress and the darkness made it difficult to see what lay ahead. They floundered on with the sound of heavy booted feet running down the lane loud in their ears. Izette burst through a hedge into a ploughed field and turned right to run along the edge in the cover of the hedge. After a moment, she realised she couldn't hear Edmund behind her. She stopped, crouched down and looked round. He had turned in the opposite direction and was running away from her, not along the edge but across the middle of the field.

'Idiot,' she thought instantly, 'what on earth is he doing?' The next moment a German appeared in the field, catching sight of Edmund instantly.

'Halt!' he shouted, 'halt or I shoot!'

She watched in horror as the soldier raised his rifle to his shoulder. Edmund suddenly stopped and turned around, raising his arms in the air.

'Don't shoot!' Edmund's unbroken voice, the voice of a child, sounded feebly though the darkness. The German lowered his rifle. Two others had joined him and together they stumbled through the ploughed earth to where Edmund was standing. Izette crawled backwards, hiding herself in the hedge and watched. Two of the Germans took hold of Edmund's arms and pulled him back towards the lane. She followed them, keeping well hidden, as they took him to where the lorries were parked and presented him to the officer in charge. The officer questioned Edmund briefly, then pointed to his staff car. A soldier opened the door and pushed Edmund into the back. After that, they turned their attention to the still burning ruin of the mill.

Izette lay where she was for another hour, watching what was going on. Eventually, the fires were extinguished and the soldiers were ordered back into the lorries. After issuing some final instructions, the officer returned to his car and got into the front with his driver. Izette watched helplessly as the convoy reformed and disappeared slowly back down the lane towards St Helier, taking Edmund with them.

She checked her watch. They would be worried at the farm. She and Edmund should have been back long ago. They might even be out looking for them. She got to her feet and started to run. As she stumbled over the fields, tears streaming down her face, she wondered how she was going to explain to her father that she had allowed Edmund to be captured.

CHAPTER 22

At the end of 30 minutes hard rowing, the pain in Tom's shoulders was unbearable and he had to stop to rest. He slumped forward over his knees. When Gunther offered to take over the oars, Tom agreed reluctantly. They couldn't allow the boat to drift with the current. Changing places in the rocking boat was difficult but they managed to crawl shakily past each other and Gunther settled himself to row while Tom took over the helm. The shore looked a long way off but they wouldn't be able to risk starting the outboard until they had rowed for at least another hour. They knew the sound would carry well over water, especially in the stillness of the night.

Gunther missed his stroke a few times until he worked out the best angle for the oars. His ankle was painful but there was no way he could avoid using both legs to brace himself. Trying to ignore the discomfort, he concentrated on maintaining a steady rhythm to his rowing.

Although the night sky was cloudy, the cloud cover was broken and moving fast, pushed along by the wind. This meant that every so often they had a period of good visibility. In the moonlight Tom kept an eye out for any German patrol boats, hoping they wouldn't have decided to send one out following the explosions. So far, they had seen nothing.

'How am I doing?' gasped Gunther after a while. 'I am no expert at this.'

'You're doing very well,' replied Tom, thinking to himself that Gunther was doing brilliantly for someone who looked as though he hadn't had a square meal in months. Tom looked back at the receding coastline. 'If you can keep going a little longer, I think we might risk starting the engine.'

Tom pulled his hat well down over his ears and wrapped his jacket tightly across his chest up to the collar. The disadvantage of not rowing was that you quickly became frozen. The wind across the water penetrated his wet clothing, chilling him to the bone. He grabbed the bailer and scooped vigorously for a time to get his circulation moving again. Then he checked his watch and the compass, giving a thumbs up sign to Gunther.

At a quarter to three, Gunther stopped rowing and Tom lowered the outboard into the water. Gunther flopped forward exhausted. The motor started after a couple of pulls, emitting what sounded like a deafening roar after the quietness of the rowing phase. Tom adjusted the fuel flow and sat back, checking their course against the compass again. Gunther was still slumped opposite.

'Here!' Tom shouted over the noise of the outboard. He was holding a small bottle of brandy.

Gunther took the bottle gratefully and drank a couple of mouthfuls before passing it back to Tom who stowed it back under the stern seat.

'Why don't you lie down and take a rest, Gunther? I'll

be fine for a while.'

Gunther pulled the oars into the boat and lay down as best he could in the limited space, pulling the tarpaulin over himself. Fortunately, the wind had dropped a little and only the occasional wave came in over the side. Tom scanned the horizon. There was nothing in sight except for the humped shadow of the island behind them. He thought anxiously about their course. Since they'd started the outboard earlier than planned, presumably they would be in the vicinity of the Ecrehous rocks sooner. Glancing up at the sky he hoped the cloud wouldn't thicken before then. In this vast expanse of water, he was having serious doubts about locating the rocks. If they had drifted just slightly off course, they could easily overshoot the rocks altogether.

*

Tom couldn't tell if Gunther had managed to get some sleep under the tarpaulin but after an hour-and-half under power, he nudged him with his foot. Gunther sat up immediately.

'We'll be coming up to the Ecrehous rocks soon, I hope,' shouted Tom. 'I think it would be better if we both keep a lookout for them.'

'Right.' Gunther flexed his shoulders and rubbed his legs to get some warmth into them. 'Are you cold, Tom?' he asked.

'Absolutely bloody frozen!'

'Do you want me to take over the helm? I'm not too bad.'

'Yes, ok. I could do to move around a bit. I feel stiff all over.'

They repeated their earlier careful shuffle and Gunther took the helm. Tom sat opposite with the tarpaulin pulled round his shoulders, scanning their port bow.

'What's that over there?' said Gunther, pointing to a shadow at the limit of their visibility. Tom peered into the darkness.

'I can't tell. Can you steer towards it?'

Gunther turned the boat to port and after a few minutes, the shadow emerged as a cluster of rocks skirted by white water.

'That must be them. Thank God for that,' said Tom with enormous relief, 'I was afraid we might miss them altogether.'

'You're not the only one,' admitted Gunther.

They continued towards the rocks, slowing the motor as they came closer.

'Shall I stop the motor and we row from here?' asked Gunther.

'No, just throttle back as far as you can. We might need it to get us out of trouble. Those waves round the rocks don't look very friendly to me.'

Gunther slowed the engine even further and they crept towards the rocks, looking for a suitable place to anchor. Tom took out the torch and leaned over the bow, shining the beam into the dark water ahead of the boat, looking for submerged rocks.

'Steer a little to starboard,' he shouted, 'now straight ahead again.' A moment later he said, 'I don't think we can get in any closer. There's...look out!'

Tom had seen a large rock loom up just below the surface on their port bow.

'Hard to starboard!' yelled Tom, throwing himself partly over the port side to fend the boat off the rock. Gunther swung the helm right over and powered up the outboard, hearing a sickening scrape on the bottom of the boat. Tom cried out in pain and fell back into the boat, clutching his hand to his chest. The boat swung away from the rocks into open water again.

'What happened?' shouted Gunther,

'Trapped my hand between the boat and a rock,' gasped Tom, 'and I lost the bloody torch.'

When he judged they were at a safe distance, Gunther cut the engine.

'Is the boat damaged, Tom?'

'I don't think so, but you'd better check for any holes. I'll make sure we don't drift too close to the rocks if you can feel around for any leaks.'

Gunther ran his hands along the plank sides of the boat in the darkness. There was some water sloshing around in the bottom but he couldn't feel the pressure of any leaks.

'I think we're ok,' he said at last, 'but we had better not go in so close again. I'm going to throw out the anchor here.'

Once the anchor was out, Gunther crawled forward to where Tom was hunched in the bow.

'How bad is it?'

'I think I've broken a couple of fingers.'

Gunther manipulated Tom's hand gently, causing him to shout out in pain again.

'I think you are right, Tom. I'll have to strap it up.'

'We didn't bring any medical stuff, remember?'

Gunther thought a moment then began to strip off his clothes. Having removed his shirt he put back on his sweater and jacket. Shivering in the cold, he took out a penknife and slashed the shirt into strips.

'I have done the medical training,' he grinned, 'now give me your hand.'

He bound Tom's hand tightly, strapping the broken fingers firmly to the others, then fashioned a sling from the shirtsleeves. By the time he had finished, Tom was feeling nauseous from the pain but thanked Gunther gratefully.

'It's nothing,' protested Gunther, 'but now I think you should finish up the brandy.'

He found the bottle and made Tom finish it, hoping it might help him get a little sleep while they waited for the tide to turn. Then he fashioned a kind of bed in the bottom of the boat.

'We should lie down together,' said Gunther, 'it will be warmer that way.'

The two men lay down beside each other and Gunther pulled the tarpaulin over the top of them both. Tom chuckled through his chattering teeth.

'We make strange bedfellows, eh, Gunther?'

'Yes, indeed. I think I would prefer you to be Irene.'

'And I'd prefer it if you were Izette.'

Gunther lifted his head in surprise. 'Is that how it is? You love Izette?'

'It took me a while to see it but yes, I do.'

'Ah, I did wonder about that. I saw the way she looked at you sometimes. You are a lucky man.'

There was a moment of silence, then Gunther said, 'So we will be the brothers-in-law?'

'If our luck's in,' Tom answered grimly.

*

Jim had the strength of a man who has spent his life in hard physical labour working the land. Nevertheless, it took all his strength to hold on to Bill to prevent him from tearing back to St Helier that very night to find out where Edmund had been taken.

'For God's sake, Bill,' he shouted as he struggled to hold on to him, 'calm down! You can't force your way into German HQ at this time of night. They'd either shoot you on the spot or lock you up, you fool!'

'That's right,' agreed Margaret, 'you won't do yourself

or Edmund any good at all if you go charging in like a raging bull.'

Bill's reaction had been just as Izette expected. When he heard what she had to say, he'd exploded every bit as violently as the mines they had detonated. It was fortunate Uncle Jim and Aunt Margaret were there; Izette wouldn't have been able to manage him on her own. When they'd calmed him and got him to sit down at last, he buried his head in his hands.

'What's Betty going to say? She'll hold me responsible, you know. She'll say I never should have let him get mixed up in all this.'

'You don't need to tell her anything just yet. Don't cross your bridges before you come to them,' said Margaret, 'the lad's very bright. He'll think up some story for the Germans. He'll probably say he was out catching rabbits. That would be a reasonable excuse for him being out at night.'

'But he was so close to the explosions Margaret.'

'That doesn't prove anything. Pure coincidence. All they could charge him with is being out after curfew, and they'll surely not waste much time on a 13-year old lad out looking for food.'

'Aye, maybe you're right, Margaret.' Bill rubbed his hands over his face wearily. 'I think I'll get some sleep now and get down to the HQ early in the morning. Poor lad, having to spend the night there. I hope they look after him all right.'

Margaret tried to reassure him. 'You know he looks younger than he is, especially with his voice not having broken yet. If they've any decency, they'll treat him kindly.'

'Decency! That's what worries me. They're not all like Gunther you know,' said Bill grimly.

Irene looked up, surprised. He's changed his tune, she thought to herself.

Bill was too distracted to notice the backhanded compliment he'd delivered. Wearily he got up from the table.

Izette ran to hug him. 'Don't worry, Dad. Edmund will be all right.'

'He'd better be,' growled Bill.

'I've been thinking. He must have led them away from me deliberately. I wondered what he was doing at the time, running across the middle of the field in full view instead of following me, but now I think he did that so that I could get away.'

'Did he, by God!'

'Yes, it seemed a crazy thing to do. I can't think of any other explanation.'

Bill was silent as he thought about this. The lad might be small but he certainly had guts. And he had a good brain, making all those crystal sets then working out how to defuse a mine...not that his mother knew anything about that yet. He could still hardly believe that Edmund had had the courage to lay those mines and return to detonate them. Grown men would baulk at such a task, let alone an adolescent boy. By God, he was proud of the lad, even if Betty gave him the length of her tongue when she heard what they had been up to.

'Come on, Izette. There's nothing more we can do now. We'd best all try to get a bit of sleep before morning.'

Bill took himself wearily off to bed for the few hours left of the night. Izette kissed him goodnight then went up to her own room. She knew she wouldn't sleep but she undressed, put on her nightdress and got into bed. As soon as she lay down, her mind was with Tom and Gunther, out there on the water somewhere in their tiny boat. Her father and Uncle Jim had stayed at the cove to watch them out of sight, so she knew the first part of the plan had been successful. There had been no alarm. By now, they might have reached the Ecrehous rocks and be resting. She reached under her pillow and withdrew a roughly folded handkerchief. Unfolding it carefully in the dark, she took out a ring, the ring Tom had pressed into her hand when he left. It was his own signet ring, gold, engraved with his initials. He had worn it for years. It was too big for her fingers so she slipped it on to her left thumb, stroking the cool metal with the fingers of her other hand. She sent up a desperate prayer that he might be kept safe, trying to fix in her mind the image of his face, the expression in his eyes when they parted. Bringing the ring to her lips, she kissed it, turned over and, contrary to her expectations, fell asleep.

*

Bill was standing outside the German HQ by nine o'clock the following morning. The building, once an impressive private house, was approached by a long, sweeping drive bounded by lawns and shrubberies leading to an imposing porticoed entrance. Bill was escorted along this drive from the entrance gate by one of the sentries on duty. The sentry led him up the wide flight of entrance steps and into a room on the left of the hall that appeared to function as a reception area. He was motioned to a row of hard backed chairs lining the wall, while his guide spoke to an officer behind one of the three desks in the room. When the sentry had left, the officer behind the desk signalled to Bill to come to the desk and asked for his identification papers. There being no chair in front of the desk, Bill was obliged to stand while the officer examined his papers.

'What is your business here, Mr Vaubert,' he asked in good English.

Bill explained that his son had not returned from hunting

for rabbits the previous night and a neighbour had seen him taken away on a German lorry.

'Your son was out after curfew then, Mr Vaubert?'

'Yes, I'm afraid so,' replied Bill, with as much humility as he could manage, 'his mother is very ill in hospital and the lad was trying to catch a rabbit for a stew to take in for her. She needs a good diet. She's in the isolation hospital, you see.'

'The boy's name and age?'

The officer wrote down the details Bill supplied.

'And where did this take place?'

Bill gave the address of the farm, adding that Edmund had been somewhere in the surrounding fields.

On hearing the location, the officer looked up and studied Bill carefully for a moment.

'Please wait over there,' he said, indicating the chairs. Bill returned to them and sat down. The German officer left the room carrying Bill's papers.

Bill looked around. He was the only civilian in the room. The other two desks were occupied by German soldiers, neither of whom had looked up from their papers while he was being interviewed. He could hear the sound of activity out in the hall but inside the room it was silent. Bill folded his arms and waited.

After about 15 minutes the door opened and the officer returned, accompanied by another German officer.

'Mr Vaubert. Will you come this way please?' said the newcomer.

Bill stood up and followed the officer out into the hall. They turned left along a narrow corridor then the officer opened a door, standing aside to let Bill precede him into the room. Inside, the room was barely furnished with a table and a number of chairs. Bill noticed the window was barred. He sat down on the chair indicated. The officer perched himself on a corner of the table.

'Mr Vaubert. I would be grateful if you would tell me exactly what happened last night that led to the disappearance of your son.'

Bill repeated the same story he had given to the first officer. The German nodded, looking at some notes he was holding.

'You know there was an incident in the vicinity of this farm last night?'

'I heard some explosions,' answered Bill, 'that's why I was worried when my son didn't come home. Are you holding him here?'

Ignoring Bill's question, the officer continued, 'What was your son doing out after curfew?'

'I've already told you,' said Bill impatiently, 'he was out after rabbits. Now, are you going to tell me if he's here or not?'

The officer raised his eyebrows. 'Oh yes, he's here, Mr Vaubert.'

'Then can I see him?'

'When I have finished,' replied the officer, getting up from the table and going round to sit on the chair opposite.

'Finished what?' Bill's patience was beginning to run out. The officer ignored him again, pulling some paper out of a drawer and placing it in front of himself on the table. He uncapped his pen and wrote some details on the top of the paper. Then he sat back in his chair and looked at Bill.

'Tell me, Mr Vaubert, does your son know anything about explosives?'

'Explosives! Don't be daft!' erupted Bill, 'He's a 13-year old schoolboy!'

'We found wire in his pockets.'

'He was rabbiting! You use wire to snare rabbits. Surely

even you know that?'

'There is no need to be abusive, Mr Vaubert,' snapped the officer.

'Then let me take my son home. He's done nothing wrong except being out after curfew and I've explained why that was. My god, I've seen your troops out at night helping themselves to other people's food...'

The officer banged his fist down on the table. 'That's enough, Mr Vaubert! I can assure you it is not German soldiers who have been stealing food. We are adequately provisioned.'

Bill gave a sarcastic snort. 'Yes, I'm sure you officers are.'

'I will not warn you again! It is not in your interests or those of your son to take this attitude. Now, will you please tell me what your son was doing near the anti-aircraft emplacement?'

A man with more self-control than Bill might have taken warning from the officer's words but Bill was thoroughly riled by now. He leaned forward and looked the officer in the eye.

'Look, matey, I'm not answering any more of your stupid questions until you let me see my son.'

The officer glared back at Bill, then appeared to come to a decision. 'Very well,' he said and stood up. He opened the door and shouted an order, then returned to his seat and began to write. Bill waited. After a few minutes he heard the sound of approaching footsteps and then the door opened. Edmund was pushed in, escorted by a huge, burly guard. Bill stood up and moved towards his son.

'Bloody hell! What have they done to you?'

Edmund looked a mess. His clothes were muddy and torn but, more significantly, one side of his face was badly bruised, the eye blackened and swollen shut. Without waiting for an explanation, Bill let out a roar and swung his fist into the officer's face, knocking him backwards off the chair and sending him flying into the corner of the room. Bill launched himself towards the guard but the man was ready for him and swung his rifle butt hard against Bill's head, sending him crashing to the floor. Hearing the noise, two more soldiers ran into the room and manhandled a stunned Bill to his feet. By this time the officer had picked himself up and was holding a handkerchief to his bleeding nose. He looked at Bill with fury.

'Lock him up!' he ordered, 'Lock them both up.'

CHAPTER 23

When Bill hadn't returned to the farm by late that afternoon, Jim, Izette and Irene set off to walk down to St Helier to find out what had happened to him. When they got to Belle View Villas they found the house empty. They knocked next door at the Birrells, to ask if they had seen Bill. Mrs Birrell answered the door and immediately hustled them inside.

'How lovely to see you all! It must be six weeks since I've seen you, Jim... and how is Margaret? Is she well? I popped in to see Betty last week. I think she's looking a little better...'

The flow was almost unstoppable but eventually Jim did manage to get across the purpose of their visit.

Mrs Birrell looked anxiously at her husband. 'No, we haven't seen Bill since he went over to your farm three days ago. He said there was something he was going to help you with. He hasn't been back here to the house, as far as we know. I think he would have looked in on us if he had. Doesn't Tom know where he is?'

Jim looked uncomfortably across at Izette and Irene. The Birrells would have to be told about Tom sooner or later. In fact, Bill had promised Tom he would tell them as soon as he got back home but that was before Edmund disappeared. Jim selected his next words carefully to avoid having to go into explanations about Tom.

'The thing is, Dorothy, Edmund went missing the other night and we think Jerry might have pulled him in for being out after curfew. Bill went down to German HQ this morning to see if he could find the lad and he hasn't come back.'

'Oh,' said Mrs Birrell, 'oh dear, I see. Well I'm afraid we can't help you there. Poor Edmund, I hope he's all right.'

Anxious not to waste time, Jim stood up, explaining that they needed to get as much done as they could before curfew and the three of them returned next door.

'It was a long shot really,' said Jim, 'I didn't think he would have called here. I expect he went straight down town.'

'I knew it was a mistake to allow Dad anywhere near that German HQ, the frame of mind he was in,' declared Irene.

'What can we do now?' asked Izette.

'I'm going to the hotel,' said Irene, 'several of the men work at HQ. Someone's bound to know what's happened to him. If I hurry, I can get there and back before curfew.'

'I'm coming with you,' announced Izette.

'Now, you girls,' said Jim, 'wouldn't it be better to wait until tomorrow? I have to get back to see to the animals so I can't come with you now. I don't like the idea of you crossing town alone.'

'Sorry, Uncle Jim, but we have to go now.'

Izette nodded in agreement with her sister. Jim looked from one to the other and sighed resignedly.

'Well, for heavens sake be careful.'

*

The girls got down to the hotel and back without incident. To avoid recognition, Irene tied a headscarf over her hair and wore one of her mother's old coats but, since they passed hardly a soul on the way, it wasn't really necessary. The staff at the hotel were surprised and pleased to see her and asked one of the soldiers whom Irene had known quite well into the kitchens to speak to her. It was an older man called Heinrich. He was genuinely concerned when Irene explained her problem.

'I will find out for you, Irene. Give me your address and I will send someone with a note to put through your door. I am sorry you no longer work here. Why did you leave so suddenly?'

Irene explained what had happened.

'Ah, I understand,' said Heinrich, 'I hear it happened it France too, but you are not one of those girls. You are a good girl, like my daughter at home…if my home is still there,' he added sadly.

Irene covered his hand with her own. He smiled appreciatively.

'By the way, do you remember Gunther?' Heinrich asked suddenly. 'He's gone, disappeared.'

Irene looked surprised.

'They think he's deserted…or committed suicide. That's not unusual now, you know. It wouldn't surprise me if we found his body brought in on the tide. He was a sensitive young man. He had morals, scruples. He thought this was all wrong. So do I,' he said, thumping his chest for emphasis, 'but I can wait. It can't be long now before we can go home, God grant it.'

Irene squeezed his hand.

'I have to go, Heinrich.'

'Yes, off you go, Irene. Don't worry about your papa. I will find out for you.'

*

Irene and Izette were tired and cold when they got home. Irene suggested they boiled water for a hot water bottle. Izette filled the kettle and went to put it on the stove, then burst into tears.

'There's no gas,' she sobbed, banging her fist on the stove, 'I'd forgotten there's no bloody gas any more.'

Irene went over and put her arms around her. These last few days had taken a heavy toll on them both.

'Here,' Irene pushed a handkerchief into Izette's hands. 'Sit down and have a good cry. I'll see what I can find for us to eat.'

Irene thought a moment then went out of the kitchen, returning a few minutes later with an axe. Izette didn't have the energy to protest as Irene set about one of the old kitchen chairs, reducing it to a pile of sticks. Disappearing again, she returned with newspaper and kindling and proceeded to light a fire in the cold grate.

'Come here, Izette, and keep an eye on this fire. Don't let it go out.'

Izette drew her chair over to the fireplace, huddling over the meagre warmth while Irene searched through the kitchen cupboards and pantry. When the fire was established, Izette balanced the old trivet on the top and put the kettle on to heat. They soon had boiling water, which Irene used to cook potatoes and cabbage, mashing them together with a little milk. Then she balanced an old cast iron frying pan on the fire and fried it all up together with a couple of eggs they had brought from the farm. Kneeling in front of the fire, Irene looked at her sister's face glowing in the firelight.

'Feeling better?'

Izette nodded. 'Cooking over an open fire. It reminds me of our campfires. Do you remember?'

'Mm. We always cooked sausages. I could kill for half a pound of sausage now.'

'Or bacon.'

'Oh, don't, Izette!'

They ate their supper by the light of the fire, heating some more water for their hot water bottles, leaving the warm hearth only when the last embers had crumbled to ash. Then, clutching their bottles, they went upstairs. Izette paused at her bedroom door.

'Irene, shall we share a bed, like we used to?'

'It would be warmer,' replied Irene.

'It's not just that.'

'No, I know,' Irene smiled sadly, 'yours or mine?'

Izette opened her bedroom door and they went in.

*

It took them three trying days to track down their father and Edmund to a cell in the Gloucester Road prison. Heinrich sent them a note the day after their visit to the hotel confirming that Edmund and his father were still being held but he hadn't managed to find out where. German HQ was still on an emergency footing and there were so many Islanders locked up waiting to be interviewed or charged the system was close to collapse. Some detainees had been released simply to make room for others. The following day a second note arrived from Heinrich asking them to meet him outside Gloucester Road prison in an hour, adding a postscript, 'bring food.'

'Does this mean he wants payment in food?' asked

Izette.

'I don't think so,' replied Irene, 'perhaps he means for Dad and Edmund.'

There wasn't much time for them to get together such food as they had and it meant that they would have to go without supper themselves that day. Irene put some spare clothes in a bag, together with her father's shaving kit.

Izette looked at the bag gloomily. 'You don't think there's a chance they'll be released then?'

'Come on, Izette, we haven't any time to waste,' replied Irene brusquely.

Heinrich was waiting outside for them, keeping an anxious eye on the road. As they approached, he beckoned to them to hurry and almost pushed them inside when they reached the entrance.

'Sorry,' he explained, 'I am not supposed to be here. Wait here and I will speak to the duty guard.'

Irene and Izette stood nervously in the corridor until Heinrich returned. He led them to a door, which he unlocked and stood aside to let them enter.

'Wait in here. Don't make a noise or open the door,' he warned, then hurried away. Within minutes he was back, accompanied by Bill and Edmund. Irene and Izette rushed to hug them.

'I apologise, I have to lock you in,' said Heinrich, 'but I'll be back in 15 minutes.'

Neither Irene nor Izette paid any attention to his words. They were both looking at their father and brother in stunned silence, horrified by their injuries.

'What have they done to you?' Izette gasped, her voice trembling as tears started to roll down her face.

'It's not as bad as it looks, love,' said Bill, 'come here to me.'

She rushed into his arms, sobbing into his chest.

'You explain, Edmund,' said Bill.

Edmund shuffled sheepishly at first, seeming reluctant to tell them.

'Go on then, lad, tell them,' said Bill.

'Well, mine was an accident really.'

'No, it bloody wasn't,' said Bill, 'they caught him down by the old mill, as you know, and one of the officers took him back to the HQ. It was pretty late by that time so, after they'd asked him a few questions, they decided to lock him up for the night and deal with him in the morning. A guard took him down into the basement and pushed him into a cell...only the fool pushed him so hard, Edmund tripped and fell against the metal bunk...And that's the result,' added Bill, pointing at Edmund's black eye.

'It was dark. He didn't put the light on,' explained Edmund.

'Oh Edmund,' said Izette, 'that must have hurt.'

'Yes,' growled Bill, 'I'd like to get my hands on that guard.'

Izette and Irene fussed around Edmund, examining his black eye, then Irene straightened up and looked at her father.

'And what about you, Dad? Your face doesn't look much better than Edmund's.'

'Ah, well, when I saw Edmund with his face looking like that, I assumed they'd knocked him about, so I took a swing at a couple of them,' admitted Bill. 'They'd been messing me about anyway, not giving me straight answers.'

Irene nodded wearily. She wasn't surprised.

'Dad sent the officer flying right across the room,' added Edmund proudly.

'And they didn't like that, of course. One of the guards laid me out with his rifle butt.'

'Well,' she said, 'I suppose we should be grateful they locked you up and didn't just shoot you on the spot. Do you know what they're going to do with you?'

Bill shook his head. He'd been talking to some of the other Islanders locked up in Gloucester Road. Apparently, those who had already been tried and sentenced were waiting to be deported to detention camps in Germany but, since the Allied advance through France, the British were blockading the sea routes between the Island and the mainland so transport had become impossible. Many others, like Bill and Edmund, were waiting to be charged or released and it seemed that their fate was pretty low down on the German priority list.

'So it looks like we'll just have to wait along with everyone else,' said Bill, 'at least there's a good spirit of camaraderie in here.'

They heard footsteps approaching. Irene and Izette quickly handed over the food and clothing they had brought. The door opened and Heinrich gestured to the girls to leave.

'We'll do everything we can, Dad. There must be some way we can get you out,' said Izette desperately.

'Don't worry, Izette. Just look after your mother. Tell her I'm sorry I've made such a mess of all this. I should be there with her instead of locked up in here for making a fool of myself.'

'Oh Dad! Don't say that. You couldn't help it.'

Izette embraced him one last time before Irene pulled her out of the room. Izette stumbled out on to the pavement, blinded by her tears. Irene gripped Izette by the elbow and hurried her along while she mopped at her eyes. Suddenly Irene stopped and turned to face Izette.

'Look, Izette,' she said harshly, 'for Heaven's sake pull yourself together! There's only you and me left now and we've got to be strong for Mum. Tomorrow we're going to have to go down to that hospital and tell her everything. We can't hide this.'

She broke off suddenly.

'I'm sorry,' she said, close to tears herself now, 'I didn't mean to lose my temper. Seeing them both like that...and I don't know how we're going to tell Mum.'

'No, neither do I,' said Izette despairingly. She looked back at the grey prison building, at the two German guards posted outside the entrance and wondered how long it would be before they saw their father and Edmund again.

'Let's go home, Irene.'

They turned and walked home together in silence.

*

Back in their overcrowded cell in the prison, Bill and Edmund ate the food the girls had brought. Prison food was poor and scanty. Many of the prisoners relied on supplies from home brought by relatives or friends, though the knowledge that someone must be going short in order to spare a little for the prisoner soured the food in the mouth. Bill made Edmund eat most of it.

'You're a growing lad, Edmund. You need your food more than I do.'

Edmund was not taken in. They sat side by side on a bunk. Four other men shared the cell, which was designed to hold two. A couple of roughly made three-tier bunks had been squeezed into the cell, replacing the original two-tier bunk. The only way to sit on a bunk was to perch on the edge, leaning forward to avoid banging your head on the bunk above. It was either that or sit on your bed blanket on the cold concrete floor. There was no room in the cell for any other furniture.

'Dad,' said Edmund quietly, fearful of being overheard

by the German guards outside in the corridor, 'I'm sorry I got you into this.'

'Sorry!' replied Bill. 'Don't talk rubbish, lad. You didn't get me into this. I'm the one who should be saying sorry to you. If I had kept my temper, we might both be at home now. No, it's my stupidity that's put us in here.'

'Well I don't agree,' said Edmund timidly. 'When you hit that guard, Dad, I was really proud of you.'

Bill looked at his son in surprise.

'Really?' Edmund nodded and grinned.

'Well, I'll be blowed!' Bill grinned back. 'I must say, I did enjoy clouting him. I've been waiting four years to thump one of them and he was asking for it.'

'That's one for the Vauberts eh, Dad?'

'Aye, but it's only a little one compared with what you did, lad. When it comes to courage and bravery...and cleverness, I can't tell you how proud I am of you.'

Edmund blushed. The other men in the cell were grinning at him and nodding in agreement with Bill. One of the first things Bill had done on arrival in their cell was to explain how they came to be there.

'Wouldn't be surprised if he got a medal,' said one of them.

'Yes, indeed,' agreed Bill. Then, addressing the other men, he said, 'I've been blessed with three children; two lovely girls and this lad here and I'm proud of all of them, but this one here,' he put his arm around Edmund, 'he's very special indeed!'

*

The following day was damp and cheerless. Irene and Izette travelled down to the isolation hospital to see their mother feeling as bleak as the weather. She would have to know. If they didn't tell her, she would wonder why Bill wasn't coming in to see her.

They entered the hospital through the dull brown-painted swing doors, their nostrils immediately filled with the smell of strong disinfectant. It would cling to their clothes long after they returned home. They walked down the long chilly corridor that led to their mother's ward. Before they could push open the doors at the end, however, a nurse hurried out of a side room and called to them. They turned, fear churning their stomachs.

'Miss Vaubert! Ah, you're both here, I see. Could you spare a moment for the doctor please?'

Without a word, they followed her into the doctor's office and sat down on the hard chairs opposite his desk. He was not there but hurried in a moment later, closing the door behind him. He looked at the frightened faces turned towards him and gave them what he hoped was an encouraging smile.

'Um, nothing to worry about...really. I just wanted to bring you up to date on your mother's condition.'

Irene reached out for Izette's hand.

'Mrs Vaubert, your mother,' he added unnecessarily, with another smile, 'is satisfactory, given the difficult circumstances under which we are operating here. I'm sure you're aware that we can't give her the nutrition we would like to but we're hopeful that the fresh air and plenty of bed rest will prove as successful as it has with many previous patients.'

He paused to let this sink in and prepare his next words.

'However, you may find her rather confused today. We think she has picked up a slight infection, which is tending to make her want to sleep most of the time. It's nothing to worry about though, I'm sure she'll be back to normal in a few days.

Um...is there anything you would like to ask me?'

Irene gave him a straight look. 'Thank you, Dr Hunter, but if you are trying to tell us that our mother's condition is worse, we would rather be told so directly.'

'I see,' replied the doctor, slightly flustered. 'Then I shall do my best to respect your wishes.'

'So,' continued Irene, 'is Mother worse?'

'It's difficult to be precise,' he replied, 'patients have good days and bad days with this illness but the good progress she has been making has been rather set back by this infection. I'm sorry, Miss Vaubert, but you will find your mother rather poorly today.'

He rose from his chair and opened the door for them to leave.

'Thank you for being so honest,' said Izette as they left his office. He inclined his head in acknowledgement.

Betty was propped up on her pillows as usual, her eyes closed. They took the opportunity to look at her closely. She didn't look any different from the last time they'd seen her. Sitting side-by-side alongside the bed, they watched her chest rise and fall steadily, listening to her breathing. Was it any more laboured? The shadows under her eyes were just as dark against the paleness of her face, her cheekbones prominent still.

Taking her hand, Izette murmured her name. Betty's eyelids twitched and then opened. Her eyes darted round the room, confused, then came to rest on the girls' faces. Reassured, she smiled weakly and squeezed Izette's fingers.

'Lovely,' she whispered. 'Glad you're here. Can't find my knitting.'

Irene and Izette exchanged glances. Betty hadn't done any knitting since she'd been admitted to hospital.

'That's all right, Mum,' said Irene, 'it's at home. I said

I would finish it for you if you remember.'

'Oh did you? I must have forgotten. Well, you'll have to hurry, Irene. Enid's baby is due in a couple of weeks. It needs to be finished soon in case the baby comes early.'

Enid's baby was now 15-months old and Betty had completed the matinee jacket in good time for the birth.

'It'll be ready, Mum. Don't worry.'

The worried expression slipped from Betty's face and she relaxed back against her pillows with a smile.

'Dad was in to see me yesterday,' she announced next, 'I must get you to darn the elbows on that jacket he was wearing. I know it's only his old gardening jacket but I don't like to see him looking scruffy.'

'I can do that, Mum,' suggested Izette.

'Good girl,' Betty murmured sleepily.

'Mum,' said Irene, thinking fast, 'Dad's gone down with a cold. Doctor Hunter says he can't come in until he's better. He doesn't want him passing it on to you. So he won't be in to see you until he's better. You're not to worry about him. He sends his love.'

'Oh? Well tell him to rub oil of camphor on his chest. There's some in the bathroom cupboard. Make sure he does it every night before going to bed, girls.'

Betty's eyes closed again and in a few moments she started snoring gently. Irene and Izette got up quietly, replaced their chairs along the wall and left the ward. It was a long walk home through the gathering gloom, made worse by the hopelessness they each felt.

'At least we won't have to tell her about Dad and Edmund,' ventured Izette, 'not yet, anyway.'

'If at all,' added Irene, bleakly.

'Don't say that, Irene. Please don't give up hope. If you give up, I don't know how I'll carry on.'

Irene sighed deeply. 'I suppose you're right, Izette. We've hung on for four years. I suppose we can keep going a little longer. But I sometimes feel as though I can't. Each day I have a little less hope and it gets harder and harder to hold on to the idea of there being any future for us. Seeing Mum as she was today feels like the last straw.'

Izette could think of nothing to say. How often had she lain awake at night recently dreading the first light of morning, precursor of another desolate day. She had no faith in talismans, yet she clasped Tom's ring tightly in her hand on such nights. If Tom was her future, his ring was the only part of him she could hold fast until he returned…if he returned.

Making a real effort, Izette turned to Irene and said, 'If we hurry, we'll be in time for the news at six o'clock. There might be some good news.'

Irene looked sceptical but admitted she didn't have any better suggestions. The two sisters linked arms and started on the long climb up to their home.

CHAPTER 24

Izette was always to remember the next few months as the worst period of waiting. An atmosphere of brooding suspense hung over Islanders and Germans alike. Everyone on the island was a prisoner in the sense that no-one was free to leave. Now that the Allies controlled the seas around the Islands, the Germans were in no less a state of siege than the Islanders. Ordinary daily life, such as it was, dragged painfully on. The daily search for food became ever more desperate since there were now no supplies at all reaching the Islands and the stocks which the Island authorities had carefully hoarded were almost at an end. Rations had been cut even further and the Germans commenced a systematic search of all the farms on the Island. All farmers had to declare the stocks of foodstuffs they were holding. Once declared and checked by the Germans, these stocks were not to be touched. This exercise also gave the Germans an opportunity to find and seize any illegal food hoards. Fortunately, word of the searches leaked out and, in common with other farmers, Uncle Jim was able to hide some of his stocks before the inspection party arrived.

Inevitably robberies of food increased. Late one afternoon in November, Izette was returning to St Helier from the farm when she was stopped on the lane by two Germans. She looked at them warily. Their faces were gaunt and unshaven, their uniforms were dishevelled and she wondered for a moment if they were deserters. She was too far from the farm to shout for help. At least their rifles were slung casually over their shoulders and not pointing at her.

'Papers,' one of them demanded.

Izette handed them over, glancing down the lane in the hope of seeing someone coming along but the lane was empty.

'What you carrying?' he then asked, pointing at her shopping bag. Izette opened the bag and pulled out a handkerchief and a pair of gloves, hoping they wouldn't insist on looking inside themselves, but the German took the bag from her arm and thrust his own hand into it.

'Ah,' he feigned surprise, 'this pretty little chicken has laid an egg for us,' he joked. Taking the eggs, four in all, out of the bag, he gave two to the other soldier and put two carefully in his own pocket, handing the empty bag back to Izette.

'You can't do that,' said Izette angrily, 'you're not allowed to steal our food.'

The German's mouth twisted into a thin smile.

'But I did not steal them, you gave the eggs to me,' he said, innocent surprise on his face, 'and I will show you my gratitude.'

Stepping forward, he grasped Izette's chin roughly and kissed her on the mouth. She sprang back from him, wiping her lips in disgust. The Germans laughed and sauntered off down the lane. She was furious, her anger fuelled more by frustration that there was nothing she could do than by the loss of the eggs, although that was bad enough.

'Scum!' she muttered to herself. She toyed with going back to the farm to tell Uncle Jim what had happened but what was the point? There was nothing he could do without getting himself into the sort of trouble her father was already in. In future, she would try to carry such things hidden in her clothes.

*

Izette and Irene no longer alternated their time at the farm and at home. There were so many robberies, some of them violent, that they felt safer if they were both in the Belle View house together. The only reason for staying there was to enable them to visit their mother in hospital and their father and Edmund in prison and since they could do all this in one day, they spent the rest of the week at the farm with Uncle Jim and Aunt Margaret. Bill was happier with this arrangement. He worried when he knew the girls were in the house by themselves.

The girls continued to help on the farm although they could no longer manage very heavy work. The lack of food was affecting everyone's energy levels and Jim had been forced to abandon all but the most essential tasks around the farm. It troubled Jim badly. He hated to see jobs left undone.

'I don't know, Margaret,' he sighed one evening, 'I feel like an old man. The land's getting into a shocking condition and I can't bring myself to do anything about it. You know what they say, "one year's seed; seven years' weeds".'

'You'll just have to bide your time, Jim. When the war ends and the soldiers come home, there'll be plenty of young men looking for work. You'll be able to get some help then. It won't take long to get the land back into shape with a bit of help.'

'But what are we going to pay them with? We've had no income to speak of since all this started.'

'We'll manage when the time comes. Everyone will be in the same boat. Perhaps the authorities will help out. Or we might find someone who'll work for bed and board until we get on our feet again. Don't give up, love.'

'Maybe,' grunted Jim.

So, against all Jim's instincts, the land was left fallow and the weeds were allowed to spread. Aunt Margaret struggled to maintain her small kitchen garden and Irene and Izette helped looked after the livestock they had left. The one bright spot on the horizon was the news that, after lengthy negotiations, the island authorities had finally arranged for the Red Cross to send emergency food supplies. At the beginning of December, they heard that a Red Cross supply ship was being sent to the Island at last.

'Look,' said Irene excitedly, 'it says in the Evening Post that a Red Cross ship will be bringing supplies to the Islands. The Bailiff says it will be leaving Lisbon on the 7th of December.'

'That's marvellous news,' said Aunt Margaret, 'but it's about time.'

Irene nudged Izette. 'You know what else this means?'

Izette had been busy darning a sock. She looked up baffled.

'It might be carrying Red Cross messages...there might be a message from Tom or Gunther.'

Due to the blockade, they had received no Red Cross messages for months. Aunt Margaret nodded in agreement. 'But don't go raising your hopes too high, you girls. You don't know what might have happened to them once they landed in France,' she warned.

Nevertheless, it was a tiny gem of hope to help them through the days and they sorely needed it during that last month of 1944. News of the whereabouts of the Red Cross ship was disturbingly contradictory. First it was reported to be coming in the next few days and would take Red Cross messages to Europe. Then they heard final arrangements had not yet been completed. A week later, the BBC announced that supplies were on their way on a Swedish ship name the Vega but a few days later, the Evening Post carried a notice, 'The Red Cross parcels: Unlikely to arrive for Christmas.' The Islanders' emotions seesawed with each new announcement and, in the end, the ship did not arrive until the end of December.

At the farm, it was hard to raise any enthusiasm for the Christmas of 1944, even though they believed it would be the last Christmas under occupation. There was an unspoken agreement that there would be no Christmas presents, not even the home-made gifts of previous years. Presents implied celebration and the family preferred to wait until they had real cause for celebration. Festivities and gaiety seemed wholly inappropriate while Bill and Edmund were imprisoned, Betty was so ill and the whereabouts of Tom and Gunther remained a mystery. Aunt Margaret did her best to produce a special meal, killing and roasting one of the chickens. Having put a lot of effort into preparing the meal, her patience finally snapped when Jim and the girls ate the food in a sombre silence.

'This is a fine to-do,' she snapped, 'it's Christmas Day and look at your faces! Anyone would think this was a wake!'

They looked at her guiltily. Izette started to apologise.

'I don't want your apologies, thank you. I don't expect this to be like other Christmases. I usually have to cook for a houseful so you don't need to remind me who isn't here today, but that doesn't mean the four of us have to mope around with mournful faces. Jim, bring that bit of sherry out of the dresser cupboard.'

'I thought we were saving that.'

'We were but I think we need it today.'

Jim brought the bottle, which was about half-full, while Margaret dusted off her best crystal glasses. She poured them each a generous measure.

'Now,' she said, standing up at the head of the table, 'it's been a long time since this table has seen so many empty chairs on a Christmas day, so we're going to drink to those who are not here today. Also, and more importantly, to next Christmas day when I believe,' and here she paused to look at them all sternly, 'the empty places will once more be filled by our loved ones.'

Margaret raised her glass. 'To our last Christmas under the German jackboot!'

They stood to repeat her toast and, as the liquid warmed their throats, a similar warmth flowed into their hearts, carrying with it the conviction that Aunt Margaret's words were prophetic. For those few moments, there was no doubt in anyone's mind that they would indeed be reunited with the missing ones. Their glasses lowered, smiles appeared on everyone's faces and they embraced each other warmly and a little shamefacedly.

'Bless you, Margaret,' Jim murmured to his wife, as he held her close, 'what would I do without you? What would any of us do without you?'

She scolded him, laughing off the compliment but she knew she'd restored their hope and she was glad.

*

Boxing Day was a bright, crisp and sunny day and, as Izette

and Irene made their way home to St Helier, their spirits were still high from the previous day.

'Last Boxing Day under the German jackboot!' they reminded each other, as they walked along.

They turned the corner into their road to see Mr Birrell leaning on his front gate, enjoying the sunshine. He straightened up as he saw them approach.

'Happy Christmas,' they shouted merrily.

He returned their greeting, adding: 'I thought you'd be back today. That's why I didn't send a message over to the farm.' Seeing their faces fall, he hastened to reassure them, 'Don't worry, your Mum's all right and your Dad and Edmund, but there's a bit of problem in the house.'

Looking at their own front door, Irene and Izette saw at once that the lock was broken and the door was very slightly ajar.

'Oh no!' groaned Izette.

'Someone must have broken in last night. They must have been very quiet. We didn't hear anything, but when I saw the door open like that this morning, I went in to take a look.'

As he spoke, the girls pushed open the front door and went in. In the kitchen, drawers and cupboard doors stood open. Irene went straight to the larder.

'Empty,' she said disgustedly, 'completely empty.'

Ted Birrell had followed them inside. 'Did they take much?'

'Everything there was, though that didn't amount to much.' Irene strode out of the kitchen angrily. 'I'll check upstairs, Izette. You check downstairs...and you'd better take a look in the garden as well.'

When every room had been checked, the final toll included every item of food in the house, together with Bill's young vegetable plants and the meagre stock of firewood that Bill had collected and stored in his greenhouse.

'Well, there's no damage except the lock on the front door,' said Izette.

'I think they must have forced it with a crowbar,' said Ted, 'it's strange, we didn't hear that though. I'm not a heavy sleeper, not any more.'

'What a mean thing to do, on Christmas Day of all days,' commented Izette.

Ted shrugged his shoulders. 'Survival is all that matters now. There's no room for decency or consideration for others. But don't worry about the door. I'll mend that for you. The lock is fine, it's just the door jamb that's splintered. I think I've got a piece of wood I could use to replace that.'

The girls expressed their thanks to Ted, then left to make their way to the hospital to visit their mother.

*

On the first day of January 1945 Izette and Irene, along with hundreds of other Islanders, hurried down to the harbour to watch the Vega dock. The last time the Islanders had assembled at the harbour had been to watch the deportations. Although that was only two years earlier, Izette felt a lifetime had passed since she last stood there amongst the crowd straining on tiptoe to see the ships. How much had changed in those two years. Even with Irene by her side today, she felt alone in a way she'd never experienced before. It was strange how loving a person brought with it a feeling of incompleteness when that person was absent. In finding Tom, she had lost her capacity for wholeness without him.

A cheer went up as the Vega entered the harbour. Some

waved Union Jacks. The Vega sounded her horn in response as she slipped into her berth. The cranes and derricks on the quayside towered over the ship, anxious to get to work on her precious cargo but it wasn't until the following day that Izette and Irene were able to collect their boxes of supplies. The boxes were heavy; about ten pounds in weight and it was hard work carrying them home up the hill. Once in the house, they put the boxes on the kitchen table, reluctant to open them and bring to an end the suspense of wondering what was inside. It brought back the excitement of earlier Christmases when mysterious surprise packages appeared under the tree on Christmas Eve.

'Come on then,' said Izette, 'let's open them. Where's the scissors?'

'We'll just open one. Save the other one for later.'

They opened the box and carefully set out the contents in a line on the kitchen table. Tins of salmon, pork and sardines, tea, butter and sugar, marmalade, milk powder and canned fruit, chocolate, soap and much more. Irene reached for the tablet of soap and pressed it to her nose.

'The first thing I'm going to do is wash my hair with this,' said Irene.

'Will that be before or after you've had a piece of chocolate?' laughed Izette.

*

A few days later, they were also able to enjoy white bread again. The Vega had brought a consignment of white bread flour for the Island's bakeries, idle for three weeks since supplies of flour had finally run out altogether. Even before that, the flour they had been using produced a heavy dusty loaf. To taste light white bread once more, after years of deprivation, was heaven indeed. The only disappointment was that the Vega brought no Red Cross messages for the Vaubert girls.

For Irene and Izette, the arrival of the food parcels also brought the hope that their mother's poor appetite might be tempted by the rare treats. They visited her soon after the distribution of the boxes. Thankfully, she had survived the infection that she contracted before Christmas but she was still very weak. The hospital's medical supplies had been virtually exhausted at the end of 1944, so the arrival of the Vega, with a fresh supply, was a godsend indeed.

When they walked into her ward, Betty greeted them with a smile.

'I've had a lovely cup of tea,' she announced, 'and a corned beef sandwich on lovely white bread with real butter.'

Izette felt tears pricking her eyes. It was such an ordinary statement, unworthy of comment normally, but it signified so much in Betty's case. She hadn't eaten any solids for a long time, surviving on soups and broths, a few spoonfuls at a time.

'I wasn't feeling hungry,' Betty continued, 'but the sandwich looked so good, I couldn't resist it.'

'That's wonderful, Mum,' Irene congratulated her, 'if you can carry on eating like that and build your strength up, we'll have you out of here in no time.'

On their way out of the hospital, they noticed Doctor Hunter was in his office. They tapped on his door. He stood up to open the door for them.

'Come in and sit down,' he said, 'I expect you've seen a little improvement in your mother?'

They confirmed that they had and asked him if this meant she was now out of danger.

'I wish I could say yes to that,' he answered, 'but you prefer me to be absolutely honest, so I have to say that there's no guarantee of that yet. However, I would say that she has turned a corner and she is definitely better than she was last week. Since the Vega arrived, we've been able to improve her nutrition and we've also received new supplies of drugs, which should help her recovery.'

Dr Hunter's optimism was infectious. As the girls left the hospital, they felt more positive than they had in months.

*

January turned out to be long, dreary and cold. The elation, caused by the food parcels and bread flour supplies, was dampened later in the month by the end of the electricity supply. Fuel for the power stations had virtually run out and supplies could only be maintained to essential services. So there was now no more electricity and, since the gas supply had run out some time ago, the Islanders had to turn to wood for cooking and heating.

Contrary to the Islanders' expectations, the Germans did not touch the Red Cross supplies. Consequently, the troops were soon in a condition of near starvation. Islanders watched them collecting limpets on the beaches and they were known to catch and eat any stray cats or dogs they came across. Inevitably, there was widespread unrest among the troops; the majority seeing no point in continuing the futile struggle and the Islanders were witness to several arguments between the men and their officers. Izette was in St Helier when a fight broke out between some German sailors and their officers on the Weighbridge. It was an ugly scene. Reinforcements arrived and dragged one of the sailors into the nearby bus garage. Izette watched in horror as the man was stood against a wall and shot. He slumped to the ground, the wall behind him splattered with blood. It was all over in less than two minutes. She was stunned. The violence was so sudden and so utterly pointless.

The Vega continued to bring supplies each month and Red Cross messages were delivered once again but none arrived for Izette or Irene.

As the gloomy winter gave way to spring and the end of the war seemed tantalizingly close, the Islanders had to endure the spectacle of the Germans celebrating Hitler's birthday on the 20th of April. Military bands played in the town squares as the Nazi flag was hoisted. Many shook their heads, believing that the island garrison should have surrendered by now but the new commander in chief, appointed in February, was a hard line Nazi and obviously determined to hang on until the bitter end.

Then news broke that stunned both Islanders and Germans alike. Hitler was dead. The news came through on the first day of May and was followed three days later by the news of the wholesale surrender of German forces in north-west Germany.

Those first few days of May were possibly the strangest since the occupation began. The German troops were still in evidence, many of them milling around the streets of St Helier and gathering in groups on corners with apparently nothing to do, while elsewhere, others were still engaged in constructing new gun emplacements. At night, guard posts continued to be manned and searchlights continued to search the skies.

While all this was going on, the Islanders were scouring the shops for Union Jacks or anything bearing the colours red, white and blue and waited outside the offices of the Evening Post for each new announcement. Wirelesses reappeared and were boldly displayed on windowsills, tuned in to the latest news from England. The air of expectancy rose with each new day, until it was finally announced that Victory in Europe Day would be celebrated on the 8th of May.

At the farm, plans were made for the entire family to go

down to St Helier for the celebrations. Aunt Margaret voiced concern for the animals.

'What happens if anyone steals the chickens, or even a pig? The Germans will expect everyone to be in town.'

'We'll take the risk,' replied Uncle Jim, 'I'm not going to miss this for anything and neither are you. I'll shut the dog in with the chickens and the pigs will have to take their chances.'

Izette and Irene agreed with Uncle Jim.

'Yes, come on, Aunt Margaret, get your glad rags on. You're coming with us,' said Irene.

'Glad rags is right,' laughed Aunt Margaret, 'we've nothing but rags left!'

In Royal Square, thousands of Islanders gathered outside the States Building to hear Churchill's speech, which was due to be broadcast at 3 p.m. Every window in the surrounding buildings was packed with listeners and loudspeakers had been erected all over town for those who couldn't squeeze into the square. In the press of the crowd, Irene and Izette stayed together by linking arms tightly. Aunt Margaret and Uncle Jim were there as well, as were the Birrells, but they had lost sight of them in the press of people.

The crowd cheered as Churchill's speech commenced but it was nothing to the repeated cheers that greeted the conclusion of the speech when the Bailiff raised the Union Jack and the Jersey flag over the Courthouse. He led the crowd in singing the National Anthem and there was wild cheering yet again at the end. Church bells rang out all over the island as the Islanders commenced their celebrations. Irene and Izette forced their way out of the square, laughing and crying alternately. The Bailiff had announced that prisoners would be released and they were determined to be outside the prison when their father and Edmund stepped out into freedom. By the time they arrived, there was already a small crowd waiting outside. An armed German guard was standing at the entrance arguing with a couple of young men. As the argument became more heated, the guard was joined by two German officers who came out of the prison. They produced a list, which they showed to the young men, then they all disappeared inside, leaving the solitary guard uncomfortably facing the impatient crowd. Within minutes, the first of the prisoners emerged and the crowd surged forward.

'What's going on, Irene? Can you see?'

Irene had climbed onto a nearby step. 'I can't see Dad or Edmund yet. There are too many people milling about. Let's get closer to the front if we can.'

Irene began to push her way through the crowd, dragging Izette along behind. Irene asked an onlooker, 'Can you tell me what's going on?'

'They've released the political prisoners first. They're saying they don't have orders to release any others yet.'

'The hell with that,' shouted another man standing close to them, 'what do orders count for now? The war's over. Let's get the rest out.'

The crowd surged forward again and the guard was pushed out of the way. Izette saw him take off his helmet, shoulder his rifle and sneak away. A small group of men pushed their way inside while the crowd waited. Then, after a few short minutes, prisoners started to appear in twos and threes, stopping on the steps of the prison in surprise at the crowd awaiting them. As each one stopped, a name would be shouted from within the crowd and the prisoner would turn to the waving arms of his relatives or friends, his face breaking into a grin as he plunged into the sea of faces.

Edmund and Bill appeared together, Bill with his arm around Edmund's shoulders.

'Here, Dad!' shrieked Izette, jumping up and down,

'here we are!'

Bill pushed a way through the press of people to Izette and Irene, where they rushed into each other's arms. All around them, people were kissing and crying and embracing, eventually dispersing to their homes. Bill guided his family away from the prison.

'Did you hear Churchill's speech, Dad?'

'Yes, someone smuggled a wireless in and the guards were too despondent to do anything about it.'

'I'd made another crystal set anyway, so that we could listen to the BBC,' added Edmund.

'How on earth did you manage to get the parts,' asked Izette.

'The German guards got stuff for me. Most of them were past caring what went on when there were no officers around.'

They made their way home to Belle View Villas, meeting the Birrells on the way. Ted was overwhelmed to see his old friend again.

'It's grand to see you free again, Bill,' he said, 'I've missed you.'

'Thank you, Ted,' Bill replied, shaking his hand vigorously, 'and thank you for keeping an eye on my girls. And mending the door!'

Ted dismissed it with a wave. 'It was nothing, a pleasure to be able to help.'

'Even so,' insisted Bill.

They let themselves into the house. Bill entered first, looking around slowly. Irene and Izette had been out collecting wild flowers in shades of red, white and blue and had arranged them around the house. The place was immaculate and there was a smell of lavender polish in the air. The kettle stood filled and ready near the fireplace. The fire was laid, ready to be lit and under a clean white cloth on the table, the tea was laid, ready to be eaten. Bill looked at Izette and Irene in turn.

'You've done a grand job here,' he said, ' and it's grand to be back home, eh Edmund?'

Edmund merely nodded, more interested in lifting up the cloth to see what was for tea.

'I'm starving,' he said.

'Then let's eat,' laughed Irene, 'we've got a lot to talk about but it can wait. We've all the time in the world now!'

CHAPTER 25

Bill sat pensively in the hospital ward holding Betty's hand. The comfort of being together again showed on both their faces. Betty was sitting up in bed, her hair freshly washed and curled by one of the nurses and there was a pink rosiness in her cheeks that spoke of health, where formerly it had indicated fever. Doctor Hunter was pleased with her progress and had said she would be able to go home in a few weeks. Privately, he was surprised she'd pulled through, a woman of her age, but you could never tell and no-one was more delighted when his patients flouted a grim prognosis to prove him wrong.

The ward was quite austere but that morning the sun was pouring in through the windows and Bill had brought some flowers to brighten up Betty's corner of it.

Betty looked at the colours appreciatively. 'Did you pick all those in our garden, Bill?'

'Most of them. Everything's starting to come into flower

now. But some are from Ted's garden. He brought them round especially for you.'

Betty smiled. 'He's a kind man.'

'They're looking forward to welcoming you home in a few weeks. I expect there'll be banners and balloons,' said Bill.

Betty laughed. 'I don't want all that fuss, Bill. You tell them not to bother. I should be embarrassed.'

'I'll do no such thing. I'll be putting them up myself!'

Betty squeezed his hand. It would be good to be back in her own home again, especially now the war was over and she wouldn't see those awful grey uniforms everywhere. That was the one advantage of being in here so long. She hadn't known what was going on outside. The girls had eventually told her about Bill and Edmund being imprisoned but, by that stage, they'd known there was no possibility of them being deported and it would only be a matter of time before they were released. She chuckled. Trust her Bill to get himself into trouble eventually. It was a wonder it hadn't happened before.

'What's so funny?' asked Bill

'Nothing,' replied Betty, 'just thinking about you hitting that officer.'

Bill grinned sheepishly. He wasn't sure now if it had been worth the eventual cost but there it was. It had worked out all right in the end.

'I've been thinking, Betty,' he said, 'when we get you home again, the time might be right for a bit of a change.'

'Oh? How do you mean?'

'Well, to tell you the truth, I've had my fill of garage work. These last few years working for Jerry have left a sour taste in my mouth somehow. Every time I go into the workshop now, I'm waiting for one of those snotty German officers to walk in as though he owns the place. It's silly but I can't seem to get it out of my mind.'

Betty looked at him with concern. These were unusual words to hear from the practical, down to earth man she was used to.

'So I think I'm going to give up the garage. I've got a few years to go before retirement but I could find some other work. There'll be a lot to do here on the island to get it back to the way it was before the occupation.'

'What will you do with the garage? Will you sell it?'

'Well, I had this idea that I would offer it to Tom. I could let him lease the business until he had the money to buy me out or some such arrangement. He'd said he fancied going into the motor trade but of course that was long before he escaped last October.'

'Has no-one heard anything from him yet?'

'No, not a word.'

A silence fell between them for a few moments, then Betty looked at her husband with a curious expression.

'I've often wondered if there was something between Tom and our Izette, Bill. I know they've always been like brother and sister but as Izette got older, I began to think that might have changed.'

Bill looked at Betty with surprise. She had put his own thoughts into words.

'I think you might be right, Betty. Margaret first mentioned the idea to me last year. Of course, I hadn't noticed anything until she pointed it out but after that I paid more attention, or at least, Margaret made sure I did,' he laughed, 'so I tried to watch them secretly, hiding behind the paper or something and I did sometimes see those little looks and smiles. You remember those, don't you, Betty?'

Betty smiled and squeezed his hand again.

'I do indeed, Bill Vaubert.'

'But how did you know, Betty? You haven't seen them

together for months and months.'

'Oh it started a long time before I came in here. I am her mother, you know. Mothers notice these things.'

'Well, if that is the way it is with them, I'd be delighted,' continued Bill. 'Tom's a good lad. He's grown up a lot these last few years. He's steadier than he used to be. Losing George made a big difference to him.'

'Yes, poor lad. What do you think the chances are that Tom will come back?'

'I just don't know, Betty. Izette's trying to join in the celebrations but she looks strained. She keeps going down to the harbour to watch the troop ships coming in. I expect she's hoping he'll be on one of them.'

They were interrupted by a nurse coming into the ward with a cup of tea and a biscuit for Betty.

'Oh, I didn't know you were here, Mr Vaubert,' she said, 'would you like a cup of tea?'

'Thank you, that would be very nice,' replied Bill.

When the nurse had left, Bill got up and stretched, then walked over to the window. He stood looking out at what had once been quite pretty gardens. This was another job that needed to be done, getting these gardens back into order. He didn't think he'd have difficulty finding work, if he was willing to try anything. Yes, he thought, it would be nice to work outside in the fresh air. That was the other idea he needed to put to Betty. He came back to the bed when the nurse brought in his cup of tea and sat down again.

'There's another matter I've been thinking about, but in this case, the decision is yours and I'll go by whatever you decide. You'll understand why in a minute.'

Bill paused and shuffled on his chair. He wanted to get his words right on this.

'It's to do with the house...our house.'

He looked at Betty anxiously, expecting to see her start to look worried but her expression remained calm.

'I don't know if it's to do with making a fresh start, putting these last few years behind us or what, and I know how important that house is to you. It's been our first home, our only home, and there's our good neighbours to take into consideration but I wonder if you would consider moving somewhere else with me?'

The last words came out in an anxious rush. Surprised, Betty paused in the act of lifting her cup to her lips.

'Where were you thinking of going?' she asked.

'Well, I've only given it a little thought but I thought we might ask Jim if we could have that old cottage on the farm. It needs quite a bit of work to make it habitable but I'd be happy doing it myself. And there's a good-sized garden. It's overgrown but I'd love getting that back into shape. We'd have the peace and quiet of the countryside and you'd only be a quarter of a mile or so from the farm.'

Betty watched Bill's face as he talked enthusiastically about his idea. His eyes sparkled as he drew a detailed picture of what the cottage could offer.

'And some of the time I could work for Jim on the farm. He'll be needing farm labourers again. You never know, he might even be able to pay me some wages eventually.'

'It sounds to me like you've give it much more than "a little thought", Bill Vaubert,' chided Betty; 'this sounds much more like a dream you've been nursing for a long time.'

Bill looked a little embarrassed. She had hit the nail on the head, as always.

'Aye, well perhaps I have,' he admitted, 'but I'd love to work in the open air, growing things, tending things. You know how I've always loved my garden. I'd grow all our vegetables. You wouldn't need to buy any and you could keep a few chickens for eggs.'

Betty burst out laughing. 'You've got it all worked out down to the last detail! Have you chosen the wallpaper for our bedroom?'

'I thought pink might...' Bill stopped. 'You're pulling my leg, aren't you?'

Betty was shaking with laughter, her hand over her mouth. Seeing Bill looked hurt, she stopped laughing and opened her arms to him.

'Come and give me a hug, Bill Vaubert, I'm not laughing at you.' She paused. 'Well, perhaps I am a little. You've prepared your case like a top barrister.'

'But the decision's yours, Betty. I said that at the outset.'

'I know, and I appreciate that. Now listen to me. I shall need some time to think about it but the way you've described it, I think I would be prepared to give it a try, provided I can choose the wallpaper, all of it!'

Bill looked at her in a way that made her heart melt, just as it had when they were courting all those years ago.

'Thank you, Betty. We'll be happy there, I promise you.'

'Don't rush me. I said I'll need time to think it all over. For instance, what would we do with the house? I don't think I'd want to sell it.'

'I've thought of that if...and I know this is a big if...but if Tom comes back safely and he and Izette get together, they could live there. And if not, we could rent it out. It would give us a little extra income.'

'I'd like to think of them starting out in that house just as we did. But I'm almost frightened to think about it. It seems like tempting providence. Let's just hope and pray that we get some word from him soon.'

'Yes, you're right, Betty. One step at a time.'

There was another factor affecting Bill's desire to leave the garage and, to a lesser extent, the house but it was one he would not be mentioning to Betty.

Although the garage had been shut for a few months, he'd gone down there a couple of days ago just to check that everything was all right. Exuberant celebrations were still going on in St Helier and there had been some minor damage done around the town, a few broken windows here and there. But he had not been prepared for the shock he received when he arrived at the garage. Across the big double doors to the workshop, in letters two feet high, someone had painted the word 'collaborator.' Bill's stomach had turned over. There'd been a lot of this going on. Girls who were known to have fraternised with the Germans had been humiliated in the streets, their hair was shorn to the scalp and some were even tarred and feathered. Similarly, businesses, which had gone out of their way to serve the Germans and had consequently made a lot of money, had had slogans and swastikas daubed on their walls. But to see that word scrawled across his own garage doors shocked and hurt him deeply.

He had hurriedly unlocked the workshop doors and went inside, straight to a shelf at the back where he stored a few cans of paint. He'd found a brush and some paint and started painting, working at a furious pace until the word was completely obliterated. Then he dropped the paintbrush and rested his aching arms. When he'd finished, his cheeks were wet with tears. Bill took the paint can and brush back into the workshop, dropping them on the floor. He took a last look around the workshop, the place that had provided him with a living all these years. He'd worked happily here alongside Tom and Donald. They'd had a few good laughs together. Until that dapper little German officer walked in.

Bill had turned and walked outside. He'd pulled the big

doors together and locked them, taking a last look at the drying paint. He might not be able to see the word now, but it would remain imprinted on his memory forever.

*

In the days following VE day, British troops began to pour into the island, sometimes taking over the billets formerly occupied by German soldiers who had been rounded up and were now imprisoned in camps, waiting to be deported. About 3,000 Germans were kept behind on the island to clear the minefields. This dangerous work started straight away but not soon enough to prevent a few island children being injured when they ventured back on to the beaches.

Izette was staying in the Belle View house with her father, Irene and Edmund, preparing for her mother's discharge from hospital. Soon, all the Vauberts would be back in the house together. Irene was looking for a job and Edmund, much to his disappointment, was sent back to school.

Izette didn't know what she wanted to do. Most days, she walked down to the harbour to watch the ships arrive, some carrying supplies, others troops. It was a bustle of activity. The shops were filling up again and it was a joy to wander round the town looking in the windows at all the items that had been absent for so long. There were no spending sprees though. Rationing was still in place and would be for quite a time.

As the barbed wire was removed from the cleared beaches, she was able to walk by the sea again. It would be a long time before the beaches could ever look the same though. Huge walls of concrete reared up behind the beaches, a sombre reminder of the fortress character the Germans had imposed on the island. Nevertheless, Izette enjoyed her solitary strolls along the tide-line.

One particularly bright morning, she finished the shopping they needed quickly and wandered down to the quay as usual. She counted eight ships moored to the dock. All the derricks were in use. The shouts of the dock workers echoed the screaming of the gulls. A steady succession of battered old lorries ground through their gears along the piers, carrying the contents of the ships' holds up to the warehouses that lined the quay. Post came ashore most days, the volume increasing day-by-day but nothing as yet had come for Izette.

Leaning on the railings at the pier head, she watched the activity for a while, then strolled off along the Esplanade towards West Park, meaning to catch a bus home. Now that supplies of motor fuel had been brought in, a few services had started up again. However, when she came to the breach in the sea wall leading down to the beach, she changed her mind. There was plenty of time. She would catch a later bus home.

From the bottom of the beach steps, she headed straight for the sea. Her shoes quickly filled with sand so she took them off and continued in her bare feet, putting her shoes in her shopping bag. The sand was cool but not cold between her toes. A gentle breeze off the sea blew her hair back from her face. The smell of the sea filled her nostrils. At the water's edge she stopped to watch the waves tumble in onto the sand. The tide was on the way out. She walked forward slowly to keep up with it. Hitching up her skirt, she stepped into the water. It was cold, but bearable. She stood still, feeling the current suck away the sand granules from around her feet. She smiled. How many times had she stood exactly like this as a child, enjoying the feeling of the sand slipping and sliding beneath her feet.

After a while, she stepped out of the water and continued

to stroll along the beach close to the waves. She walked contentedly for about half-an-hour, unaware of time passing. By keeping her eyes on the line of the incoming waves, she could pretend the ugly sea wall was not there and the beach was as it used to be. In fact...she stopped and turned around. Although it looked very different now, this couldn't be far from the place she and Nancy were playing when those first German planes came over to bomb the harbour. How long ago that seemed. There was a rock a little way ahead breaking through the sand. She would sit there for a few minutes before the return walk back.

She dusted the loose sand off the rock, put down her bag and sat down. She had the long stretch of beach to herself, except for a distant figure walking at the harbour end. It was taking time for people to resume their old habits. As yet, there were only a few dogs to be exercised daily along the beach. She looked out into the bay where several ships lay at anchor, waiting for their turn to enter the harbour. One of them might be carrying the letter she was waiting for, just a sheet of paper in an envelope tucked away in a sack in one of the holds. Surely it wasn't too much to hope for? She had taken to wearing Tom's ring on a chain around her neck since it was too large to stay on her finger. Pulling it outside her dress she fingered it pensively. Please don't let this be all there is, she whispered to herself.

The breeze was turning colder and she shivered a little. Checking her watch, she realised she would have to hurry to catch the later bus. She had lost track of the time. Looking up, she noticed the other figure on the beach was now much closer. They must be walking briskly, she half-registered. Picking up her shopping bag, she slung the strap over her shoulder and started to walk back the way she had come. She followed her own footprints in the sand, noting how some had filled with water, yet others were as clear as if they had just been made.

The next time she looked up the figure was much closer. It was a man, a British soldier, and she could see now that he was running. She walked on. He seemed to be running straight towards her, but it could be that he was just running along the water's edge for exercise. Then she froze and stopped dead, a sensation of prickling running up her arms. She knew that shape, that movement. The man stretched out his arms as the gap between them lessened while she waited in confusion. A few feet away, he stopped and lowered his arms to his sides.

'Izette?'

She broke out of her trance and threw herself into his arms, sobbing. Tom held her tightly, stroking her hair, breathless from his long run across the sand. He let her cry.

'Oh Tom, I've cried so much,' she sobbed, 'now you're here at last and all I can do is cry again!'

He chuckled and hauled a large handkerchief out of the pocket of his khaki battledress. She wiped her eyes and blew her nose. Now her face was no longer buried in his chest, he could take a good look at her. His eyes swept over her face, taking in every longed-for detail.

'I can't explain how much I've missed you, Izette. I've only been half alive.'

He tipped up her chin and kissed her tenderly. She clung to him, still sniffling.

'How did you find me here on the beach?'

'My ship docked about an hour ago. I raced up to your house and your parents told me where they thought you'd be. I ran straight back here.'

'Didn't you even speak to your Mum and Dad?'

'No but I made Bill promise not to let on he'd seen me.'

Izette shook her head. 'Tom,' she said sternly, 'that was wrong.'

'I know,' he admitted, 'but I was so desperate to see

you. And we'll be home in another half-hour. Let me look at you, feast these poor starved eyes on you.'

Holding her away from him, he laughed at her red-rimmed eyes and pink shiny nose. It was so good to hear that laugh again. Then, looking her up and down, he announced that she was too thin.

'Well, it has been rather difficult here while you, by the look of you, have been tucking into roast beef and Yorkshire pudding,' she accused him.

'And fish and chips, and sausages and bacon and egg and...'

'Stop it,' she groaned, 'that isn't fair. We're still on rations.'

'So were we but there's rations and rations,' he laughed. 'Come on, let's walk, it's getting chilly.'

Tom picked up Izette's bag and they began to walk back along the beach, arms around each other.

'So where have you been, Tom Birrell, and why didn't you send us a message?'

'Ah, I knew I would be in trouble. Mum and Dad are going to ask exactly the same thing.'

'So what stopped you from putting pen to paper?' she insisted.

'I did but the British blockade stopped all messages getting through. I didn't hear about the Vega coming here until it was too late...and in my defence, the army has kept me just a little busy.'

Tom went on to tell her what had happened since the night of the escape. He told her how he'd broken his fingers on the rocks, which meant that Gunther had to row the entire way to the French coast.

'He collapsed when we finally managed to drag the boat out of the water. As soon as it was safe, he just passed out like a light. I had to leave him while I went to find help. He was still unconscious when I got back with an old French farmer and his son. We had to drag him up the beach between us. They put him to bed and he slept for a full 12 hours. The old woman bandaged his hands. They were raw and bleeding.'

'So what happened to Gunther?'

'The farmer directed me to the nearest Allied unit, which turned out to be American. They came and picked us up. After hearing our story, they arranged for me to be sent on to London. Gunther had to be treated as a prisoner of war. I don't know where they sent him but I made sure they knew what he had done. I couldn't have made it without him.'

In London, Tom had faced extensive questioning and was able to hand over the information he had collected about the German defences.

'They were very anxious to know what conditions were like on the island but when it came to the German military information, I got the impression they were listening out of politeness. Before I left here, I assumed the Allies would invade the islands once the French mainland was secure but now I don't think they ever had any intention of attacking. I think they'd already decided to starve Jerry out and the Islanders would have to survive as best they could. It makes me furious to think about it.'

Tom stopped talking, absorbed in his thoughts for a few moments.

'And then?' prompted Izette.

'Then I was allowed to join up. They sent me up to some place in Yorkshire for training and then my unit was sent back to France again to help with the clearing up. I kept my ear to the ground for any mention of the Channel Islands then, after VE day, I volunteered to come back here. They were very understanding about us Islanders. I expect they thought our local knowledge would be useful as well.'

'So here you are...and all in one piece!'

Tom raised his hand to show her. 'Except for these fingers. I still can't bend them properly.'

'As long as you can hold me, I don't care,' said Izette.

'Oh, I can manage that all right,' said Tom, taking her in his arms again, 'and quite a bit more, I hope.'

'I can't wait to find out,' Izette murmured in his ear.

'How about a wedding first?' Tom suggested.

'If you insist.'

Tom looked at her in mock surprise. 'You brazen little hussy, Izette Vaubert! I think you were always one step ahead of me, even when we were kids.'

'I knew I loved you before you knew you loved me.'

Tom gave this some thought.

'You're right, you did. But now you'll have to give me the opportunity to make up for lost time.'

'We've all the time in the world.'

Tom kissed her again, lingeringly, stroking her cheek with his fingers. Then they turned together for home. Their home and their future...at last.

Bibliography:

Histories

Bunting, Madeleine, '*The Model Occupation*', Harper Collins, 1995
Cruikshank, Charles, '*The German Occupation of the Channel Islands*', Oxford University Press, 1975
Freeman-Keel, Tom, '*From Auschwitz to Alderney and Beyond*', Seek Publishing, 1995
Harris, Roger E, '*Islanders Deported*', Channel Islands Specialists Society, 1983
Keiller, Frank, '*Prison without Bars*', Seaflower Books, 2000
Le Moignan, Luke, '*Stories of an Occupation*', La Haule Books - Jersey, 1995
Maugham, R.C.F, '*Jersey under the Jackboot*', W.H.Allen & Co Ltd, 1946
Mayne, Richard, '*Channel Islands Occupied*', Jarrold and Sons Ltd, 1981
Mayne, Richard, '*Operation Nestegg*', Channel Islands Historical Photo Agency, n.d.
McLoughlin, Roy, '*Living with the Enemy*', Starlight Publishing, 1995
Shipley, Rob, '*The Liberation of Jersey*', Guiton Publishing and Marketing, 1985
Stoney, Barbara, '*Sybil, Dame of Sark*', Burbridge Ltd, 1984
Thomas, Roy, '*Lest We Forget*', La Haule Books - Jersey, 1992
Toms, Carel, '*Hitler's Fortress Islands*', The New English

Library Ltd, 1967
Wood, Alan and Mary Seaton, '*Islands in Danger*', Evans Brothers, 1955

Diaries and Memoirs

Anquetil, Audrey F, '*Wartime memories*', privately published, n.d.

Bihet, Molly, '*A Child's War*', The Guernsey Press Co Ltd, 1985

Boleat, Peggy, '*A Quiet Place*', Villette Publishing Ltd, 1993

de Carteret, '*An Island Trilogy*', Redberry Press, n.d.

Hillsdon, Sonia, '*Jersey Occupation Remembered*', Jarrold Publishing, 1986

Lewis, Dr John, '*A Doctor's Occupation*', Starlight Publishing, 1982

Le Quesne, Edward, '*The Occupation of Jersey Day by Day*', La Haule Books – Jersey, 1999

Le Ruez, Nan, '*Jersey Occupation Diary*', Seaflower Books, 1994

Le Sueur, Francis, '*Shadow of the Swastika*', The Guernsey Press Co Ltd, 1990

Manning, John, '*Grandpa v Germany*', The Guernsey Press Co Ltd, 1995

Sinel, Leslie, '*The German Occupation of Jersey*', Villette Publishing Ltd, 1995

Stroobant, Frank, '*One Man's War*', Burbridge Ltd, 1967

Vaudin, Margaret, '*A Garland of Daisies*', Regency Press Ltd, 1984

Other Sources

The Channel Islands Occupation Society, '*Channel Islands*

Occupation Review' and *'Occupation Camera'*.
Societe Jersiaise, *'The German Occupation of Jersey, 1940-45'*, Ralph Mollet, 1954
The German Underground Hospital, *'The First Casualty and Jersey's Occupation Experience'*,
    Sanctuary Inns Ltd, 1991
Money, June, *'Aspects of War'*, published for the Education Development Centre, Guernsey,
    1993-1995
'Channel Islands Occupied', Commemorative Liberation Video, Tomahawk Films.
'Moments in Time', Jersey Film Archive, Jersey Museums Service, 1990-1993

General

Bourke, Joanna, *'The Second World War'*, Oxford University Press, 2001
Bowman, John S, *'Chronicle of 20th Century History'*, Magna Books, 1989
Pitt, Barrie and Francis, *'The Chronological Atlas of World War II'*,
Ponting, Clive, *'1940: Myth and Reality'*, Hamish Hamilton Ltd, 1990
Shaw, Antony, *'World War II, Day by Day'*, Grange Books plc, 2000
Macmillan London Ltd, 1989